As Good As Dead

Also by Holly Jackson

A Good Girl's Guide to Murder series

A Good Girl's Guide to Murder

Good Girl, Bad Blood

As Good as Dead

Kill Joy (a Good Girl's Guide to Murder novella)

Five Survive

The Reappearance of Rachel Price

Not Quite Dead Yet

The Final

***A Good Girl's Guide to Murder* novel**

HOLLY JACKSON

Delacorte Press

This one is for all of you.

Thank you for sticking with me to the end.

Delacorte Press
An imprint of Random House Children's Books
A division of Penguin Random House LLC
1745 Broadway, New York, NY 10019
penguinrandomhouse.com
GetUnderlined.com

Editor: Kelsey Horton
Cover Designer: Casey Moses
Interior Designer: Megan Shortt
Production Editors: Colleen Fellingham and Kelly Taylor
Managing Editor: Tamar Schwartz
Production Manager: Shameiza Ally

Library of Congress Cataloging-in-Publication Data is available upon request.
ISBN 978-0-593-37985-1 (trade) — ISBN 978-0-593-37987-5 (ebook) —
ISBN 978-0-593-37988-2 (pbk.) — ISBN 979-8-217-11738-3 (deluxe edition)

Originally published in paperback and in slightly different form by Electric Monkey, an imprint of Egmont UK Limited, London, in 2021. Subsequently published in hardcover in the United States by Delacorte Press, an imprint of Random House Children's Books, a division of Penguin Random House LLC, New York, in 2021.

Closed folder by ralko/stock.adobe.com, wooden background by LIGHTFIELD STUDIOS/stock.adobe.com, binder clip by gearstd/stock.adobe.com, grunge metal texture by anammarques/stock.adobe.com, old lined paper by macondos/stock.adobe.com, torn paper with paper clip by Konstantin G/stock.adobe.com, folded piece of paper by Sharpshot/stock.adobe.com, open folder with papers by ralko/stock.adobe.com, ripped torn paper edges by chathuporn/stock.adobe.com.

Manufactured in Italy
10 9 8 7 6 5 4 3 2 1
2025 Deluxe Edition

The authorized representative in the EU for product safety and compliance is Penguin Random House Ireland, Morrison Chambers, 32 Nassau Street, Dublin D02 YH68, Ireland, https://eu-contact.penguin.ie.

Random House Children's Books supports the First Amendment and celebrates the right to read.

PART I

ONE

Dead-eyed. That's what they said, wasn't it? Lifeless, glassy, empty. Dead eyes were a constant companion now, following her around, never more than a blink away. They hid in the back of her mind and escorted her into her dreams. *His* dead eyes, the very moment they crossed over from living to not. She saw them in the quickest of glances and the deepest of shadows, and sometimes in the mirror too, wearing her own face.

And Pip saw them right now, staring straight through her. Dead eyes encased in the head of a dead pigeon sprawled on the front drive. Glassy and lifeless, except for the movement of her own reflection within them, bending to her knees and reaching out. Not to touch it, but to get just close enough.

"Ready to go, pickle?" Pip's dad said behind her. She flinched as he shut the front door with a sharp clack, the sound of a gun hiding in its reverberations. Pip's other companion.

"Y-yes," she said, straightening up and straightening out her voice. *Breathe, just breathe through it.* "Look." She pointed needlessly. "Dead pigeon."

He bent down for a look, his black skin creasing around his narrowed eyes, and his pristine three-piece suit creasing around his knees. And then the shift into a face she knew too well: he was about to say something witty and ridiculous, like—

"Pigeon pie for dinner?" he said. Yep, right on cue. Almost every other sentence from him was a joke now, like he was working that much harder to make her smile these days. Pip relented and gave him one.

"Only if it comes with a side of mashed rat-ato," she quipped, finally letting go of the pigeon's empty gaze, hoisting her bronze backpack onto one shoulder.

"Ha!" He clapped her on the back, beaming. "My morbid daughter." Another face shift as he realized what he'd said, and all the other meanings that swirled inside those three simple words. Pip couldn't escape death, even on this bright late-July morning in an unguarded moment with her dad. It seemed to be all she lived for now.

Her dad shook off the awkwardness, only ever a fleeting thing with him, and gestured to the car with his head. "Come on, you can't be late for this meeting."

"Yep," Pip said, opening the door and taking her seat, unsure of what else to say, her mind left behind as they drove away, back there with the pigeon.

It caught up with her as they pulled into the parking lot for the Fairview train station. It was busy, the sun glinting off the regimented lines of commuter cars.

Her dad sighed. "Ah, that fuckboy in the Porsche has taken my spot again." "Fuckboy": another term Pip immediately regretted teaching him.

The only free spaces were down at the far end, near the chain-link fence where the cameras didn't reach. Howie Bowers's old stomping ground. Money in one pocket, small paper bags in the other. And before Pip could help herself, the unclicking of her seat belt became the tapping of Stanley Forbes's shoes on the concrete behind her. It was night now, Howie not in prison but right there under the orange glow, downward shadows for eyes. Stanley reaches him, trading a handful of money for his life, for his secret. And as he turns to face Pip, dead-eyed, six holes split open inside him, spilling gore down his shirt and onto the concrete, and somehow it's on her hands. It's all over her hands and—

"Coming, pickle?" Her dad was holding the door open for her.

"Coming," she replied, wiping her hands against her smartest pants.

The train into Grand Central was packed, and she stood shoulder to shoulder with other passengers, awkward closed-mouth smiles substituting *sorrys* as they bumped into one another. There were too many hands on the metal pole, so Pip was holding on to her dad's bent arm instead, to keep her steady. If only it had worked.

She saw Charlie Green twice on the train. The first time in the back of a man's head, before he shifted to better read his newspaper. The second time, he was a man waiting on the platform, cradling a gun. But as he boarded their car, his face rearranged, lost all its resemblance to Charlie, and the gun was just an umbrella.

It had been three months and the police still hadn't found him. His wife, Flora, had turned herself in to a police station in Duluth, Minnesota four weeks ago; they had somehow gotten separated while on the run. She didn't know where her husband was, but the rumors circulating online were that he'd managed to make it across the border to Canada. Pip looked out for him anyway, not because she wanted him caught, but because she needed him found. And that difference was everything, why things could never go back to normal again.

Her dad caught her eye. "You nervous about the meeting?" he asked over the screeching of the train's wheels as it slowed into Grand Central. "It will be fine. Just listen to Roger, OK? He's an excellent lawyer. Knows what he's talking about."

Roger Turner was an attorney at her dad's firm who was *the best* at defamation cases, apparently. They found him a few minutes later, waiting outside the old redbrick conference center, where the meeting room was booked.

"Hello again, Pip," Roger said, holding out his hand to her. Pip quickly checked her hand for blood before shaking his. "Nice weekend, Victor?"

"It was, thank you, Roger. And I have leftovers for lunch today, so it's going to be an excellent Monday too."

"I suppose we better head in, then, if you're ready?" Roger asked Pip, checking his watch, his other hand gripping a shining briefcase.

Pip nodded. Her hands felt wet again, but it was sweat. It was only sweat.

"You'll be fine, darling," her dad told her, straightening out her collar.

"Yes, I've done thousands of mediations." Roger grinned, swiping back his gray hair. "No need to worry."

"Call me when it's done." Pip's dad leaned down to bury a kiss in the top of her hair. "I'll see you at home tonight. Roger, I'll see you in the office later."

"Yes, see you, Victor. After you, Pip."

They were in meeting room 4E, on the top floor. Pip asked to take the stairs because if her heart was hammering for that reason, it wasn't hammering for any other reason. That's how she rationalized it, why she now went running anytime she felt her chest tighten. Run until there was a different kind of hurt.

They reached the top, old Roger puffing several steps behind her. A smartly dressed man stood in the corridor outside 4E, smiling when he saw them.

"Ah, you must be Pippa Fitz-Amobi," he said. Another outstretched hand, another quick blood check. "And you, her counsel, Roger Turner. I'm Hassan Bashir, and for today I am your independent mediator."

He smiled, pushing his glasses up his thin nose. He looked kind, and so eager he was almost bouncing. Pip hated to ruin his day, which she undoubtedly would.

"Nice to meet you," she said, clearing her throat.

"And you." He clapped his hands together, surprising Pip. "So, the other party is in the meeting room, all ready to go. Unless you have any questions beforehand." He glanced at Roger. "I think we should probably get started."

"Yes. All good." Roger sidestepped in front of Pip to take charge as Hassan ducked back to hold open the door to 4E. It was silent inside. Roger walked through, nodding thanks to Hassan. And then it was Pip's turn. She took a breath, arching her shoulders, and then let it out through gritted teeth.

Ready.

She stepped into the room and his face was the first thing she saw. Sitting on the opposite side of the long table, his angular cheekbones in a downward point to his mouth, his messy swept-back blond hair. He glanced up and met her eyes, a hint of something dark and gloating in his.

Max Hastings.

TWO

Pip's feet stopped moving. She didn't tell them to; it was like some primal, unspoken knowledge, that even one more step would be too close to *him.*

"Here, Pip," Roger said, pulling out the chair directly opposite Max, gesturing her down into it. Beside Max, across from Roger, was Christopher Epps, the same attorney who'd represented Max in his trial. Pip had last come face to face with this man on the witness stand; she'd been wearing this exact same suit while he hounded her with that clipped bark of a voice. She hated him too, but the feeling was lost, subsumed by her hatred for the person sitting opposite her. Only the width of a table between them.

"Right. Hello, everyone," Hassan said brightly, taking his assigned chair at the head of the table, in between the two parties. "Let's get the introductory bits out of the way. My role as mediator means I'm here to help you reach an agreement and a settlement that is acceptable to both parties. My only interest is to keep everyone here happy, OK?"

Clearly Hassan had not read the room.

"The purpose of a mediation is essentially to avoid litigation. A court case is a lot of hassle, and very expensive for all involved, so it's always better to see if we can come to some arrangement before a lawsuit is even filed." He grinned, first to Pip's side of the room, and then to Max's. A shared and equal smile.

"If we cannot reach an agreement, Mr. Hastings and his counsel intend to bring a libel lawsuit against Miss Fitz-Amobi, for a tweet and a blog post shared on April thirtieth of this year, which they claim consisted of a defamatory statement and audio file." Hassan glanced at his notes. "Mr. Epps, on behalf of the claimant, Mr. Hastings, says the defamatory statement has had a very serious effect on his client, both in terms of mental well-being and irreparable reputational damage. This has, in turn, led to financial hardship, for which he is seeking damages."

Pip's hands balled into fists on her lap, knuckles erupting out of her skin like a prehistoric backbone. She didn't know if she could sit here and listen to all this, she didn't fucking know if she could do it. But she breathed and she tried, for her dad and Roger, and for poor Hassan over there.

On the table, in front of Max, was his obnoxious water bottle, of course. Cloudy dark-blue plastic with a flick-up rubber spout. Not the first time Pip had seen him with it; turns out that in a town as small as Fairview, running routes tended to converge and intersect. She'd come to expect it now, seeing Max out on his run when she was on hers, almost like he was doing it on purpose somehow. And always with that fucking blue bottle.

Max saw her looking at it. He reached for it, clicked the button to release the spout with a snap, and took a long, loud sip from it, swilling it around his mouth. His eyes on her the entire time.

Hassan loosened his tie a little. "So, Mr. Epps, if you would like to kick things off here with your opening statement."

"Certainly," Epps said, shuffling his papers, his voice just as sharp as Pip remembered. "My client has suffered terribly since the libelous statement Miss Fitz-Amobi put out on the evening of April thirtieth, especially since Miss Fitz-Amobi has a significant online presence, amounting to more than 300,000 followers at the time. My client has a top-tier education from a very reputable college, meaning, he should be a very attractive candidate for graduate jobs."

Max sucked from his water bottle again, like he was doing it to punctuate the point.

"However, these last few months, Mr. Hastings has struggled to find employment at the level to which he deserves. This is directly due to the reputational harm that Miss Fitz-Amobi's libelous statement has caused. Consequently, my client still has to live at home with his parents, because he cannot find an appropriate job and therefore cannot pay rent to live in New York."

Oh, poor little serial rapist, Pip thought, speaking the words with her eyes.

"But the harm has not been my client's alone," Epps continued. "His parents, Mr. and Mrs. Hastings, have also suffered from the stress, and have even recently had to leave town to stay at their second home in Santa Barbara for a couple of months. Their house was vandalized the very same night Miss Fitz-Amobi published the defamatory statement; someone graffitied the front of their home with the words 'Rapist, I will get you—' "

"Mr. Epps," Roger interrupted, "I hope you are not suggesting that my client had anything to do with that vandalism. The police have never even spoken to her in connection with it."

"Not at all, Mr. Turner." Epps nodded back. "I mention it because we can surmise a causal link between Miss Fitz-Amobi's libelous statement and the vandalism, as it occurred in the hours proceeding that statement. Consequently, the Hastings family does not feel safe in their own home and have had to fit security cameras to the front of the house. I hope this goes some way in explaining not only the financial hardship Mr. Hastings has suffered, but also the extreme pain and suffering felt by him and his family in the wake of Miss Fitz-Amobi's malicious, defamatory statement."

"Malicious?" Pip said, heat rising to her cheeks. "I called him a rapist and he *is* a rapist, so—"

"Mr. Turner," Epps barked, voice rising, "I suggest you advise your client to keep quiet and remind her that any defamatory statements she makes now could be classified as slander."

Hassan held up his hands. "Yes, yes, let's just everyone take a breather. Miss Fitz-Amobi, your side will have the chance to speak later." He loosened his tie again.

"It's all right, Pip, I've got this," Roger said quietly to her.

"I will remind Miss Fitz-Amobi," Epps said, not even looking at her, his gaze on Roger instead, "that three months ago my client faced trial in court and was found *not guilty* on all charges. Which is all the proof you need that the statement made on April thirtieth was, in fact, defamatory."

"All that being said"—Roger now stepped in, shuffling his own papers—"a statement can only be libelous if it is presented as fact. My client's tweet reads as follows: *Max Hastings trial final update. I don't care what the jury believes: he is guilty.*" He cleared his throat. "Now, the phrase *I don't care* clearly places the following statement as a subjective one, an opinion, not fact—"

"Oh, don't give me that," Epps cut in. "You're trying to fall back on the opinion privilege? Really? Please. The statement was clearly worded as fact, and the audio file presented as though it were actually real."

"It is real," Pip said. "Wanna hear it?"

"Pip, please—"

"Mr. Turner—"

"It's clearly doctored," Max spoke up for the first time, maddeningly calm, folding his hands in front of him. His eyes focused only on the mediator. "I don't even sound like that."

"What, like a rapist?" Pip spat across at him.

"MR. TURNER—"

"Pip—"

"OK, everyone!" Hassan stood up. "Let's take this down a notch. We will all get our chance to speak. Remember, we are here to make sure everyone is happy with the outcome. Mr. Epps, could you take us through the damages your client is seeking?"

Epps bowed his head, pulling out a sheet of paper from the bottom of the pile. "For special damages, considering my client should have been in employment for the last three months, at a monthly salary level we would expect for someone in his position, this would have been at least five thousand dollars. This places the financial loss at fifteen thousand dollars."

Max sucked at his water bottle again, the water sloshing around his throat. Pip would have liked to take that fucking water bottle and smash it into his face. If there was to be blood on her hands, it should be his.

"Of course, no monetary figure can be put on the pain and mental anguish suffered by my client and his family. But we feel a sum of eight thousand dollars should be adequate, bringing the total to twenty-three thousand dollars."

"Ridiculous," Roger said, shaking his head. "My client is only eighteen years old."

"Mr. Turner, you should allow me to finish," Epps sneered, licking his finger to turn the page. "However, in discussion with my client, it is his opinion that his ongoing suffering is caused by the fact that the libelous statement has not been retracted and no apology issued, which would actually be of greater value to him than any monetary damages."

"Miss Fitz-Amobi deleted the post weeks ago, when your initial letter of demand was sent," said Roger.

"Mr. Turner, please," Epps replied. If Pip had to hear him say *please* like that one more time, she might just smash his face in too.

"Deleting the tweet after the fact does not mitigate the reputational harm done. So, our proposal is thus: Miss Fitz-Amobi releases a statement on the same public account, in which she retracts her original defamatory statement with an admission of wrongdoing and apologizes for any hurt her words have caused my client. In addition, and this is the most important sticking point, so do pay close attention: in this statement, she must fully admit that she doctored the audio clip in question and that my client never said those words."

"Fuck off."

"Pip—"

"Miss Fitz-Amobi," Hassan pleaded, struggling with his tie like it was tightening around his neck, chasing its own tail.

"I will ignore your client's outburst, Mr. Turner," said Epps. "If those demands are met, we shall apply a discount, as it were, to the monetary damages, bringing them down to thirteen thousand dollars."

"OK, that's a good starting point," Hassan nodded, trying to regain control. "Mr. Turner, would you like to respond to the proposal?"

"Thank you, Mr. Bashir," Roger said, taking the floor. "The proposed damages are still too high. You make great assumptions about your client's potential employment status. I don't see him as a particularly spectacular candidate, especially in the current jobs market. My client is just eighteen. Her only income is from ad revenue from her true crime podcast, and she starts college in a few weeks, where she will incur large student debt. In light of this, the demand is unreasonable."

"OK, ten thousand," Epps said, narrowing his eyes.

"Five thousand," Roger countered.

Epps glanced quickly at Max, who gave an ever-so-slight nod, slouching sideways in his chair. "Seven thousand would be agreeable to us," Epps said, "in conjuncture with the retraction and apology."

"OK, we seem to be getting somewhere." A cautious smile returned to Hassan's face. "Mr. Turner, Miss Fitz-Amobi, could we get your thoughts on those terms?"

"Well," Roger began, "I think the—"

"No deal," Pip said, pushing her chair back from the table, the legs screaming against the polished floor.

"Pip." Roger turned to her before she could get to her feet. "Why don't we go discuss this somewhere and—"

"I will not retract my statement and I will not lie and say the audio file was doctored. I called him a rapist because he is a rapist. I will be dead before I ever apologize to you." She bared her teeth at Max, the rage curling her spine, coating her skin.

"MR. TURNER! Control your client, please!" Epps slapped the table.

Hassan flapped, unsure what to do.

Pip stood up. "Here's the thing about you suing me, Max." She spat out his name, unable to bear it on her tongue. "I have the ultimate defense: the truth. So go on, then, file the lawsuit. I dare you. I'll see you in court. And you know how that goes, don't you? It will have to prove whether my statement was true, which means we get to redo your rape trail. All the same witnesses, the victim testimonies, the evidence. There won't be any criminal charges, but at least everyone will know what you are, forever. Rapist."

"Miss Fitz-Amobi!"

"Pip—"

She planted her hands and leaned across the table, her eyes ablaze, boring into Max's. If only they could start a fire in his, burn up his face while she watched. "Do you really think you can pull it off a second time? Convince another jury of twelve peers that you're not a monster?"

His gaze cut back into hers. "You've lost your mind," he sneered.

"Maybe. So you should be terrified."

"Right!" Hassan stood and clapped his hands. "Perhaps we should have a break for some coffee and cake."

"I'm done," Pip said, shouldering her backpack, opening the door so hard it ricocheted into the wall.

"Miss Fitz-Amobi, please come back." Hassan's desperate voice followed her out into the corridor. Footsteps too. Pip turned. It was only Roger, fumbling his papers back into his briefcase.

"Pip," he said, breathlessly, "I really think we should—"

"I'm not negotiating with him."

"Wait a moment!" Epps's bark filled the corridor as he hurried over to join them. "Just give me one minute, please," he said, re-neatening his gray hair. "We won't file for another month or so, OK? Avoiding a court case is really in everyone's best interest. So, have a few weeks to think it over, when things aren't so *emotional*." He looked down at her.

"I don't need to think it over," Pip said.

"Please, just . . ." Epps fumbled in his suit pocket, pulling out two crisp ivory-colored business cards. "My card," he said offering them to her and Roger. "My cell phone number is on there too. Have a little think, and if you change your mind, call me anytime."

"I won't," she said, reluctantly taking his card, stuffing it into the unused pocket of her jacket.

Christopher Epps studied her for a moment, eyebrows lowered in an approximation of concern. Pip held his gaze; to look away was to let him win.

"And maybe just one word of advice," Epps said. "Take it or leave it. But I've seen people in a self-destructive spiral before. Hell, I've represented many of them. In the end, you'll only end up hurting everyone around you, and yourself. You won't be able to help it. I urge you to turn back before you lose everything."

"Thank you for your unbiased advice, Mr. Epps," she said. "But it appears you have underestimated me. I would be willing to lose everything, destroy myself, if it also meant destroying your client. That seems a fair trade. Now you have a good day, Mr. Epps."

She shot him a smile, sweet and acidic, as she turned on her heels. She quickened her pace, the clicking of her shoes beating almost in time with her turbulent heart. And there, just beneath her heartbeat, under layers of muscle and sinew, was the sound of a gun going off six times.

THREE

He caught her staring: at the fall of his dark hair, at the dimpled line in his chin where her little finger fit, at his dark eyes and the flame dancing inside them from her mom's new Autumn Spice candle. His eyes were always bright somehow, dazzling, like they were lit from within. Ravi Singh was the opposite of dead-eyed. The antidote. Pip needed to remind herself of that sometimes. So she watched him, took him all in, left none of him behind.

"Hey, perve." Ravi grinned across the sofa. "What are you staring at?"

"Nothing." She shrugged, not looking away.

"What does *perve* actually mean?" Josh's small voice chirped up from the rug, where he was assembling some unidentifiable shape out of Lego. "Someone called me that on *Fortnite.* Is it worse than, you know, the f-word?"

Pip snorted, watching Ravi's face unroll into panic, his lips pursed, eyebrows disappearing beneath his hair. He checked over his shoulder toward the kitchen door, where Pip's parents were clattering about, clearing up the dinner she and Ravi had made.

"Um, no, it's not that bad," he said as casually as he could. "Maybe don't say it, though, yeah? Especially not in front of your mom."

"But what do perves do?" Josh stared up at Ravi, and for a fleeting moment, Pip wondered whether Josh knew exactly what he was doing, enjoying watching Ravi squirm on the spot.

"They, um . . ." Ravi broke off. "They watch people, in a creepy way."

"Oh." Josh nodded, seeming to accept the explanation. "Like the guy who's been watching our house?"

"Yes. Wait . . . no," said Ravi. "There isn't a perve watching your house." He glanced toward Pip for help.

"Can't help you," Pip whispered back with a smirk. "Dug your own grave."

"Thanks, Pippus Maximus."

"Yeah, can we actually retire that new nickname?" she said, launching a cushion at him. "Not a fan. Can we go back to just Sarge? I like Sarge."

"I call her Hippo Pippo." Josh again. "She also hates that one."

"But it suits you so well," Ravi said, prodding her in the ribs with his toes. "You are the maximum amount of Pipness that any Pip could be. The Ultra-Pip. I'm going to introduce you to my family this weekend as Pippus Maximus."

She rolled her eyes and jabbed him back with her toe, in a place that made him squeal.

"Pip's already met your family loads of times." Josh looked up, confused. He seemed to be going through a new pre-eleven stage, where he had to insert himself into every single conversation going on in the house. Even had an opinion on tampons yesterday.

"Ah, this is the *extended* family, Josh. Much more scary. Cousins and even, dare I say it, *the aunties*," Ravi said dramatically, haunting the word with his waggling fingers.

"That's OK," Pip said. "I'm well prepared. Just got to read over my spreadsheet a couple more times and I'll be fine."

"And also it's . . . Wait." Ravi stalled, eyebrows eclipsing his eyes. "What did you just say? Did you just say *spreadsheet*?"

"Y-yeah." She shifted, cheeks growing warm. She hadn't intended to tell him about that. Ravi's favorite hobby in the whole world was winding her up; she didn't need to give him any more ammunition. "It's nothing."

"No, it's not. What spreadsheet?" He sat up straight. If his smile were any wider it might actually split his face.

"Nothing." She crossed her arms.

He darted forward before she could defend herself, got her right in the place she was most ticklish: where her neck met her shoulder.

"Ow, stop." Pip laughed; she couldn't help it. "Ravi, stop. I have a headache."

"Tell me about the spreadsheet, then," he said, refusing to relent.

"Fine," she choked breathlessly, and finally Ravi stopped. "It's . . . I've just been making a spreadsheet, to keep a record of the things you've told me about your family. Just little details, so I remember. And so when I meet them, they might, you know, like me." She refused to look at his face, knowing what expression would await her there.

"Details like what?" he said, voice brimming with hardly contained amusement.

"Things like, um . . . oh, your auntie Priya—who is your mom's younger sister—she also really likes true crime documentaries, so it would be good to talk to her about those. And your cousin Deeva, she's really into running and fitness, if I'm remembering right." She hugged her knees. "Oh, and your auntie Zara won't like me no matter what I do, so not to get too disappointed by that."

"It's true," Ravi laughed, "she hates everybody."

"I know, you said."

He studied her for a lingering moment, the laugh playing silently across his face. "I can't believe you've been secretly taking notes." And in one fluid movement, Ravi stood up, scooped his arms under her, and lifted her up. He swung her around while she protested, saying, "Under that big, tough exterior we've got ourselves a cute little weirdo over here."

“Pip’s not cute.” Josh’s necessary input.

Ravi let her go, delivering her back to the sofa. “Right,” he said with an upward stretch. “I should head off. Not everyone has to get up at disgusting o’clock tomorrow morning for their internship at a law firm. But my girlfriend’s probably going to need a good lawyer one day, so . . .” He winked at her. The very same thing he’d said after she told him how the mediation went.

It was his third week at the summer internship, and Pip could already tell he loved it, despite his protestations about the early wake-up. For his first day, she’d given him a T-shirt that said *Lawyer Loading . . .*

“Right, goodbye, Joshua,” he said, nudging him with his foot. “My favorite human being.”

“Really?” Josh beamed up at him. “What’s Pip, then?”

“Ah, she’s a close second,” Ravi said, returning to her. He kissed her on the forehead, his breath in her hair and—when Josh wasn’t looking—moved down to press his lips against hers.

“I heard that,” Josh said anyway.

“I’ll just go say bye to your mom and dad,” Ravi said. But then he paused and pivoted, came back to whisper in Pip’s ear: “And let your mother know that, unfortunately, you are the reason your ten-year-old brother now thinks a pervert is watching your house. Nothing to do with me.”

Pip squeezed Ravi’s elbow, one of their secret *I love you*s, laughing to herself as he walked away.

The smile stayed a little longer this time, after Ravi was gone. It did. But when Pip walked upstairs, standing alone in her bedroom, she realized it had already left her without saying its goodbyes. She never knew how to bring it back.

The headache was starting to pinch at her temples now, as her eyes focused beyond the window, at the thickening darkness outside. The clouds amassing into one dark, lurking shape. Nighttime. Pip checked the time on her phone; it had just passed nine. Wouldn't be long now until everyone was in bed, lost to sleep. Everyone but her. The lone pair of eyes in a sleeping town, begging the night to pass on by.

She'd promised herself no more. Last time was the last time. She'd repeated it in her head like a mantra. But even as she tried to tell herself that now, even as she balled her fists against her temples to out-hurt the pain, she knew it was hopeless, that she would lose. She always lost. And she was tired, so tired of fighting it.

Pip crossed to her door and gently closed it, in case anyone walked by. Her family could never know. And not Ravi. Especially not Ravi.

At her desk, she placed her iPhone between her notebook and her bulky black headphones. She opened the drawer, the second one down on the right, and began to pull out the contents: the pot of pins, her rewound red string, an old pair of white earphones, a glue stick.

She removed the pad of lined paper and reached the bottom of the drawer. The false bottom she'd made out of white cardboard. She dug her fingertips in at one side and pried it up.

There, hidden below, were the burner phones. All six of them, arranged in a neat line. Six prepaid phones bought with cash, each from a different store, a cap pulled low over Pip's face as she'd handed over the money.

The phones stared blankly up at her.

Just one more time, and then she was done. She promised.

Pip reached in and took out the one on the left, an old gray Nokia. She held the power button down to turn it on, her fingers shaking with the pressure. There was a familiar sound hiding in the beat of her heart. The phone lit up with a greenish backlight, welcoming her back. In the simple menu, Pip clicked onto her messages, to the only contact saved in this phone. In any of them.

Her thumbs worked against the buttons, clicking number one three times to get to *C*.

Can I come over now? she wrote. She pressed send with one last promise to herself: this was the very last time.

She waited, watching the empty screen below her message. She willed the response to appear, concentrated only on that, not on the growing sound inside her chest. But now that she'd thought about it, she couldn't unthink it, couldn't unhear it. She held her breath and willed even harder.

It worked.

Yes, he replied.

FOUR

It was a race between her ticking heart and the pounding of her sneakers on the sidewalk. Her body alive with sound, from her chest to her feet, dulled only by the noise cancellation of her headphones. But Pip couldn't lie to herself that one was caused by the other; she'd been running for only four minutes and already she was here, turning onto Beacon Close. The heart had preceded the feet.

She'd told her parents she was going out on a quick run, as she always did—dressed in her navy leggings and a white sports top—so at least running here left her with a shred of honesty. Shreds and scraps were all she could hope for. Sometimes running itself was enough, but not tonight. No, tonight there was only one thing that could help her.

Pip slowed as she approached number thirteen, lowering her headphones to cradle her neck. She planted her heels and stood still for a moment, checking whether she really needed to do this. If she took one more step—there was no going back.

She walked up the drive to the terraced house, past the gleaming white BMW parked at an angle. At the dark red door, Pip's fingers passed over the doorbell, balling into a fist to knock on the wood. The doorbell wasn't allowed; it made too much noise and the neighbors might notice.

Pip knocked again until she could see his outline in the frosted glass, growing taller and taller. The sound of the sliding bolt and then the door opening inward, Luke Eaton's face in the crack. In the darkness, the tattoos climbing up his neck and the side of his face looked like his skin had come apart, strips of flesh rebuilding to form a net.

He pulled the door just wide enough for her to fit through.

"Come on, quickly," he said gruffly, turning to walk down the hall. "Got someone coming over soon."

Pip closed the front door behind her and followed Luke around the bend into the small, square kitchen. Luke was wearing the exact same pair of dark basketball shorts he'd been wearing the first time Pip met him, when she'd come here to talk to Nat da Silva about the missing Jamie Reynolds. Thank god Nat had gotten away from Luke; the house was empty now, just the two of them.

Luke bent down to open one of the kitchen cabinets. "Thought you said last time was it. That you wouldn't be back again."

"I did say that, didn't I?" Pip replied flatly, picking at her fingernails. "I just need to sleep. That's all."

Luke rustled around in the cupboard, coming back up with a paper bag clenched in his fist. He opened the top and held it out so Pip could see inside.

"They're two-milligram pills this time," Luke said, shaking the bag. "That's why there aren't as many."

"Yeah, that's fine," Pip said, glancing up at Luke. She wished she hadn't. She always found herself studying the geography of his face, searching for the ways he was similar to Stanley Forbes. Both of them had been Charlie Green's final suspects for Child Brunswick, narrowed down from all the men in Fairview. But Luke had been a wrong turn, the wrong man, and lucky for him because he was still alive. Pip had never seen his blood, never worn it the way she'd worn Stanley's. It was on her hands now, the feel of cracking ribs below the pads of her fingers. Dripping onto the linoleum floor.

No, it was just sweat, just a tremor in her hands.

Pip gave her hands something to do to distract them. She reached into the waistband of her leggings and pulled out the cash, flicking through the notes in front of Luke until he nodded. She passed the money over and then held out her other hand. The paper bag went into it, crinkling under her grip.

Luke nodded again, but then he stalled, a new look in his eyes. One that seemed dangerously close to pity. "You know," he said, doubling back to the cupboard, returning with a small, clear baggie. "If you're struggling, I have something stronger than Xanax. Will completely knock you out." He held up the baggie and shook it; it was filled with oblong tablets of a light mossy-green hue.

Pip stared at them, bit her lip. "Stronger?" she asked.

"Definitely."

"Wh-what is it?" she asked, her eyes transfixed.

"This"—Luke gave it another shake—"is Rohypnol. Stuff puts you right out."

Pip's gut tightened. "No thanks." She dropped her eyes. "I've had experience." By which she meant she'd had it pumped out of her stomach when Becca Bell had slipped it into her drink nine months ago. Pills that Becca's sister, Andie, had been selling to Max Hastings before she died.

"Suit yourself," he said, pocketing the small bag. "Offer's there if you want it. More expensive, though. Obviously."

"Obviously," she parroted him, her mind elsewhere.

She turned to the door to see herself out. Luke Eaton didn't do goodbyes, or hellos for that matter. Maybe she should turn back, though; maybe she should tell him that actually *this* was the last time and he'd never see her again. How else would she stick to it? But then her mind came back to her with a new thought and she followed it, spinning on her heels to return to the kitchen, and something else came out of her mouth instead.

"Luke," she said, sharper than she'd meant. "Those pills—the Rohypnol—are you selling them to someone in town? Does someone here buy them from you?"

He blinked at her.

"Is it Max Hastings? Does he buy those from you? He's tall, longish blond hair, well-spoken. Is it him? Is he the one buying those pills from you?"

He didn't answer.

"Is it Max?" Pip said, the urgency cracking her voice.

Luke's eyes hardened, the pity a thing of the past. "You know the rules by now. I don't answer questions. I don't ask 'em and I don't answer 'em." There was the slightest smirk on his face. "Rules apply to you too. I know you think you're special, but you're not. See you next time."

Pip crushed the bag in her hand as she walked out of the house. She thought to slam the door behind her, a flash of rage beneath her skin, but then thought better of it. Her heart beat even faster now, battering against her chest, filling her head with the sound of cracking ribs. And those dead eyes, they were hiding just over there in the shadows from the streetlamps. If Pip blinked, they'd be waiting for her in the darkness there too.

Was Max the one buying those pills from Luke? He used to buy them from Andie Bell, who got them from Howie Bowers. But Luke had always been the one supplying Howie, and he was all that was left, the two lower links in the chain now gone. If Max was still buying, it would have to be from Luke; that made the most sense. Were he and Pip almost crossing paths at Luke's front door like they did on their runs? Was he still slipping pills into the drinks of women? Was he still ruining lives, like he had done to Nat da Silva and Becca Bell? The thought made her stomach churn, and oh god, she was going to be sick, right here in the middle of the road.

She doubled over and tried to breathe through it, the bag rattling in her shaking hands. It couldn't wait any longer. She stumbled to the other side of the road, under the covering of the trees. She reached inside the paper bag for one of the see-through baggies, struggling to unfasten it because her fingers were coated in blood.

Sweat. Just sweat.

She pulled out one of the long white pills, different from the kind she'd taken before. Scored into one side were three lines and the word "Xanax," and on the other a *2*. At least it wasn't fake, then, or cut with anything else. A dog barked from somewhere close by. *Hurry up.* Pip snapped the pill along the center line and pushed the half through her lips. Her mouth had already filled with saliva and she swallowed it dry.

She tucked the bag under her arm just as a dog walker and small white terrier came around the corner. It was Gail Yardley, who lived down her road.

"Ah, Pip," she said, her shoulders relaxing. "You surprised me." She looked her up and down. "I swear I just saw you outside your house, coming back from one of your runs. Mind playing tricks on me, I guess."

"Happens to the best of us," Pip said, rearranging her face.

"Yes, well." Gail laughed awkwardly through her nose. "I won't keep you." She walked away, the dog stopping to sniff Pip's sneakers before the leash grew taut, and it shuffled off after her.

Pip rounded the same corner Gail had come from, her throat sore from where the pill had scratched on its way down. And now the other feeling: guilt. She couldn't believe she'd done this again. *Last time,* she told herself as she walked toward home. *Last time, and then you're done.*

At least she'd get some sleep tonight. It should come on soon, the unnatural calmness, like a warm shield across her thinning skin, and the relief when the muscles in her jaw finally unclenched. Yes, she would sleep tonight—she had to.

The doctor had put her on a course of Valium, back after it first happened. The first time she saw death and held it in her hands. But it wasn't long before he took her off, even when she'd begged him. She could still recite what he'd said, word for word:

You need to come up with your own strategies to cope with the trauma and stress. This medication will only make it harder to recover from the PTSD in the long-term. You don't need it, Pippa, you can do this.

How wrong he'd been. She did need the pills, needed them as much as she needed sleep. This *was* her strategy. And at the same time, she knew. She knew he was right, and she was making everything worse.

The most effective treatment is talk therapy, so we're going to continue your weekly sessions.

She'd tried, she really had. And after seven sessions she'd told everyone she was feeling much better, really. She was fine. A lie practiced well enough now that people believed her, even Ravi. She thought if she had to go to one more session, she might just die. How could she *talk* about it? It was an impossible thing that escaped language or sense.

On one hand, she could tell you, from the very bottom of her heart, that she didn't believe Stanley Forbes had deserved to die. That he deserved life and she had done all she could to bring him back. It wasn't unforgivable, what he'd done as a child, what he'd been made to do. He was learning, trying every day, to be a better man. Pip believed this with every part of her being. That and the terrible guilt that she'd been the one to lead his killer to him, luring Stanley out to that abandoned farmhouse after learning he was Child Brunswick.

Yet, at the same time, she believed in the very opposite thing.

And this one came from somewhere even deeper. Her soul, maybe, if she'd believed in those sorts of things. Though he had been a child, Stanley was the reason Charlie Green's sister had been murdered. Pip had asked herself: If someone picked out her little brother and delivered him to a killer, to die the most horrific death imaginable, would she spend two decades chasing justice, hunting them down to kill them? The answer was yes. She knew she would, without hesitation; she would kill the person who took Josh away, no matter how long it took. Charlie had been right: they were the same. There was an understanding between them, this . . . this sameness.

That's why she couldn't talk about it, not to a professional, not to anyone. Because it was impossible, incompatible. It had torn her in two and there was no way to stitch those parts back together. It was untenable. Beyond sense. No one could understand, except . . . maybe *him*. She hesitated at her driveway, looking to the house just beyond it.

Charlie Green. That's why she needed him to be found, not caught. He'd helped her once before, opened her eyes about right and wrong and who decided what those words meant. Maybe . . . maybe if she could talk to him, he'd understand. He was the only one who could. He must have found a way to live with what he'd done, and maybe he could show Pip how to live with it too. Show her a way to fix everything, how to put herself back together again. But Pip was of two minds about this as well; it made perfect sense and it made none.

A rustle in the trees across the road from her house.

Pip's breath caught in her throat as she whipped around and stared, trying to shape the darkness into a person, the wind into a voice. Was there someone there, hiding in the trees, watching her? Following her? Tree trunks or legs? Charlie? Was it him?

She strained her eyes, trying to draw out individual leaves and their skeletal branches.

No, there couldn't be anyone there. Don't be stupid. It was just another of those things that lived in her head now. Scared of everything. Angry at everything. It wasn't real and she needed to learn the difference again. Sweat on her hands, not blood. She walked up to her house, glancing back only once. *The pill will take it away soon,* she told herself. Along with everything else.

HOME > REAL-CRIME > CRIME-SCENE-INVESTIGATION > ESTIMATING-TIME-OF-DEATH

How do pathologists determine time of death in a homicide case?

The most important thing to note is that time of death can only ever be an estimated range; a pathologist cannot give a specific time of death, as we sometimes see in movies and TV shows. There are three main mortis factors used to determine the estimated time of death, and some of these tests are performed at the crime scene itself, as soon as possible after the victim is found. As a general rule, the sooner a victim is found postmortem, the more accurate the time-of-death estimate.[1]

1. Rigor Mortis

Immediately after death, all the muscles in the body relax. Then, typically around two hours postmortem, the body starts to stiffen due to a buildup of acid in the muscle tissues.[2] This is rigor mortis. It begins in the muscles in the jaw and neck, proceeding downward to the body and the extremities. Rigor mortis is normally complete within six to twelve hours, and then starts to disappear approximately fifteen to thirty-six hours after death.[3] As this stiffening process has a roughly known time of occurrence, it can be very useful in estimating time of death. However, there are a few factors that can impact the onset and timeline of rigor, such as temperature. Warm temperatures will increase the rate of rigor, whereas cold temperatures will slow it down.[4]

2. Livor Mortis

Also known as "lividity," livor mortis is the settling of the blood inside the body due to gravity and the loss of blood pressure.[5] The skin will become discolored with a red-purple tinge where the blood has pooled internally.[6] Livor mortis starts to develop two to four hours after death, becomes nonfixed up to eight to twelve hours after death, and fixed after eight to twelve hours from the time of death.[7] "Nonfixed" refers to whether the skin is blanchable: this means that—when lividity is present—if the skin is pressed, the color will disappear, a bit like when you press your own skin now.[8] But this process can be affected by factors such as temperature and changing body position.

3. Algor Mortis

Algor mortis refers to the temperature of a body. After death, the body starts to cool until it reaches equilibrium with the ambient temperature (wherever the body is discovered).[9] Typically, the body will lose about 1.5° F per hour, until it reaches the environmental temperature.[10] At the crime scene—in addition to making observations about the rate of rigor and lividity—a medical examiner will also likely take the body's internal temperature and that of the environment, in order to calculate approximately when the victim was killed.[11]

Although these processes cannot tell us the exact minute a person died, they are the main factors a pathologist uses when estimating a range for the time of death.

FIVE

Death stared back at her. Real death, not the clean, idealized version of it. The purpling, pockmarked skin of a corpse, and the eerie, forever-whitened imprint of a too-tight belt they must have worn as they died. It was almost funny, in a way, Pip thought as she scrolled down the page on her laptop. Funny in the way that if you thought about it too long, you'd go mad. We all end up like this eventually, like these postmortem images on a badly formatted webpage about body decomposition and time of death.

Her arm was resting on her notebook, steadily filling up with her scribbles. Underlines here and highlighted parts there. And now she added another sentence below, glancing up at the screen as she wrote: *If the body feels warm and stiff, death occurred three to eight hours prior.*

"Are those dead bodies?!"

The voice pierced through the cushion of her noise-canceling headphones; she hadn't heard anyone come in. Pip flinched, her heart jumping to her throat. She dropped her headphones to her neck and sound came rushing back in, a familiar sigh behind her. These headphones blocked almost everything out, that's why Josh kept stealing them to play *FIFA,* so he could "noise-cancel Mom." Pip lurched forward to switch to another tab. But, actually, none of them was any better.

"Pip?" Her mom's voice hardened.

Pip spun her desk chair, overstretching her eyes to cover their guilt. Her mom was standing right behind her, one wrist cocked against her hip. Her blond hair was manic, sections folded up into foil like a metal Medusa. It was highlighting day. They happened more frequently now that her roots were starting to show gray. She still had on her clear latex gloves, smudges of hair dye on the fingers.

"Well?" she prompted.

"Yes these are dead bodies," Pip said.

"And why, dear daughter, are you looking at dead bodies at eight a.m. on a Friday morning?"

Was it really only eight o'clock? Pip had been up since five.

"You told me to get a hobby," she said, shrugging.

"Pip," her mom said sternly, although the turn of her mouth had a hint of amusement in it.

"It's for my new case," Pip conceded, turning back to the screen. "You know that Jane Doe case I told you about? The one who was found by the Hudson nine years ago? I'm going to investigate it for the podcast while I'm at college. Try to find out who she was and who killed her. I've already been lining up interviews over the next few months. This is relevant research, I swear," she said, hands up in surrender.

"Another season of the podcast?" Pip's mom raised a concerned eyebrow. How could one eyebrow communicate so much? She'd somehow managed to fit around three months' worth of worry and unease into that one small line of hair.

"Well, I've somehow got to fund the lifestyle to which I have grown accustomed. You know, expensive future libel trials, lawyer fees . . ." Pip said. *And illegal, unprescribed benzodiazepines,* she thought secretly. But those weren't the real reasons; not even close.

"Very funny." Her mom's eyebrow relaxed. "Just . . . be careful with yourself. Take a break if you need it, and I'm always here to talk if . . ." She reached out for Pip's shoulder, forgetting about the hair-dye-covered gloves until the very last second. She stalled, lingering an inch above, and maybe Pip imagined it, but she could somehow feel the warmth from her mom's hovering hand. It felt nice, like a small shield against her skin.

"Yeah" was all Pip could think of to say.

"And let's keep the graphic dead bodies to a minimum, yes?" She nodded at the screen. "We have a ten-year-old in the house."

"Oh, I'm sorry," Pip said. "I forgot about Josh's new ability to see through walls, my bad."

"Honestly, he's everywhere at the moment," her mom said, lowering her voice to a whisper, checking behind her. "Don't know how he does it. He overheard me saying *fuck* yesterday, but I could've sworn he was on the other side of the house. Why is it purple?"

"Huh," Pip said, taken aback until she followed her mom's eyes to the laptop screen. "Oh, it's called 'lividity.' It's what happens to the blood when you die, it pools on the . . . Do you really want to know?"

"Not really, sweetie, I was feigning interest."

"Thought so."

Her mom turned toward the door, hair foil crinkling. She paused at the threshold. "Josh is walking in with Sam today; Lynne will be here any minute to pick him up. How about when he's gone, I make a nice big breakfast for the two of us?" She smiled hopefully. "Pancakes or something?"

Pip's mouth felt dry, her tongue like an overgrown aberration sticking to the roof of her mouth. She used to love her mom's pancakes, thick and so syrupy they might just glue your mouth together. Right now, the thought of them made her feel a little sick, but she fixed a matching smile onto her face. "That would be nice. Thanks, Mom."

"Perfect." Her mom's eyes crinkled, glittering as her smile stretched into them. A smile too wide.

Pip's gut twisted with guilt; this was all her fault. Her family forced into a performance, trying twice as hard with her because she could barely try at all.

"It'll be about an hour, then." Pip's mom gestured to her hair. "And don't expect to see your haggard mother at breakfast; instead there will be a newly blonded bombshell."

"Can't wait," Pip said, trying. "I hope the bombshell's coffee is slightly less weak than my haggard mother's."

Her mom rolled her eyes and wandered out of the room, muttering under her breath about Pip and her dad and their strong coffee that tastes like shi—

"I heard that!" Josh's voice sailed through the house.

Pip sniffed, running her fingers around the padded cushions of her headphones cradling her neck. She traced her finger up the smooth plastic of the headband, to the part where the texture changed: the roughened, bumpy sticker wrapped around its width. It was an *A Good Girl's Guide to Murder* sticker, with the logo from her podcast. Ravi had had them made as a present when she released the final episode of season 2, the hardest one to record yet. The story of what happened inside that old abandoned farmhouse, now burned to the ground, a trail of blood through the grass that they'd had to hose away.

So sad, commenters would say.

Don't know why she sounds upset, said others. *She asked for this.*

Pip had told the story, but she never really told the heart of it: that it had broken her.

She pulled the headphones back over her ears and blocked out the world. No sound, only the fizzing inside her own head. She closed her eyes too, and pretended there was no past, no future. It was just this: absence. It was a comfort, floating there free and untethered, but her mind was never quiet for long.

And neither were the headphones. A high-pitched ping sounded in her ears. Pip flipped her phone over to check the notification. An email had come through the form on her website. That same message again: *Who will look for you when you're the one who disappears?* From anonymous987654321@gmail.com. A different email address again, but the same exact message. Pip had been getting them on and off for months now, along with the other colorful comments from trolls. At least it was more poetic and reflective than the straight-cut rape threats.

Who will look for you when you're the one who disappears?

Pip stalled, her eyes lingering on the question. In all this time, she'd never thought to answer it.

Who would look for her? She'd like to think Ravi would. Her parents. Cara Ward and Naomi. Connor and Jamie Reynolds. Nat da Silva. Detective Hawkins? It was his job, after all. Maybe they would, but maybe no one should.

Stop it, she told herself, blocking the way to that dark and dangerous place. Maybe another pill now might help? She glanced at the second drawer down, where the pills lived, beside the burner phones under the false bottom. But, no, she already felt a little tired, unsteady. And they were for sleep, they were just for sleep.

Besides, she had a plan. Pip Fitz-Amobi always had a plan, whether hastily thrown together or spun slowly and agonizingly. This had been the latter.

This person, this version of who she was, it was only temporary. Because she had a plan to fix herself. To get her normal life back. And she was working on it right now.

The first painful task had been to look inside herself, to trace the fault lines and find the cause, the why. And when she worked it out, she realized just how obvious it had been all along. It was everything she had done this last year. All of it. The two intertwined cases that had become her life, her meaning. And they had both been off, somehow. Wrong. Twisted. They weren't clean, they weren't clear. There had been too much gray area, too much ambiguity, and all meaning had become clouded and lost.

Elliot Ward would sit in prison for the rest of his life, but was he an evil man? A monster? Pip didn't think so. He wasn't *the* danger. He'd done a terrible thing, several terrible things, but she believed him when he said some of it was done out of love for his daughters. It wasn't all wrong and it certainly wasn't all right, it was just . . . *there.* Drifting messily in the middle somewhere.

And Max Hastings? Pip saw no gray here at all: Max Hastings was black-and-white, clear-cut. He *was* the danger, the danger that had outgrown the shadows and now made its home behind an expensive, disarming smile. Pip clung to this belief like she would fall off the world if she didn't. Max Hastings was her cornerstone, the upturned mirror by which she defined everything, including herself. But it was meaningless, twisted, because Max had won; he would never see the inside of a prison cell. The black-and-white smudged back out to gray.

Becca Bell still had fifteen months left of her custodial sentence. Pip wrote a letter to her after Max's trial, and Becca's scrawled reply had asked if she wanted to come visit. Pip had. She'd been there three times now, and they spoke on the phone every Thursday at four p.m. Yesterday they'd talked about cheese for the full twenty minutes. Becca seemed to be doing OK in there, maybe even close to happy, but did she deserve to be there at all? Did she need to be locked up, kept away from the rest of the world? No. Becca Bell was a good person, a good person who was thrown into the fire, into the very worst of circumstances. Anyone might have done what she did if pressure was applied to just the right place, to each person's secret breaking point. And if Pip herself could see that, after what she and Becca went through, why couldn't anyone else?

And then, of course, came the greatest knot in her chest: Stanley Forbes and Charlie Green. Pip couldn't think about them too long or she would unravel, come apart at the seams. How could both positions be both wrong and right at the very same time? An impossible contradiction that she would never settle. It was her undoing, her fatal flaw, the hill she would die and decay on.

If that was the cause—all these ambiguities, these contradictions, these gray areas that spread and engulfed all sense—how could Pip rectify that? How could she cure herself from the aftereffects?

There was only one way, and it was maddeningly simple: she needed a new case. And not just any case—a case built only from black and white. No gray, no twisting. Straight, uncrossable lines between the good and the bad and the right and the wrong. Two sides and a clear path running through them for her to tread. That would do it. That would fix her, set things right. Save her soul, if she'd believed in those sorts of things. Everything could go back to normal. *She* could go back to normal.

It had to be the right case.

And here it was: an unknown woman between twenty and twenty-five found naked and mutilated near the Hudson River. No one had looked for her when she disappeared. Never claimed, so never missed. It couldn't have been clearer: this woman deserved justice for the things done to her. And the man who had done them, he could never be anything other than a monster. No gray, no contradictions or confusion. Pip could solve this case, save Jane Doe, but the most important point was that Jane Doe would save her.

One more case would do it, put everything right.

Just one more.

SIX

Pip didn't see them until she was standing right on top of them. She might never have seen them if she hadn't stopped to retie the laces on her sneakers. She lifted her foot and stared down. What the . . .

There were faint lines, drawn in white chalk, right at the foot of the Amobis' driveway, where it met the sidewalk just beyond. They were so faded that maybe they weren't chalk at all, maybe they were salt marks left behind from the rain.

Pip rubbed her eyes. They were scratchy and dried out from staring at her ceiling all night. Even though yesterday evening with Ravi's family had gone well and her face actually ached from smiling, she hadn't earned back her sleep. There'd been only one place to find it, in that forbidden second drawer down.

She removed her balled-up fists from her eyes and blinked, her gaze just as gritty as before. Unable to trust her eyes, she bent to swipe a finger through the nearest line, held it up against the sun to study it. Definitely seemed like chalk, felt like it too, between the bulbs of her fingers. And the lines themselves, they didn't seem like they could be natural. They were too straight, too intentional.

Pip tilted her head to look at them from another angle. There seemed to be five distinct figures; a repeating pattern of crossing and intersecting lines. Could they . . . could they be birds, maybe? Like how children drew birds from a distance, squashed Ms mounting candy-cotton skies? No, that wasn't right, too many lines. Was it some kind of cross? Yeah, it looked like a cross, maybe, where the longer stem split into two legs nearer the bottom.

Oh wait—she stepped over them to look from the other side. They could also be little stick people. Those were their legs, the trunks of their bodies, crossed through with their over-straightened arms. The small line above was their neck. But then, nothing . . . they were headless.

So—she straightened up—either a cross with two legs, or a stick figure with no head. Neither particularly comforting. Pip didn't think Josh had chalk in the house, and he wasn't the kind of kid who enjoyed drawing anyway. Must be one of the neighborhood kids, then, one with a somewhat morbid imagination. Although, who was she to comment on that.

Pip checked as she walked up Thatcher Road; there were no chalk lines on anyone else's driveway, nor on the sidewalk or road. Nothing out of the ordinary, in fact, for a Sunday morning in Fairview. Other than an innocuous square of duct tape that had been stuck onto the black-and-white road sign, so it now instead read *Thatcher Poad.*

Pip shrugged the figures off as she turned onto Main Street, chalked it up to the Yardley children from six doors down. And anyway, she could see Ravi up ahead, approaching the café from the other end.

He looked tired—normal tired—his hair ruffled and the sun flashing off his new glasses. He'd found out over the summer that he was ever-so-slightly nearsighted, and you can bet he made as much fuss as he could at the time. Though now he sometimes forgot to even put them on.

He hadn't spotted her yet, in his own world.

"Oi!" she called from ten feet away, making him jump.

He stuck out his bottom lip in exaggerated sadness. "Be gentle," he said, "I'm delicate this morning."

Of course, Ravi's hangovers were the worst hangovers the world had ever seen. Near-fatal every time.

They made it to each other outside the café door, Pip's hand finding its home in the crook of Ravi's elbow.

"And what's this 'Oi' we've started?" he pressed the question into her forehead. "I have an array of beautiful and flattering nicknames for you, and the best you can come up with is 'Oi'?"

"Ah, well," Pip said. "Someone very old and wise once told me that I am entirely without pizzazz, so . . ."

"I think you meant very wise and very handsome, actually."

"Did I?"

"So," he paused to scratch his nose with his sleeve, "I think last night went really well."

"Really?" Pip said tentatively. She thought it had too, but she didn't entirely trust herself anymore.

He broke into a small laugh, seeing her worried face. "You did good. Everyone loved you. Genuinely. Rahul even messaged this morning to say how much he liked you. And," Ravi lowered his voice conspiratorially, "I think even Auntie Zara might have warmed to you."

"No?!"

"Yes," he said, grinning. "She scowled about twenty percent less than her normal rate, so I call that a raging success."

"Well, I'll be damned," Pip said, leaning into the café door to push it open, the bell jangling overhead. "Hi, Jackie," she called as usual to the woman who owned the café, who was currently restocking the sandwich shelves.

"Oh, hello dear," Jackie said with a quick glance back, almost losing a Brie-and-bacon roll to the floor. "Hi, Ravi."

"Morning," he said, a thickness to his voice until he cleared his throat.

Jackie freed herself from the packaged sandwiches and turned to face them. "I think she's out back, in a fight with the temperamental sandwich toaster. Hold on." She backed up behind the counter and called, "Cara!"

Pip spotted the topknot first, bobbing atop Cara's head as she walked out from the employees' entrance to the kitchen, wiping her hands on her green apron.

"Nah, it's still on the fritz," she said to Jackie, eyes focused on a crusted stain on her apron. "Best we can offer are marginally warm paninis for the time—" She finally glanced up, eyes springing to Pip's, a smile following close behind. "Miss Sweet F-A. Long time, no see."

"You saw me yesterday," Pip replied, catching on too late to Cara's waggling eyebrows. Well, she should have waggled first, then spoken; they established these rules long ago.

Jackie smiled, as though she could read the hastened conversation happening between their eyes. "Well, girls, if it's been a whole day, you probably have a long overdue catch-up, no?" She turned to Cara. "You can start your break early."

"Oh, Jackie," Cara said, with an over-flourished bow. "You are too good to me."

"I know, I know," Jackie waved her off. "I'm a saint. Pip, Ravi, what can I get you?"

Pip ordered a strong coffee; she'd already had two before leaving the house and her fingers were fast and fidgety. But how else would she make it through the day?

Ravi pursed his lips, eyeballing the ceiling like this was the hardest decision he'd ever faced. "You know," he said, "I could be tempted by one of those marginally warm paninis."

Pip rolled her eyes. Ravi must have forgotten he was dying of a hangover; he had absolutely zero willpower in the presence of sandwiches.

Pip settled at the far table, Cara taking the seat beside her, shoulders brushing together. Cara had never understood the concept of personal space, and yet, sitting here now, Pip was grateful for it. Cara wasn't even supposed to be here anymore, in Fairview. Her grandparents had planned to put the Wardses' house up for sale at the end of the school year. But minds changed and plans changed: Naomi found a job nearby in Stratford, and Cara had decided to take a gap year to go traveling, working at the café to save up money. Suddenly, taking the Ward sisters out of Fairview was more complicated than leaving them here, so the grandparents were back in New Jersey, and Cara and Naomi were still here. At least until next year. Now Cara would be the one left behind, when Pip left for Columbia in a few weeks.

Pip couldn't believe it would really happen, that Fairview would ever let her get away.

She nudged Cara back. "So, how's Steph?" she asked.

Steph: the new girlfriend. Although it had been almost two months now, so maybe Pip shouldn't think of her as new anymore. The world moved on, even if she couldn't. And Pip liked her; she was good for Cara, made her happy.

"Yeah, she's good. Training for a triathlon or something because she's actually insane. Oh wait, you'd take her side now, wouldn't you, Miss Runs-a-Lot."

"Yep." Pip nodded. "Definitely Team Steph. She'd be a great asset in a zombie apocalypse."

"So would I," Cara said.

Pip pulled a face at her. "You would die within the first half hour of any apocalypse scenario, let's be honest."

Ravi came over then, placing a tray down carrying their coffees and his sandwich. He'd already taken a massive bite before bringing it over, of course.

"Oh, so," Cara lowered her voice, "big drama here this morning."

"What?" Ravi asked between bites.

"We suddenly had a bit of a rush, so there was a line, and I was at the register taking orders. And then," her voice was a whisper now, "Max Hastings came in."

Pip's shoulders arched and her jaw tensed. Why was he everywhere? Why could she never get away from him?

"I know," Cara said, reading Pip's face. "And obviously I wasn't going to serve him, so I told Jackie I'd clean the milk frother while she dealt with the customers. She took Max's order, and then someone else came in." She paused for dramatic effect. "Jason Bell."

"Oh, really?" Ravi said.

"Yeah, he was standing in line behind Max. And even though I was trying to hide from them, I could see him kind of eyeballing the back of Max's head."

"Understandably," Pip said. Jason Bell had just as much reason to hate Max Hastings as she did. Whatever the outcome of the trial, Max had drugged and raped his youngest daughter, Becca. And as horrific and unspeakable as that was, it was even worse than that. Max's actions were the catalyst for Andie Bell's death. You might even say a direct cause. Everything came back to Max Hastings, when you really thought about it: Becca traumatized, letting Andie die in front of her and covering it up. Sal Singh dead, believed to be Andie's killer. That poor woman in Elliot Ward's attic. Pip's project. Her dog, Barney, buried in the backyard. Howie Bowers in prison, sharing whispers about Child Brunswick. Charlie Green arriving in town. Layla Mead. Jamie Reynolds missing. Stanley Forbes dead and blood on Pip's hands. She could trace it all back to Max Hastings. The origin. Her cornerstone. And maybe Jason Bell's too.

"I mean, yeah," Cara said, "but I wasn't expecting the next part. So, Jackie handed Max his drink, and as he was turning to walk away, Jason held out his elbow and nudged right into Max. Spilled coffee all down his T-shirt."

"No?" Ravi stared at Cara.

"I know." Her whispers strained into an excitable hiss. "And then

Max was like, 'Watch where you're going' and shoved him back. And Jason grabbed Max's collar and said, 'You stay out of my way,' or something like that. But anyway, by this point, Jackie had inserted herself between them, and then this other customer escorted Max out of the café and apparently he was going on about 'You'll hear from my lawyer' or something."

"Sounds like Max," Pip said, pushing the words through her gritted teeth. She shivered. The air felt different now that she knew he'd been here too. Stuffy. Cold. Tainted. Fairview was just not big enough for both of them.

"Naomi's been wondering what to do about Max," Cara continued, so quiet you couldn't even call it a whisper anymore. "Whether she should go to the police, tell them about New Year 2014, you know, the hit-and-run. Even though she'll get in trouble, she's saying at least it will get Max in trouble too, as he was the one driving. Maybe it's a way of putting him behind bars, at least for a short while, so he can't hurt anyone else. And put an end to this ridiculous lawsuit thi—"

"No," Pip cut across her. "Naomi can't go to the police. It won't work. She'll only be hurting herself and nothing will happen to *him*. Max will win again."

"But at least the truth will be out and Naomi—"

"The truth doesn't matter," Pip said, digging her nails into her thigh. The Pip from last year wouldn't recognize this one today. That lively-eyed girl and her school project, naively clinging to *the truth,* wrapping it around herself like a blanket. But the Pip sitting here was a different person and she knew better. The truth had burned her too many times; it couldn't be trusted. "Tell her not to, Cara. She didn't hit that man and she didn't want to leave him, she was coerced. Tell her I promise I will get him. I don't know how, but I will do it. Max will get exactly what he deserves."

Ravi stretched an arm around Pip's shoulder, giving it a gentle squeeze. "Or, you know, instead of revenge plots, we could focus our energy on going off to college in a few weeks," he said brightly. "You haven't even picked out a new comforter; I'm told that's a very important milestone."

Pip knew that Ravi and Cara had just flashed each other a look. "I'm fine," she said.

Cara looked like she was about to say something more, but her eyes drew up as the bell jangled above the café door. Pip turned to follow her gaze. If it was Max Hastings, she didn't know what she might do, she—

"Ah, hello, gang," said a voice Pip knew well.

Connor Reynolds. She smiled and waved at him. But it wasn't just Connor; Jamie was here too, closing the café door with another chime of the bell. He spotted Pip a moment later and a grin split his face, wrinkling his freckled nose. Frecklier now, after the summer. And she would know; she'd spent that entire week he was missing studying photos of his face, searching his eyes for answers.

"Fancy seeing you guys here," Jamie said, overtaking Connor as he strolled over to their table. He placed a fleeting hand on Pip's shoulder. "Hey, how're you doing? Can I get you guys a drink or something?"

Sometimes Pip saw that same look in Jamie's eyes too, haunted by Stanley's death and the parts they'd both played in it. A burden they would always share. But Jamie hadn't been there when it happened, he didn't have blood on his hands, not in the same way.

"Why is it whenever I'm on shift, the whole frickin' circus turns up?" Cara said. "Do you guys think I'm lonely or something?"

"No, mate." Connor flicked her topknot. "We think you need the practice."

"Connor Reynolds, I swear to god if you order one of those iced pumpkin macchiatos today, I will murder you dead."

"Cara," Jackie called cheerily from behind the counter, "remember lesson number one: we don't threaten to kill customers."

"Even if they're ordering the most complicated thing just to annoy you?" Cara stood up, with an exaggerated side-eye at Connor.

"Even then."

Cara growled, calling Connor a "basic white bitch" under her breath as she made her way toward the counter. "One iced pumpkin macchiato coming up," she said with the fakest of enthusiasm.

"Made with love, I hope," Connor laughed.

Cara glowered. "More like spite."

"Well, as long as it's not spit."

"So," Jamie said, taking Cara's empty seat, "Nat told me about the mediation meeting."

Pip nodded. "It was . . . eventful."

"I can't believe he's suing you." Jamie's hand tightened into a fist. "It's just . . . it's not fair. You've been through enough."

She shrugged. "It'll be fine, I'll work it out." Everything always came back to Max Hastings; he was on every side and every angle, pressing in on her. Crushing her. Filling her head with the sound of Stanley's cracking ribs. She wiped the blood off her hands and changed the subject. "How's paramedic training going?"

"Yeah, it's going well," he nodded, broke into a smile. "I'm actually really enjoying it. Who would have thought I would ever enjoy hard work?"

"I think Pip's disgusting work ethic might be contagious," Ravi said. "You should stay back, for your own safety."

The bell clanged again, and from the sudden way Jamie's eyes glowed, Pip knew exactly who had just walked in. Nat da Silva stood in the doorway, her silver hair tied up in a small, stubby ponytail, though most of the hair had made a break from the scrunchie, fanning around her long neck.

Nat's face lit up as she surveyed the room, rolling up the sleeves of her plaid shirt.

"Pip!" Nat made a beeline straight for her. She bent down and wrapped a long arm around Pip's shoulders, hugging her from behind. She smelled like summer. "Didn't know you'd be here. How are you?"

"Good," Pip said, their cheeks pressed together, Nat's skin cold and fresh from the breeze outside. "You?"

"Yeah, we're doing good, aren't we?" Nat straightened up and walked over to Jamie. He stood up to offer her his chair, pulling over another for himself. They paused as they collided, Nat's hand pressed to his chest.

"Hey you," she said, and kissed him quickly.

"Hey you, yourself," Jamie said, the color rising to his already red cheeks.

Pip couldn't help but smile, watching the two of them together. It was . . . what was the word? . . . *nice,* she supposed. Something pure, something good that no one could take away from her—to have known each of them at their lowest and to see how far they'd come. On their own and together. A part of their lives, and they a part of hers.

Sometimes good things did happen in this town, Pip reminded herself, her gaze catching on Ravi, finding his hand under the table. Jamie's glowing eyes and Nat's fierce smile. Connor and Cara bickering over pumpkin spice. This was what she wanted, wasn't it? Just this. Normal life. People you could count on your fingers who cared about you as much as you cared about them. The people who would look for you if you disappeared.

Could she bottle this feeling, live off it for a while? Fill herself with something good and ignore the slick of blood on her hands, not think about the gun in the sound of that cup hitting the table or those dead eyes waiting for her in the darkness of a blink?

Oh, too late.

SEVEN

Pip couldn't see, sweat stinging the corners of her eyes. She might have pushed herself a little too hard this time. Too fast. Like she'd been running away, not just running.

At least she hadn't seen Max out this time. She'd looked for him, ahead and over her shoulder, but he never appeared. The roads were hers.

She lowered her headphones to her neck and walked home, catching her breath as she passed the empty house next door. She turned up her driveway and stopped. Rubbed her eyes.

They were still here, those chalk figures. Five little stick people without their heads. Except, no, that couldn't be right. It had rained yesterday, hard, and they definitely hadn't been here when Pip left for her run. They hadn't, she swore. And there was something else too.

She bent to get a closer look. They had moved. On Sunday morning they'd been at the intersection between sidewalk and driveway. Now they had shuffled several inches over, down the brickwork, moving closer to the house.

Pip was certain: these figures were new. Drawn in the hour she'd been out on her run. She closed her eyes to focus her ears, listening to the white-noise sound of trees dancing in the wind, the high whistle of a bird overhead, and the growling sound of a lawn mower somewhere close by. But she couldn't hear the squawking sounds of the neighborhood kids. Not one peep.

Eyes open, and yes, she hadn't imagined them. Five small figures. She should ask her mom if she knew what they were. Maybe they weren't supposed to be headless people; maybe they were something entirely innocent and her wrung-out head was twisting them into something sinister.

She straightened up, the muscles in her calves aching and a sharper sensation in her left ankle. She stretched out her legs, and continued toward the house.

But she only made it two steps.

Her heart picked up, knocking against her ribs.

There was a gray lump farther along the driveway. Near the front door. A feathered gray lump. She knew before she even got close what it was. Another dead pigeon. Pip approached it slowly, steps careful and silent, as though not to wake it, bring it crashing back to life. Her fingers fizzed with adrenaline as she towered over the pigeon, expecting to see herself again reflected in its glassy, dead eyes. But she wasn't there. Because there were no dead eyes.

Because there was no head.

A clean, tufted stump where it should be, hardly any blood.

Pip stared at it. Then up at the house, and back to the headless pigeon. She took herself back to last Monday morning, peeled away the week, sorting through her memories. There she was, rushing out the door in her smart suit, stopping as she caught sight of the dead bird, fixating on its eyes, thinking of Stanley.

It had been here. Right here. Two dead pigeons in exactly the same place. And those strange, shifting chalk figures with arms and legs and no heads. This couldn't be a coincidence, could it? Pip didn't believe in those at the best of times.

"Mom!" she called, pushing open the front door. "Mom!" Her voice rebounded down the hall, the echo mocking her.

"Hi, sweetie," her mom replied, leaning out of the kitchen doorway, a knife in her hands. "I'm not crying, I promise, it's these damn onions."

"Mom, there's a dead pigeon out on the drive," Pip said, keeping her voice low and even.

"Another one?" Her mom's face fell. "For goodness sake. And, of course, your father's out *again,* so I'm the one who has to do it." She sighed. "Right, just let me get this stew on and then I'll deal with it."

"N-no," Pip stammered. "Mom, you're not getting it. There's a dead pigeon in exactly the same place as the one last week. Like someone put it there on purpose." It sounded ridiculous even as she said it.

"Oh, don't be silly." Her mom waved her off. "It's just one of the neighbors' cats."

"A cat?" Pip shook her head. "But it's in exactly the same pl—"

"Yes, probably this cat's new favorite killing spot. The Williamses have a big tabby cat; I see it in our yard sometimes. Poops in my herb garden." She mimed stabbing it with her knife.

"This one doesn't have a head."

"Huh?"

"The pigeon."

Her mom's mouth turned down at the corners. "Well, what can I say, cats are disgusting. Don't you remember the cat we had before we got Barney? When you were very small?"

"You mean Socks?" Pip said.

"Yes. Socks was a vicious little killer. Brought dead things in the house almost every day. Mice, birds. Sometimes these great big rabbits. Would chew their heads off and leave them somewhere for me to find. Trails of guts. It was like coming home to a horror show."

"What you guys talking about?" Josh's voice called down the stairs.

"Nothing!" Pip's mom yelled back. "You mind your own business!"

"But, this . . ." Pip sighed. "Can you just come look?"

"I'm in the middle of dinner, Pip."

"It will take two seconds." She tilted her head. "Please?"

"Uh, fine." Her mom backtracked to place the knife on the counter. "Quietly, though. I don't want Mr. Nosy coming down and getting involved."

"Who's Mr. Nosy?" Josh's small voice followed them out the front door.

"I'm getting that kid some earplugs, I swear to god," Pip's mom whispered as they walked out onto the drive. "Right, yes, I see it. A headless pigeon, exactly as I imagined it. Thanks for the preview."

"It's not just that." Pip grabbed her arm and walked her down the driveway. She pointed. "Look, those little chalk figures. They were here a couple of days ago too, nearer the sidewalk. The rain washed them away, but they're back, and they've moved. They weren't here when I left on my run."

Pip's mom bent over, leaning on her knees. She screwed her eyes.

"You see them, right?" Pip asked her, doubt stirring in her stomach, cold and heavy.

"Er, yeah, I guess," she said, squinting even harder. "There are some faded white lines."

"Yeah, exactly," Pip said, relieved. "And what do they look like to you?"

Her mom stepped closer, tipped her head to look at them from another angle.

"I don't know, maybe it's a tire tread from my car or something. I did drive to a building site today, so there could have been dust or chalk around."

"No, look harder," Pip said, her voice spiking with irritation. She narrowed her own eyes; they couldn't just be tire treads, could they?

"I don't know, Pip, maybe it's dust from the mortar joints."

"The . . . what?"

"The lines between the bricks." Her mom blew out a funneled breath, and one of the little figures all but disappeared. She straightened up, running her hands over her skirt to smooth out the creases.

Pip pointed again. "You don't see stick people? Five of them. Well, four now, thanks. Like someone has drawn them?"

Pip's mom shook her head. "Don't look like stick people to me," she said. "They don't have he—"

"Heads?" Pip cut her off. "Exactly."

"Oh, Pip." Her mom eyed her with concern, that eyebrow slipping up her forehead again. "They aren't connected. I'm sure it's just something from my tires, or maybe the mail carrier's truck." She studied them again. "And if someone did draw those, it's probably just the Yardleys' kids. That middle one seems a bit, well, you know." She pulled a face.

It made sense, what her mom was saying. It was just a cat, of course, just tire treads or a kid's innocent doodle. Why had her mind jumped so far ahead, thinking they must be connected? She felt the creep of shame under her skin, that she'd even considered the idea someone had left them both here. Even more shameful, that they'd left them just for her. Why would she think that? Because she was scared of everything now, the other side of her brain answered. She had a fight-or-flight heart, felt danger pressing in on her when there was none, could hear gunshots in any sound if she wanted to, scared of the night but not of the dark, even scared to look down at her own hands. Broken.

"Are you OK, sweetie?" Her mom had abandoned the chalk figures, studying her face instead. "Did you get enough sleep last night?"

Almost none. "Yes. Plenty," Pip said.

"You look pale, is all." The eyebrow stretched even higher.

"I'm always pale."

"Lost a bit of weight too."

"Mom—"

"I'm just saying, sweetie. Here." She slotted her arm through Pip's, leading her back toward the house. "I'll get back to dinner and I'll even make tiramisu for dessert. Your favorite."

"But it's a Tuesday?"

"So?" Her mom smiled. "My little girl's going off to college in a few weeks, let me spoil her while I still have her."

Pip gave her mom's arm a squeeze back. "Thanks."

"I'll deal with that pigeon in a minute, you don't need to worry about it," she said, shutting the front door behind them.

"I'm not worried about the pigeon," Pip said, though her mom had already moved away, back to the kitchen. Pip listened to her clattering around in there, tutting about these *industrial-strength onions.* "I'm not worried about the pigeon," Pip said again quietly, just to herself. She was worried about who might have left it there. And then worried that she'd thought that at all.

She turned to the stairs, walking up to see Josh perched on the top step, chin between his hands.

"What pigeon?" he asked as Pip rested her hand on his head, navigating around him.

"Seriously," she muttered, "maybe I should let you borrow these more often." She tapped the headphones cradled around her neck. "Glue them to your head."

Pip went into her room, leaning against the door to close it behind her. She freed her arm from the Velcro phone holder and let it drop to the floor. She peeled her top off, the material clinging to her sweat-sticky skin, getting tangled around the headphones. They came off together, now in a heap on her carpet. Yeah, she should definitely shower before dinner. And . . . she glanced at the second drawer down in her desk. Maybe just take one, to calm her down and settle her spiking heart, keep the blood off her hands and her mind off of headless things. Her mom was starting to suspect something was wrong; Pip needed to be good at dinner. Just like her old self.

A cat and tire marks. Those made sense, perfect sense. What was wrong with her? Why did she need it to be something bad, like she was looking for trouble? She held a breath. Just one more case. Save Jane Doe and save yourself. That's all it would take, and she wouldn't be like this anymore: misplaced inside her own head. She had a plan. Just stick to the plan.

Pip quickly checked her phone. A text from Ravi: *Would it be weird to have chicken nuggets ON TOP of pizza?*

And an email from Roger Turner: *Hi Pip. Should we have a chat sometime this week, now you've had a chance to think about the offer from the mediation? Best wishes, Roger Turner.*

Pip exhaled. She felt sorry for Roger, but her answer was the same. Over her dead body. What was the most professional way of saying that?

She was about to open the email when a new notification slotted in beneath. Another message had come through the form on her website, to AGGGTMpodcast@gmail.com. The preview read: *Who will look for you . . .* and Pip knew exactly what the full text would say. Yet again.

She opened up the message from anon to delete it. Maybe she could set up some kind of blocker that would send them straight to spam? The message opened and Pip's thumb hovered over the trash icon.

Her eyes stopped her just in time, catching on one word.

She blinked.

Read the message in full.

Who will look for you when you're the one who disappears?

Ps. remember to always kill two birds with one stone.

The phone slipped from her hands.

EIGHT

The soft thud of her phone falling to the carpet was the shot of a gun, aiming through her chest. Echoing five times, until her heart captured the sound and carried it on.

She stood there for a moment, numb to everything except the violence erupting beneath her skin. Great thunderclaps of gunshots and cracking bones, the sucking sound of blood between her fingers, and a scream: hers. The words rupturing at the edges as they threw themselves around her head: *Charlie, please don't do this. I'm begging you!*

The cream walls of her room peeled away, revealing burning and blackened timbers, collapsing in on themselves. The abandoned farmhouse resurrected in her bedroom, filling her lungs with smoke. Pip closed her eyes and told herself she was here and now, she wasn't there and then. But she couldn't do it, not alone. She needed help.

She staggered through the fire, arm up to shield her eyes. To her desk, fingers fumbling, finding the second drawer on the right. She pulled it out, completely, tipped the drawer out on the burning floor. Red string unraveled from her, papers fluttered, pins scattered, tangling in white headphone wires. The cardboard bottom that hid her secrets flipped away, and out came the six burner phones, falling out of their carefully structured order. Last out was the small clear bag.

Pip ripped it open with shaking fingers. How were there so few left already? She tipped out one pill and swallowed it dry, her eyes watering as it scraped her throat.

She was here and now. Not then and there. Here and now.

It wasn't blood, it was just sweat. See? *Wipe it on your leggings and see.*

Not then and there.

Here and now.

But was here and now any better? She stared at her phone, abandoned on the floor over there. *Kill two birds with one stone.* Two dead pigeons on the driveway, one with dead all-seeing eyes, and one with none. That wasn't a coincidence, was it? Maybe it wasn't a cat, maybe someone really had put them there, along with those chalk figures drawing closer and closer. The same someone who was desperate for Pip to answer that one question: *Who will look for you when you're the one who disappears?* Someone who knew where she lived. A stalker?

She'd been looking out for trouble, and so it had found her.

No, no, stop. She was doing it again, taking things too far, seeking danger where maybe there was none. *Kill two birds with one stone.* It was a very common phrase. And she'd been receiving that question from anon for a long time, and nothing had happened to her so far, had it? She was here, she hadn't disappeared.

She crawled along the floor and turned her phone over, the device recognizing her face and unlocking. Pip swiped into her emails, clicking into the search bar. She typed in *"Who will look for you when you're the one who disappears? + anon."*

Seven emails, eight including the one she just got, all from different accounts, all asking her that same question. Pip scrolled up. She'd received the first one on May 8, the messages starting out further apart, getting closer and closer together, only four days between the final two. May 8? Pip shook her head; that didn't seem right. She remembered getting the first one earlier than that, around the time Jamie Reynolds had disappeared and she'd been the one looking for him. That's why the question had stuck out to her.

Oh wait. It might have been on Twitter. She pressed the blue icon to open the app, tapping into the advanced search options. She typed in the question again, in the field for *this exact phrase,* and her podcast handle in the *to these accounts* section.

She pressed search, her eyes spooling along with the loading circle.

The page filled with results: nine separate tweets sent to her, asking her that exact question. The most recent from just seven minutes ago, with the same P.S. as the email. And at the bottom of the page was the very first time: *Who will look for you when you're the one who disappears?* Sent on Sunday, the twenty-sixth of April, in response to Pip's tweet announcing the second season of *A Good Girl's Guide to Murder: The Disappearance of Jamie Reynolds.* That was it. The beginning. More than three months ago.

That felt so long ago now. Jamie had been missing for only one day. Stanley Forbes was walking around, alive, without six holes in him; Pip had spoken to him that very day. Charlie Green was just her new neighbor. There'd been no blood on her hands, and sleep didn't always come easy, but it had come nonetheless. Max was on trial and Pip had believed, down into the very deepest part of who she was, that he would face justice for what he'd done. So many beginnings on that bright April morning, beginnings that had led her here. The first steps along a path that had turned on her, twisting around itself until it only led down. But had something else begun on that exact day, too? Something that had been growing for three months and was only now rearing its head?

Who will look for you when you're the one who disappears?

Pip pushed to her feet, back in her room now, the abandoned farmhouse locked away at the back of her mind. She fell onto her bed. The question, the chalk figures, the two dead birds. Could they be connected? Could this be about her? It was tenuous at best, but had there been anything else? Anything she'd thought strange at the time, but her mind had abandoned it to chance? Oh . . . There had been that letter several weeks ago. Well, not even a letter. It had been just an envelope, *Pippa Fitz-Amobi* scribbled on the front in scratchy black ink. She remembered thinking there was no address, no stamp, so someone must have pushed it through the front door. But when she'd opened it—Dad standing beside her, asking whether it was "old-fashioned nudes from Ravi"—there'd been nothing inside at all. Empty. She'd put it in the recycling bin and never thought about it again. The mystery letter had been forgotten as soon as another letter had arrived with her name on it: the letter of demand from Max Hastings and his lawyer. Was it possible that envelope had been connected to all this?

And now she was thinking maybe there'd been something else before that. The day of Stanley Forbes's funeral. When the ceremony was over and Pip returned to her car, she'd found a small bouquet of roses tucked inside the driver's-side mirror. Except every flower head had been picked off, red petals strewn over the gravel below. A bouquet of thorns and stems. At the time, Pip thought it must have been one of the protesters at the funeral, who hadn't disbanded until the police were called. But maybe it wasn't any of the protestors, not Ant's dad or Mary Scythe or Leslie from the Stop & Shop. Maybe it had been a gift, from the same person who wanted to know who would look for her when she disappeared.

If it was—if these incidents were connected—then this had been going on for weeks. Months, even. And she hadn't realized. But maybe there was a reason for that. Maybe she was reading too much into everything now, all because of that second dead bird. Pip didn't trust herself and she didn't trust her fear.

Only one thing was clear: *if* these all were from the same person—from dead flowers to dead pigeons—then it was escalating. Both in severity but also occurrence. Pip needed to track it somehow, collect all the data points and see if there were any connections, if she really did have a stalker or if she was finally losing it. *A spreadsheet,* she thought, imagining the smirk on Ravi's face. But it would help to see it all neatly laid out, help her work out if this was real or only real in the dark place at the back of her head, and if it *was* real, where it all might lead, what the endgame was.

Pip made her way across the room to her desk, stepping over the tipped-out contents of the drawer; she would tidy that up later. She pulled her laptop open, double-clicked on Google Chrome, and pulled up a blank tab. She typed "stalker" into the search bar and pressed enter, scrolling down the list of results. *Report a stalker* on a government website, a Wikipedia page, a site about types of stalkers, Inside the Mind of a Stalker, psychology sites, and crime statistics. Pip clicked on the first result and started to read through it all, turning to a fresh page in her notebook.

She wrote: *Who will look for you when you're the one who disappears?* Underlined it three times. She couldn't help but feel the quiet rage embedded in that sinister question. She did think about disappearing sometimes, running away and leaving Pip behind. Or disappearing inside her own head, in those rare moments when her mind was quiet, an absence she could just float in, free. But what did "disappear" mean, really, when it came down to it? Define "disappear."

Sometimes people came back from being disappeared. Jamie Reynolds was one example, and Isla Jordan, the young woman Elliot Ward had kept for five years thinking she was someone else. They had un-disappeared. But then Pip's mind went back to the beginning, back to Andie Bell, to Sal Singh, to the victims of Scott "the Monster of Rochester" Brunswick, to Jane Doe, to every true crime podcast and documentary she'd ever lost herself in. And in most cases, "disappear" meant "dead."

"Pip, dinner!"

"Coming!"

File Name:

Potential Stalker Incidents.xlsx

Date	Days Since Last Incident	Type	Incident	Severity Scale (1-10)
04/26/2020	n/a	Online	Tweet: *Who will look for you when you're the one who disappears?*	1
05/08/2020	12	Online	Email and Tweet: (same question)	2
05/17/2020	9	Offline	Dead flowers left on car	4
05/31/2020	14	Online	Email: (same question)	1
06/11/2020	11	Online	Tweet: (same question)	1
06/21/2020	10	Online	Tweet: (same question)	1
06/30/2020	9	Offline	Empty envelope posted through door. Addressed to me.	4
07/08/2020	8	Online	Email: (same question)	1
07/15/2020	7	Online	Email and Tweet: (same question)	2
07/22/2020	7	Online	Email and Tweet: (same question)	2
07/27/2020	5	Offline	Dead pigeon left on driveway (with head)	7
07/27/2020	0	Online	Email and Tweet: (same question)	3
07/31/2020	4	Online	Email and Tweet: (same question)	2
08/02/2020	2	Offline	5 chalk figures drawn at foot of driveway (headless figures?)	5
08/04/2020	2	Offline	5 chalk figures farther up the driveway, closer to the house	6
08/04/2020	0	Offline	Dead pigeon left on driveway (without head)	8
08/04/2020	0	Online	Email and Tweet: (same question) with added *PS. Remember to always kill two birds with one stone*	5

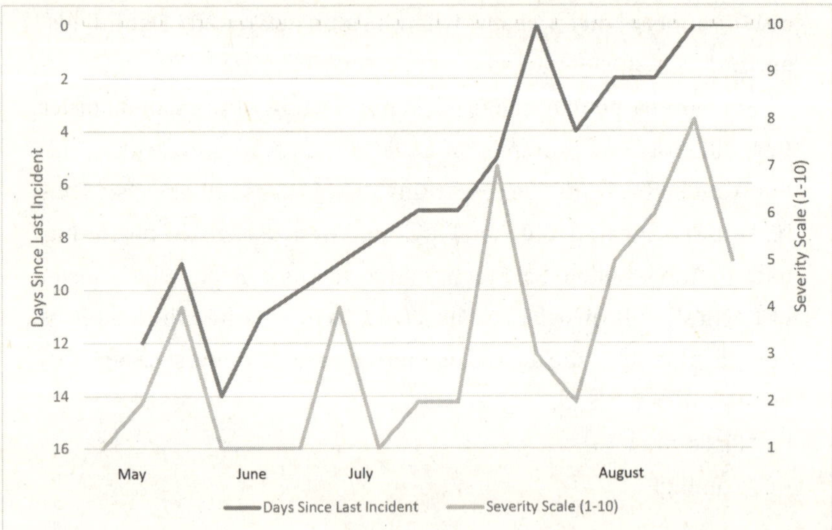

NINE

There was something stuck to her shoe. Clacking against the sidewalk with every step, the gummy pull unbalancing her tread.

Pip slowed to a jog, then a walk, right down to a stop, wiping her forehead on her sleeve. She raised her leg to inspect the bottom of her sneaker. There was a crinkled piece of duct tape stuck to the middle of her heel. The silver finish on the tape had smeared to a dirty gray. Pip must have run over it somewhere on her route, unknowingly picked it up.

She pinched her fingers around the filthy piece of tape, peeling it off as the tacky side clung to the dark sole of her shoe. It came free, leaving little specks of gluey white behind, specks she could still feel as she picked up her pace and started running again.

"Great," she hissed to herself, trying to get her breathing in order again. *In, step, two, three, out, step, two, three.*

She was taking her longer route this evening, up around Lodge Wood. Long. Fast. Exhaust herself so maybe she wouldn't need to take anything to fall asleep. This plan never worked out, never had and probably never would, and she believed her own lies even less now. The last two nights had been the worst in a long time. That doubt keeping her awake, that niggling idea that someone might be out there watching her. Someone who might even be counting down the days until she disappeared. No, stop. She'd come on a run to get away from those thoughts. Pip pushed herself even harder, out of control, rounding the corner too fast.

And there *he* was.

On the other side of the road. Blue water bottle gripped in one hand.

Max Hastings.

And just as she saw him, he saw her. Their eyes met, only the width of one road between them as they approached each other.

Max slowed his pace, pushing his blond hair back from his face. Why was he slowing down? Shouldn't he want to get this over and done with too, the moment they had to pass each other? Pip pushed her legs harder, a pain in her ankle, and their mismatched steps became a kind of music, a chaotic percussion that filled the unknowing street, accompanying the high-pitched howl of the wind in the trees. Or did that sound come from inside her head?

There was a tightening in her chest as her heart outgrew its cage, unrolling under her skin, filling her with angry red until it was all behind her eyes. She watched him draw close and her view shifted to red, the scene speeding up before her. Something takes over, pulls Pip by the hand across the road, guiding her feet. And she isn't scared anymore, she is only rage. Only red. And this is right, this is supposed to be, she knows it.

She's across the road in six strides, and up onto his side. He's just feet away when he stops, stares at her.

"What are you do—" he begins to ask. She doesn't let him finish.

Pip closes the gap between them and her elbow crashes into Max's face. She hears a crack, but it isn't Stanley's ribs this time, it's Max's nose. The sound is the same, it's all she knows. Max bends double and howls into his hands as the nose falls crooked on his face. But she isn't finished. Pip rips his hands away and hits him again, slamming her fist into his sharp cheekbones. His blood, it slides between her knuckles onto her palm, right where it belongs.

And still she isn't finished. There's a truck coming, a semi; there are never trucks that size on this small country lane, they wouldn't fit. But this one is almost here, and now is her chance. Pip grabs Max, twisting her hands into the fabric of his sweat-stained top. And in that passing moment, Max's eyes widen in fear, and they both know it: she has won. The truck's horn screams but Max doesn't have a chance to. Pip throws him out into the road in front of the too-big truck and he explodes, raining red down on her as she stands there, smiling.

A car passed, in real life, and the sound brings her back. The red falls from her eyes and Pip returned to herself. To here and now. Running down this path. Max was over there on his side of the road, and she here on hers. Pip looked down and blinked, trying to shake loose the violence inside her own head. If she should be scared of anything, it was of that.

She glanced up again at Max, keeping her eye on him as he regained his speed, water bottle pumping at his side. The moment was coming, the moment they would pass each other, cross paths, overlap. They were still running toward each other, and then it happened, the pass, the split second of convergence, and then they were running away from each other, their backs turned.

At the end of the lane, Pip checked back over her shoulder. Max was gone and she could breathe a little easier, without his steps haunting hers.

She was getting worse; she could step outside of herself and recognize that. The panic attacks, the pills, the rage so hot it might just burn the world down with it. She was slipping ever further from that normal life she was so desperate to crawl back to. To Ravi, to her family, her friends. But it would be OK, because she had a plan for how to get there. To fix everything. Save Jane Doe, save herself.

But there might be a new obstacle now, she realized as she looped down the far end of Thatcher Road, past the broken lamppost, her usual marker to slow for the wind-down walk home. If she really did have a stalker, whoever they were, whatever they wanted to do to her—whether it was just to scare her, or whether they really did want her to disappear—they were now in her way too. Or maybe it was Pip getting in her own way. What had Epps called it? A self-destructive spiral. Maybe there was no stalker, maybe there was just her and an overspill of violence from that dark place at the back of her head. Finding danger only because she was looking for it.

That's when she walked over it, on the sidewalk between the Yardleys' house and the Williamses,' her own still in the distance. She caught it as a blur in the corner of her eye, white intersecting lines and a large smudge of chalk, but she had to backstep before she realized what it really was. There, across the width of the sidewalk, smeared by her own sneakers, were three large words written in chalk:

DEAD GIRL WALKING

Pip's head whipped around. She was alone on the street, and the neighborhood was dinnertime-quiet. She turned back to study the words beneath her feet. "Dead girl walking." She had been the one to walk over them. Was this for her? It wasn't on her driveway, but it was on her route. A feeling in her gut, an instinct. It was a message for her, Pip knew it.

She was the dead girl walking.

No, don't be ridiculous. It wasn't even on her drive, it was on a public street. This could have been left for anyone, by anyone. And why was she listening to her instincts anyway? They put blood on her hands and a gun in her heart and danger in shadows when there was nothing there. But part of her felt she shouldn't dismiss it either, torn in two, between Stanley and Charlie, between having a stalker and inventing one herself. Pip struggled with the strap on her arm, releasing her phone. She straightened up to take a photo of the words, a sliver of her sneaker at the bottom of the frame. Evidence, just in case. She didn't have one of the chalk figures; they'd been gone by the time she finished her shower the other day, wiped away by the wheels of her dad's car. But she had a photo now, another data point for the spreadsheet. Just in case. Data was clean and it didn't take sides. And if this really were a message for her, this would be assigned a higher number, an eight, maybe a nine; it might even be considered a direct threat.

And with that, Pip felt closer to this unknown person who might or might not exist, felt she understood them a little better. They agreed on something: "disappear" meant "dead." At least they had cleared that up.

Up ahead, she saw a car turning in to her drive. Ravi. Her other cornerstone. Pip stepped over the chalk words and hurried along the sidewalk. Step after step toward home, and she couldn't help being what the words wanted her to be, the dead girl walking. But if she sped up, she would be running instead.

"Oh, hello!" Ravi's voice found her as she turned onto the drive, lowering her headphones to her neck. He climbed out of his car. "Look who it is, my sporty girlfriend!" He smiled and flexed his arms, chanting "sports sports sports" until she reached him. "You OK?" he asked, running his hand around her waist. "Good run?"

"Um, well, I saw Max Hastings again. So . . . no."

Ravi gritted his teeth. "Another run-in? He's still alive, I presume," he said, trying to lighten the mood.

"Only just." Pip shrugged, afraid that Ravi could see into her head, see all those violent things that swirled inside it. But he should be able to see in there; he was the person who knew her best. And if he loved her, then she couldn't be all bad. Right?

"Hey, what's up?" he said. Oh no, he could definitely tell. But that was good, she reminded herself, she shouldn't keep secrets from him. He was her person. Except those secrets she was most ashamed of, the ones that lived in the second drawer down in her desk.

"Er, this was on my route, just down the road." She pulled up the photo on her phone and held it out to Ravi. "Someone wrote that on the sidewalk in chalk."

"'Dead girl walking,'" he muttered, and hearing it in someone else's voice changed the meaning somehow. Made her see it differently. Proof that it did exist outside of her own head. "Do you think this was for you? Connected to the pigeons?" he asked.

"It was on my running route, right after the point where I normally start walking to cool down before home," she said. "If someone's been watching me, they would know that."

Why would someone be watching her, though? It sounded more ridiculous when she said it out loud.

Ravi shook his head. "OK, I really don't like this."

"It's fine, sorry, it's probably nothing to do with me," Pip said. "Just being stupid."

"No you're not," he said, voice hardening. "OK, fine, we don't know for sure if you have a stalker or not, but this tips it for me. I mean it now, and I know what you're going to say, but I think you should go to the police."

"Wh— And they'll do what, Ravi? Nothing, as usual." She could feel the anger spiking again. *No, not with him, control yourself.* She breathed and swallowed it down. "Especially when I don't even know myself."

"If this is the same person emailing you, the same one who left the chalk and the pigeons, then this person is threatening you," he said, widening his eyes in the way that told her he was serious. "They might be dangerous." He paused. "It might be Max." Another pause. "Or Charlie Green."

It wasn't Charlie, could never be Charlie. But Pip had thought of Max, his face flashing into her mind when she'd first read the words. Who else would know her running route so well? And if Max hated her as much as she hated him, well then . . .

"I know," she said. "But maybe they aren't connected, and if they are it might just be someone messing with me." Her instincts told her that wasn't true, even as she said it, she just wanted to take the worry out of his eyes, bring back the smile. And she didn't want to go back to that police station; anything but that.

"I guess it all depends," Ravi said.

"On?"

"On whether they just found those dead birds or . . . whether they killed them. There's a world of difference there."

"I know," she exhaled, hoping he would keep his voice down, in case Josh could somehow hear. A new feeling in her gut now that Ravi and instinct were taking the same side against her. She didn't want this to be real. She preferred the other option, that she was seeing a pattern where there was none, her brain too fine-tuned to danger, because that would soon be fixed along with everything else. Save Jane Doe, save yourself.

"We shouldn't take the chance." Ravi ran his thumb across her collarbone. "You leave for college in a couple of weeks, so I think everything will be OK and this will probably die down. But if it is the latter, if this person is dangerous, then this is not something you can deal with on your own. You need to report this. Tomorrow."

"But I can't—"

"You're Pippa Fitz-Amobi"—he smiled, brushed the flyaway hairs from her eyes—"there's nothing you *can't* do. Even if it's biting your tongue and asking Detective Hawkins for help."

Pip growled, dropped her head to roll around her neck.

"That's the spirit," Ravi said, patting her on the back. "Well done. Now can you show me where this chalk was? I want to see it."

"OK."

Pip turned to lead him away from the house, his hand grabbing for hers, fingers sliding into the gaps between her knuckles. Holding on. Hand in hand: the boy with a dimple in his chin, and the dead girl walking.

File Name:

Dead girl walking photo.jpg

TEN

Pip hated this place. As she stepped toward the entrance, catching sight of the blue-painted waiting room beyond, she could feel her skin recoiling from it, unwrapping from her flesh, begging her to turn back. Retreat. The voice in her head too. This was a bad place, a bad, bad place. She shouldn't be here.

But she'd promised Ravi, and her promises still meant something to her. Especially with him.

And so she was here, Fairview Police Station, the sign glaring down at her, covered in a thin layer of windswept grime. The automatic doors jumped open and swallowed her whole.

She passed the regimented lines of cold metal chairs facing the reception desk. A man and a woman sat against the back wall, swaying slightly, as though the police station were at sea. Drunk, clearly, at eleven a.m. Though Pip had had to take a Xanax to work up the nerve to even come here, so who was she to judge them?

Pip approached the desk, hearing the drunk man whisper an almost affectionate "Fuck you," immediately parroted by the slurred voice of the woman. To each other, not to Pip, though it might as well have been: everything inside this building was hostile, a bad memory, a *fuck you* from the garish, flickering bulbs and the scream of the polished floor beneath her shoes. It had squealed just the same way when she was here months ago, asking Hawkins to look for Jamie

Reynolds so she didn't have to. Begging him. How different things would be now if only he had said yes.

Just as she reached the desk, Eliza, the detention officer, strolled out of the attached office with a sharp "Right, you two!" She looked up and jumped at the sight of Pip. Pip didn't blame her; she must look terrible. Eliza's face softened, a pitying smile as she fiddled with her gray hair. "Pip, sweetie, didn't see you there."

"Sorry," Pip said quietly. But Eliza *had* seen her, and now Pip saw her too. Not here and now, in the reception area with the drunk couple behind, but on *that night*, back inside the belly of the police station. That very same pitying expression on Eliza's face as she helped Pip peel off her blood-drenched clothes. Gloved hands packing them away into clear evidence bags. Pip's top. Her bra. The pinkish smears of dead Stanley all over her skin as she stood there, bare and shivering, in front of this woman. A moment that bound them forever, hanging like a ghost at the corners of Eliza's smile.

"Pip?" Eliza's eyes had narrowed. "I said, what can I do for you today?"

"Oh." Pip cleared her throat. "I'm here to see *him* again. Is he here?"

Eliza exhaled, or had it been a sigh? "Yes, he is," she said. "I'll go tell him you're here. Please, take a seat." She gestured at the front row of metal chairs before disappearing to the back office.

Pip wouldn't take a seat; that would be surrender. This was a bad, bad place and she couldn't let it have her.

The sound came sooner than she was expecting; the harsh grating buzz as the door to the back half of the station opened and Detective Hawkins stepped through, in jeans and a light shirt. "Pip," he called, though he didn't need to, she was already following him, through the door and into the worse, worse part of the station.

The door closed and locked behind her.

Hawkins glanced back with a jerk of his head that might have been a nod. Down this very same corridor, past Interview Room 1, the same journey she had walked back then, in new, bloodless clothes. She never found out whose they were. She'd followed Hawkins then too, into a small room off to the right, with a man who never said his name, or he had and Pip never heard. But she remembered Hawkins's grip on her wrist, to help her as she pressed each finger into the ink pad and then onto the correct square on the paper grid, the patterns of her fingerprints like never-ending mazes, made only to trap you. *It's just to rule you out. To eliminate you.* That's what Hawkins had said back then. And all Pip remembered saying back was, *I'm fine.* No one could have thought she was fine.

"Pip?" Hawkins's voice brought her back to now, back into this even heavier body. He had stopped walking, was holding the door open to Interview Room 3.

"Thank you," she said flatly, ducking under the archway of his outstretched arm and into the room. She wouldn't sit in here either, just in case, but she slid the straps of her backpack from her shoulders and placed it down on the table.

Hawkins crossed his arms and leaned against the wall.

"You know I will call you when it happens, right?" he said.

"What?" Pip narrowed her eyes.

"Charlie Green," Hawkins said. "We have no more information on his whereabouts. But when we do catch him, I will call you. You don't have to come here to ask."

"It's not . . . that's not why I'm here."

"Oh?" he said, the sound from his throat rising, turning it into a question.

"It's something else, really, that I thought I should tell you . . . report to you." Pip shifted awkwardly, pulled her sleeves down to cover her naked wrists. Leave nothing bare or exposed, not in this place.

"Report something? What is it? What happened?" Hawkins face rearranged, all sharp lines from his raised eyebrow to his tightened lips.

"It's . . . well, it's possible I have a stalker," Pip said, the final syllable clicking in her throat. She was only imagining it, but it felt like she could hear that click bounding around the room, ricocheting off the plain walls and the dull metal table.

"A stalker?" Hawkins said, and the click had gotten into his throat too somehow. His face shifted again, new lines and a new curve to his mouth.

"A stalker," Pip repeated, reclaiming the click as her own. "I think."

"OK." Hawkins sounded unsure too, scratching his graying hair to buy him some time. "Well, in order for us to look into this, there needs to have been—"

"A pattern of two or more behaviors," Pip interrupted him. "Yes, I know. I've done my research. And there have been. More than that, in fact. Both online and . . . in real life."

Hawkins coughed into his hand. He pushed off the wall and crossed the room, his shoes sliding across the floor, hissing like they had a secret message just for Pip. He perched against the metal table and crossed his legs.

"OK. What were these incidents?" he asked.

"Here," Pip said, reaching for her bag. Hawkins watched her as she opened it and dug inside. She shifted her bulky headphones out of the way and pulled out the folded sheets of paper. "I made a spreadsheet of all the potential incidents. And a graph. A-and there's a photo," she added, opening the pages and handing them to Hawkins.

Now was her turn to watch him, studying his downturned eyes as they flicked across the spreadsheet, up and down and up again.

"There's quite a lot here," he said, more to himself than to her.

"Yeah."

"Who will look for you when you're the one who disappears?"

Hawkins read out the burning question, and the hairs rose up the back of Pip's neck, hearing it out loud in his voice. "So, it started online, did it?"

"Yes," she said pointing at the top half of the page. "It started with just that question online, and quite infrequently. And then, as you can see, the incidents have become more regular, and then things started happening offline. And if they are connected, then it is escalating: first the flowers on my car, and it has progressed to the—"

"Dead pigeons," Hawkins finished for her, running his finger across the graph.

"Yes. Two of them," Pip said.

"What's this severity scale here?" He glanced up from the column.

"It's a rating, of how severe each possible incident is," she said plainly.

"Yes, I understand that. Where did you get it from?"

"I made it up," Pip said, her feet heavy through the bottoms of her shoes, sinking into the floor. "I did my research and there isn't a lot of official information about stalking, probably as it isn't seen as a policing priority despite it often being a gateway to more violent crimes. I wanted a method of cataloging the potential incidents to see if there's a progression of threat and implied violence. So I made one up. I can explain to you how I did it; there's a three-point difference between online and offline behavior and—"

Hawkins waved his hand to cut her off, the pages fluttering in his grip. "But how do you know these are all connected?" he asked. "The person online asking you that question and these . . . other incidents?"

"Well, of course I don't know for sure. But the thing that made me consider it was the *'kill two birds with one stone'* message, the day the second pigeon was left on my drive. Without a head," she added.

Hawkins's throat made a sound, a new and different click. "Well, it's a very common expression," he said.

"But the two dead pigeons?" Pip said, straightening up. She knew, she already knew where this was going, where it was always destined to go. The look in Hawkins's eyes against the look in hers. He wasn't sure and she wasn't either, but Pip could feel something shifting inside her, changing, heat sliding around under her skin, starting by her neck, claiming her one vertebra at a time.

Hawkins sighed, attempted a smile. "You know, I have a cat, and sometimes I come home to two dead things in one day. Often without heads. One left in my bed just last week."

Pip felt defensive, tightening a fist behind her back.

"We don't have a cat." She hardened her voice, sharpened it at the edges, readying to cut him with it.

"No, but one of your neighbors probably does. I can't really open an investigation because of two dead pigeons."

Was he wrong? That's exactly what she'd told herself too.

"What about the chalk figures? Twice now, getting closer to the house."

Hawkins flicked through the pages.

"Do you have a photograph of them?" He looked up at her.

"No."

"No?"

"They disappeared before I could."

"Disappeared?" He narrowed his eyes.

And the worst thing was, she knew exactly how this all sounded. How unhinged she must seem. But that's what she had wanted too, preferred to think of herself as broken, seeing danger where there wasn't. And yet, a fire was starting in her head, lighting up behind her eyes.

"Washed away before I had a chance," she said. "But I *do* have a photo of something that might be a direct threat." Pip controlled her voice. "Written on the sidewalk on my running route. 'Dead Girl Walking.' "

"Well, yes, I understand your concern." Hawkins shuffled the pages. "But that message wasn't left at your house, it was on a public street. You can't know that you were its intended target."

That's exactly what Pip had first told herself. But that's not what she said now:

"But I do know. I know it was left for me." She didn't before, but standing across from Hawkins now, listening to him say the same things she'd said to herself, it pushed her the other way, splintering off to the same side as instinct. She knew now, with bone-deep certainty, that all these things were connected. That she had a stalker and, more than that, this person meant her harm. This was personal. This was someone who hated her, someone close by.

"And, of course, these online messages from trolls are very unfortunate," Hawkins said. "But this is the kind of thing that happens when you make yourself a public figure."

"Make myself a public figure?" Pip stood a step back, to keep the fire away from Hawkins. "I didn't make myself a public figure, Hawkins, that happened because I had to do your job for you. You would've been happy to let Sal Singh carry the guilt for killing Andie Bell forever. That's why everything has happened the way it has. And this person clearly isn't just someone who's listened to the podcast, an online troll. They're close by. They know where I live. This is more than that." It was. It was.

"I understand that's what you believe," Hawkins said, holding up his palms, trying to placate her. "And it must be very scary to be an online figure and have strangers think it's their right to have access to you. To send you hurtful messages. But you must have expected that, on some level? And I know you aren't the only one to have received hurtful messages from the public because of your podcast. I know Jason Bell has too, after you released season one. He told me in an unofficial capacity; we play tennis sometimes," he said in explanation. "But anyway, I'm sorry, I'm just not seeing a clear connection between these online messages and these other *incidents.*" He said that last word differently, leaned on it a little too hard so that it came out of his mouth sideways.

He didn't believe her. Even after everything, Hawkins didn't believe her. Pip had known this was how it would be—she'd warned Ravi—but faced with it now, in the moment, she couldn't believe he didn't believe her, now that she believed herself. And the heat under her skin became something else: the cold, heavy downward pull of betrayal.

Hawkins lowered the papers to the table. "Pip," he said, his voice softer, gentler, like how he might talk to a lost child. "I think that, after everything you've been through and . . . I truly am sorry for my part in that, that you had to take all this on, alone. But I think you might be seeing a pattern that isn't here, and it's completely understandable after everything you've been through, that you might see danger around every corner, but . . ."

She'd thought the same thing about herself not so long ago, and yet his words still felt like a punch to the gut. Why had she allowed herself even a shred of hope that this would go another way? Stupid, *stupid.*

"You think I'm making it up," she said. It wasn't a question.

"No, no, no," he said quickly. "I think that you are dealing with a lot, and still processing the trauma you went through, and maybe that's affecting how you are looking at this. You know"—he paused, pinched the skin on his knuckles—"when I first saw someone die in front of me, I wasn't OK for a long, long time. It was a stabbing victim, young woman. That sort of thing, it stays with you." His eyes softened as he glanced up finally and held Pip's gaze. "Are you getting help? Talking to someone?"

"I'm talking to you right now," Pip said, her voice rising. "I was asking you for help. My mistake, I should have known better. It wasn't so long ago that we were standing in a room just like this and I asked you for help, to find Jamie Reynolds. You said no then too, and look where we all are now."

"I'm not saying *no,*" Hawkins said, a small cough into his balled-up fist. "And I *am* trying to help you, Pip, I really am. But a couple of dead pigeons and a message written on a public sidewalk . . . there's not a lot I can do with that, you must be able to understand that. Of course, if you think you know who might be responsible, we can look into issuing them a warn—"

"I don't know who it is, that's why I'm here."

"OK, OK," he said, his words starting loud and ending quiet, as though he were trying to hook onto Pip's voice and bring it back down too. "Well, perhaps you can go and have a little think of anyone you know who might be responsible for something like this. Anyone who might have a grudge against you or—"

"You mean a list of enemies?" Pip gave an amused sniff.

"No, not enemies. Again, I don't see anything here that indicates these events are necessarily connected, or that someone is targeting you specifically, or that they wish you harm. But if you have any thoughts on someone you know who might pull something like this, to mess with you, I can certainly look into having a chat with them."

"Fantastic," Pip barked with an empty laugh. "I'm so glad that you'll *look into* looking into it." She clapped her hands, once, making Hawkins flinch. "You know, this is exactly why more than fifty percent of stalking crimes go unreported, this exact conversation we've had here. Congratulations on another episode of excellent police work." She darted forward to snatch her papers from the table beside him, the pages ripping at the air between them, cutting the room into his side against hers.

She did have a stalker. And now that she thought it through, maybe this could be it: exactly what she needed. Not Jane Doe, but this. One more case, the right one, and opportunity had handed it right to her.

The universe might have aligned, for once, in her favor. This stalker could be the one. A case without that suffocating gray area, one with a clear moral right and a clear moral wrong. Someone out there hated her, wanted to hurt her, and that made them bad. On the other side was her, and maybe she wasn't all good, but she couldn't be all bad. Two opposing sides, as clean as she could hope for. And this time, *she* was the subject. If she got things wrong again, there would be no collateral, no blood on her hands. Only hers. But if she got it right, maybe this could be the thing to fix her.

It couldn't hurt to try.

Pip felt a little more room inside her chest as it loosened around her heart, a feeling of resolve steel-cold in her stomach. She welcomed it back like an old friend.

"Now, Pip, don't be like that—" Hawkins said, the words too careful and too soft.

"I will be however I am," she spat, stuffing the papers back into her bag, the angry-wasp sound of her pulling up the zip. "And you"—she stopped to wipe her nose across her sleeve, the breath heavy in her chest—"I have you to thank for that too." She shouldered her bag, pausing at the door out of Interview Room 3. "You know," she said, her hand stalling above the handle, "Charlie Green taught me one of the most important lessons I've ever learned. He told me that sometimes justice must be found outside of the law. And he was right." She glanced back at Hawkins, his arms wrapped around his chest to protect it from her eyes. "But, actually, I think he didn't go far enough. Maybe justice can only *ever* be found outside of the law, outside of police stations like this, outside of people like you who say you understand but you never do."

Hawkins unwrapped his arms and opened his mouth to answer, but Pip didn't let him.

"He was right, Charlie Green," she said. "And I hope you never find him."

"Pip." There was a bite to Hawkins's voice now, a hard edge that she'd goaded to the surface. "That's not helpf—"

"Oh, and," she cut him off, her fingers gripping the handle too hard, like she might just bend the metal, leave her prints in it forever, "do me a favor. If I disappear, don't look for me. Don't even bother."

"Pi—"

But the door slamming behind her cut off the end of her name, filling the corridor outside with the sound of old gunshots. Six of them, burrowing down past her skin and her ribs, rebounding around her chest, exactly where they belonged.

A new sound joined in, tapping in between the echoes of the gun. Footsteps. Someone walking up the hallway toward her, in a dark uniform, his long brown hair pushed back from his face, and his eyes widening as he spotted her.

"Are you OK?" Dan da Silva asked as she stormed past, the tunnels of their disturbed air colliding as she did. Pip barely caught the concerned look on his face before she was moving on. There wasn't time to answer, to stop, or nod, or to say she was fine when it was clear she wasn't.

She just needed to get out of here. Out of the belly of this station where the gun first decided to follow her home. This very corridor where she'd walked the other way, wearing the blood of a dead man she couldn't save. There was no help for her here and she was on her own, again. But she had herself now, and Ravi. She just needed to get out of this bad, bad place, and never, ever come back.

File Name:

List of potential enemies.docx

- **Max Hastings—**Has the most reason to hate me = number one suspect. He is dangerous, we all know this. I didn't know I could hate anyone as much as I hate him. But if it is Max and he is planning to get me I WILL GET HIM FIRST.
- **Max's parents**—?
- **Ant Lowe—**Definitely hates me. Only attempted to speak to him once since I got suspended for shoving him up against the lockers. He was always the prankster in the group, even when it crossed the line. Could this be him? Revenge for when I snapped on him? But the first *Who will look for you* message was sent before we all fell out?
- **Lauren Gibson—**Same reasons as above. She's definitely petty enough to do something like this, especially if it was something Ant suggested. Dead birds aren't her style, though. Connor, Cara, and Zach don't speak to Ant or Lauren anymore and Lauren blames me for that. Her fucking boyfriend shouldn't have called me a liar, then. Liar liar lair liar li ala li la r lar
- **Tom Nowak—**Lauren's ex-boyfriend. Gave me false information about Jamie Reynolds just to get on the podcast. Used me and I fell for it. In return, I humiliated him in front of the entire school, and online. He deleted his socials after season 2 aired. Definite reason to hate me. He's still in town; Cara has seen him in the café.
- **Daniel da Silva—**Even though Nat and I are close now, her brother *has* been a suspect of mine twice before, in both Andie's case and Jamie's case. I admitted this publicly on the podcast, so he definitely knows. I might have caused

trouble between him and his wife for revealing that he was talking to Layla.

- **Leslie from the Stop & Shop—**Don't even know her last name. But she hates me after the incident with Ravi. And she was one of the protestors at Stanley's funeral. I screamed at her. Why were they there? Why couldn't they just leave him alone?
- **Mary Scythe—**another protestor. And she was one of Stanley's friends, volunteered with him at the *Fairview Mail*. She said this was "our town" and he shouldn't be buried in it. Maybe she'd want me out of *her town* too.
- **Jason Bell—**I found the truth of what really happened to Andie Bell, and yet it only caused more pain for the Bell family, to learn that their younger daughter, Becca, had been involved all along. Plus, it brought a huge amount of press and media attention back into their lives five years after Andie died. Jason and Detective Hawkins play tennis together, apparently, and Jason complained to Hawkins about harassment he'd received because of the podcast, because of me. Jason's second marriage broke down—was that because of my podcast too? He's now back living with Andie's mom, Dawn, in the house where Andie died.
- **Dawn Bell—**Same reasoning as above. Maybe she didn't want Jason back in the house. My investigation indicated that Jason isn't a good man: he was controlling and emotionally abusive to his wife and daughters. Becca won't really talk about him. Could Dawn blame me for having him back in her life? Did I do that to her? I didn't mean to.
- **Charlie Green—**It's not him. I know it's not him. He never intended to hurt me. He set that fire because he wanted me to leave Stanley there, to make sure he died. I know

that's why. Charlie wouldn't want to hurt me: he looked out for me, helped me, even if he had his own reasons why. But the objective part of my brain knows he should be on the list because I am the *only* witness to him committing first-degree murder and he is still a fugitive. Without me to testify, would a jury find him guilty? Logic dictates he should be on here. But it isn't him, I know it.

- **Detective Richard Hawkins—**Fuck him.

Is it normal for one person to have this many enemies? I'm the problem, aren't I?

How did it get so late already?

I understand why they all hate me.

I might hate me too.

ELEVEN

Chalk dust on her fingers, gritty and dry. Except there wasn't, because she was awake now, her eyes cracking open, dragging her from the dream. Her eyes felt gritty and dry, but her fingers were clean. Pip sat up.

It was still dark in her room.

Had she been asleep?

She must have been asleep, otherwise how had she dreamed?

It was all still there, thrumming around her head, like it had all been lived only moments before. But not lived, only imagined, right?

It had felt so real. The weight of it in her cupped hands. Still warm, keeping away the cold of the dark night. Its feathers so soft, so sleek against the cage of her fingers. Pip had locked eyes with it, or she would have if it had had a head. She hadn't thought that strange at the time. That was the way it was supposed to be, as she carried the small dead pigeon across the driveway. So soft she almost didn't want to let it go. But she had to, and rested the dead bird down on the brick driveway, shifting it so the space where its head should have been was pointing toward her bedroom window. Looking in through the gap in the curtains to watch Pip asleep in her bed. Both here and there.

But it hadn't finished there. There was more to do before she could rest. Another task. The chalk had already been in her hand, not nearly as nice to hold as the dead pigeon. Where had it come from? Pip didn't know, but she knew what she was supposed to do with it.

She'd retraced her steps, remembering where the last ones had been. Then she stepped forward three times, toward the house, to find their new home.

Knees on the cold driveway, the chalk in her hand ground down to a stub, her fingers red and raw as she dragged it along the lines of the bricks. Downward legs. Upward body. Sideway arms. No head. She carried on until there were five stick figures, dancing together, slowly making their way to Pip asleep in her bed to ask her to join them.

Would she join them? She didn't know, but she was finished, and the chalk had dropped from her hands with a tiny clatter. Chalk dust on her fingers, gritty and dry.

And then Pip had pulled herself out of the dream, studying her fingers to know what was real and what wasn't. Her heart was fluttering, wing-beat fast, winding up the rest of her. She'd never sleep again now.

She checked the time. It was 4:32 a.m. She really should try to sleep; she'd only climbed into bed two hours ago. Time was always cruel to her in these early hours. She wouldn't be able to do it, not without help.

Pip glanced through the darkness at the drawer in her desk. There was no point fighting it. She threw off her comforter, the cold air full of invisible jaws biting at her exposed skin. She rummaged through the drawer, prying up the false bottom, her fingers scrabbling below for the small plastic bag. Not many left now. She'd have to text Luke Eaton again soon, ask him for more, those burner phones lined up and ready.

What happened to one last time, then?

Pip swallowed the pill and bit her lip. These past months had been filled with *one last time*s and *just one more*s. They weren't lies; she'd truly meant them at the time. But she always lost in the end.

It didn't matter, it wouldn't matter soon. Because she had the plan, the new plan, and after that she'd never lose again. Everything would go back to normal. And life had handed her exactly what she needed. Those chalk figures, those dead pigeons, and the person who'd left them there for her. It was a gift, and she should remember that, prove Hawkins wrong. One last case, and it had landed right on her doorstep. It was her against them this time. No Andie Bell, no Sal Singh, no Elliot Ward or Becca Bell, no Jamie Reynolds or Charlie Green or Stanley Forbes, and no Jane Doe. The game had changed.

Her against them.

Save herself to save herself.

TWELVE

There was a kind of thrill in it, watching someone when they didn't know you were there. Invisible to them. Disappeared.

Ravi was walking up the drive to her house, she at her bedroom window where she'd been for hours, watching. His arms were swinging, his hair morning-messy, and a strange movement in his mouth like he was chewing the air. Or singing to himself. She'd never seen him do that before, never around her. This was a different Ravi, one who thought he was alone, unobserved. Pip studied him and all the subtle differences to the Ravi he was when he was around her. She smiled to herself, wondered what he was singing. Maybe she could love this Ravi just as much, but she'd miss that look in his eyes when he was looking back at her.

And then the moment was over. Pip faintly heard his familiar knock, long-short-long, but she couldn't move, needed to stay here and watch the drive. Her dad was here anyway, he would let Ravi in. He liked his small moments of time alone with Ravi. He'd make some sort of inappropriate joke, segue into a conversation about football or Ravi's internship, finishing off with an affectionate pat on the back. All while Ravi took off his shoes and neatly lined them up by the door, stuffing the laces inside too, and that special laugh he saved for her dad. That was it, what she wanted: to live those small, normal moments again. The scene would change, somehow, if she were there to disturb it.

Pip blinked, her eyes watering from staring too long at that spot on the driveway, the sun glaring through the window. She couldn't look away; she might miss it.

She heard Ravi's gentle tread up the steps, his clicking knees, and her heartbeat picked up. The good kind of fast heart, not like that other trigger-happy kind. No, don't think about that now. Why did she have to ruin every nice moment?

"Hello, Sarge," he said, the creaking sound of him pushing the door fully open. "Agent Ravi here, reporting for boyfriending duties."

"Hello, Agent Ravi," Pip said, her breath fogging up the glass in front of her. The smile was back, fighting her until she gave in.

"I see," he said, "not even a glance back, or one of your scornful looks. Not a hug, not a kiss. Not an *Oh, Ravi, darling, you look devilishly handsome today and you smell like a spring dream.* Oh, Pip, my dear, you are too kind to notice. It's a new deodorant I'm trying." A pause. "No, but seriously, what are you doing? Can you hear me? Am I a ghost? Pip?"

"Sorry," she said, eyes straight. "I'm just . . . I'm watching the driveway."

"You're what?"

"Watching the drive," she said, her own reflection getting in the way.

She felt a weight on the bed next to her, gravity pulling her toward him as Ravi lowered to his knees on the far side of the mattress, his elbows up on the windowsill and eyes to the glass, just as Pip's were.

"Watching for what?" he said. Pip dared one fleeting look at him, at the sun lighting up his eyes.

"For . . . for the birds. The pigeons," she said. "I've put bits of bread out there on the drive, in the same spot I found those pigeons. And I put little pieces of ham in the grass on either side of the drive too."

"Right," Ravi said, drawing out the word, confused. "And why have we done that?"

She gave him a quick jab with her elbow. Wasn't it obvious? "Because," she said, overemphasizing the word, "I'm trying to prove Hawkins wrong. It can't be a neighbor's cat. And I've laid the perfect bait to test that. Cats like ham, don't they? He's wrong, I'm not crazy."

The harsh summer light through the crack in her curtains had woken her earlier than she'd planned, pulling her out of the after-pill fog. This experiment had seemed a good idea at the time, on three hours' sleep, although now, checking in with Ravi's uncertain eyes, she wasn't sure. Lost her footing again.

She could feel his gaze on her, warm against her cheek. No, what was he doing? He should be watching out for the birds, helping her.

"Hey," he said quietly, his voice hovering just above a whisper.

But Pip didn't hear what he said next, because there was a dark shape in the sky, a winged shadow growing on the drive below. Pip's eyes caught it as it swooped down, landing on its twig legs and hopping over to the scattered bread.

"No," she breathed out. It wasn't a pigeon. "Stupid crow," she said, watching as it scooped up a small square of bread in its beak, and then another, the sun glinting off its sleek black feathers.

"At least it's only one," said Ravi. "Last thing we want is a *murder* out there. You know, a murder of crows."

"We have plenty of that in Fairview already," Pip replied as the bird helped itself to a third piece of bread. "Hey!" she shouted suddenly, surprising herself too, banging on the window with her fist. "Hey, go away! You're ruining it!" Her knuckles hit against the glass so hard, she didn't know which would crack first. "Go away!" The crow jumped into the air and flew off.

"Whoa, whoa, whoa," Ravi said quickly, grabbing her hands away from the window, holding them tightly inside his grip. "Whoa, hey," he said, shaking his head at her. His voice hard, but his thumb soft as he ran it against her wrist.

"Ravi, I can't see the window, the birds," she said, straining her neck to try to look outside and not at him.

"No, you don't need to look outside." He tucked his finger under her chin, guided it back. "Look at me, please. Pip." He sighed. "This isn't good for you. It really isn't."

"I'm just trying—"

"I know what you're trying. I understand."

"He didn't believe me," she said quietly. "Hawkins didn't believe me. No one believes me." Not even her sometimes, a new wave of doubts after her dream last night, wondering again whether it was possible she was doing this to herself.

"Hey, that's not true." Ravi held her hands even tighter in his. "I believe you. I will always believe you, whatever it is. That's my job, OK?" He held her eyes, and that was good because hers suddenly felt wet and heavy, too heavy to hold alone. "It's me and you, Trouble. Team Ravi and Pip. Someone left those birds for you, and the chalk; you don't have to try to prove otherwise. Trust yourself."

She shrugged.

"And Hawkins is an idiot, frankly," Ravi said with a small smile. "If he hasn't learned by now that you're—annoyingly—*always* right, then he never will."

"Never," Pip repeated.

"It's going to be OK," he said, drawing lines in the valleys between her knuckles. "Everything will be OK, I promise." He paused, staring at the space below her eyes a little too long. "Did you get much sleep last night?"

"Yes," she lied.

"Right." He clapped his hands together. "I think we need to get you out of the house. Come on. Up, up. Socks on."

"Why?" she said, sinking into the bed as Ravi stood.

"We're going out for a walk. *Oh, what a fantastic idea, Ravi, you're so smart and handsome.* Oh, Pip, I know I am, but do try to keep it in your pants, your father is downstairs."

She threw a pillow at him.

"Come on." He dragged her out of bed by her ankles, giggling as she and the comforter slid to the floor. "Come on, Sporty Spice, you can put your sneakers on and run circles around me if you really want."

"I already do," Pip quipped, fighting her feet into a pair of discarded socks.

"Oooh, sick burn, Sarge." He clapped her on the backside as she stood up. "Let's go."

It worked. Whatever Ravi was doing, it worked. Pip didn't think about disappearing or dead birds or chalk lines or Detective Hawkins, not on the way down the stairs, not when her dad stopped them to ask her where all the wafer-thin ham had gone, not even as they walked down the driveway, Ravi's fingers hooked onto her jeans, heading for the woods. No pigeons, no chalk, no six gunshots disguised in the beating of her heart. It was just the two of them. Team Ravi and Pip. No thoughts beyond the first inane things that came into her head. No deeper, no darker. Ravi was the fence in her head that kept it all back.

A grumpy-faced tree that she insisted looked like Ravi when he woke up.

Planning when he would first come to visit her at college; maybe the weekend after Orientation Week? Was she nervous to go? What books did she still need to buy?

They followed the winding path through the woods. Ravi recreated their first walk together beneath these same trees, a high-pitched impression of Pip as she took him through her initial theories on the Andie Bell case. Pip laughed. He'd remembered almost every word. Barney had been with them on that first walk, a golden flash through the trees. Herding them together. Tail wagging as Ravi had teased him with a stick. Thinking back on it now, maybe that's the moment Pip knew. Had it been a tightening in her gut, or maybe that drunk feeling behind the eyes, or could it have been that glow below her skin? She hadn't realized it at the time, hadn't known what it was, but maybe some part of her had already decided she would love him. Right then. In a conversation about his dead brother and a murdered girl. It all came back to death, in the end. Oh, there you go, she'd gone and ruined it. The fence was down.

Pip's attention was drawn up and away as a dog from here and now crashed through the undergrowth toward them, barking as it jumped up to plant its paws on her legs. A beagle. She recognized this dog, just as he had recognized her.

"Oh no," she muttered, giving him one quick pat on the head, as the other sound reached them: a double set of footsteps. Two voices she knew.

Pip stopped as they walked around a knot of trees and finally came into view.

Ant-and-Lauren, arm in arm. Eyes in unison, widening when they realized it was her.

Pip didn't imagine it. Lauren actually gasped, coughing into her hand to cover it. They stopped too. Ant and Lauren over there, Pip and Ravi back here.

"Rufus!" Lauren screamed, her wild voice echoing through the trees. "Rufus, come here! Get away from her!"

The dog turned and tilted his head.

"I'm not going to hurt your dog, Lauren," Pip said, leveling her voice.

"Who knows with you," Ant said darkly, stuffing his hands into his pockets.

"Oh, come on." Pip sniffed. One part of her itched to pet Rufus again, just to really set Lauren off. *Go on, do it.*

It was as though Lauren had read her mind and the glint in her eye. She screamed for the dog again until he bounded back over to her on his unsure little legs.

"No!" Lauren turned her voice on him now, giving him a one-fingered tap on the nose. "You don't go up to strangers!"

"Ridiculous," Pip said, with a hollow laugh, swapping a look with Ravi.

"What was that?" Ant barked, straightening up. Pointless, really, because Pip was still taller than him; she could take him. She already had once before, and she was stronger now.

"I said that your girlfriend was ridiculous. Should I repeat it a third time?" she said.

Pip could feel Ravi's arm tensing against hers. He hated confrontation, hated it, and even so, Pip knew he would go to war for her if she ever asked. She didn't need him now, though; she had this. Almost like she'd been waiting for this encounter, felt herself coming alive with it.

"Well, don't talk about her like that." Ant brought his hands back out, flexed them at his sides. "When are you leaving for college?"

"Why?" Pip said. "Are you waiting for me to . . . *disappear*?"

She studied their faces carefully. The wind whipped Lauren's red hair across her forehead, strands catching across her narrowed eyes. She blinked. One side of Ant's mouth pulled up in a sneer.

"What the fuck are you talking about?" he said.

"No, I know." Pip nodded. "You must feel really embarrassed. You accused me, Connor, and Jamie of orchestrating his disappearance for money, just hours after we all found out a serial rapist walked free. Are you the ones who spoke to that reporter? I guess it doesn't matter anymore. And now Jamie's alive but another man is dead, and you must feel really quite stupid about the whole thing."

"Deserved to die, though, didn't he, so I guess it all worked out nicely in the end."

He winked.

He fucking winked at her.

The gun was back in Pip's heart, pointing through her chest at Ant. Backbone curling and her teeth bared. "Don't you ever say that again." She pushed the words through her teeth, dark and dangerous. "Don't you ever say that in front of me."

Ravi retook her hand, but she didn't feel it. She wasn't in her body anymore, she was standing over there, that same hand around Ant's throat. Tightening, tightening, squeezing it all out into Ravi's fingers.

Ant seemed to sense this, taking one step back from her, almost tripping over the dog. Lauren hooked her arm through Ant's again and locked their elbows together. A shield. But that wouldn't stop Pip.

"We used to be friends. Do you really hate me enough to want me to die?" she said, the wind carrying her voice away from her.

"What the fuck are you talking about?" Lauren spat, drawing more strength from Ant. "You're a psycho."

"Hey." Ravi's voice floated in from somewhere beside her. "Come on now, that's not nice."

But Pip had an answer of her own. "Maybe," she said. "So, you should make sure your doors are locked up real nice and tight at night."

"OK," Ravi said, taking charge. "We're going this way." He pointed beyond Ant and Lauren. "You go that way. See you around."

Ravi led her off-path, his fingers tight around hers, anchoring her to him. Pip's feet were moving, but her eyes were on Ant and Lauren, blinking the moment they passed, shooting them with the gun in her chest. She watched over her shoulder as they moved away through the trees, in the direction of her house.

"My dad said she was fucked up now," Ant said to Lauren, loud enough for them to hear, turning back to meet Pip's eyes.

She tensed, her heels turning, catching in the long grass. But Ravi's arm folded around her waist, holding her into him. His mouth brushing the hair at her temple. "No," he whispered. "You're OK. They aren't worth it. Really. Just breathe."

So she did. Concentrated only on air in, air out. One step, two step, in, out. Every step carrying her farther away from them, the gun retreating back into its hiding place.

"Should we go home?" she said when it was gone, between breaths, between steps.

"No." Ravi shook his head, staring straight ahead. "Forget about them. You need some fresh air."

Pip circled his hot palm with her trigger finger, one way then the other. She didn't want to say, but maybe there was no such thing in Fairview. No fresh air. It was all tainted, every breath of it.

They looked both ways and crossed the road to her house, the sun finding them again, warming their backs.

"Anything?" Pip smiled at Ravi.

"Yes, anything you want," he said. "This is a full-on cheer-up-Pip day. No true crime documentaries, though. Those are banned."

"And what if I said I really wanted a Scrabble tournament?" she said, sticking her finger through his sweater into his ribs, their steps clumsily winding in and out of each other's across the drive.

"I'd say, game on, bitch. You underestimate my pow—" Ravi stopped suddenly, and Pip collided into him. "Oh fuck," he said, little more than a whisper.

"What?" she laughed, coming around to face him. "I'll go easy on you."

"No, Pip." He pointed behind her.

She turned and followed his eyes.

There, on the driveway, beyond the pile of bread crumbs, were three little chalk figures.

Her heart turned cold, dropped into her stomach.

"They were here," Pip said, letting go of Ravi's hand and darting forward. "They were just here," she said, standing over the little chalk people. The figures had almost reached the house now, scattered just in front of the potted shrubs that lined the left side. "We shouldn't have left, Ravi! I was watching. I would have seen them." *Seen them, caught them, saved herself.*

"They only came because they knew you weren't here." Ravi joined her, his breath fast in his chest. "And those definitely aren't tire marks." This was the first time he'd seen them. Time and rain had taken the last ones away before she'd had a chance to show him. But he could see them now. He saw them and that made them real. She hadn't made them up, Hawkins.

"Thank you," Pip said, glad that he was with her.

"Looks like something out of *The Blair Witch,*" he said, bending to get a closer look, drawing the crisscross shapes with his finger, hovering a few inches above.

"No." Pip studied them. "This isn't right. There's supposed to be five of them. There were five both other times. Why three now?" she asked of Ravi. "Doesn't make sense."

"I don't think any of this makes sense, Pip."

Pip held her breath, scouring the driveway for the two lost figures. They were here, somewhere. They had to be. Those were the rules in this game between her and them.

"Wait!" she said, catching something in the corner of her eye. No, it couldn't be, was it? She stepped forward, up to one of her mom's potted plants—*pots come all the way from Venezuela, can you believe?*—and brushed the leaves aside.

Behind it, on the wall of her house. Two little headless figures. So faint they were hardly there at all, hidden almost entirely among the mortar between the bricks.

"Found you," Pip said with an outward breath. Her skin was alive and electric as she pushed her face right up close to the chalk, some of the white dust scattering from her breath. But was she pleased or was she scared? She couldn't, in this moment, tell the difference.

"Up on the wall?" Ravi said behind her. "Why?"

Pip knew the answer before he did. She understood this game, now that she was playing. She stepped back from the two headless figures, the leaders of their pack, and looked directly up, following their journey. They'd mounted the wall to climb, up past the study and up and up, toward her bedroom window.

The bones cracked in her neck as she turned back to Ravi.

"They're coming for me."

File Name:

The chalk figures (3rd instance).jpg

THIRTEEN

Darkness consumed her, the last chink of sunlight through the curtains glowing down her face before Ravi pulled them shut, tucking one half behind the other to be extra sure.

"Keep these closed, OK?" he said, just a shadow in the blacked-out room until he crossed the floor to switch on the light. Unnaturally yellow, a poor imitation of the sun. "Even during the day. In case someone is watching you. I don't like the idea of someone watching you."

Ravi stopped by her elbow, placed his thumb under her chin. "Hey, you OK?"

Did he mean about Ant and Lauren, or the little chalk figures climbing up to her room?

"Yeah." Pip cleared her throat. Such a meaningless half word.

She was sitting at her desk, fingers resting on the keyboard of her laptop. She'd just saved a copy of the photo she'd taken of the chalk figures. Finally, she'd gotten there before the rain or tires or feet could wash them away, disappear them. Evidence. She herself might be the case this time, but she still needed evidence. And, more than that, it was proof. Proof that she wasn't haunting herself, that she couldn't be the one drawing the figures and killing those pigeons during the foggy sleepless nights, could she?

"Maybe you can come stay at my house for a few nights," Ravi said, spinning her chair until they were face to face. "Mom wouldn't mind. I'd have to leave early from Monday, but that's OK."

Pip shook her head. "It's fine," she said. "I'm fine." She wasn't fine, but that was the whole point. There was no running away from this; she'd asked for it. She needed it. This was how she would make herself fine again. And the scarier it got, the more perfect the fit. Out of the gray area, into something she could comprehend, something she could live with. Black and white. Good and bad. *Thank you.*

"You're not fine," Ravi said, running his fingers through his dark hair, long enough now that it had started to curl at the ends. "This isn't fine. I know it's easy to forget, after all the fucked-up things we've been through, but this isn't normal." He stared at her. "You know this isn't normal, don't you?"

"Yes," she said. "I know that. I went to the police yesterday like you wanted, I tried to do the normal thing. But I guess it's down to me again, to fix it." She pulled a line of loose skin along one fingernail, a bubble of blood greeting her from the deep. "I'll fix it."

"How are you going to do that?" Ravi asked, a harder edge in his voice. Was that doubt? No, he couldn't lose faith in her too. He was the last one left. "Does your dad know about this?" he asked.

She nodded. "He knows about the dead birds; we found the first one together. Mom told him it was the Williamses' cat, though; that's the logical solution. I told him about the chalk marks but he never saw them. They were gone by the time he got home—I think him driving over them was why they disappeared, even."

"Let's go show him now," Ravi said, the edge in his voice more slippery now, more urgent. "Come on."

"Ravi," she sighed. "What's he going to do about it?"

"He's your dad," he said with an exaggerated shrug, like it was the most obvious thing in the world. "And he's six-foot-six. I'd definitely want him on my team in any fight."

"He's a corporate lawyer," she said, turning, catching sight of her far-off eyes in the sleeping face of her laptop. "If this were a problem about mergers and acquisitions, yeah, he'd be the guy. But it's not."

She took a deep breath, watched the dark mirrored version of herself do the same. "This is for me. This is what I'm good at. I can do this."

"This isn't a test for you," Ravi said, scratching the phantom itch at the back of his head. He was wrong; that's exactly what it was. A trial. A final judgment. "This isn't a school project, or a season of the podcast. This isn't something you can win or lose."

"I don't want to argue," she said quietly.

"No, hey, no." He bent down until his eyes were level with hers. "We're not arguing. I'm just worried about you, OK? I want to keep you safe. I love you, always will. No matter how many times you almost give me a heart attack or a nervous breakdown. It's just . . ." He drew off, his voice guttering out. "It's scary, to know that someone might want to hurt you, or make you scared. You're *my* person. My little one. My Sarge. And I'm supposed to protect you."

"You do protect me," she said, holding his eyes. "Even when you're not here." He was her life raft, her cornerstone for what good truly meant. Didn't he know that?

"Yeah, OK, and that's great," he said, clicking finger guns at her. "But it's not like I'm a muscleman with biceps the size of tree trunks and a secret Olympic-standard knife-throwing habit."

A smile stretched into her mouth, fully formed without her say-so. "Oh, Ravi," she clipped her finger under his chin, the same way he always did to her. Pressed a kiss into his cheek, brushing the side of his mouth. "You know brains always beat brawn, any day of the week."

He straightened up. "Well, I just squatted for too long, so I probably have glutes of steel now anyway."

"That'll show the stalker." She laughed, but it became a hollow, raspy sound as her mind wandered away from her.

"What?" Ravi asked, noticing the shift.

"It's just . . . it's clever, isn't it?" She laughed again, shaking her head. "So clever."

"What?"

"All of it. The faint, almost-not-there chalk figures that fade as soon as it rains, or someone drives over them. The first two times, I didn't take photos before they were gone, so when I told Hawkins about them, he thought I was insane or seeing things that aren't there. Discrediting me right from the get-go. I even wondered whether I *was* seeing things. And the dead birds." She clapped her hands against her thigh. "So clever. If it were a dead cat, or a dead dog"—she flinched at her own words, Barney flashing into her mind—"it would be a different story. People would pay attention. But it's not, it's pigeons. No one cares about pigeons. Almost as common to us dead as they are alive. And of course, the police would never do anything about a dead pigeon or two, because it's normal. No one else can see it but me, and you. They know all this, they designed it that way. Things that look normal and explainable to everyone else. An empty envelope; just an accident. And the 'Dead Girl Walking' down the road, not at my house. I know it was for me, but I'd never be able to convince anyone else, because if it *really* were for me, it would have been at my house. So subtle. So clever. The police think I'm crazy and my mom thinks it's nothing—just a cat and some dirty tires. Cutting me off, isolating me from help. Especially because everyone already thinks I'm *fucked up*. Very clever."

"Kinda sounds like you admire them," Ravi said, sitting back on Pip's bed, arm out for balance. His face looked uneasy.

"No, I'm just saying it's clever. Thought-out. Like they know exactly what they are doing."

Her next thought was only natural, only logical, and she could see from Ravi's eyes that he had arrived at the same idea, chewing on it, the muscles tensing in his cheek.

"Almost like they've done this before," she said, completing the thought, the slightest nod of agreement from Ravi.

"Do you think they *have* done this before?" He sat up.

"It's possible," she said. "Likely, even. The statistics certainly indicate that serial stalking is common, particularly if the stalker is a stranger or an acquaintance, rather than a current or former partner."

She'd read through pages and pages of information on stalkers last night, hour after hour, instead of sleeping, scrolling through numbers and percentages and nameless, countless cases.

"A stranger?" Ravi doubled down on the word.

"It's unlikely to be a stranger," Pip replied. "Nearly three out of four stalking victims know their stalker in some capacity. This is someone who knows me, someone I know, I can feel it." She knew more statistics too, could reel them off the top of her head, burned into the backs of her eyes from the white light of her laptop screen. But there were some she couldn't tell Ravi, especially not the one that said more than half of female homicide victims reported stalking to the police before they were killed by their stalkers. She didn't want Ravi to know that one.

"So, it's someone you know, and they are pretty likely to have done this to someone else, before?" Ravi asked.

"I mean, yes, if we go along with the statistics." Why hadn't she thought of this herself? She was too inside her own head, too fixated on the idea of *her* against them that she hadn't considered the involvement of anyone else. *Not all about you,* said the voice that lived in her head, beside the gun. *It's not always about you.*

"And you always favor a science-based approach, Sarge." He doffed an imaginary cap at her.

"Yes, I do." Pip chewed her lip, thinking. Her mind guided her hands to the laptop, checking in with her only after she'd already awoken the computer and brought up Google. "And the first stage in a science-based approach is . . . research."

"The most glamorous part of crime-solving," Ravi said, pushing up from the bed to come stand behind her, hands resting on her shoulders. "And, also, my cue to go get snacks. So . . . like, how are you going to research this?"

"Yeah, not really sure, actually." She hesitated, fingers hovering above the keys while the cursor blinked at her. "Maybe just . . ." She typed in: *chalk lines chalk figure dead pigeon stalker stalk Fairview, Connecticut.* "It's a stab in the dark," she said, thumbing the enter button, and the page of results filled her screen.

"Oh awesome," Ravi said, pointing at the top result. "We can go clay-pigeon shooting at Chalk Farm in Hartford for *only* ninety-five dollars each. What a bargain."

"Shhh."

Pip's eyes scanned the entry below: a story from last year, about SAT results from a nearby school where two teachers just happened to be called Miss Chalk and Mr. Stalker.

She felt Ravi's breath on her neck as he leaned closer, head against hers as he said, "What's that one?" And the low vibrations of his voice felt like they were coming from within her. She knew which one he meant, fifth result down.

DT KILLER STILL AT LARGE

AFTER CLAIMING FOURTH VICTIM

It had four matches to her search items: *Connecticut, pigeon, stalk, chalk lines.* Small snippets from a *Newsday* article, truncated sentences separated by three little dots.

" 'The DT Killer,' " Ravi read aloud, voice catching on something in his throat. "What the fuck is that?"

"It's nothing, that's an old story. Look." Pip underlined the date with her finger: the article was from February 5, 2014. More than six and a half years ago. This wasn't news—Pip knew this case, how it had ended. She could tell you at least two true crime podcasts that had covered it in the last few years. "You don't know this story?" she asked, reading the answer from his dread-widened eyes. "It's OK," she laughed at him, nudging him with her elbow. "He's not still *at large*. He killed another woman after this, a fifth victim, and then they caught him. He confessed. Billy, um, something. He's been in prison since."

"How do you know that?" he asked, his grip loosening a little.

"How do you not?" She looked up at him. "It was big news when it was going on. Even I remember and I was, like, eleven, twelve. Oh—I," she stuttered, stroking the bones in his hand. "It was around the time that Andie and Sal . . ." She didn't need to finish.

"Right," he said quietly. "I was a little distracted at the time."

"It all happened pretty close by," Pip said. "The towns where the victims were from, the places where their bodies were found. In fact, almost everywhere nearby *except* Fairview."

"Had our own murders going on back then," he said flatly. "What does 'DT Killer' even mean?"

"Oh, it was the media's name for him. You know, a serial killer's got to have a creepy name. Sells more papers. Short for the Duct Tape Killer." She paused. "The local newspapers used to refer to him as the Stratford Strangler—keep it close to home, y'know—but that never caught on with the national press. Not as catchy," she said, smirking. "Also, not very accurate, seeing as only two victims were found nearish Stratford, I think."

And just saying those words, Stratford Strangler, took her back to the last time she'd said them. Sitting in this very chair, on a call with Stanley Forbes, interviewing him about Andie Bell's coroner's inquest. She'd brought up the article he'd recently written about the Stratford Strangler, marking five years since his arrest. Stanley down the end of the phone, alive, but not for long because his blood is dripping out of the edges of her phone, covering her hands and—

"Pip?"

She flinched, wiping her bloody hands on her jeans. Clean, *they're clean.* "Sorry, what did you say?" Pip hunched her back, folding her chest around her hummingbird heart.

“I said click on it, then. The article.”

“But . . . it’s got nothing to do with—”

“It’s matched four of your search terms,” he said, grip tightening again. “Pretty coincidental for a *stab in the dark.* Just click on it and see what it says.”

NEWSDAY

US>Connecticut>News>Crime

DT Killer Still at Large After Claiming Fourth Victim

LINDSEY LEVISON FEBRUARY 5, 2014

Like

Last week, police found the body of Julia Hunter, 22, now officially confirmed as the fourth victim of the DT Killer. Julia—who was living with her parents and her sister in Stamford, Connecticut—was killed on the evening of January 28, her body discovered the following morning on a golf course just north of Stratford.

The DT Killer began his crime spree two years ago, murdering his first victim, Phillipa Brockfield, age 21, on February 8, 2012. Ten months later, the body of Melissa Denny, 24, was found after a week of extensive police searches. She went missing on December 11 and forensic experts believe she was killed that same night. On August 17, 2013, Bethany Ingham, age 26, became the third victim of the DT Killer. Now, more than five months later, after much media speculation, police have confirmed that the serial killer has struck again.

The DT Killer—short for the Duct Tape Killer—is so called because of his distinctive MO: he not only binds the wrists and ankles of his victims in duct tape to restrain them, but their faces too. Each woman was found with her head fully wrapped in standard gray duct tape, covering her eyes and mouth, "almost like a mummy," commented one police officer who wished to remain anonymous. The duct tape itself is not the murder weapon in these horrific crimes; in fact, it appears the DT Killer intentionally leaves the nostrils of his victims free so they do not suffocate that way. The cause of death in each case has been strangulation by ligature, and police theorize that the killer leaves his victims bound in the duct tape for a while before killing them, and then dumps their bodies in a different location.

There have been no arrests in the case, and with the DT Killer still at large, police are scrambling in their efforts to identify him before he kills again.

"This is an incredibly dangerous man," said Lieutenant David Nolan, Detective Division Commander of the Bridgeport Police Department, speaking outside the station today. "Four young women have very sadly lost their lives, and it's clear this individual poses a significant risk to the general public. We are doubling our efforts to identify this offender—known as the DT Killer—and we have today released a composite sketch from a potential witness at the scene where Julia's body was found. We urge the public to please contact the police on the case hotline if you recognize the man in the sketch."

Police release composite sketch of the DT Killer

In addition to the sketch, police today have also released a list of personal items that were missing from the victims, items they had on them at the time of abduction, as identified by their families. Police believe the killer took these items as trophies for each murder, and that they are very likely still in his possession. "Trophy-taking is common among serial killers like this," commented Lieutenant Nolan. "The trophies allow the killer to relive the thrill of the crime and to sustain his dark urges, lengthening the time before he feels compelled to kill again." From Phillipa Brockfield, the killer took a necklace, which police describe as "a gold chain with an antique coin-style pendant." It was a "lilac or light-purple paddle-shaped hairbrush" from Melissa Denny, which she carried everywhere in her purse. A "gold stainless-steel Casio watch" from Bethany Ingham, and now, from Julia Hunter, a "pair of rose-gold earrings with light-green stones." Police are asking the public to keep an eye out for these items.

Newsday spoke with Adrienne Castro, a criminal profiler who used to work with the FBI and today consults on popular true crime show *Forensic Time*. Ms. Castro gave us her expert opinion on the DT Killer, based on all the information police have released so far:

"As ever, profiling is not an exact science, but I think we can draw some tentative conclusions from this criminal's behavior and his choice of victim. This is a white man who could be anywhere between his early twenties to his mid-forties. These aren't compulsive acts: these murders are planned and methodical, and our killer likely has an average to high IQ. This man would seem to be perfectly normal, unremarkable—charming, even. He outwardly appears to be an upstanding member of society, with a good job where he's used to a level of control, maybe a management position. I think it's very likely he has a partner or a wife, and potentially even a family too, who have no idea about his secret life.

"There is an interesting observation to make about his spatial behavior too. In serial killers, we find that an offender will have a natural aversion to committing crimes too close to home, their buffer zone. And yet, conversely, they also have a comfort zone: a nearby area they know very well that isn't too close to home and where they feel secure committing these acts. We refer to this as the Distance Decay Theory. It's interesting to note that these victims were all from different towns and cities in Fairfield County, and their bodies too were all spread out in different locations in the comfort-zone area. This leads me to believe that our killer lives in a different nearby location, one that hasn't yet come up in the investigation, his untouched buffer zone.

"As to his motive, I think what we have here is something that underpins a lot of serial killings: misogyny, essentially. This man has very strong feelings about women—he hates them. These victims are all attractive, educated, intelligent young women, and there is something there that this killer finds utterly intolerable. He sees these killings as his own personal mission. I find the wrapping of their heads in tape particularly interesting, like he is denying them even their own faces, cutting off their ability to speak or see before he kills them. These killings come down to power and humiliation, and the sadistic pleasure the offender takes from that. It's likely the signs were there from a young age, and he started out by harming family pets as a boy. I would not be surprised if, somewhere in his possession, he keeps a manifesto with all his thoughts about women and how they should look or behave in order to be acceptable.

"The police have not released any information about whether he stalks his victims beforehand, but I would say, given how meticulous the victim selection appears to be, that there is a degree of surveillance before he abducts them. I think that's part of the thrill for him. He may even make direct contact with them, and it's possible the killer has had intimate relationships with these victims."

Outside Julia Hunter's family home this evening, her eighteen-year-old sister, Harriet, stopped briefly to speak to reporters. When asked about the possibility of Julia being stalked before her death, a tearful Harriet had this to say: "I'm not sure. She never told me she was scared or anything. I would've helped her if she had. But she did mention a few weird things in the couple of weeks before. She talked about seeing some lines, chalk lines, I think, that looked like three stick figures, near the house. I never saw them and it was probably just our neighbor's kids. Also, a couple of dead birds—pigeons—had been brought into the house through the cat flap. But Julia thought that was strange because our cat is very old now and hardly goes outside. She also mentioned getting a few prank calls. That was in the week before she went missing, but she didn't seem frightened by them. If anything, she found them annoying. But [. . .] looking back on those few weeks before, *everything* seems weird to me now, now that she's gone."

A memorial service for Julia Hunter will be held on February 21 at her local church.

FOURTEEN

Ravi must have reached the end first, a sharp intake of breath right by her ear, like a windstorm trapped inside her head. Pip held up one finger to put him on pause until she was done, reached the very last word.

And then: "Oh," she said.

Ravi jerked away from her, standing up to his full height. "Oh?" he said, voice higher and scratchier than it should be. "Is that all you have to say about that? *Oh?*"

"What are you . . ." She spun her chair to watch him. His hands were dancing nervously, tucked under his chin. "What are you freaking out about?"

"What are you *not* freaking out about?" He tried not to raise his voice, but he should have tried harder. "A serial killer, Pip."

"Ravi." His name broke apart in her mouth, into a small laugh. His eyes flashed angrily at her. "This is from six and a half years ago. The DT Killer confessed. I'm pretty sure he pleaded guilty in court too. He's been in prison all this time, and there were no more murders after his arrest. The DT Killer is gone."

"Yeah, well, what about the dead pigeons?" Ravi said, his arm in a straight and quivering line, pointing back to the screen. "And the chalk lines, Pip? Those two exact things in the weeks before he killed Julia." Ravi dropped to his knees in front of her, holding one hand up to her face, thumb and little finger folded down. *"Three,"* he hissed, bringing his three raised fingers even closer. "Three chalk stick figures. Julia was the *fourth* victim, Pip. Three before her. And now there have been five women killed, and there are five little stick figures outside your house right fucking now."

"Look, calm down," she said, taking his raised hand, tucking it between her knees to hold it still. "I've never heard of those things Julia Hunter's sister said there, not in any articles or podcasts. Maybe the police decided they weren't relevant in the end."

"But they *are* relevant to you."

"I know, I know, I'm not saying that." She locked onto his eyes, tilted her chin. "Obviously there's a connection, between what Harriet Hunter said and what's happening to me. Well, I haven't had any mysterious phone calls—"

"Yet." Ravi cut across her, his hand trying to escape.

"But the DT Killer is in prison. Look." She released his hand, and turned back to the laptop, typing *DT Killer* into a new search page and pressing enter.

"Ah, Billy Karras, yes, that's his name," she said, scrolling down the page of results to show Ravi. "See. Age thirty when he was arrested. He confessed in a police interview and—see—yep, he also pleaded guilty to all five murders. No need for a trial. He's in prison and will be for the rest of his life."

"Doesn't really look like the police sketch," Ravi sniffed, his hand finding its own way back between her knees.

"Well, kind of." She squinted at Billy Karras's mug shot. Greasy dark-brown hair pushed back from his forehead, green eyes that almost jumped right out of his face, startled by the camera. "No one ever really does, anyway."

That seemed to help Ravi a little, putting a face to the name, the proof unrolling before his eyes as Pip clicked onto the second page of results.

She stopped, scrolled back up. Something had caught her eye. A number. A month.

"What?" Ravi asked her, a tremor in his hand that passed through to her.

"Oh, it's nothing," she said, shaking her head so he knew she meant it. "Nothing really. Just . . . I never realized before. The final victim of the DT Killer, Tara Yates, she was killed on April eighteenth, 2014."

He looked at her, the same glint of recognition in his eyes, mirroring back her own. She watched herself, the warped version of her trapped in the darks of his eyes. Well, one of them had to say it out loud.

"The same night Andie Bell died," she said.

"That is weird," he said. He dropped his gaze and the Pip that lived in them slipped away. "This is all weird, all of it. OK, he's in prison, but so why is someone doing the exact same to you as happened to Julia Hunter before she died? To all of the victims, potentially. And don't tell me it's a coincidence, because that's a lie: you don't believe in coincidences."

He had her there.

"No, I know. I don't know." She stopped to laugh at herself, unsure why she had—it didn't belong here. "Obviously that can't be a coincidence. Maybe someone wants me to think I'm being stalked by the DT Killer."

"Why would someone want that?"

"Ravi, I don't know." She felt defensive all of a sudden, hot, the fence going up again, but this time to keep Ravi out. "Maybe someone wants to drive me crazy. Push me over the edge."

They wouldn't have to push very hard at all. She'd walked herself right up to the edge, toes hanging over the drop. One sharp breath to the back of her neck would probably do it. Just one question between her and that long fall down: *Who will look for you when you're the one who disappears?*

"And no one has been killed since this Billy guy was arrested?" Ravi double-checked.

"No," Pip said. "And it's a very distinctive MO, the duct tape around the face."

"Move over a sec," Ravi said, rolling her chair away from the desk, her hands falling from the laptop.

"Hey."

"I'm just seeing something," he said, kneeling in front of the screen. He flicked to the top of the page, deleted the current search items and typed in: *Billy Karras innocent?*

Pip sighed, watching him scroll quickly through the results. "Ravi. He confessed and he pleaded guilty. The DT Killer is behind bars, not outside my house."

There was a crackling sound in Ravi's throat, somewhere between a gasp and a cough. "There's a Facebook page," he said.

"For what?" Pip dug in her heels to scoot the chair back.

"A page called Billy Karras Is Innocent." He clicked on it, and Billy Karras's mug shot filled the screen as the banner image. His face looked softer the second time, somehow. Younger.

"Well, of course there is," Pip said, pulling up at Ravi's side. "I bet there's a Facebook page proclaiming the innocence of every single serial killer. I'd bet there's even one for Ted Bundy."

Ravi hovered the arrow above the about tab, pressed his thumb into the trackpad to bring it up. "Oh shit," he said, scanning the page. "It's run by his mom. Look. Maria Karras."

"Poor woman," Pip said quietly. "Of course she thinks her own kid is innocent."

"*'On May 16, 2014, after sitting in a police interview room for nine hours without a break, my son gave a false confession to crimes he did not commit, a confession coerced by intense—and illegal—police interrogation tactics,'*" Ravi read from the screen. "*'He immediately recanted the next morning, after some sleep, but it was already too late. The police had what they needed.'*"

"A false confession?" Pip said, looking into Billy Karras's eyes as though the question were for him. No, it couldn't be. Those were the eyes of the DT Killer staring back at her . . . they had to be. Otherwise—

"*'Serious systemic failings in our criminal justice system . . .'*" Ravi started skipping, into the next paragraph. "*'Need three thousand signatures on the petition to congresswoman'*—oh man, she only has twenty-nine signatures so far—*'trying to bring Billy's case to the attention of The Innocence Project so we can appeal the conviction . . .'*" He stopped. "Oh look, she's even put her phone number in the contact info section. '*Please contact me if you have any legal experience or media connections and think you can help me with Billy's case, or would like to help collect signatures. Please note: prank callers will be reported to the police.*'" He turned from the screen, locked eyes with Pip.

"What?" she said, reading the answer in the downturn of his mouth. "Well, of course she thinks he's innocent. She's his mom. That's not proof."

"But it's a question mark," he said firmly, dragging Pip and the chair closer. "You should call her. Talk to her. See what her reasons are."

Pip shook her head. "I don't want to disturb this poor woman. Give her false hope for no reason. She's clearly been through enough."

"Yeah." Ravi ran his hand up her leg. "The very same thing my mom went through, that I went through, when everyone thought Sal killed Andie Bell. And how did that come to an end again?" he said, tapping a finger to his chin while he pretended to grapple for the memory. "Oh yeah, with an unsolicited knock at the door from an overly persistent Pippus Maximus."

"That was entirely different," she said, turning away from him, because she knew if she looked at him any longer, he'd convince her to do it. And she couldn't do it. Could not. Because if she called that poor woman, that would be admitting there was a chance. A possibility.

That the wrong man was sitting in prison. And the right man? He was outside her house, drawing headless stick figures of the women he'd already killed, coming for her, beckoning her to join them. Number six. And that would be a game she wasn't ready for. A stalker was one thing, but this . . .

"OK, never mind." Ravi shrugged. "How about we sit here twiddling our thumbs instead, just wait and see how this whole *stalker* thing pans out? The passive approach. Never thought I'd see you opt for a passive anything, but we'll just hang tight, kick back. No biggie."

"I didn't say that." She rolled her eyes at him.

"But what you did just say," he said, "was that this was for you, that you can do this alone. This is what you are good at. Investigating."

He was right, she had just said that. Her test. Her trial. Her final judgment. Save herself to save herself. That was all still true. Even more so if there was that chance, that possibility, that there was a right man and a wrong man.

"I know," she said quietly, conceding with a long outward breath. She'd known as soon as she'd finished reading the article what she had to do, had only needed Ravi to draw it out.

"So . . ." He smiled the little smile that always got her, and he dropped her phone into her hand. "*Investigate* it."

FIFTEEN

Pip had stared at the numbers so long they were burned into the underside of her eyes. *475-555-0183.* A lilting tune inside her head that she could now repeat back, without looking. An ever-repeating loop that had played through her mind all night as she'd begged for sleep. Down to her last four pills now.

Her thumb hovered over the green call button again. She and Ravi had tried it five times yesterday, but it rang out each time, no voice mail. Maria Karras must have been busy. Maybe even visiting her son, they'd guessed. Pip said she would try again in the morning, but now she was stalling, afraid, even. Because once she pressed that button, and Maria picked up on the other end, there'd be no going back. No unknowing what she knew, or unhearing or unthinking it. But already the idea had burrowed deep, settling down inside her head next to Stanley's dead eyes and Charlie's gray gun. And even now, as she clicked a ballpoint pen in one hand, she heard something in the click and unclick. Two distinct notes, two letters. *DT. DT. DT.* And yet, she kept on clicking.

Her hand was resting against her notebook, a new page, after her notes on body decomposition and livor mortis. Maria Karras's number scribbled there. She couldn't escape it.

Pip finally pressed the call button and put the phone on speaker. It rang, the shrill sound riding up and down her spine, just as it had yesterday. But then—

Click.

"Hello? Karras residence?" said a muffled voice, the words softened by a Greek accent.

"Oh, um, hi," Pip said, recovering, clearing her throat. "I'm looking for Maria Karras?"

"Yes, that's me," the voice replied, and Pip imagined the woman behind it: heavy eyes and a sad smile. "How can I help you?"

"Hi, Maria," she said, fiddling nervously with the pen again. *DT. DT. DT.* "Sorry to disturb you on a Sunday. My name is Pip Fitz-Amobi, and I—"

"Oh my god," Maria cut across her. "You finally got my message?"

Pip stuttered, felt her eyebrows pulling together. What message? "Oh, I . . . um, your message?"

"Yes, the email I sent through your website, oh, back in April, it must have been. I also tried to send you a message on Tweeter but I can never work these things on my own. But you finally got it?" she said, her voice climbing in pitch.

Pip had never seen this email. She considered for half a moment, deciding to go with it. "Y-yes, your email," she said. "Thank you so much for reaching out to me, Maria, and apologies it's taken me so long to respond."

"Oh, sweetheart, please," Maria said, a rustle down her end as she repositioned the phone. "I know you must be terribly busy, and I'm just so happy you got it at all. I didn't know if you would be doing any more of this podcast, but I wanted to reach out anyway, in case you were looking for another local case. You're really very brilliant, your parents must be very proud of you. And I just knew this is exactly what we need for Billy, to bring some media attention, which you and your podcast would very much do. It's very popular, my hairdresser listens to it too. As my email said, we are trying to get The Innocence Project to help us with Billy."

Maria paused to take a breath, and Pip stepped in, before she lost her chance.

"Yes," Pip said. "And, Maria—I have to be up-front with you—this call doesn't mean I will necessarily be covering your son's case on the podcast. I'd need to do some extensive research before I make any decisions on that front."

"Oh, sweetheart, yes, I understand, of course," Maria said, and it was almost as though Pip could feel the warmth of her voice, radiating out of the phone. "And maybe you are still thinking my son is guilty. He's the DT Killer, the Stratford Strangler, whichever name it is. Almost everybody does. I would not blame you."

Pip cleared her throat again, to buy herself some time. She certainly hoped Billy Karras *was* guilty, for her own sake, but she couldn't say that.

"Well, I haven't looked into all the details of the case yet. I know your son confessed to all five murders, and then pleaded guilty in court, which isn't the easiest position to begin with."

"It was a false confession," Maria said with a sniff. "It was coerced by the officers interviewing him."

"So why didn't Billy then plead innocent, take the case to trial? Do you think you could talk me through the details, the evidence, why you think Billy is not guilty?"

"Of course, darling, I do not mind," Maria said. "And I can tell you a secret. I thought Billy was guilty too. For the first year or two. I thought eventually he would tell me the truth, but he kept telling me, *Mama, Mama, I did not do it, I promise you.* For two years. So then I started to look into it, and that's when I realized he was telling the truth: he's innocent. And you would think so too if you could see the police interview. Oh wait, I can send it to you!" More rustling down the line. "I got copies of all these police documents, years ago. Through that, what do they call it again . . . oh, the Freedom of Information Act. I have the whole interview, his *confession.* The transcript is over a hundred pages; did you know they had him in that room for nine hours?

He was exhausted, terrified. But I tell you what: I can go through it and highlight the most important parts, send a scan to you? I think I know how to use that scanner. It might take me a while to go through it all, but I can send that to you, tomorrow latest."

"Yes, please," Pip said, making a scribbled note on her page. "If you could, that would be very helpful, thank you. But there's no rush, really." Except there definitely was. Five little stick women, their heads gone because they were all wrapped up in tape, climbing up to Pip's room to meet their number six. The end in sight. Unless that's just what someone wanted her to think, of course.

"Yes, I will," said Maria. "And you can see exactly what I mean. All the answers they feed to him. He knows nothing. They tell him they have all this evidence against him, they even imply they have someone who saw him during one murder, which wasn't true. Billy got so confused, bless him. I know he's my son, but he was never the sharpest tool in the shed, as they say. He had a bit of a drinking problem too, back then, sometimes would black out in the evening. And these officers convince him that he's committing the murders while he's blacked out, that's why he doesn't remember. I think Billy started to believe it of himself, even. Until he finally got some sleep in the cell, and then he recanted the confession right away. You know, false confessions are a lot more common than you think. Of the three hundred and sixty-five people The Innocence Project have helped exonerate in recent decades, more than a quarter of them had confessed to their alleged crime."

Maria must have recited that fact from the top of her head, and that's when Pip fully realized: This was her entire life. Every breath and every thought dedicated to her son. To Billy. He had new names now, though: the DT Killer, the Stratford Strangler, a monster. Pip's chest ached for this woman, but not quite enough to want her to be right. Anything but that.

"I did not know that statistic," Pip said. "And I'm very interested to see Billy's interview. But, Maria, if he recanted the next morning, why did he then plead guilty?"

"His lawyer," Maria said, a hint of reproach tainting her soft voice. "He was a public defender; I did not have money to hire a lawyer. If only I had . . . It is one of my biggest regrets. I should have tried harder." Maria paused, her breath crackling through the speaker. "This lawyer basically told Billy that because he had already confessed to all five murders, and the police had this confession on tape, that there was no point in going to trial. He would lose. They had other evidence too, but the confession was the thing. The jury would believe that tape over Billy any day. Well, the lawyer wasn't wrong; they say that a confession is the most prejudicial piece of evidence."

"I see," Pip said, because she couldn't think of what else to say.

"But we should have tried," Maria continued. "Who knows what might have come up in a trial, to save Billy. What evidence. You know, there was an unidentified fingerprint on the second victim, Melissa Denny. The print does not match Billy's and they don't know who it belongs to. And—" She broke off. Paused. "On the night that Bethany Ingham was murdered, the third victim, I think Billy was here, with me. I can't be certain, but I think on that night, Billy came over to my house in the evening. He'd been drinking, a lot. Could not string one sentence together. So I made him sleep in his old bedroom, took his keys so he wouldn't try to get in the car again. I don't have any evidence of this; I have searched and searched. Phone records, security cameras down the road, everything. I don't have evidence, but in a court, my testimony would have been evidence. How could Billy have murdered Bethany if he was home with me?" She exhaled. "But the lawyer told Billy that if he pleaded guilty, the judge might let him serve in a prison closer by, so that I could visit him more easily. Which then didn't happen, of course. Billy lost hope—that's why he said he was guilty. He thought the game was already lost before it began."

Pip had been scribbling as Maria spoke, her words slanted, letters trampling each other in her haste to get it all down. She realized Maria had stopped, was waiting for her to speak.

"Sorry," Pip said. "So, other than the confession, what other evidence did the police have that made them think Billy is DT?"

"Well, there were a few things," Maria said, and Pip could hear shuffling down her end, as though Maria were flicking through papers. "The main one was that Billy was the person who found Tara Yates, the final victim."

"He found her body?" Pip asked. She vaguely remembered that now, from one of the podcasts she'd listened to, remembered how they'd framed it as the big twist.

"Yes. He found her like that. Tape around her ankles and wrists, wrapped around her face. I couldn't ever imagine, seeing another human being like that. It was at work, where he found her. Billy worked for a grounds maintenance company: cutting lawns, trimming hedges, picking up trash, that sort of thing. It was early in the morning, and Billy was on the grounds of this hotel, one of his company's sites, cutting the grass. He spotted Tara in the trees around the edge of the site." She cleared her throat. "And Billy . . . Well, the first thing he does is run over to her. He thought she might still be alive. Couldn't see her face, you see. He shouldn't have gone over, should have left her there and called the police straightaway. But that's not what Billy did . . ."

Maria trailed off.

"What did he do?" Pip prompted her.

"He tried to help her," Maria exhaled. "He thought the tape on her face was keeping her from breathing, so he started to unwrap it. Touching her and the tape with his bare hands. Then, when he realized that she wasn't breathing anyway, he attempted CPR, but he didn't know what he was doing, had never learned what to do." A small cough. "He knew he needed help, so he ran back to the hotel and told one of the employees to call the police, to come help him. He had his cell on him, he just forgot about it in the moment. I guess maybe he was in shock? I don't know what that does to you, seeing another person like that."

Pip knew exactly what it did to you, though she could never try to explain it.

"So the result of that," Maria continued, "was that Billy's DNA, his sweat and saliva, were all over poor Tara. And his fingerprints. Silly boy," she said quietly.

"But the police would have known that was from him discovering the body. Trying to save Tara, even if he didn't realize it was too late and he was only contaminating the scene."

"Yes, well, maybe that's what they believed initially. But, you know, I've done a lot of research into serial killers these last few years. I would even go as far as to say I am an expert in them now. And with this kind of criminal—DT—it is very common that the killer would try to insert himself into the police investigation somehow. Calling in with ideas or tips, or offering to help search parties, that sort of thing, even trying to get information to see how safe they are from suspicion. That's what the police thought this was, eventually. Billy inserting himself into the investigation by *discovering* Tara's body, to appear helpful, innocent. Or maybe to cover himself in case he had left any DNA on her while committing the murder." Maria sighed. "You see now, how everything is twisted to fit the story?"

With a sinking feeling in her gut, Pip realized she had just nodded. No, what was she doing? She didn't want it to go this way, because if there was a chance Billy was innocent, then . . . Fuck. Oh fuck.

Luckily, Maria had resumed talking, and Pip didn't have to listen to the voice in her head anymore.

"Maybe this would have been OK on its own," she said, "but there were other details that tied Billy into this whole mess. He knew one of the victims. Bethany Ingham, number three, she was his supervisor at work. He was very sad after he learned about her death, said she was always so nice to him. And the first victim, Phillipa Brockfield, her body was found on a golf course just outside Bridgeport. It was another site that had a contract with the company Billy worked at, and Billy was on the team assigned there. His work van was seen driving to the golf course on the same morning Phillipa's body was left there, but, of course, he was just driving to work. And the duct tape . . . well, it was the exact same kind Billy had access to at work, so . . ."

Pip could feel that part of her awakening, the spark in her brain, questions rolling over each other, gathering speed. The world slowing as her mind picked up, double pace. She shouldn't, she knew what this path meant for her, but she couldn't stop it, and one of the questions came loose.

"So, all of these details tying Billy to the murders, they're related to his job," Pip said. "What's the name of the company he worked for?"

Too late. Just asking it meant it was already too late for her. That, on some level, she must think it possible, that she might not be speaking to the mother of the DT Killer at all.

"Yes, that is where the connections seem to come from," Maria said, voice even faster now, more excitable. "The company is called Green Scene Limited. Scene, not like eyes, like the kind in a film."

"Got it, thanks," Pip said, writing the name of the company at the bottom of her page. She tilted her head, studied the words from another angle. She thought she recognized the name. From where, though? Well, if the company operated nearby, she'd probably seen its logo on vans driving through Fairview.

"And how long had Billy worked there?" Pip asked as she swiped her finger across her laptop's trackpad, the screen springing back to life. She typed in *Green Scene Ltd Connecticut* and hit enter.

"Since 2009, it was."

The first result was the company's website and, yes, Pip did recognize the cone-shaped tree of its logo. An image she knew, that already existed in her brain somewhere. But why? The Home page told her about Green Scene's *specialist and award-winning grounds-maintenance services,* with a slideshow of photos. Lower down the page was a link to another site, its sister company, *Clean Scene Ltd.,* which offered cleaning services for *offices, housing associations, and more.*

"Hello?" Maria said tentatively, breaking the silence, and Pip had almost forgotten she was even there.

"Sorry, Maria," she said, scratching her eyebrow. "For some reason, I recognize the company's name. And I can't figure out why."

Pip clicked on the menu item labeled Our Team.

"Oh, I know why you'll recognize it, sweetheart," Maria said. "It's because the—"

But the page loaded, and the answer was there in front of her, before Maria could say it. A grinning photo of a suited man at the top, introducing the managing director and owner of Green Scene Ltd. and Clean Scene Ltd.

It was Jason Bell.

"It's Jason Bell's company," Pip said in an outward breath, the pieces connecting in her head. Yes, that was it. That's how she knew it.

"Yes, dear," Maria said softly. "Andie Bell's father, and, of course, you know all about Andie Bell. We all do now, because of your podcast. Poor Mr. Bell was going through his own unthinkable tragedy around the same time."

Exactly the same time, Pip thought: Andie died the same night Tara Yates was murdered. And here Andie had come up yet again, back from the dead. Billy Karras worked at Jason Bell's company, and his connection to the DT killings in each case was also tied to his job.

If Pip had to admit it to herself, right here, right now, that there was even the faintest possibility Billy Karras was innocent—that there might be a wrong man and a right man—Green Scene Ltd. was where she should look first. If this were a case with no other complications, no ties to her, no dead pigeons or stick figures at her doorway, that would be her first step. And yet, that step seemed so much harder this time, so much heavier.

"Maria," Pip said, her voice rough and gravelly, "just one last thing. After Billy was arrested, the killings stopped. How do you explain that?"

"As I said, I've learned a lot about serial killers in the last few years," she said. "And one thing most people don't realize is that sometimes serial killers just stop. Sometimes they age out, or they have life events going on that mean they don't have the urge, or the time anymore. Say a new relationship, or maybe the birth of a child. So maybe that's what happened here. Or maybe the killer saw an easy way out, after Billy's arrest."

Pip's pen dragged to a stop, her mind too full. "Maria, thank you so much for taking the time to talk to me today. This has all been very"—*don't say helpful, don't say terrifying*—"interesting," she said.

"Oh, sweetheart, please, thank *you* for taking the time." Maria sniffed. "There's no one I can talk to about this, no one who listens, so thank you for that. Even if it goes no further, I understand, darling. You know how hard it is to appeal a conviction once it is made? It is almost hopeless, we know this. But Billy will be so touched to even know you reached out. And I will get right on to scanning the transcript of Billy's interview, so you can see for yourself."

Pip wasn't sure she wanted to see for herself. There was a part of her that wanted to clasp her hands over her eyes and wish this all away. Wish herself away. Disappear.

"Tomorrow," Maria said firmly. "I promise. Shall I send to your podcast email address?"

"Y-yes, that would be perfect, thank you," Pip said. "And I'll be in contact soon."

"Goodbye, darling," Maria said, and Pip thought she heard it in her voice then, the smallest stirrings of hope.

She thumbed the red button on her phone, and the silence grated in her ears.

It was a maybe.

It was possible.

And that possibility, it began with Green Scene Ltd.

And it ended—the voice in her head interrupted—with her dead.

The sixth victim of the DT Killer.

Pip tried to speak over that voice in her head, distract it. *Don't think about the end for now, just the next step. One day at a time.* But how many more of those did she have?

Shut up, leave her alone. First step: Green Scene. The echo of those two words sounding in her head, morphing into the click of her pen. *DT. DT. DT.*

And that's when she realized: Jason Bell wasn't the only person she knew who was connected to Green Scene Ltd. There was someone else too: Daniel da Silva. Before he became a police officer, he'd worked at Jason Bell's company for a couple of years. Maybe even worked directly *with* Billy Karras.

This case, which just yesterday had seemed so far away from her, so remote, it was creeping closer and closer to home, just like those chalk figures climbing up her wall. Closer and closer, like it was leading her right back to Andie Bell and to the very beginning of everything.

There was a sudden sound, a harsh buzzing.

Pip flinched.

It was only her phone, vibrating against the desk with an incoming call.

Pip glanced at the screen as she picked up the phone. *No Caller ID.*

"Hello?" she said.

There was no answer down the other end. No voice, no sound, other than the faintest trace of static.

"Hello?" Pip said again, holding onto the *o* sound. She waited, listened. Could she hear someone breathing, or was that just her own? "Maria?" she said. "Is that you?"

No answer.

A telemarketing call, maybe, with a bad connection.

Pip held her breath and listened. Closed her eyes to focus her ears. It was faint, but it was there. Someone was there, breathing into the phone. Couldn't they hear her speaking?

"Cara?" Pip said. "Cara, I swear if you think this is funny, then—"

The call ended.

Pip lowered the phone and stared at it. Stared at it for far too long, as though it might explain itself to her. And it wasn't her own voice in her head now, it was Harriet Hunter who spoke to her, in an imagined voice Pip created for her, talking about her murdered sister from that article about DT. *She also mentioned getting a few prank calls. That was in the week before she went missing.*

Pip's heart reacted, and the gun went off inside her chest. Billy Karras might be the DT Killer. And he might not. And *if*—an *if* that circled Pip like a black hole—*if* Billy wasn't DT, then the game had changed again. Into the final round. And now a timer was ticking down.

The week before.

Who will look for you when you're the one who disappears?

File Name:

Download: Billy Karras police interview.pdf

Page 41

LT. NOLAN: Come on, Billy, let's stop messing around here. It's going to be OK. Look at me. Let's stop playing this game, hey? You will feel so much better when you just say it. Trust me. Everything will be better for you if you just tell me what happened. You probably didn't mean for any of this to happen, right? And you didn't mean to hurt any of those girls, I understand that. Maybe they wronged you in some way, did they? Were they mean to you, Billy?

BK: No, sir, I don't know any of them. I didn't do it.

LT. NOLAN: See, you're lying to me now, Billy, aren't you? Because we know you knew Bethany Ingham. She was your supervisor at work, wasn't she?

BK: Yes, sorry, I meant I didn't know the other women. I knew Bethany, though. I didn't mean to lie, sir, I'm just so tired. Could we have a break soon?

LT. NOLAN: Did you hate Bethany, Billy? Did you think she was attractive? Did you want to sleep with her, and did she turn you down? Is that why you killed her?

BK: No, I— Please, can you stop asking so many questions so fast? I–I'm trying to not get confused, to not accidentally lie again. I didn't hate Bethany at all. I liked her, but not like how you're saying. She was nice to me. She brought in a cake to the office for my birthday last year, made everyone sing for me. People aren't normally nice to me like that, except my mom.

LT. NOLAN: So, you're a loner, are you, Billy? Is that what you're saying? You don't have a girlfriend, do you? Do women make you uncomfortable because you're lonely? Does it make you angry that they don't want to be with you?

BK: No, I . . . Sir, I just, I can't keep up. Please, I'm trying. I'm not a loner, I just don't have many friends at the moment, maybe some of the guys at work. ████████, who used to work with me in Bethany's team too, he's actually a police officer now. And I have nothing but respect for women. My mom raised me, a single mother, and she's always taught me that.

LT. NOLAN: You can't remember?

BK: I just mean that sometimes, when I've drunk a lot, I black out. I can't really remember what I've done. I think I have a problem. I'm going to get help with it, I promise.

LT. NOLAN: So you're saying that you don't remember any of the nights that these women died? You can't remember where you were on any of these dates?

BK: No, I would have been at my house, I just don't remember exactly. I was explaining to you sometimes the reason why I don't remember.

LT. NOLAN: But, Billy, if you don't remember, isn't it possible that you weren't at home? That you did kill these women, while you were blacked out?

BK: I-I-I'm not sure, sir. I don't . . . I guess it is possible—

LT. NOLAN: It *is* possible that you killed these women? Just say it, Billy.

BK: No, I di— Just, if I don't remember, then I can't say what I was or wasn't doing, that's all. Can I get some water or something? My head hurts.

LT. NOLAN: Just tell me, Billy. And then this can all stop, and yes, you can have some water, get some sleep. Come on, we're both tired. You will feel so much better, so much lighter. The guilt must just be eating you up. Just tell me you did it. You can trust me, Billy, you know that. You've already gone from saying *I didn't do it* to *I don't remember*. Come on, let's just go one step further, tell me the truth.

BK: That is the truth. I didn't do it, but I don't remember those nights.

LT. NOLAN: Stop lying to me, Billy. Your van was captured driving to the site where Phillipa Brockfield's body was dumped, on that same morning. Your DNA is all over Tara Yates's body. Look, I have a file as thick as my arm of evidence against you. It's over. Just tell me what you did and I can make this all go away.

BK: I shouldn't have touched her. Tara. I'm sorry. I thought she was alive. I was trying to help her. That's why my DNA is on her.

LT. NOLAN: Someone saw you, Billy.

BK: S-saw me? Doing what?

LT. NOLAN: You know what, Billy. You know exactly what. Let's stop pretending here. You've been caught. Just tell me, so we can give the families of these poor girls some peace.

BK: S-someone saw me? With Tara . . . before? At night? But I don't remember, I don't . . . How could I not remember if . . . This doesn't make sense.

LT. NOLAN: What doesn't make sense, Billy?

BK: Well, from everything you're telling me . . . all the evidence you have, it sounds like . . . maybe, I must have done it. But I don't understand how.

LT. NOLAN: Maybe you blocked it out, Billy. Maybe you didn't want to remember, because you feel so sorry for what you've done.

BK: Maybe, but I don't remember. I don't remember anything. But someone saw me?

LT. NOLAN: I'm going to need you to say it out loud, Billy. Tell me what you did.

BK: I think, maybe . . . it must have been me. I don't understand how, but it was me, wasn't it? I was the one who hurt those women. I'm sorry. I don't . . . I wouldn't ever do anything like that. But it must have been me.

LT. NOLAN: Well done, Billy. That's really good. There's no need to cry, now. I know how sorry you must feel. Come on, now, here's a Kleenex. There you go. Right, I'll go and get you some water now, but when I'm back, we need to carry on this conversation, OK? Get everything, all the details out in the open. You've done really well now, Billy. You must feel better already.

BK: Not really. Are you . . . is my mom going to find out?

Page 91

LT. NOLAN: How did you kill them, Billy?

BK: It's the tape around their faces. They couldn't breathe, that's how.

LT. NOLAN: No, Billy. That's not how they died. Come on, you know the answer. How did you kill them? It wasn't the duct tape.

BK: I . . . I don't know, sir. I'm sorry. Did I, did I strangle them? Y-yes, I strangled them.

LT. NOLAN: Good, Billy.

BK: With my hands.

LT. NOLAN: No, it wasn't with your hands, was it, Billy? You used something. What did you use?

BK: Um . . . I don't . . . maybe, a rope?

LT. NOLAN: Yes, it was. Blue rope. We found fibers that match the exact type of rope in your van.

BK: It's the kind we use at work. Especially with the tree surgeon teams. I must have taken it from work, did I?

LT. NOLAN: As well as the duct tape.

BK: I guess.

LT. NOLAN: Where did you kill them, Billy? After you abducted them, where did you take them to kill them?

BK: Um, I don't . . . my work van, maybe? And then I could drive them straight to where they were found.

LT. NOLAN: You left each of them for a while, though, didn't you? After you bound them in the duct tape, before you returned to strangle them. A few of the women had managed to loosen the tape around their wrists, tear it in places, which suggests you left them unsupervised for a little while. Where did you go, in that time?

BK: I . . . just drive around, I suppose.

Page 102

LT. NOLAN: Good, that's right, Billy. And what did you take from Melissa Denny? As a trophy.

BK: Another bit of jewelry, I think.

LT. NOLAN: No, it wasn't, that time. It was something else. Something else a woman might carry in her purse.

BK: Oh, maybe her wallet? H-her driver's license?

LT. NOLAN: No, Billy. You know what it was. Something she probably used every day.

BK: Oh. A lipstick?

LT. NOLAN: You might have taken a lipstick too, Billy. But there was something else missing from her bag. Something bigger than that, something her family told us she took everywhere.

BK: What—oh . . . something . . . h-hair, a hairbrush? Is that what you mean by that?

LT. NOLAN: Yes, it was a hairbrush, wasn't it, Billy? One of those wider brushes. She had a lot of hair, Melissa, long blond hair. Is that why you wanted to keep the brush?

BK: I guess. That makes sense.

LT. NOLAN: And what color was the brush?

BK: P-pink?

LT. NOLAN: Hmm, I'd describe it more as a purple, myself. A light purple. Lavender-ish.

BK: L-like lilac?

LT. NOLAN: Yes, that's exactly it. So, where are you keeping the trophies, Billy? Phillipa's necklace, Melissa's hairbrush, Bethany's watch, Julia's earrings, and Tara's key rings. We've searched your house and your van, and we couldn't find them.

BK: I think I must have thrown them away, then. I don't remember.

LT. NOLAN: Threw them in the trash?

BK: Yeah. Wrapped them up and threw them in the trash.

LT. NOLAN: You didn't want to keep them?

BK: Can I please go to sleep now? I'm just so tired.

SIXTEEN

The town was sleeping but Pip was not. And neither was someone else.

An alert on her phone. A new message through her website. A notification on Twitter.

Who will look for you when you're the one who disappears?

SEVENTEEN

Her blood didn't feel right. It was too fast, foaming uncomfortably as it crashed in and out of her chest. Maybe those two coffees in a row at the café had been a mistake. But Cara had offered, said Pip looked tired at this *ungodly* hour of the morning. Now Pip's hands were shaking, and her blood was fizzing as she walked from the café toward Church Street.

She was running on empty, no sleep at all last night, none. Even though she'd taken a full pill, a double dose. It was wasted on her, after reading through Billy Karras's interview transcript. More times than she could count, sounding out the voices in her head like a play, the pauses filled with static from the recorder. And the voice she'd imagined for Billy . . . it didn't sound like a killer at all. He sounded scared, confused. He sounded like her.

Every shadow in her room had taken on the shape of a man, watching her wrapped up in her comforter. Every blinking electronic light was a pair of eyes in the dark: the LEDs on her printer and the Bluetooth speaker on her desk. It was even worse after the new message came through at two-thirty, the world shrinking to just her and those prowling shadows.

Pip had lain there, eyes growing scratchy and dry as she stared up at the black ceiling. If she was being honest with herself, truly honest, she could hardly even call that a confession at all. Yes, the words had come out of Billy's mouth. Yes, he'd said *I was the one who hurt those women.* But the context changed everything. The lead-up and the aftermath. They stripped the meaning right out of those words.

Maria hadn't been exaggerating, hadn't been twisting the truth because she'd read the transcript through a mother's eyes. She was right: the confession did seem coerced. The detective had trapped Billy into a corner by talking in circles, catching him in lies he never meant to tell. No one had seen Billy with Tara Yates the night before, that wasn't true. And yet Billy had believed it of himself, believed a made-up person over his own memory. Lieutenant David Nolan had fed him everything, all the details of the murders. Billy didn't even know how he'd killed his own victims before being told.

There was a chance it was all an act. A clever ploy by a manipulative killer. She'd tried to comfort herself with that thought. But that was overshadowed when placed beside the other possibility: that Billy Karras was an innocent man. Now that she'd read his *confession,* it was no longer just possible, no longer a weak maybe. In her gut she could feel it tilting, abandoning *maybe* to reach for other words. *Likely. Plausible.*

And there must be something wrong with her, because part of her had felt relieved. No, that wasn't the right word, it was more like . . . excited. Her skin prickling, the world shifting into half speed around her. This was it, her other drug. A twisted and writhing knot for her to untie. But she couldn't believe that part without accepting the other, the one that came with it, hand in hand.

Two halves of the same truth: if Billy Karras was innocent, then the DT Killer was still out there. Out here. He was back. And Pip had one week left before he made her disappear.

So, she would just have to find him first. Find whoever was doing this to her, whether it was the DT Killer or someone pretending to be.

The key was Green Scene Ltd., so that's where she would begin. Had already begun. Last night, as the clock on her dashboard ticked past 4:00 a.m. and on, Pip had scrolled through her old documents.

Searching through files and folders until she found the document she needed. The one that had snuck up on her brain like an itch, reminding her of its existence, of its importance, as she'd tried to think through everything she knew about Jason Bell's company.

Back into My Documents and the folder labeled Schoolwork. Into Senior Year, and the folder sat halfway between her AP classes.

Senior Capstone Project.

Pip clicked into it, revealing the rows and rows of Word documents and sound files she'd made one year ago. Photos and .jpgs: the pages of Andie Bell's academic planner spread open on her desk and an annotated map of Fairview Pip had drawn herself, following Andie's last-known movements. She'd scrolled down through all the Capstone Project Log documents until she found the one. The itch. *Capstone Project Log—Entry 20,* the one with the interview with Jess Walker.

Yes, that was it. Pip had reread it, her heart kicking up as she realized its relevance. How strange, that a throwaway detail back then could be so vital now. Almost like all of this had been inevitable, since the very beginning. A path Pip didn't know she'd been following all along.

Next, she'd researched where Green Scene Ltd. and Clean Scene Ltd. were based: a yard and office complex in Weston, near Devil's Den Nature Preserve, about a twenty-five-minute drive from Fairview. She'd even visited, through Street View on Google Maps while she sat on her bed, virtually driving up and down the road outside. The complex was off a small country road, surrounded by tall trees, captured here on some past cloudy day. She couldn't see much from the road, apart from a couple of industrial-looking buildings, parked cars and vans, all encased within a tall metal fence painted forest green. There was a sign on the front gate with the colorful logos for both sister companies. Up and down she'd gone, haunting the pixelated place like a ghost out of time. She could stare at it all she wanted, but it wouldn't give her the answers she needed. There was only one place she'd get those. Not in Weston, but in Fairview.

Right here, right now, in fact, as she glanced up and realized she'd almost arrived. And something else too. There was a woman walking toward her, a face she knew. Dawn Bell, Andie and Becca's mom. She must have just left the house, an empty plastic bag swinging from her arm. Her dark blond hair was pulled back from her face and her hands were lost in the arms of her oversize sweater. She looked tired, too. Maybe that's just what this town did to people?

They were about to pass each other. Pip smiled and dipped her head, not knowing whether to say hello or not, or to tell her she was just about to knock on her door to speak to her husband. Dawn's mouth flickered, as did her eyes, but she didn't stop, looking instead at the sky while she slid her fingers beneath the gold chain of her necklace, fiddling the pendant back and forth so it caught the morning light. They passed each other and carried on. Pip checked over her shoulder as she went, and so did Dawn, their eyes meeting for one awkward moment.

But the moment went out of Pip's head as she reached her destination, staring up at the house, her eyes following the crooked roofline to each of its three chimneys. Old, stippled bricks overwhelmed by shivering ivy, and a chrome wind chime mounted beside the front door.

The Bells' house.

Pip held her breath as she crossed the road toward the house, glancing at the green SUV parked in the drive, beside a smaller red car. Good, Jason must be here, then, not already on his way to work. There was a strange feeling at the base of her spine, uncanny and otherworldly, like she wasn't really here, but in the body of herself from one year ago. Displaced, out of her own time, as everything came back full circle. Here, at the Bell house once more, because there was only one person who had the answers she needed.

She rapped her knuckles against the glass on the front door.

A shape emerged in the frosted glass, a blurred head, as a chain scraped against the front door and it was pulled open. Jason Bell stood in the threshold, buttoning the top of his shirt, smoothing down its creases.

"Hi, Jason," Pip said brightly, her smile feeling tight and rubbery. "Sorry to disturb your morning. H-how are you?"

Jason blinked at her, registering who it was standing on his doorstep.

"What, er, what do you want?" he asked, dropping his gaze to do up the buttons on his cuffs too, leaning against the doorframe.

"I know you're heading off to work," Pip said, her voice jolting nervously. She fiddled her hands together, but that was a bad idea because they were sweating, and now she had to look down to check it wasn't blood. "I, um, well, I just wanted to ask you a couple of questions. About your company, Green Scene."

Jason ran his tongue over his teeth; Pip could see the bulge of it through the skin of his top lip. "What about it?" he said, eyes narrowing now.

"About a couple of your ex-employees." She swallowed. "One of those being Billy Karras."

Jason looked taken aback, his neck receding into his shirt. His mouth formed around his next words before he finally spoke them. "You mean the DT Killer?" he said. "Is that your next *thing*, is it? Your next cry for attention?"

"Something like that," she said with a fake smile.

"I obviously have no comment on Billy Karras," Jason said, something stirring at the corners of his mouth. "I've done everything I can to try to distance the company from the things he did."

"But they are intrinsically connected," Pip countered. "The official narrative is that Billy got the duct tape and the blue rope from work."

"Listen to me," Jason said, raising his hand, but Pip spoke over him before he could derail the conversation. She needed answers, whether he liked it or not.

"Last year, I spoke to one of Becca's friends from high school, Jess Walker, and she told me that on April eighteenth, 2014—the night Andie went missing—you and Dawn were at a dinner party. But you had to leave at some point because the security alarm was going off at Green Scene; you had an alert on your phone, I assume."

Jason stared blankly at her.

"That was the very same night the DT Killer murdered his fifth and final victim, Tara Yates." Pip didn't stop to breathe. "So, I was wondering whether that was *it*: DT breaking into your offices to take the supplies and accidentally setting off the burglar alarm. Did you ever find out who it was? Did you see anyone there when you went to check it out and turn off the alarm? Do you have security cameras?"

"I didn't see . . ." Jason trailed off. He glanced up at the sky behind her for a moment, and when he looked back at her, his face had changed, angry lines arranging themselves around his eyes. He shook his head. "Listen to me," he spat, "that is enough. Enough. I don't know who you think you are, but this is unacceptable. You need to learn . . . Don't you think you've interfered enough in people's lives, in our lives?" he said, slapping one hand into his chest, wrinkling his shirt. "Both of my daughters are gone now. Reporters are back, lurking around my house, trying to get quotes for their stories. My second wife left me. I'm back in this town, in this house. You've done enough. More than enough, believe me."

"But, Jason, I—"

"Never try to contact me again," he said, gripping the edge of the door, his skin overstretched across the whites of his knuckles. "Or anyone in my family. That's enough."

"But—"

Jason closed the door on her. Not a slam—he did it slowly, his eyes holding Pip's until the door broke them apart. Detached them. The click of the lock. But he was still there, standing at the door; Pip could see the shape of him through the frosted glass. She imagined she could feel the heat of his eyes on hers, though she couldn't see them anymore. And still his outline hadn't moved.

He wanted her to leave first, to watch her walk away, she realized. And so she did, hoicking up the straps on her bronze backpack, her sneakers scraping on the front path.

It might have been wishful thinking to have brought her microphones, her laptop, and her headphones. She should have expected that reaction, really, given what Hawkins had told her. She didn't blame Jason; she wouldn't be welcome on a lot of doorsteps in this town. But she really needed those answers. Who had set off the alarm at Green Scene Ltd. that night? Was it Billy, or was it someone else? Her heart was still going too fast, much too fast, and now the beat sounded to her like a timer, ticking down to its own end.

Halfway down the road, Pip checked over her shoulder, looking back at the Bells' house. Jason's silhouette was still there, in the doorway. Did he really need to watch until she was out of sight? She got the message; she would never go back there. It had been a mistake.

She rounded the corner onto Main Street and her phone started vibrating in her front pocket. Was it Ravi? He should be on the train at this time. She slid her hand into her jeans and pulled out the buzzing phone.

No Caller ID.

Pip stopped walking, stared at the screen. Another one. A second one. It might just be a robocall, but it wasn't, she knew. But what should she do? She had only two options here: red button or green.

She pressed green and held the phone up to her ear.

The line was silent.

"Hello?" she said, her voice coming out too strong, crackling at the edges. "Who is this?"

Nothing.

"DT?" she said, eyeing some children squabbling across the street, recognizing one from Josh's soccer team. "Are you the DT Killer?"

A sound. It might have been the car driving past her, or it might have been a breath in her ear.

"Will you tell me who you are?" she said, scared she would drop the phone because her hands were suddenly slick with Stanley's blood. "What do you want from me?"

Pip stepped out into the road, into the crossing, holding her breath so she could hear his instead.

"Do you know me?" she said. "Do I know you?"

The line crackled and then it cut out. Three loud beeps in her ear, her heart spiking at each one. He was gone.

Pip lowered the phone and stared down at it, two steps from the curb. The outside world blurred, disappeared for her as she stared at her empty lock screen, where he had just been moments ago. There was no mistaking who the calls were from now.

Her against him.

Save yourself to save yourself.

Pip heard the crackling of the engine too late.

The screaming wheels behind her.

She didn't need to see to know what was happening. But in that half second, instinct grabbed hold of her, launched her legs forward, reaching for the sidewalk.

A screeching sound filled her ears and filled her bones and her teeth as the car swerved away from her. One foot landed and skidded out from under her.

She crashed to her knee, catching herself with one elbow, the phone skittering out of her hand across the pavement.

The screeching broke into a growl, fading as the car turned right and sped away, before she'd even had a chance to look up.

"Oh my god, Pip!" called a bodiless, high-pitched voice somewhere in front of her.

Pip blinked.

Blood on her hands.

Actual blood, from a scrape across her palm.

She pushed herself up, one leg still jutted out onto the road, as a set of footsteps hurried toward her.

"Oh my god."

A hand came out of nowhere, held in front of her.

She looked up.

Layla Mead. No, she blinked, not Layla, Layla hadn't been real. It was Stella Chapman standing over her, Stella-from-school, her almond eyes downturned with concern.

"Fuck, are you OK?" she said as Pip took her offered hand and let Stella pull her to her feet.

"I'm fine, I'm fine," Pip said, wiping the blood off onto her jeans. This time it left a mark.

"That dickhead wasn't even looking," Stella said, her voice still high and panicked as she bent down to scoop up Pip's phone. "You were at the crossing, for fuck's sake."

She placed the phone into Pip's hand, remarkably unscratched.

"Must have been going at least sixty." Stella was still talking, too quickly for Pip to keep up. "On fucking Main Street. Sports cars think they own the damn road." She ran her hand nervously through her long brown hair. "So close to hitting you."

Pip could still hear the screeching of the wheels, left behind as a ringing in her ears. Had she hit her head?

". . . going so fast I couldn't even *attempt* to read the license plate. It was a white car, though, I could see that. Pip? Are you OK? Are you hurt? Should I call someone for you? Ravi?"

Pip shook her head and the ringing in her ears faded. Turned out it was just in her head after all. "No, it's OK. I'm fine. Really," she said. "Thank you, Stella."

But as she looked at Stella, at her kind eyes and her tan skin and the lines of her cheekbones, she became someone else again. A new person but the same person. Layla Mead. The same as Stella in every way, except her brown hair was now a dusty, ashy blond. And when she spoke next, it was in Charlie Green's voice.

"How've you been, anyway? I haven't seen you in months."

And Pip wanted to scream at Charlie and tell him about the gun he had left behind in her heart. Show him the blood on her hands. But she didn't want to scream, actually. She wanted to cry and ask him to help her, help her understand everything, understand herself. Beg him to come back and show her how to be OK with who she was again. Tell her, in his calm, soothing voice, that maybe she was losing this fight because she was already lost.

The person in front of her was now asking her when she was off to college. Pip asked the same question back, and they stood there on the street, talking carelessly about a future Pip wasn't sure she'd have anymore. It wasn't Charlie standing in front of her, talking about leaving home. And it wasn't Layla Mead. It was Stella. Only Stella. But, even so, it was hard to look at Only Stella.

EIGHTEEN

"Another one?" Ravi didn't move, the expression on his face held there like he was suspended in time, on that one patch of carpet. As though to move either way, forward or back, would confirm the thing he didn't want to hear. If he didn't move, it might not be real.

He'd only just walked through her bedroom door; it was the first thing Pip had said to him. *Don't freak out but I got another blocked call today.* She hadn't wanted to text him earlier, distract him while he was working, but the waiting had been hard, the secret burrowing around under her skin, looking for its own way out.

"Yeah, this morning," she said, watching his face as it finally shifted, eyebrows climbing up his forehead, away from his glasses that he'd remembered again. "Didn't say anything. Just breathing."

"Why didn't you tell me?" He stepped forward, closing the gap between them. "And what happened to your hand?"

"I'm telling you now," she said, running a finger down his wrist. "And nothing, really. Car nearly hit me as I was crossing the road. It's fine, it's just a scrape. But, look, this call is a good thing because—"

"Oh, it's *good,* is it? Getting calls from a potential serial killer. *Good.* Well, that's a relief," Ravi said, hand raised to theatrically mop his brow.

"Can you listen?" she said, rolling her eyes. Such a drama queen when he wanted to be. "It's *good* because I've spent all afternoon looking this up. And look, see. I've downloaded this app." Pip held up her home screen to show him. “It’s called CallTrapper. And what it does is, once you’ve activated it—which I now have—and paid the frickin’ six dollar subscription fee, when you get a call from a blocked number, it will unmask it. So you know the number that’s calling you.” She smiled up at him, hooked her finger onto his belt loop, like he always did to her. “I should have installed it after the first call, really, but I wasn’t sure what it was at the time. Thought it might have been a random butt dial. Never mind, I have it now. And next time he calls me, I’ll have his phone number.” She was being too cheery, she could tell. Overcompensating.

Ravi nodded, and his eyebrows climbed back down just a little. “There’s an app for everything these days,” he said. “Great, now I sound like my dad.”

“Look, I’ll show you how it works. Call me with star-six-seven at the front to block your number.”

“OK.” She watched Ravi pull out his phone and tap away at the screen. It was sudden and unexpected, the feeling that stirred in her chest, watching him. A feeling that dawdled there, took its sweet time. A slow burn. It was just an unexpected nice thing, to know that he knew her number by heart. That some parts of her lived inside him too. Team Ravi and Pip.

He would look for her if she disappeared, wouldn’t he? He might even find her.

The feeling was interrupted by her phone buzzing in her hands. *No Caller ID.* She held it up to show Ravi.

“So what I do is, I press this button twice to decline the call,” she said, demonstrating. Her phone returned to its lock screen, but only for half a second before it lit up with another call. And this time, Ravi’s phone number scrolled along the top. “See, it diverts it to CallTrapper, where the number is unmasked and then they redirect the call back to me. And the caller has no idea on their end,” she said, pressing the red button.

"Can't believe you just hung up on me."

She put down her phone. "See, I have technology on my side now."

Her first victory in the game, but not one to linger over: she was already way behind.

"OK, I'm not going to go as far as to say that that's *good,*" Ravi said. "Not referring to anything as *good* after reading Billy's police interview and realizing that a serial killer the whole world thinks has been locked up for six years might actually be hanging around, threatening to brutally murder my girlfriend, but it's something." He wandered over to her bed, sat down inelegantly on the comforter. "What I don't get, really, is how this person has *your* phone number."

"Everyone has my phone number."

"I damn well hope not," he replied quickly, appalled.

"No, I mean, from the posters." She couldn't help but laugh at his face. "We put up missing posters for Jamie all over town with my phone number on them. Anyone in Fairview could have my phone number. Anyone."

"Oh right," he said, chewing his lip. "We weren't thinking about future stalkers slash serial killers at the time, were we?"

"Hadn't crossed our minds."

Ravi sighed, dropped his face into his cupped hands.

"What?" she asked him, swiveling in her chair.

"Just, don't you think you should go back to Hawkins? Show him that DT article with the pigeons, and Billy's interview. This is too big for us."

It was Pip's turn to sigh now. "Ravi, I'm not going back there," she said. "I love you, and you are perfect in all of the ways you aren't like me and I would do anything to make you happy, but I can't go back there." She slotted one hand through the other, tightened them into a knot of crisscrossing fingers. "Hawkins basically called me crazy to my face last time, told me I was imagining it all. What's he going to do if I go back and tell him that, actually, my stalker—who he doesn't think is real in the first place—is an infamous serial killer who has been in prison for six years, who both confessed and pleaded guilty, except he might not actually have done it? He'd probably put me in a straitjacket right then and there." She paused. "They won't believe me. They never believe me."

Ravi peeled his fingers away, uncovered his face to look at her. "You know, I've always thought you were the bravest person I've ever met. Fearless. I don't know how you do it sometimes. And whenever I'm feeling nervous about anything, I always think to myself, *What would Pip do in this situation?* But"—he exhaled—"I don't know if this is the time to be brave, to do what Pip would do. The risk is too high. I think . . . I think, maybe, you're being reckless and . . ." He trailed off into a wordless shrug.

"OK, look," she said, opening up her hands. "At the moment, the only evidence we have is a bad feeling. When I get a name, some *concrete* evidence, a phone number, even," she said, picking up her phone to wave it at him, "then I will go back to Hawkins, I promise. And if he doesn't believe me, then I'll go public with the information, I don't care about any more lawsuits. I'll put it out all over social media, on the podcast, and *then* they will listen. No one's going to try to hurt me if I've told hundreds of thousands of people who they are and what they're planning to do. That's our defense."

There was another reason she had to do this and do this alone, of course. But she couldn't tell Ravi; he wouldn't understand because it didn't make sense, it was beyond that. It couldn't fit into words, even if she tried. Pip had asked for this, wished for it, begged for it. One last case, the right one, to fix all of the cracks inside herself. And if Billy Karras *was* innocent, and if the man who wanted her to disappear *was* DT, then she couldn't have wished for something more perfect. There was no gray area here, none at all, not even a trace. The DT Killer was the closest thing to evil the world could offer her. There was no good in him at all: no mistakes, no good intentions twisted, no redemption, nothing like that. And if Pip were the one to finally catch him, to free an innocent man, that would be an objectively *good* thing. No ambiguity. No guilt. Good and bad set right inside her again. No gun in her heart or blood on her hands. This would fix everything so it could go back to normal. To Team Ravi and Pip living their normal lives. Save herself to save herself. That's why she had to do this her way.

"Is that . . . is that better?" she asked him.

"Yes." He gave her a weak smile. "That's better. So, *concrete evidence.*" He clapped his hands. "I'm guessing Jason Bell didn't tell you anything useful?"

"Ah, that," she said, clicking her pen again, and all she could hear was *DT DT DT.* "Yeah, no, he didn't give me anything and basically told me to never darken their doorway again."

"I thought it might go that way," Ravi said. "I think they like their privacy, the Bells. Andie never even invited Sal over when they were together. And, of course, you are Chief Doorway Darkener, Sarge."

"But," she said, "I do think the security alarm at Green Scene that night is key. That it was DT breaking in to get the duct tape and the rope he needed, for Tara. And he must have left before Jason Bell got there to check it out. Whether it was Billy or . . . someone else."

"Someone else," Ravi said absently, chewing on the phrase. "So that FBI profiler from that article, before Billy was caught, said that the DT Killer was a white man who could be anywhere from their early twenties to mid-forties."

Pip nodded.

"I guess that rules Max Hastings out." He sniffed.

"Yeah," she said grudgingly. "He would have been just seventeen at the time of the first murder. And the night Tara died, and Andie Bell too, Max had Sal and Naomi Ward and the others round his house. He could have left when the others were asleep, but I don't think it fits. And he has no connection to Green Scene. So, yeah, not him, as much as I want to put Max Hastings away for life."

"But Daniel da Silva used to work at Green Scene, right?" Ravi asked.

"Yes, he did," she said, her teeth gritted. "I just worked out the timeline this afternoon." She flipped through the scribbles in her notebook. She knew Daniel da Silva's exact age, because he'd been one of the men in town who'd matched Charlie Green's age profile for Child Brunswick. "Had to scroll back *really* far on his Facebook. He worked as the janitor at school from 2010 to 2011, when he was around twenty years old. Then he started working at Green Scene at the end of 2011, and he stayed there until October-ish 2013, I think, when he started his police training. So, he was twenty-one when he started at Green Scene, and twenty-three when he left."

"And he was still working there when the first two DT murders happened?" Ravi said, pressing his lips into a thin line.

"The first three, actually. Bethany Ingham was killed in August 2013. I think she used to be Dan's supervisor, as well as Billy's. The name redacted in the police transcript, I think that's Daniel Billy's talking about. Then Jason Bell gave Dan a job in the office—rather than out on the field, as it were—and that was at the start of 2013, as far as I can tell. Oh, and he married his wife, Kim, in September 2013. They'd been together for years before that."

"Interesting," Ravi said, running his hand over Pip's curtains, checking they were fully closed.

She grunted in agreement, a dark sound at the back of her throat, as she flipped back to her to-do list in the notebook. Most of the crudely drawn boxes beside the list were now filled with check marks. "So, if Jason won't talk to me, I've had a look to see if there are any ex-employees of Green Scene or Clean Scene, people who worked in the office who might know more about that security alarm on April eighteenth, 2014. I found a couple on LinkedIn and I've sent them a message."

"Good thinking."

"I think I should see if I can talk to Lieutenant Nolan too; he's retired now. Oh, I also tried to get in contact with some family members of the victims," she said, running her pen down those items on the list. "I thought I found an email address for Bethany Ingham's dad, but the email bounced. I did find an Instagram profile for Julia Hunter's sister, Harriet—you know, the one who mentioned the pigeons. It looks like she hasn't posted in months," she said, opening Instagram on her phone to show him. "Maybe she doesn't go on it anymore. But I sent her a DM just in c—"

Pip's eyes stalled, caught on the red notification that had just popped up above the messages tab.

"Oh shit," she hissed, clicking on it, "she's just replied. Harriet Hunter's just replied!"

Ravi was already up on his feet, his hands finding their way to her shoulders. "What did she say?" His breath tickled the back of her neck.

Pip scanned the message quickly, her eyes so tired, so dried out, she thought they might creak in their sockets. "She . . . she says she can meet with me. Tomorrow."

Pip felt herself smiling before she could help it. Luckily, Ravi was behind her and couldn't see; he would frown at her, tell her this wasn't a time for celebrating. But it felt like it, in a way. It was another win for her. Save herself to save herself.

Your move, DT.

NINETEEN

That must have been her, walking through the café door now, her head unsure upon her shoulders, swiveling this way and that.

Pip held up one hand and waved to her.

Harriet's face broke into a relieved smile as she spotted the raised hand and followed it to Pip's eyes. Pip watched her as she wound her way politely through all the tables and people rammed into this small Starbucks, around the corner from the Stamford train station. She couldn't help but notice how much Harriet looked like Julia Hunter had, before the DT Killer stole her face and wrapped it up in tape. The same dark blond hair and full, arching eyebrows. Why was it that sisters looked so much alike when one of them was dead? Andie and Becca Bell. Now Julia and Harriet Hunter. Two younger sisters, carrying around a ghost wherever they went.

Pip untangled herself from her laptop charger to stand as Harriet approached.

"Hi, Harriet," she said, offering her hand awkwardly.

Harriet smiled, shaking Pip's hand, her skin cold from being outside in the breeze. "I see you're already set up." She pointed down at Pip's laptop, trailing wires connecting it to the two microphones, Pip's headphones already cradled around her neck.

"Yes, it should be quiet enough here in the back corner," Pip said, retaking her seat. "Thank you so much for meeting me on such short notice. Oh, I got you an Americano." She gestured to the steaming mug across the table.

"Thank you," Harriet said, shedding her long coat and taking the chair opposite. "I'm on my lunch break, so we have about an hour." She smiled, but it didn't quite lift into her eyes, the corners of her mouth twitching anxiously. "Oh," she said suddenly, digging around for something in her purse. "I signed that consent form you sent." She passed it over.

"That's great, thank you," Pip said, slotting it into her bronze backpack. "Could I actually just check the levels?" She slid one of the microphones closer to Harriet, and then held one of the cradles of her headphones against her own ear. "Can you say something? Just talk normally."

"Yes . . . um, hello, my name is Harriet Hunter and I'm twenty-four years old. Is that . . . ?"

"Perfect," Pip said, watching the blue lines spike on her audio software.

"So you said you wanted to talk about Julia, and the DT Killer. Is this for another season of your podcast?" Harriet asked, her fingers twisting the ends of her hair.

"I'm just doing some background research at this stage," Pip said. "But yes, potentially." And making sure she collected concrete evidence, if Harriet happened to give her DT's name.

"Oh, right, of course." She sniffed. "It's just, you know, with the other two seasons of your podcast, the cases were ongoing, or closed, but with this . . . with Julia, we know who did it and he's in prison, facing justice. So, I guess I'm just not sure what your podcast would be about." Her voice trailed up, turning the sentence into a question.

"I don't think the story has ever been told in full," Pip said, skirting the reason.

"Oh, right, because there wasn't a trial?" Harriet asked.

"Yes, exactly," Pip lied. They slid easily off her tongue now. "And what I really wanted to talk to you about was a statement you gave to a reporter from *Newsday* on the fifth of February 2014. Do you remember it? I know it was a long time ago, now."

"Yeah, I remember." Harriet paused to take a sip of her coffee. "They all ambushed me outside the house on my way home from school. It was my first day back too, had only been a week or so since Julia was killed. I was young and stupid. I thought you *had* to talk to reporters. Probably told them a whole load of nonsense. I was crying, I remember that. My dad was furious after."

"Specifically, I wanted to ask you about two things you said on that occasion." Pip picked up a printout of the article and passed it to Harriet, lines of bright pink highlighter at the bottom. "You mentioned some weird occurrences in the weeks leading up to Julia's murder. The dead pigeons in the house, and those chalk figures. Could you tell me about those?"

Harriet nodded slightly as she scanned the page, reading back her own words. Her eyes looked heavier when she glanced up again, cloudier. "Yeah, I don't know, it was probably nothing. Police didn't seem that interested in it. But Julia definitely found it weird, enough to comment on it to me. Our cat was old then, basically housebound, used to shit in the living room instead of going outside. He definitely wasn't in his hunting prime, put it that way." She shrugged. "So killing two pigeons and dragging them through the cat flap did seem weird. But I guess it was probably one of the neighbor's cats or something, leaving us a present."

"Did you see them?" Pip asked. "Either of the dead birds?"

Harriet shook her head. "Mom cleared up one, Julia did the other. Julia only found out about the first one when she was complaining about having to mop the blood off the kitchen floor. Her one didn't have a head, apparently. I remember my dad getting mad at her because she'd put the dead pigeon in the recycling bin," she said with a sad sniff of a smile.

Pip's stomach lurched, thinking of her own headless pigeon. "And the chalk figures, what about those?"

"Yeah, I never saw those either." Harriet took another sip, the microphone picking up the sound. "Julia said they were up on the street, near our drive. I guess they washed away before I got back. We lived near a young family then, so it was probably those kids."

"Did Julia mention seeing them again? Getting closer to the house, maybe?"

Harriet stared at her for a moment.

"No, don't think so. She did seem bothered by them, though, like they were on her mind. But I don't think she was scared."

Pip's chair creaked as she shifted. Julia should have been scared. Maybe she was, and she'd hid it from her little sister. She must have seen them, mustn't she? Those three headless stick figures, creeping closer and closer to the house, to her, their number four. Did she think she was imagining them, like Pip had? Had she also questioned whether she was drawing them for herself when sleep-deprived and drugged up?

Pip had been silent too long. "And," she said, "those prank calls you mentioned, what were they?"

"Oh, just calls from blocked numbers, not saying anything. It was probably just someone trying to sell her something. But, you know, these reporters were really pushing for me to tell them anything out of the ordinary in the last few weeks, put me on the spot. So I just told them the first things that came to mind. I don't think they were related to Bil—the DT Killer."

"Do you remember how many calls she got in that week?" Pip leaned forward. She needed at least one more, one more to catch him.

"I think it was three, maybe. At least. Enough for Julia to comment on," said Harriet, and her answer was a physical thing, coaxing up the hairs on Pip's arms. "Why?" she said. She must have noticed Pip's reaction.

"Oh, I'm just trying to work out whether the DT Killer had contact with his victims beforehand. Whether he stalked them, and that's what those calls were, and the pigeons and the chalk," she said.

"I dunno." Harriet's fingers were lost in her hair again. "He never said anything about that in his confession, did he? If he confessed to everything else, why wouldn't he admit that too?"

Pip chewed her lip, running the scenarios through her head, how best to play this. She couldn't tell Harriet that she thought it possible the DT Killer and Billy Karras were two different people; that would be irresponsible. Cruel, even. Not without concrete evidence.

She changed tactic.

"So," she said, "was Julia single around the time she was killed?"

Harriet nodded. "No boyfriend," she said. "Only one ex and he was in Mexico the night she was killed."

"Do you know if she was seeing anyone? Dating?" Pip pressed.

A noncommittal croak from Harriet's throat, a corresponding jump in the blue audio line on-screen. "I don't think so, really. Andie always asked me that question too, at the time. Julia and I didn't talk much about boys at home, because Dad would always hear and want to be included to try to embarrass us. She *was* going out for dinner with friends a lot around then; maybe that was code for something. But it obviously wasn't Billy Karras—the police would have found a trail on her phone. Or his, even."

Pip's mind stuttered, stumbling over one word. She hadn't heard anything else Harriet said after that.

"I'm sorry, did you just say A-Andie?" she asked with a nervous laugh. "You don't mean Andie B—"

"Yeah, Andie Bell." Harriet smiled sadly. "I know, it's a small world, huh? And what are the chances that two different people in my life were murdered? Well, sort of—I know Andie was an accident."

Pip felt it again, that creeping feeling up her spine, cold and inevitable. Like everything was playing out the way it was always supposed to from the start. Coming full circle. And she was simply a passenger inside her own body, watching the show play out.

Harriet was eyeing her, a concerned look on her face. "Are you OK?" she asked.

"Y-yes, fine," Pip coughed. "Just trying to work out how you knew Andie Bell. It's thrown me a little, sorry."

"Yeah, no"—her mouth flicked up sympathetically—"it kind of threw me too, came a little out of nowhere. It was after Julia died, a couple weeks after, and I got this email out of the blue from Andie. I didn't know her before then. We were the same age, at different schools, but we had a few mutual friends. I think she got my email from my Facebook profile, back when everyone was on Facebook. Anyway, it was a really sweet message, saying how sorry she was about Julia, and if I ever needed someone to talk to, I could talk to her."

"Andie said that?" Pip asked.

Harriet nodded. "So I replied and we started talking. I didn't really have a *best friend* at the time, someone who I could talk to about my feelings, about Julia, and Andie was really great. We became friends. We scheduled phone calls about once a week, and we used to meet up, in *here,* actually," she said, glancing around the coffee shop, her eyes catching on a table over by the window. That must have been where they used to sit. Harriet Hunter and Andie Bell. Pip still couldn't wrap her head around it, this strange convergence. Why would Andie have reached out to Harriet out of the blue? That didn't sound much like the Andie Bell she'd grown to know five years after her death.

"And what did you used to talk about?" said Pip.

"Everything. Anything. She was like my sounding board, and I hope I was one for her too, although she didn't talk about herself much. We talked about Julia, about the DT Killer, how my parents were, et cetera. She died the same night Billy Karras killed Tara Yates, did you know that?"

Pip gave her a slight nod.

"Weird, horrible coincidence," Harriet said, biting her lip. "We talked about it so much, and she didn't live to find out who he was. She was desperate to know too, I think, for my sake. And I feel terrible—I didn't know about all the *stuff* going on in her life."

Pip's eyes flicked side to side as her mind tried to catch up with this unexpected path, splintering from DT back to Andie Bell again. Another connection: her dad's company, and now this friendship with Harriet Hunter. Had the police known about this convergence at the time, this strange link between two ongoing cases? If it was an email account Andie's family knew about, then Detective Hawkins must have learned about it after her disappearance, unless . . .

"D-do you know the email address Andie first used to contact you?" she said, her chair creaking as she leaned forward.

"Oh yeah," Harriet said, reaching into the pocket of her jacket, slung over the chair. "It was a weird one, all random letters and numbers. I initially thought it was an automated bot or something." She swiped at her phone. "I starred the emails after she died, so I'd never lose them. Here, this is them, before we exchanged numbers."

She slid her phone across the table, the Gmail app open, with a row of emails lined up the screen. Sent from A2B3FV96@gmail.com, with the subject line: *Hi.*

Pip scanned down the previews of each message, reading them out in Andie's voice, bringing her back to life. *Hello Harriet, you don't know me but my name is Andie Bell. I go to Fairview High, but I think we both know Chris Parks. . . . Hi Harriet, thanks for getting back to me and for not thinking I'm a creepy weirdo for reaching out, I'm so sorry about your sister. I have a sister too. . . .* All the way down to the last one: *Hey HH, would you want to talk on the phone instead of emailing, or even meet up some time. . . .*

Something stirred at the back of Pip's mind, pushing her eyes back to those two letters: *HH.* She asked her mind what she was supposed to be seeing here; it was just Harriet's initials.

"I'm glad you found out the truth of what happened to her," Harriet interrupted her thoughts. "And that your podcast was kind to her. Andie was a complicated girl, I think. But she saved me."

Even more complicated now, Pip thought, scribbling down Andie's email address. Harriet was right: it was a strange email address, almost like it was obscure on purpose. Almost like it had been a secret. Maybe she'd made it for this very reason, just to reach out to Harriet Hunter. But why?

"Are you going to talk to him?" Harriet asked, bringing Pip's attention back to the room, this table, the microphones set out in front of them. "Are you going to talk to Billy Karras?"

Pip paused, ran her finger across the plastic of her headphones, round and round her neck. "I hope I get to speak to the DT Killer, yes," she answered. She'd meant it to be tactful, so she didn't have to lie to Harriet, but there was something else beneath those words. Something creeping and ominous. A dark promise. To herself, or to him?

"Listen," Pip said, clicking the stop button on her recording software. "We're running out of time for today. Do you think we can schedule another interview soon, where you can talk more about Julia, what she was like? You've given me lots to go on today for my research, so thank you for that."

"I have?" Harriet said, the skin above her nose crinkling in confusion.

She had, but she didn't know it. She'd given Pip a lead, in the most unlikely of places.

"Yes, it's been very informative," Pip said, unplugging the microphones, those two letters, *HH,* still playing on her mind, sounding them out in Andie's voice, a voice she'd never even heard.

She and Harriet shook hands again as they said goodbye, and Pip hoped she hadn't noticed the tremor in her hands, the shiver that had made itself at home beneath her skin. And as Pip pushed the coffee shop door—holding it open for Harriet—the cold wind hit her, and so did one realization, tangible and heavy. That, even after all this time, Andie Bell still had one mystery left in her yet.

File Name:

Andie planner photo March 10–16 2014.jpg

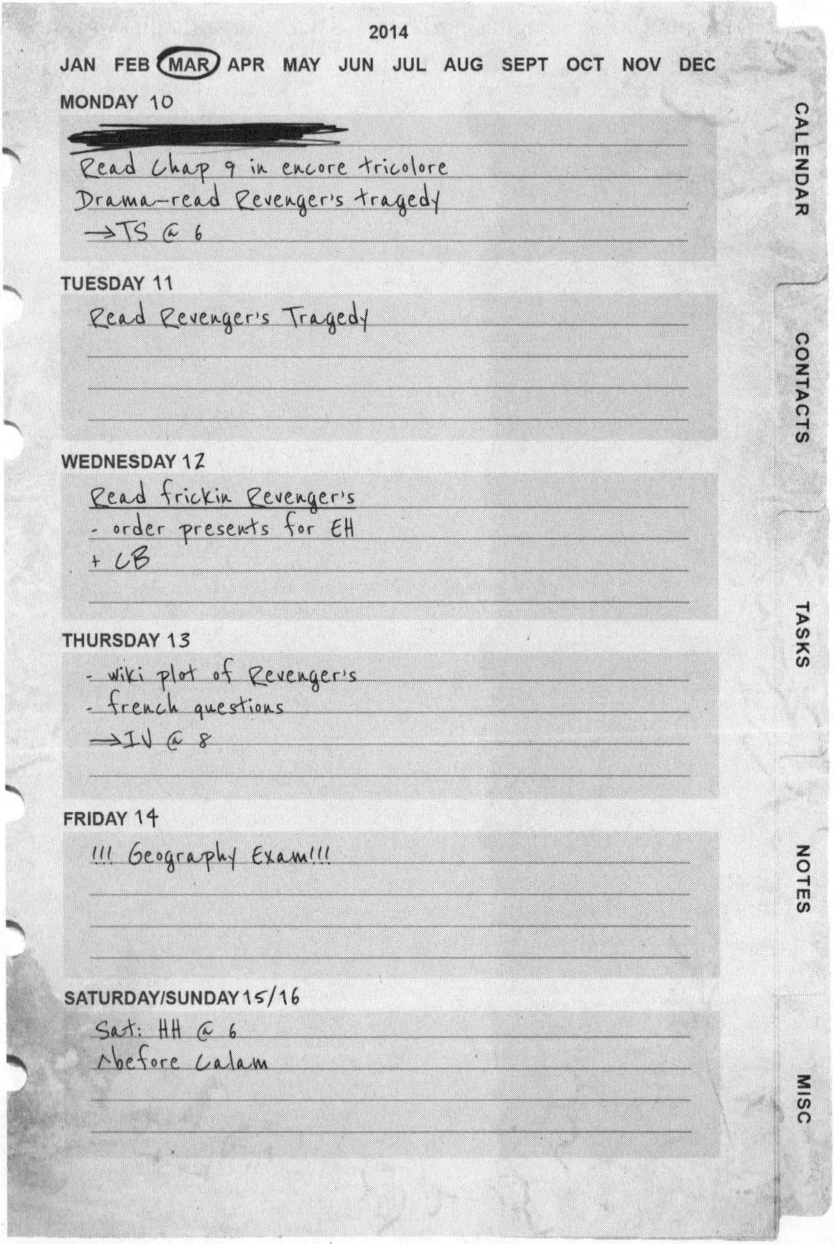

TWENTY

Pip found it, the itch at the back of her head, the one that scraped forward and back, sounding like two hissed letters. *HH.*

She stared at the file open in front of her. *Andie planner photo March 10–16 2014.jpg.* A photo she'd copied and pasted into Capstone Project Log–Entry 25 last year. One of the photos she'd taken of Andie's school planner when she and Ravi broke into the Bell house, just under a year ago, searching for a burner phone they'd never find.

The full photo, the original before Pip had cropped it, showed more of Andie's cluttered desk. A makeup case with a pale-purple hairbrush resting on top, her blond hairs still wound around the bristles. Beside it was a Fairview High academic planner for the year 2013–2014, open to this mid-March week, a little more than a month before Andie had died.

And there it was. *HH* scribbled in on this Saturday, and in the other photos they'd taken: the weeks before and after. Pip thought she'd worked out Andie's code at the time. That *HH* referred to "Howie's house," just as *TS* meant the train station parking lot, where Andie would meet Howie Bowers to pick up a new stash or drop off money. But she'd been wrong. *HH* had nothing to do with Howie Bowers. *HH* meant Harriet Hunter. Whether it was a phone call or a meet-up, it was hard to say. But it had been Harriet all along, and here was proof. Andie reaching out to the sister of the DT Killer's fourth victim.

The itch in Pip's head became an ache, sharpening at her temples as she tried to understand what this meant. The idea thrashed against her as she tried to make it make sense. What did Andie Bell have to do with all this, with DT?

There was only one place she might find the answers. Andie's email address, one Pip suspected had been a secret. Andie had had lots of those in her short life.

Pip finally looked away from the planner page, opening her browser instead. She logged out of her account on Gmail, and then clicked sign in again.

She typed in Andie's address *A2B3FV96@gmail.com* and then paused, her mouse hovering over the password box. There was no way she'd be able to guess it. She guided the mouse instead to the prompt that said *Forgotten password?*

A new screen popped up, asking Pip to *Enter the last password you remember.* The cursor blinked in the input box, mocking her. She traced her fingers down the trackpad, skipping over the password box to the *Try a different question* button.

Another option blinked up on-screen, offering to send a code to the recovery email address AndieBell96@gmail.com. Pip's stomach lurched: so Andie did have another email address, likely her main one. The one people knew about. But Pip didn't have access to that one either, so she couldn't recover the verification code. Andie's secret email address might just remain a secret forever.

But hope wasn't all gone yet. There was another option, another *Try a different question* at the bottom of the page. She clicked it, closing her eyes for a half second, begging the machine to *please please please work.*

When she reopened them, the page had changed again.

Answer the security question you added to your account:

Name of first hamster?

Below it was another input box, asking Pip to *Enter your answer.*

That was it. There were no other options, no try again buttons on the screen. She had reached the end. Stalemate.

And how on earth was she supposed to find out the name of the Bells' first hamster? A hamster that, presumably, existed pre-social media. She couldn't exactly knock on their door again to ask Jason; he'd told her to leave them alone for good.

Wait a second.

Pip's heart kicked against her chest. She grabbed her phone to check the day. It was Wednesday. Tomorrow at four p.m., Becca Bell would call her from prison, like she did every Thursday.

Yes. Becca was the solution. She would know the hamster Andie had been referring to here. And Pip could ask her if she knew anything about Andie's second email address, and why she might have needed one.

But four p.m. tomorrow was twenty-five hours away. Twenty-five hours felt like an entire lifetime, which it might be. Hers. Pip didn't know how much time was left, only DT knew that, or the person pretending to be him. A race against a timer she couldn't see. But there was nothing she could do about it except wait.

Becca would know.

And in the meantime, she could chase the other open leads. Send follow-up messages to those ex-Green Scene employees about the security alarm. Arrange an interview with the now-retired Lieutenant Nolan. He'd replied to her email this morning saying he would be happy to discuss the DT case for her podcast. There were still things Pip could do, moves she could play against him in these next twenty-five hours.

Her hands were shaking now. Oh no. Next would come the blood, leaking from the lifelines across her palm. Not now, please not now. She needed to calm down, slow down, take a break from being inside her own head. Maybe she should go out for a run? Or . . . She glanced at the second drawer down in her desk. Or maybe both?

The half pill was bitter on her tongue as she dry-swallowed it, tried to chase it down with air. *Breathe, just breathe.* But now she couldn't breathe because there were only two and a half pills left in the small clear bag and she needed more, she needed them, or she wouldn't sleep at all, and if she didn't sleep then she wouldn't be able to think, and if she couldn't think then she wouldn't win.

She didn't want to. Last time was supposed to be it, she'd promised. But she needed them now, to save herself. And then she'd never need them again. That was the deal she made as she picked up the first burner phone in the line and turned it on, the Nokia symbol lighting up the screen.

She navigated to her messages, to the only number saved in any of these phones. She sent Luke Eaton just three words: *I need more.*

Pip laughed at herself then, hollow and dark, as she realized this very thing in her hands was yet another link back to Andie Bell. Walking in her footsteps, six years behind. And maybe secret hidden phones weren't the only things she and Andie Bell would share.

Luke replied within seconds.

Last time again is it? Ill tell you when I have them.

There was a flash of rage up the skin of her neck. Pip bit down on her lower lip until it hurt, as she held down the off button and returned the phone and Luke to their secret compartment at the bottom of her drawer. Luke was wrong. This was different; this really would be the last time.

The Xanax hadn't kicked in yet, though; her heart was still hummingbird-fast in her chest, no matter what bargain she tried to make with it. She could go for a run. She *should* go for a run. It might help her think, help her work out what Andie's connection to Harriet Hunter and DT was.

She wandered over to her bed and the window behind it, glancing through the glass at the afternoon sky beyond. It didn't look much like summer. It was a slow, churning gray, and there were spots on the driveway from another bout of rain. Never mind, she liked running in the rain. And there were worse things someone could find on their driveway, like five headless stick figures, coming for her. There'd been no more; Pip checked every time she left the house.

But there was something else out there now, a flash of movement pulling at Pip's gaze. A person, jogging on the sidewalk past their house, past their driveway. It was only three seconds before they were gone, out of sight again, but three seconds were all Pip needed to know exactly who it was. Blue water bottle gripped in one hand. Blond hair pushed back from his angular face. One quick glance over his shoulder at her house. He knew. He knew this was where she lived.

Pip saw red again, an eruption of violence behind her eyes as her mind showed her all the ways she might kill Max Hastings. None of them was bad enough; he deserved much worse. She cycled through them all, her thoughts chasing him down the road, until a sound brought her back to the room.

Her phone, vibrating against the desk.

She stared at it.

Fuck.

Was it *No Caller ID*? DT? Was this it, the moment she found out who was doing this to her? The CallTrapper app ready and waiting to go, to turn the disembodied breath into a real person, into a name. She didn't need to learn what Andie Bell's connection to all this was; the final answer would be in front of her.

Quick. She'd hesitated too long already. She darted across the room to pick up the phone.

No, it wasn't *No Caller ID.* There was a sequence of numbers scrolling above the incoming call: a cell phone number she didn't recognize.

"Hello?" she said, holding the phone too tight against her ear.

"Hello," said a deep, crackling voice down the line. "Hi, Pip. It's me, Detective Richard Hawkins."

Pip's chest loosened around her too-fast heart. Not DT.

"O-oh," she said, recovering. "Detective Hawkins."

"You were expecting someone else," he said with a sniff.

"I was."

"Well, I'm sorry to disturb you." Now a cough. Another sniff. "It's just that, well, I have some news, and I thought it best to call you right away. I know you'd want to know."

News? About the stalker he didn't believe in? Had they made the connection to DT on their end too? She felt a new lightness then, starting from her gut and working up, bare heels lifting from the carpet. He believed her, he believed her, he believed—

"It's about Charlie Green," he said, filling the silence.

Oh. She sank again.

"Wh-what . . ." Pip began.

"We've got him," Hawkins said. "He was just arrested. He had managed to make it to Canada. Interpol has him now. But we've got him. He'll be extradited back and officially charged tomorrow."

She was still sinking. How was she still sinking? There was only so deep she could go, until she fell right through the ground into nothing.

"I—I," she stuttered. Sinking. Shrinking. Watching her feet so they couldn't disappear down through the carpet.

"You don't have to worry anymore. We've got him," Hawkins said again, his voice softening. "Are you OK?"

No, she wasn't. She didn't understand what he wanted from her. Did he want her to thank him? No, this wasn't what she wanted. Charlie didn't belong in a cage; how could he help her from a cage, tell her what was right and wrong, what to do to fix it all? Why would she want this? *Should* she want this? Is that how a normal person would be feeling right now, instead of this black hole inside and her bones caving in around it?

"Pip? There's nothing to be scared of anymore. He can't get to you."

She wanted to scream at him, tell him that Charlie Green was never a danger to her, but Hawkins wouldn't believe her. He never believed her. But maybe it wouldn't matter, maybe there was still a way here to fix herself, to safely step off this spiral before it reached its end. Because that was where this was all heading, she could feel it, and yet she couldn't stop herself. But maybe Charlie could.

"C-can I . . . ," she began, hesitating. "Can I please talk to him?"

"Excuse me?"

"To Charlie," she said, louder now. "Can I please talk to Charlie? I'd really like to speak to him. I—I need to speak to him."

A sound came down the line, a croak of disbelief from Hawkins's throat. "Well, um . . . ," he said, "I'm afraid that that won't be possible, Pip. You're the only eyewitness to a murder he allegedly committed. And if there's a trial, obviously you'll be called as the prosecution's lead witness. So, I'm afraid it's not going to be possible for you to talk to him, no."

Pip sank even farther, bones fusing with the structure of the house. Hawkins's answer was a physical thing, sharp and lodged inside her chest. She should have known.

"OK, that's fine," she said quietly. It wasn't fine, it was anything but fine.

"How's the . . . how's that other thing going?" Hawkins asked, a hint of uncertainty in his voice. "The stalker you came to me about. Have there been any other incidents?"

"Oh, no," Pip said flatly. "Nothing else. That's all sorted now. That's fine, thank you."

"OK, well, I just wanted to let you know about Charlie Green, before you saw it in the press tomorrow." Hawkins cleared his throat. "And I hope you're doing better."

"I'm fine," Pip said, and she hardly had the energy to even pretend, her words coming out in a flat line. "Thanks for your call, Detective Hawkins." She lowered the phone, her thumb finding the red button.

Charlie was caught. It was over. The one possible salvation she'd had left, other than this dangerous game against DT. At least she could officially cross Charlie's name from the list of people who might hate her enough to want her to disappear. She'd always known it wasn't him, and now it really couldn't have been: he'd been in Canada all this time.

Pip glanced at her computer screen again, at the page asking her to name Andie Bell's first hamster, and it was almost funny, just how ridiculous it was. Just as funny, as ridiculous, as the notion of decomposing bodies and the way we all become one. Disappearing wasn't mysterious, it wasn't thrilling; it was cold bodies with stiff limbs and purpling patches as the blood inside pooled. What Billy Karras must have seen when he found Tara Yates. What Stanley Forbes must have looked like in the morgue, though how could he have had any blood left in him when it was all over her hands? Sal Singh too, dead in the woods outside her house. Not Andie Bell, though; she was found too late, when she was almost entirely gone, disintegrated. That was the closest thing to disappearing, Pip supposed.

And yet, Andie hadn't disappeared, not at all. Here she was again, six and a half years after she died, and she was Pip's only remaining lead. No, not a lead, a lifeline: some strange unknowable force connecting them across time, though they'd never met. Pip wasn't there to save Andie, but maybe Andie was there to save her.

Maybe.

But still, Pip had to wait. And Andie Bell would remain a mystery at least for the next twenty-four and a half hours.

TWENTY-ONE

"This is a Tel-Co Link prepaid call from . . . Becca Bell . . . *an inmate at FCI Danbury. Please note, this call will be recorded and is subject to monitoring at any time. To accept this call, press one. To block all futu—"*

Pip pressed *1* so fast, she almost pushed the phone right out of her hands.

"Hello?" She raised it to her ear again, her leg bouncing uncontrollably against her desk, rattling the cup of pens on top. "Becca?"

"Hey," Becca's voice came through, faint at first. "Hey, Pip, yeah, I'm here. Sorry, there was a bit of a line. How're you doing?"

"Yeah, good," Pip said, her chest constricting uncomfortably with every breath. "Good, yeah, fine."

"You sure?" Becca said, a hint of concern pulling up her voice. "You sound a bit jittery."

"Oh, too much coffee, you know me," Pip said with a hollow laugh. "How are you? How's French going?"

"Good, yeah," she said, then added, "Très bon," with an amused sniff. "And they just started up yoga classes this week."

"Oh, that's fun."

"Yeah, and I went with my friend, remember I told you about Nell?" Becca said. "So yeah, that was fun, although it's made me realize how incredibly not-bendy I am. Something to work on, I suppose."

Becca's voice was bright; it always was. Pip might even describe it as close to happy. She found it strange, the idea that Becca might be happier in there than she would be out. Because she *had* chosen to be there, in a way: she'd pleaded guilty even though her defense team had been confident that if they went to trial, they could have avoided jail time. It always struck Pip as odd that someone would choose to be there, as Becca had. Maybe it wasn't a cage, not to her.

"So," Becca continued, "how is everyone? How's Nat?"

"Yes, good," Pip said. "I saw her a week and a bit ago. Her and Jamie Reynolds. They seem to be doing really well, actually. Happy."

"That's good," Becca said, and Pip could hear the smile accompanying her words. "I'm glad she's happy. And have you made any decision about the libel lawsuit yet?"

Truthfully, she'd almost forgotten about it. DT taking up too much of her brain, winding round and round it like tape. Christopher Epps's card was still sitting, ignored, in that same jacket pocket.

"Well," Pip said, "I haven't spoken to my lawyer since, or Max's. I've been a bit distracted. But I already told them my answer. I'm not recanting and I'm not apologizing to him. If Max wants to go to a full trial, that's on him. But he won't get away with it twice; I won't let him."

"I'll testify," Becca said, "if it happens. I know I already told you that. People need to know what he is, even if it's not a criminal trial, not *real* justice."

Justice. The word that always tripped Pip up, brought the blood out on her hands. That word was her prison, her cage. One glance down and yes, there Stanley was, bleeding out across her hands. She could talk to Becca about him if she wanted to, someone else who knew him as more than Child Brunswick. Becca and Stanley had even gone out twice before deciding to just be friends. Becca could listen, even if she couldn't understand. But, no, Pip didn't have time for that, not now.

"Becca, um, I'm . . . ," she began unsteadily. "I actually needed to ask you something. Quite urgent. I mean, it's not going to sound urgent. But it is. It's important but I can't really explain why to you, not on the phone."

"OK," Becca said, some of the shine now gone from her voice. "Are you OK?"

"Yes, fine," Pip replied. "It's just, well, I need to know what Andie called her first hamster."

Becca snorted, taken aback. "What?"

"It's . . . it's a security question. Do you remember what she called her first hamster?"

"A security question for what?" Becca asked.

"I think Andie had an email account. A secret one. One the police never found."

"AndieBell94," Becca said the words in one quick stream. "That was her email address. The police definitely asked about it at the time."

"This is another account she used. And I can't get on it unless I answer the security question."

"Another account?" Becca hesitated. "Why are you looking into Andie again? Wha . . . why? What's going on?"

"I don't think I can say," Pip said, holding down her knee to stop her leg from rattling. "This call is being recorded. But it might be something . . . important to me." She paused, listening to the light swell of Becca's breathing. "Life or death," she added.

"Roadie."

"What?" Pip said.

"Roadie, that was Andie's first hamster." Becca sniffed. "I don't know where she got that name from. She got him for her sixth birthday, I think. Maybe seventh. I got one a year later and called him Toadie. Then we got our cat, Monty, who ate Toadie. But her hamster, he was Roadie."

Pip's fingers thrummed, ready.

"R-O-A-D-Y?" she asked.

"No. I-E," Becca said. "Is this . . . is everything OK? Really?"

"It will be," Pip said. "I hope. D-did Andie ever mention someone called Harriet Hunter to you? A friend?"

Silence down the line, the background hum of nearby voices. "No," Becca said eventually. "I don't think she did. I never met anyone called Harriet. Not that Andie ever really had people over at the house. Why? Who is she?"

"Becca, listen," Pip said, her fingers fidgeting against the phone. "I'm going to have to go, I'm sorry. There's something . . . and I might not have much time. But I will explain everything to you when it's over, I promise."

"Oh, yeah . . . that's OK," she said, her voice less close to happy now. "Are you still coming to visit, next Saturday? I've put you down on the log."

"Yes," Pip said, her mind already straying away from Becca, back to the computer screen and the security question waiting for her. "Yep, I'll be there," she said, absently.

"Good luck," Becca said, "with . . . and, let me know you're OK. When you can."

"I will," Pip said, and she could hear it now too, the jittering edge in her own voice. "Thanks, Becca. Bye."

She did drop the phone this time, pushing the button too hard, the phone sliding right off her blood-slick palm. Pip left it there, on the floor, her fingers finding their way to the keyboard. To *R* and then *O* and on. Roadie. Andie Bell's first hamster.

Invisible blood smears across the trackpad as Pip guided the on-screen arrow to the Next button.

A page loaded, telling her to create a new password, and to retype it in the box below to confirm. The feeling in her chest changed again, fizzing as it came into contact with her skin. What password should she use? Anything. Anything, just hurry up.

The first thing that came into her mind was *DTKiller6.*

At least she wouldn't forget it.

She retyped it and clicked to confirm.

An inbox opened up, not enough emails to even fill the screen.

Pip exhaled. Here it was. Andie Bell's secret email account. Preserved after all this time. Untouched, except by her. Pip had that feeling again in her spine, like she was out of her own time, untethered.

It was immediately clear why Andie had made this account. The only emails she'd ever sent and received were to and from Harriet Hunter. That must have been the reason Andie made the account, but it still wasn't clear why, what her connection to Harriet and DT was.

Pip clicked through the emails, reading the same messages Harriet had showed her, from Andie's side this time. Nothing new here. No explanations. No lifelines. There were only eight messages back and forth, all under that same subject line: *Hi.*

There had to be something else here. Anything. Andie had to help her, she had to. That's why everything was leading back to her, coming full circle.

Pip clicked out of the primary inbox, into social. There was nothing here, just a blank page. She tried the third option—promotions—and the page filled with lines and lines of emails. All from the same sender: Self-Defense Tips. Andie must have subscribed to their email list at some point. She'd been getting the emails, one every week, long after she was already dead. Why was Andie looking at a self-defense newsletter? Pip shivered. Had Andie believed she was in danger? Had part of her known she wouldn't make it past seventeen? That same inevitable feeling that lived inside Pip's gut.

Pip checked down the side bar. There was nothing in the trash: no deleted emails. Damn. *Come on, Andie.* There had to be something here. Had to be. There was a connection here, and Pip was the person supposed to find it. She knew it, that unknowable thing. Things falling in line the way they were always supposed to.

Her hand drew up suddenly as her eyes caught on a number in the side bar. A small *1* hiding next to the Drafts folder. So small and slight, like it had been trying to hide from Pip's prying eyes.

An unsent draft. Something Andie wrote. What was it—an unfinished message to HH? Maybe nothing at all, maybe just blank. Pip clicked to open the Drafts folder, and there it was, waiting for her at the top. One unsent email and she could already see it wasn't blank. The date on the right-hand side marked it as being saved on February 19, 2014. The subject line said: *from anon.*

Pip's chest constricted, and there was a strange rattling in her breath now, as she wiped away the blood from one hand and opened the draft.

New message

Recipients

Subject: from anon

To whom it may concern,

I know who the DT Killer is.

I've never said it out loud, not to anyone, not even just to myself. It's only been a thought in my head, growing and growing, taking up more space until it's all I can think about. Even writing it out here feels like a big step, makes me feel slightly less alone in this. But I am alone in this. All alone.

I know who the DT Killer is.

Or the Stratford Strangler. Whatever the name, I know who he is.

And I wish I could actually send this email. Send in an anonymous tip to the police with his name—don't even know if police stations have email addresses. I could never call. I could never say it. I'm so scared. Every single second that I'm awake, and when I'm asleep too. It's getting harder to pretend, when he's inside the house, talking with us all like everything is normal, around the dinner table. But I know I can't send this. How could I ever send this? Who would believe me? The police won't. And if he found out what I said, he would kill me, just like he killed them. Of course he'd find out. He's practically one of them.

This is just a practice, and maybe it will make me feel better, knowing that I *could* send this, even though I can't. Talking it through with myself, outside of my head.

I know who the DT Killer is.

I saw him. I saw him with Julia Hunter. I know it was her, 100%. They were holding hands. I saw him kiss her cheek too. He doesn't know I saw them. And I wasn't that surprised to see them together. But then, six days later, she's dead. He killed her. I know he did. I knew it as soon as I saw her face on the news. Everything fits now, all of those other details. I should have worked it out before this.

I don't know why I contacted HH. I thought maybe she might know too, or have suspicions about who killed her sister, and I could have someone to talk about it with. Work out what to do together. But she doesn't know. She doesn't know anything. And, I don't know why, but I feel like I have a responsibility to her, to make sure she's OK. Because I know who killed her sister and I don't know how to tell her. If someone touched Becca, I would be broken.

I can't tell Sal. He probably already thinks I'm fucked-up enough. There's so much I have to hide from him, because he's one of the only good things I have left, and he has to be protected. He can never come over, just in case.

I have this overwhelming sense of dread all the time, that if I don't escape this town, it's going to kill me. *He's* going to kill me. He's already started looking at me differently, or maybe that started years ago. I hope he doesn't look at Becca like that. But I have a plan, have had a plan for a while now, just need to keep my head down. I've been saving up all the cash from Howie for almost a year. It's hidden, no one will find it. I fucked up school, though, so fucking stupid of me. That would have been the easiest way to escape, a college far away. No one would suspect a thing. But the only one I got into is here, and I'd have to stay in Fairview. I can't stay at home.

Sal got into Yale. I wish I could go with him. It's not so far away, but it's far enough. Maybe there's something I can do to go too. If it's not too late. I have to do anything to get out of here. Anything. I know Mr. Ward helped him get his place, maybe he can help me too. Anything. At all costs.

And when I'm away and I'm safe, I'll come back for Becca. She has to finish school first, she has to, she's smart. But if I'm set up somewhere far away from here, she can come live with me, and when we are away and safe, maybe that's when I tell the police who he is. Maybe that's when I finally send this email, from anon, when he can no longer get to us, doesn't know where we are.

That's the plan, at least. I have no one to talk it through with, except myself, but it's the best I can do. I'll have to delete this now, just in case.

This feels too big for me, but I think I can do it. Save us. Keep Becca safe. Survive.

I just have to m

Send

TWENTY-TWO

Ravi scrolled up and down again, shaking his head, and Pip could see the reflection of Andie's words in the dark of his eyes. Even clearer now that they were filling with tears. The weight of her ghost inside him too, not just in her. A dead girl shared, a dead girl halved, and they were the only two people in the word who knew. These weren't Andie Bell's final words, but they sure felt like it.

"I don't believe it," he said finally, cupping his hands around his face. "I can't believe it. Andie, she . . . This changes everything. Everything."

Pip sighed. There was an unutterable sadness in her gut, and still she was sinking through the floor, dragging Andie's ghost with her. But she took Ravi's hand, holding tight to anchor them all together. "I mean, it changes everything, and it changes nothing," she said. "Andie didn't survive. It wasn't DT who killed her, but it was everything she tried to do to escape him that did. Howie Bowers. Max Hastings. Elliot Ward. Becca. This is why it all happened. Everything. Full circle," she added quietly. The beginning was the end and the end the beginning, and DT was both.

Ravi wiped his eyes on his sleeve. "I just . . ." His voice croaked, stifling his next words. "I don't know how I feel about this. It's . . . it's too sad. And we, we've all been wrong about her. I couldn't really understand what Sal saw in her before, but . . . oh god, she must have been so terrified. So alone." He glanced up at Pip. "And this is it, isn't it?

The nineteenth of February: it was right after this that she first approached Mr. Ward, and . . ."

"At all costs," Pip said, echoing Andie's words, and she felt that uncanny closeness to her again. Five years apart and they'd never met, yet here she was, carrying Andie around in her chest. Two dead girls walking, more alike than Pip could ever have realized. "She was desperate. I never really understood why, but I never would have guessed this. Poor Andie."

Such an inadequate thing to say, but what else was there?

"She was brave," Ravi said in a small voice. "Reminds me of you a little bit." A small smile to match the small voice. "The Singh brothers clearly have a type."

But Pip's mind had left her, spinning back to last year. To Elliot Ward standing across from her, the police on their way. "Elliot said something to me last year, and I never really understood it until now." She paused, replaying the scene in her head. "He told me that when Andie went round to his house—before he pushed her off and she hit her head—she told him that she had to get away from home, from Fairview, because it was killing her. The signs were there . . . I—I didn't see them."

"And it did," Ravi said, his eyes back on the screen, on the final trace of Andie Bell, her last mystery laid bare. "It did kill her."

"Before *he* did," she said.

"Who is he?" Ravi said, running an unclicked pen down the laptop screen. "There's no name, but there's a lot of information, Pip. There must be a smoking gun here. So, it's someone the whole Bell family knew, including Andie and Becca. Which makes sense with the connection to Jason's company Green Scene, right?"

"Someone who used to go over to their house, even have dinner with them," Pip said, underscoring the line with her finger. She clicked her tongue as another old thought stirred, came back to life.

"What?" Ravi asked.

"Last year, I went to speak to Becca at the *Fairview Mail* office. This was back when Max and Daniel da Silva were my main suspects for Andie. We talked about Dan, because I found out he was one of the officers who did the initial search of their house when Andie went missing. And Becca told me Daniel was close with her dad. Jason got him a job at Green Scene, then promoted him to the office, and also was the one who suggested Dan apply to be a police officer." Pip was untethered again, floating through time, from then to now, the start to the end. "She said that Daniel was often coming round theirs after work, sometimes stayed for dinner."

"Oh, right," Ravi said gravely.

"Daniel da Silva." Pip said his name again, testing it out on her tongue, trying to somehow fit all the syllables inside DT.

"And there's this bit." Ravi scrolled back up the email draft. "When she talks about going to the police, but she's scared they won't believe her and that *he* might find out. There's this part that trips me up." He pointed it out. "*Of course he'd find out. He's practically one of them.* One of what?"

Pip ran the sentences through her head, tilting them to see them from a different angle. "A police officer, it sounds like. Not sure what the *practically* means."

"Maybe she meant a newly trained police officer, like Daniel da Silva was." Ravi completed her thought.

"Daniel da Silva," Pip said again, testing it out, watching her breath dissipate around the room, taking his name with it. *And what about Nat?* asked the other side of her brain. She and Dan weren't the closest of siblings, but he was still her big brother. Could Pip really think that of him? She'd certainly considered him before, for Andie's murder, and in Jamie's disappearance. What was different now? She and Nat were close, bonded, tied together: that's what was different now. And he had a wife. A baby.

"I thought you were speaking to that retired detective today too?" Ravi said, a tug at her sweater to bring her attention back to him.

"Yeah, he canceled on me last-minute," Pip said with a sniff. "Rescheduled for tomorrow afternoon."

"OK, that's good." Ravi nodded absently, eyes returning to Andie's never-sent email.

"I just need my phone to ring," Pip said, staring down at it lying inconspicuously on her desk. "DT just has to call me one more time. Then CallTrapper will give me his number and then I can find out who he is, if it is Daniel or . . ." She broke off, narrowing her eyes at her phone, begging it to ring, wishing so hard she could almost hear the echoes of her ringtone.

"And then you can go to Detective Hawkins," Ravi said. "Or go public."

"And then it's over," Pip agreed.

More than just over. Normal. Fixed. No blood on her hands, or pills to keep it all at bay. She will be saved. Normal. Team Ravi and Pip, who can talk about normal things like new college bed sheets and movie theater times and tentative, half-shy discussions of the future. Their future.

Pip had asked for a way out, one last case, and something had answered her. Now it was even more perfect, even more fitting. Because DT was the origin. The end and the beginning. The monster in the dark, the creator, the source. Everything that had happened traced right back to him.

All of it.

Andie Bell knew who DT was and she was terrified, so she sold drugs for Howie Bowers to save up money to escape, to get far away from Fairview. She sold Rohypnol to Max Hastings, who then used those drugs to rape her little sister, Becca. Andie pursued Elliot Ward in her desperate plan to escape to Yale with Sal. Elliot thought he accidentally killed Andie, so he murdered Sal to cover it up, Ravi's brother dead in the woods. But Elliot didn't kill Andie, not really; it was Becca Bell, too angry and shocked at her sister's role in her own tragedy that she froze and let Andie die from her head injury, choking on her own vomit. Five years went by and then Pip came along, uncovered all those truths. Elliot in prison, Becca in prison though she shouldn't be, Max not in prison though he should be. And, most importantly, Howie Bowers in prison. Howie told his cellmate that he knew the real Child Brunswick. The cellmate told his cousin, who told a friend, who told a friend, who put the rumor online. Charlie Green read that rumor and came to Fairview. Layla Mead, wearing the face of Stella Chapman. Jamie Reynolds missing. Stanley Forbes with six holes blown in him, bleeding out on Pip's hands.

Three different stories, but one interconnected knot. And in the center of that writhing knot, grinning at her from the dark, was DT.

File Name:

Interview with Lieutenant Nolan about DT.wav

PIP: Thank you so much, Mr. Nolan, for agreeing to this interview. And sorry for stealing you away from your Friday afternoon.

LT. NOLAN: Oh please, call me David. And yes, no worries at all. Sorry I had to cancel our call yesterday. Last-minute golf game, you know how it is.

PIP: Of course, yes, no worries. Not like there's a time limit or anything. So, firstly, how long have you been retired?

LT. NOLAN: Three years now. Yes, it was 2017 when I left. I know: golfing, reliving my glory days, I'm a retired-cop cliché. I've even tried pottery-making, my wife made me.

PIP: Sounds lovely. So, as I said in my emails, today I wanted to talk to you about the DT Killer case.

LT. NOLAN: Yes, yes. Biggest case of my career, that was. A great way to go out. I mean, terrible, of course, what he did to those women.

PIP: It must have been memorable. Serial killers aren't that common.

LT. NOLAN: Certainly not. And there hadn't been a case like this round here in decades, in living memory. DT was a very big deal for us all. Luckily we had the case because the first victim was from Bridgeport, and she was found just outside the city. DT was a huge deal. And the fact that we managed to get him to confess. That was my proudest moment, I think. Well, other than the birth of my daughters. [Laughs]

PIP: Billy Karras sat in that interview room for over five hours overnight before he started to confess. He must have been tired, exhausted. Do you ever have doubts about his confession? I mean, he recanted first thing in the morning after he'd had some sleep.

LT. NOLAN: No doubts. None. I was in the room with him when he confessed. No one's going to say they did those awful things if it's not true. I was exhausted too, and I didn't confess to being a serial killer, did I? And, you won't understand this, but after so many years working as a detective, of heading up the division, I could tell he was telling me the truth. It's in the eyes. I can always tell. You know when you're in the presence of evil, believe me. Billy recanted in the morning because he'd had time to think of all the consequences. He's a coward. But he definitely did it.

PIP: I've spoken to Billy Karras's mother, Maria—

LT. NOLAN: Oh man.

PIP: Why'd you say that?

LT. NOLAN: Just, I've had several run-ins with her. She's a strong woman. You can't blame her, of course; no mother is going to think their son capable of the horrific things Billy did.

PIP: Well, she's done a lot of research on the literature surrounding false confessions. Is there any part of you that thinks it possible that Billy's confession was false? That he only said those things because of the pressure applied in the interview?

LT. NOLAN: Well, yes, I think he only cracked *because* of the pressure I applied in the interview, but that doesn't mean the confession isn't good. If it were the only piece of evidence, then I might entertain the idea, but there was other evidence tying Billy to the murders: forensic and circumstantial. And he pleaded guilty, remember. This isn't what your podcast is about this time, is it? Trying to prove Billy innocent?

PIP: No, not at all. I'm just trying to tell the true story of the DT Killer, in all its detail.

LT. NOLAN: OK, good, because I wouldn't have agreed to this interview otherwise. I don't want you to try to make me look stupid.

PIP: Oh, I wouldn't dream of it, David. So, a lot of the evidence tying Billy to the case seems to be connected with his job. He worked at a grounds-maintenance company called Green Scene Limited. I just wondered whether you were aware of Green Scene's connection to the murders, before Billy became your number one suspect.

LT. NOLAN: Yes. We certainly *were* looking into Green Scene before that. It was after Bethany Ingham—the third victim—was killed, because she worked there. Then, when Julia Hunter was killed, we made the connection that a couple of the dump sites were places where Green Scene was contracted. We asked to search the premises, and I remember the owner being very helpful and considerate, and that's when we discovered they used the exact same brand of blue rope and duct tape as used by DT. So that was sort of the slam dunk, really, and we started to look into current employees. But there's only so much looking you can do without probable cause. Then Billy Karras came along, was the one who *found* Tara Yates, and we knew pretty quickly he was our guy.

PIP: Did you have any suspects before Billy? Before Tara was killed? Anyone connected with Green Scene?

LT. NOLAN: I mean, we had a few persons of interest, but nothing concrete or substantial.

PIP: I suppose you're not going to tell me any names, are you?

LT. NOLAN: I don't even remember them, to be honest.

PIP: Fair enough. So, I've spoken to Harriet Hunter, Julia's younger sister, and she told me about some weird occurrences at their house, in the weeks before Julia died. Some dead pigeons brought into the house, chalk figures drawn near their house, and prank phone calls. Was this ever a focus of your investigation? And had the families of the other victims reported similar incidents?

LT. NOLAN: Oh yes, I remember the dead pigeons now. Yes, the younger sister, she told us about them at the time. And we asked the friends and family of the previous victims, but they'd never heard anything of the sort. We asked Billy if he had had contact with the victims before abducting them. He told us that he watched them, so he knew when they were alone, et cetera, but he didn't make contact with them, not with dead birds or phone calls or any other method. So, it's unrelated to the case, unfortunately. Though it makes for a more compelling story, I give you that.

PIP: Got it, thanks. So, now on to the trophies. You know exactly what item the DT Killer took from each victim. Something personal they had on them when he abducted them: earrings, a hairbrush, and so on. But you never found these trophies in Billy's possession, did you? Does that concern you?

LT. NOLAN: No. He told us he threw them away. They're probably all in a landfill somewhere in the country. We would never have found them.

PIP: But isn't the whole point of a trophy that it's something you keep with you? To remind you of the violent crime, and to delay the compulsion to kill again? Why would he throw them away?

LT. NOLAN: He didn't say, but it's obvious, isn't it? He knew we were zeroing in on him after Tara, and he got rid of the evidence before we got a warrant to search his house. I don't think he *wanted* to throw the trophies away.

PIP: Got it, OK. But, going back to Tara: why would Billy draw attention to himself like that, staging that he found her body? He might not have really been on your radar before then; why would he draw attention to himself like that? That's essentially what got him caught.

LT. NOLAN: This goes back to something that has been observed in a lot of serial-killer cases similar to this. The killers will show a lot of interest in their own cases, will follow coverage on the news, discuss it with all their friends and family. I'm no psychiatrist, but it's a narcissism thing, I believe. Thinking they are so clever and it's right under everyone's noses. And some of these killers, they even try to insert themselves into the police investigation somehow, offering tips or to help with search parties and the like. That's what Billy was doing, being the hero and *finding* Tara so he could insert himself into the investigation, maybe find out what we knew so far.

PIP: Right.

LT. NOLAN: I know, it doesn't make much sense to you or me, to normal people. But it's one of the things we were already on the lookout for in this investigation. It's quite funny actually [laughs], but this was already on our minds because we had an officer from a nearby town who kept asking lots and lots of questions about the case. He wasn't involved in the investigation, he was a newly trained officer, as I remember, but he was showing a little too much interest in what had happened and what we were doing, if you know what I mean. He was new and just very curious, I'm sure, but it certainly raised a couple of red flags. Before Billy came along, that is. That's why we were sort of primed and ready for some kind of insertion from the perpetrator.

PIP: Oh really? Where was this officer based?

LT. NOLAN: I think it was Dari—oh, no, it was Fairview Police Department, I remember now. Yes, because I remember talking about this officer with one of my old colleagues who was based there. Still is. I think you know him, actually. Detective Hawkins. Good man. But, yeah, that's an amusing little anecdote for your show there. An eager newbie police officer and we thought the worst [laughs].

PIP: This officer . . . was his name Daniel da Silva?

LT. NOLAN: [Coughs] Well, of course, I can't tell you the officer's name. And you wouldn't be able to air it on your show anyway, data protection and all that. How many more questions do you have? I'm afraid I might have to go soo—

PIP: But it was Daniel da Silva, right?

TWENTY-THREE

No head. The dead pigeon in her hands has no head. But it's too spongy, giving way, her fingers indenting its sides. That's because it's the comforter twisted up in her fist, not a dead bird, and Pip was awake now. In bed.

She'd fallen asleep. She'd actually fallen asleep. It was dead-of-night dark and she'd been asleep.

Why was she awake now, then? She woke up like this all the time, sleep so shallow that she dipped in and out. But this felt different. Something had pulled her out.

A noise.

It was there now.

What was that?

Pip sat up, comforter falling to her waist.

A hissing sound, but a gentle one.

She rubbed her eyes.

A *sputt-sputt-sputt,* like a slow-moving train, nudging her back to sleep.

No, not a train.

Pip blinked again, the room taking shape with a ghostly glow. She got out of bed, the air stinging her bare feet.

The hiss was coming from over there, by her desk.

Pip stopped, focused her gaze.

It was her printer.

Something was coming out of the wireless printer on her desk, LEDs blinking from its panel.

Sputt-sputt-sputt.

A piece of paper emerged from the bottom, fresh black ink printed upon it.

But . . .

That was impossible. She hadn't sent anything to print today.

Her sleep-fogged head could not follow. Was she still dreaming?

No, the pigeon was the dream. This was real.

The printer finished, spitting out the piece of paper with a final clunk.

Pip hesitated.

Something pushed her forward. A ghost at her back. Maybe Andie Bell.

She walked over to the printer and reached out, like she was taking someone's hand. Or someone was taking hers.

The page was printed upside down; she couldn't read it from here.

Her fingers closed around it, and the page fluttered in her grip like the wings of a headless pigeon.

She turned it around, the words righting themselves.

And part of her knew before she read them. Part of her knew.

Who will look for you when you're the one who disappears?

p.s. I learned this trick from you, season 1 episode 5.
Ready for my next trick?

The page was covered in Stanley's not-there blood, leaking from Pip's not-there hands. No, the hands were there. But her heart had gone, throwing itself down the ladder of her spine, curdling in the acid of her gut.

Nonononononononononono.

How?

Pip swung around, her eyes wild, her breath wilder, taking in every shadow. Each one was DT before it was not. She was alone. He wasn't here. But how . . .

Her frantic gaze landed back on the printer. Wireless printer. Anyone within range could send something through.

Which meant he had to be close by.

DT.

He was here.

Outside or inside the house?

Pip checked the screwed-up page in her hand. *Ready for my next trick?* What did he mean by that? What was the trick—make her disappear?

She should look out the window. He might be there, on the drive. DT standing in a ring of dead birds and chalk figures.

Pip turned and—

A metallic scream filled the room.

Loud.

So impossibly loud.

Pip clasped her hands to her ears, dropping the page.

No, not a scream. Guitars, screeching and crying, up and down too fast while a drumbeat hammered alongside them, shaking the room, implanting its pulse down into the floor and up her heels.

Now came the screaming. Voices. Deep and demonic, barking behind her in an inhuman surge.

Pip cried out and she could not hear herself. She was sure it was there, but her voice was lost. Buried.

She turned to where the screaming was loudest, listening through her hands. It was her desk. The other side this time.

LEDs blinking at her.

Her speakers.

Her Bluetooth speakers on full volume, blaring death metal in the dead of night.

Pip screamed, fighting forward through the sound, tripping over her own feet as she dropped to her knees.

She had to uncover one ear, the sound a physical sensation, tunneling into her brain. She reached for the four-way extension cord under her desk. Grabbed the plug. Pulled it out.

Silence.

But not really.

A tinny after-sound, just as loud in her aching ears.

And a shout from the now-open doorway.

"Pip!"

She screamed again, fell back against the desk.

A figure standing in the threshold. Too big. Too many limbs.

"Pip?" DT said again in her dad's voice, and then a yellow glow burst into the room as he turned on the light. It was her mom and dad, standing at her door in their pajamas.

"What the *fuck* was that?" her dad asked her. His eyes wide. Not just angry. Frightened. Had Pip ever seen him frightened before?

"Victor," her mom said in a soothing voice. "What happened?" a sharper one for Pip.

Another sound joined the tinny ghost in Pip's ears, a small wail down the hall, breaking into sobs.

"Josh, honey," Pip's mom opened her arms and folded him in as he appeared in the doorway too. His little chest shuddered. "It's OK. I know it was a big shock." She kissed the top of his head. "You're OK, sweetheart. Just a loud noise."

"I—I th-thought i-it was a b-bad man," he said, losing control to the tears.

"What the f— What the heck was that?" Pip's dad asked her. "Will have woken up *all* the neighbors."

"I don—" But her mind wasn't focused on forming words. It skipped from *neighbors* to *outside* to *within range.* DT had connected to her speakers by Bluetooth. He must be right outside her window, on the driveway.

Pip scrambled to her feet, launched herself across her bed, and pulled open the curtains.

The moon hung low in the sky. Its light cast an eerie silver edge on the trees, on the cars, on the man running away from their drive.

Pip froze, a half second too long and the man was gone.

DT.

Dark clothes and a dark fabric face.

He'd been wearing a mask.

Standing right outside her window.

Within range.

Pip should go, she should chase after him. She could run faster than that. She'd had to learn to outrun all kinds of monsters.

"Pip!"

She turned. She would never be able to get past her parents. They were blocking the way and it was already too late.

"Explain yourself," her mom demanded.

"I—I," Pip stuttered. *Oh, it was just the man who's going to kill me, nothing to worry about.* "I don't know any more than you do," she said. "It woke me up too. My speakers. I don't know what happened. My phone must have been connected to them, and maybe, maybe it was an ad on YouTube or something. I don't know. I didn't do it." Pip didn't know how she'd managed to say so many words without any breath. "I'm sorry. I've unplugged the speakers. They must be faulty. It won't happen again."

They asked more questions. More and more, and she didn't know what to tell them. But it would be all her fault if the neighbors complained, she was told, and if Josh was in a foul mood tomorrow.

Fine, that was all her fault.

Pip climbed into bed and her dad switched off her light with a slightly strained "Love you," and her scorched-out ears listened to the sounds of them trying to coax Josh back into bed. He wouldn't go. He would only sleep with them.

But Pip . . . she wouldn't sleep at all.

DT had been here. Right here. Now he was gone in the dark. And she, she was his number six.

TWENTY-FOUR

The screaming was still there inside, inhuman and angry, trapped in Pip's bones. The *sputt-sputt-sputt* of a phantom printer in her ears. Both fighting against the gun in her heart. Not even a run could take them away or distract her. A run so hard she thought it might split her in two, all the violence and darkness within leaking out onto the pavement. Checking over her shoulder for Max Hastings, with his slicked-back hair and his gloating eyes, but he hadn't been there.

The run was a bad idea. Now she felt like she couldn't move, lying here on the rug in her bedroom. Cocooned in cold air. Embalmed. She hadn't slept at all. She'd taken the last of the Xanax almost immediately after her parents left her room last night. She'd closed her eyes and time had skipped, but it hadn't felt like sleep. It felt like drowning.

Now she had none. Nothing at all. No crutch.

That got her to move, finally, picking herself up, cold sweat in the waistline of her leggings. She staggered toward her desk, plugs hanging loose beneath it. She'd unplugged everything in the room. The printer. The speakers. Her laptop. Her lamp. Her phone charger. All lifeless, trailing wires.

She opened the second drawer, snaked her hand inside, and pulled out the burner phone at the front of the line. The same she'd used to text Luke on Wednesday. It was Saturday now, and she'd still not heard back from him. And now she was all out.

She turned on the phone and began to type, frustrated at how slow it was, pressing *4* three times just to get to *I*.

I'm out. Need more ASAP

Why hadn't Luke replied yet? He normally would have by now. This couldn't go wrong too, not on top of everything else. She had to sleep tonight; she could already feel her brain moving too slow, sluggish in connecting thought to thought. She replaced the burner phone in the drawer, startled by a buzz from her real phone.

Ravi again. *You back from your run?*

He'd insisted on coming over when she'd called him earlier, still slurry from the pills as she told him about the printer and the speakers. But Pip said no. She needed a run to clear her head. And then she needed to go talk to Nat da Silva about her brother. Alone. Ravi had eventually relented, as long as she kept checking in with him all day. And there was no question about it: Pip was staying over at his house tonight. Dinner too. No question at all, he'd told her in his serious voice. Pip supposed it was a sensible idea, but what if DT somehow knew?

Look, one thing at a time. Tonight was a lifetime away, and so was Ravi. She texted him a quick: *yes, I'm fine. Love you.* But now she had to focus on her next task: talk to Nat.

It was the first thing she had to do, and the last thing she wanted to. Talking to Nat, speaking it out loud, would make it real. *Hey, Nat, do you think it's at all possible that your brother is a serial killer? Yes, I know, I have a history of accusing you and your family members of murder.*

They were close now, she and Nat. Found family. *Found,* that is, in violence and tragedy, but *found* nonetheless. Pip counted Nat on her fingers as one of the people who would look for her if she disappeared. Losing Nat would be far worse than losing that finger. What if this talk pushed that bond just a little too far, pushed it to breaking point?

But what choice did she have? All the signs were pointing to Daniel da Silva: he fit the profile, he used to work at Green Scene and could very well have been the one who set off that security alarm while Jason Bell was at a dinner party, his red-flag interest in the case as a fellow officer, *practically one of them,* someone close to the Bells who Andie could have been afraid of, someone who had reason to hate Pip.

It all fit. The path of least resistance.

Gunshots in her chest. Quick couplets that sounded like *DT. DT. DT.*

Pip glanced at her phone again. Fuck. How was it just past three o'clock? She hadn't emerged from her bed—the last safe place—until midday, the pills too heavy in her chest to stand before then. And the run had been long, too long. Now she was hesitating, talking herself into it when she just needed to go.

No time for a shower. She peeled off her sweaty top and replaced it with a gray hoodie, zipping it up over her sports bra. It didn't feel like mid-August outside today, the sun trapped behind a cover of cloud, the wind a little too insistent. Pip placed her water bottle and her keys in her open backpack and removed the USB microphones; this conversation with Nat was not one for anyone else's ears. Ever. Then she remembered she was staying at Ravi's tonight: she grabbed a pair of underwear and some clothes for tomorrow, fetched her toothbrush from the bathroom. Although she might actually come back here first, to check the burner phone and see whether Luke had any pills for her. The idea was hot and shameful. Pip zipped up the bag and shouldered it, grabbing her headphones and her phone before she left the room.

"Going to go see Nat," she told her mom at the bottom of the stairs, rubbing Stanley's blood off her hands onto her dark leggings. "Then I'm going to the Singhs' for dinner, and I might stay over, if that's OK?"

"Oh. Yes, fine," her mom said, sighing as Josh started whining about something else from the living room. "You'll have to be back tomorrow morning, though. We've told Josh we're going to Adventureland tomorrow. Cheered him up for all of two seconds."

"Yeah, OK," Pip said. "Sounds fun. Bye." She hesitated by the front door. "Love you, Mom."

"Oh." Her mom looked surprised, turning back to her with a smile, one that reached into her eyes. "I love you too, sweetie. See you in the morning. And say hi to Nisha and Mohan from me."

"Will do."

Pip closed the front door. She glanced up at the brick wall beneath her window, standing exactly where *he* might have stood. It had rained again this morning, so she couldn't tell, but there were little white disembodied marks up the wall. Maybe they'd always been there, maybe they hadn't.

She hesitated by her car, and then walked on past it. She shouldn't drive; it probably wasn't safe. The pills were still in her system, weighing her down, and the world felt almost like a dream unrolling around her. Out of time, out of place.

She placed her headphones over her ears as she left the drive and started walking down Thatcher Road. She didn't even want to listen to anything, just flicked on the noise-cancellation button and tried to float in that free, untethered place again. Disappeared. Where the gunshots and the *sputt-sputt* and the screaming music couldn't find her.

Down Main Street, past the Book Cellar and the library. Past the café and Cara inside, handing someone two takeout cups, and Pip could read the words on her best friend's lips: *Careful, they're hot.* But Pip couldn't stop. Past Church Street on her left, which wound round the corner up to the Bells' house. But Andie wasn't in that house, she was here now, with Pip. Turn right. Down Chalk Road, and onto Cross Lane.

The trees shivered above her. They always seemed to do that here, like they knew something she didn't.

She walked halfway up, her eyes fixating on the painted blue door as it came into view. Nat's house.

She didn't want to do this.

She had to do this.

This deadly game between her and DT led here, and she was one move behind.

She stopped on the sidewalk just in front of the house, let her backpack fall to the crook of one elbow so she could place her headphones inside. Zipped it back up. Took a breath and edged toward the front path.

Her phone rang.

In the pocket of her hoodie. Vibrating against her hip.

Pip's hand darted into the pocket, fumbled with the phone as she pulled it out, and stared down at the screen.

No Caller ID.

Her heart dragged its way back up her spine.

This was him, she knew it.

DT.

And now she had him. Checkmate.

Pip hurried past Nat's house, the phone still buzzing against her cupped hands. Out of sight of the da Silvas' house, she held it up and pressed the side button twice, to redirect the incoming call to Call-Trapper.

The phone went dark.

One step.

Two.

Three.

The screen lit up again with an incoming call. Only this time, it didn't say *No Caller ID.* A cell phone number scrolled across the top of her screen, unmasked. A number Pip didn't recognize, but that didn't matter. It was a direct link to DT. To Daniel da Silva. Concrete evidence. Game over.

She didn't need to accept the call; she could just let it ring out. But her thumb was already moving to the green button, pressing against it and bringing the phone up to her ear.

"Hello, DT," Pip said, walking down Cross Lane, to where the houses faded away and the trees thickened over the road. They weren't just shivering anymore; they were waving to her. "Or do you prefer the Stratford Strangler?"

A sound down the line, jagged yet soft. It wasn't the wind. It was him, breathing. He didn't know it was game over, that she'd already won. That this third and final call was his fatal flaw.

"I prefer DT, I think," Pip said. "It's more fitting, especially as you're not from Stratford. You're from here. Fairview." Pip carried on, the canopy now hiding the stifled sun from her, a road of flickering shadows. "I enjoyed your trick last night. Very impressive. And I know you have a question for me: you want to know who would look for me if I disappeared. But I have a question for you instead."

She paused.

Another breath down the line. He was waiting.

"Who will visit you when you're in a cage?" she asked. "Because that's where you're going."

A guttural sound down the line, the breath stuck in his throat.

Three loud beeps in Pip's ear.

He'd ended the call.

Pip stared down at her phone, the corners of her mouth stretching in an almost-smile. Got him. The relief was instant, prying up the terrible weight from her shoulders, tethering her back to the world, the real world. A normal life. Team Ravi and Pip. She couldn't wait to tell him. It was within her grasp now; she just had to reach out and take it. A sound somewhere between a cough and a laugh pushed through her lips.

She navigated into her Recent Calls menu and her eyes flicked across his phone number again. It was most likely a burner phone, considering he'd never been caught before, but maybe it wasn't. Maybe it was his actual phone, and maybe he'd pick it up without thinking, answer with his name. Or a voice mail would give it away. Pip could go to Hawkins with this number, right now, but she wanted to know first. She wanted to be the one to find him, to finally know his name and know all of it. Daniel da Silva. DT. The Strangler. She'd earned that. She'd won.

And maybe he should know what it feels like. The fear, the uncertainty. His screen lighting up with *No Caller ID.* That hesitation between answering and not. He wouldn't know it was her. She would be masked, just like him.

Still walking the road beneath the deepening trees, Nat's house forgotten long behind her, Pip copied and pasted his phone number into her keypad. Before the number, she typed in **-6-7,* the mask. Her thumb fizzed as it hovered above the green button.

This was it. The moment.

She pressed the button.

Raised the phone to her ear once more.

She heard it ringing, through the phone.

But, wait, no. That wasn't right.

Pip stopped walking, lowered the phone.

It wasn't only through her phone that she could hear it ringing.

It was in the other ear. Both of them. It was here.

The shrill chime of the call, ringing right behind her.

Louder.

And louder.

There wasn't time to scream.

Pip tried to turn, to see, but two arms reached out of the unknown behind her. Took her. Phone still ringing as she dropped hers.

A hand collided with her face, over her mouth, blocking the scream before it could live. An arm around her neck, bent at the elbow, tightening, tightening.

Pip struggled. One breath but no air. She tried to rip his arm away from her neck, his hand away from her mouth, but she was weakening, her head emptying.

No air. Cut off at the neck. Shadows deepened around her. She struggled. *Breathe, just breathe.* She couldn't. Explosions behind her eyes. She tried again and felt herself separating from her own body. Peeling away.

Darkness. And her, disappearing down into it.

TWENTY-FIVE

D

A

A R K D A R K D A R K

K

D

A

R

K K

D D

A A

R R

K K

TWENTY-SIX

Pip came through the darkness, one cracked eye at a time. It was a sound that led her out, something slamming by her ear.

Air. She had air. Blood flowing to her brain again.

Her eyes were open but she couldn't make sense of the shapes around her. Not yet. A disconnect between what she saw and what she understood. And all she understood right then was pain, splitting open her head, writhing against her skull.

But she could breathe.

She could hear herself breathing. And then she couldn't: the world growled and roared beneath her. But she knew that sound. She understood it. An engine starting. She was in a car. But she was lying down, on her back.

Two more blinks and suddenly the shapes around her made sense, her mind reopening its doors. A tight enclosed space, rough carpet beneath one cheek, a slanting cover secured above her, blocking out the light.

She was in the trunk of a car. *Yes, that's it,* she told her newborn brain. And it was the rear door slamming shut; that's what she'd heard.

She must have only been out for seconds. Half a minute at most. He'd been parked right behind her, ready. Dragged her. The trunk open and yawning, to swallow her inside.

Oh yes, that was the most important thing to remember, her mind now catching up.

DT had taken her.

She was dead.

Not now: she was alive now and she could breathe, thank god she could breathe. But she was dead in all the ways that mattered. As good as.

Dead girl walking. Except she wasn't walking; she couldn't get up.

Panic riled up in her, warm and frothing, and she tried to let it out, tried to scream. But wait, she couldn't. Only the muffled edges escaped, not enough to even call it a scream. There was something covering her mouth.

She reached up to see what it was . . . but wait, she couldn't do that either. Her hands were clasped behind her. Stuck there. Stuck together.

She twisted one hand as much as she could, folded down her index finger to feel what was bound around her wrists.

Duct tape.

She should have known that. There was a strip of it across her mouth. She couldn't move her legs apart; her ankles must be wrapped too, though she couldn't see that far down, even when she lifted her head.

Something new, unraveling from the pit of her stomach. A primal feeling, ancient. A terror beyond any words that could contain it. It was everywhere: behind her eyes, beneath her skin. Too strong. Like all the million, million pieces of her disappearing and reappearing at once, flickering in and out of existence.

She was going to die.

Shewasgoingtodieshewasgoingtodieshewasdeadshewasdead-shewasgoingtodie.

She might just die from this feeling alone. Her heart so fast it no longer sounded like a gun, but it couldn't keep going like this. It would give out. It would surely give out.

Pip tried to scream again, pushing the word "help" against the duct tape, but it pushed it right back. A hopeless cry in the dark.

But there was still a spark of herself inside of all that terror, and she was the only one here who could help. *Breathe, just breathe,* she tried to tell herself. How could she breathe when she was going to die? But she took a deep breath, in and out of her nose, and she felt herself rallying inside, gathering in numbers, pushing that too-strong feeling into the dark place at the back of her mind.

She needed a plan. Pip always had a plan, even if she was going to die.

The situation was this: it was a Saturday, around four o'clock in the afternoon, and Pip was in the trunk of his car—the DT Killer. Daniel da Silva. He was driving her to the place where he planned to kill her. Her hands were bound, her feet were bound. Those were the facts. And she had more; Pip always had more facts.

The next one was particularly heavy, particularly hard to hear even if it came from her own mind. Something she'd learned from one of those many true crime podcasts, something she never thought she'd need to know. The voice in her head repeated it to her plainly, no pauses, no panic: *If you are ever abducted, you must do everything you can to avoid them taking you to a secondary location. Once you are in a second location, your chances of survival go down to less than one percent.*

Pip was being taken to a second location right now. She'd missed her chance, that small window of survival in the first few seconds.

Less than one percent.

But for some reason, that number didn't bring back the terror. Pip felt calmer, somehow. A strange quieting, as though putting a number to it made it easier for her to accept.

It wasn't that she was going to die, but that she was very, very likely to die. An almost certainty, not enough left over for hope.

OK, she breathed. So, what could she do about it?

She wasn't at the second location yet.

Did she have her phone on her? No. She'd dropped it when he grabbed her, heard it crack on the road. Pip raised her head and surveyed the trunk, juddering as they swung down a rougher road. There was nothing in here except her. He must have taken her backpack. *OK, what next?*

She should have been trying to visualize the route they were taking, make mental notes of the turns the car made. She'd been taken at the far end of Cross Lane, where the trees grew thick. She'd heard him start the engine, and she hadn't felt the car turn, so he must have carried on down that road. But that terror, it had blinded everything else while she'd flickered in and out, and she hadn't been paying attention to the journey. She would guess they'd been driving for five minutes already. They might not even be in Fairview anymore. But Pip didn't see how any of that could help her.

OK, so what could help her? *Come on, think.* Keep her mind busy, so it didn't go looking for that dark place at the back, where the terror lived. But a different question occurred to her instead. *That* question.

Who will look for you when you're the one who disappears?

Now she'd never know the answer, because she'd be dead. But, no, that wasn't right, she told herself, shuffling onto her side to release the pressure on her arms. She did know the answer, a knowledge that was bone-deep, a knowledge that would outlive her. Ravi would look for her. Her mom. Her dad. Her baby brother. Cara, more a sister than a friend. Naomi Ward. Connor Reynolds. Jamie Reynolds, just as she'd looked for him. Nat da Silva. Becca Bell, even.

Pip was lucky. So lucky. Why hadn't she ever stopped to think about how lucky she was? All those people who cared about her, whether she deserved them or not.

A new feeling now. Not panic. It was less bright than that, heavier, sadder, slow-moving, but it hurt so much more. She was never going to see them again. Any of them. Not Ravi's lopsided smile or his ridiculous laugh, or any of the hundred ways he had of telling her he loved her. Never hear him call her Sarge again. Never see her family, not her friends. All those last moments with all of them, and Pip hadn't known those were her final goodbyes.

Her eyes welled up and spilled over, running down her face to the rough carpet. Why couldn't she sink through the ground now, disappear, but disappear to somewhere DT couldn't get to her?

At least she'd told her mom she loved her before she walked out the door. At least her mom had that small moment to hold on to. But what about her dad? When had she last said it to him, or to Josh? Would Josh even remember what she looked like when he was all grown-up? And what about Ravi: when was the last time she told Ravi she loved him? Not enough, never enough. What if he didn't truly know? This was going to destroy him. Pip cried harder, tears gathering around the tape across her mouth. Please don't let him blame himself. He was her best thing, and now she would always be the worst thing that had happened to him. A pain in his chest he'd never forget.

But he would look for her. And he wouldn't find her, but he would find her killer, Pip was sure of it. Ravi would do that for her. Justice: that slippery word, but they would need it, so they could all eventually learn to move on without her, lay flowers at her grave once a year. Wait, what was the date today? She didn't even know the date of the day she was going to die.

She cried and cried harder, until those more rational parts of herself took over, pulled her back from despair. Yes, Ravi would find her killer, would know who he was. But there was a difference between knowing and being able to prove it. A world of difference between those two things; Pip had learned the hard way.

That was something she could do, though. A plan, to keep her mind busy. Pip could help them to find her killer, to lock him away in a cage. She just needed to leave enough of herself behind, in this trunk. Hair. Skin. Anything with her DNA. Cover his car with the last remaining traces of her, her final mark upon the world, an arrow straight to *him.*

Yes, she could do that. That was something she could do. She stretched back and rubbed her head against the carpet. Harder. Harder, until it hurt and she could feel the hairs pulling from her scalp. She shuffled lower and did it again.

Next: skin. There wasn't much exposed that she could use. But she had her face and she had her hands. She twisted her neck, pushed her cheek into the carpet, and she grated it back and forth. It hurt and she cried, but she kept going, the bone in her cheek raw and grazed. If it bled, that was even better. Leave blood behind, see *him* try to get away with that. Then her hands, moving awkwardly against the duct tape. She scraped her knuckles into the carpet and against the backs of the passenger seats.

What else could she do? She cast her mind back through all the cases she'd ever studied. Three syllables came to her, a word so obvious she didn't know how she hadn't thought of it first. Fingerprints. The police already had her fingerprints on file, to eliminate her after Stanley died. Yes, that was it. The swirling spiderweb prints of her fingers would be the net she left behind, to tighten and tighten around DT until he was caught. But she needed a hard surface; carpet wouldn't work.

Pip glanced around. There was the back window, but she couldn't get to it because of the dark cover slanting down over the trunk. Wait.

The sides of the car by her head and her feet were encased in plastic. That would work. Pip drew her legs in close and pushed her sneakers against the carpet, sliding herself up and round, and again, until she was curled up small against the side, the plastic within reach of her bound hands.

She did one hand at a time. Placing and pressing each finger into the plastic, several times. Up and down, wherever she could reach. The thumbs were the hardest, because of the tape, but she managed to make contact with the very tops of them. That was a partial print, at least.

OK, what next? The car itself seemed to answer, jumping as the wheels drove over something. Another sharp turn. How long had they been driving now? And what would Ravi's face look like when he was told she was dead? *No, stop that.* She didn't want that image in her head. She wanted to remember him smiling, in her last hours.

He'd told her she was the bravest person he knew. Pip didn't feel brave now. Not at all. But at least the version that lived in Ravi's head was, the one he turned to to ask *What would Pip do now?* Pip tried it herself, with the Ravi who lived inside her head. She turned to him and she asked: What would you tell me to do, if you were here with me?

Ravi answered.

He would tell her not to give up, even if that's what the statistics and logic told her to do. "Fuck that less than one percent. You're Pippa Fricking Fitz-Amobi. My little Sarge. Pippus Maximus. And there's nothing you can't do."

"It's too late," she said back to him.

He told her it wasn't too late. She wasn't at the second location yet. There was still time, and there was still fight left in her.

"Get up, Pip. Get up. You can do this."

Get up. She could do this.

She could. Ravi was right. She wasn't at the second location yet;

she was still in the car. And she could use this car to her advantage. Her chances of surviving a car crash were far higher than her chances of surviving a second location. The car seemed to agree with her, the wheels growing louder against a gravel road, urging her on.

Make him crash the car. Survive. That was the new plan.

Her eyes darted to the bottom of the trunk door. There wasn't a latch she could use here to open the door and roll out. The only way was through the back passenger seats, and from there, throw herself at him, make him lose control of the wheel.

OK: two options. Kick at the backseat, hard enough to break it, fold it down. Or she could climb over the top, in the gap above the headrests. And to do that, all she had to do was remove this cargo cover above her.

Pip went with option two. The cover was rigid—she felt it with her knees—but it could only be attached on two sides by a hook or a mechanism. She just needed to readjust her position, slide down, and then kick up at that corner until it came loose.

The car slowed to a stop.

A stop too long to be just a turn. Fuck.

Pip's eyes widened. She held her breath so she could hear. There was a sound—a car door opening.

What was he doing? Was he leaving her somewhere? She waited for the slam of the door, but the follow-up sound didn't come, at least not for several seconds. And when it did, the car peeled off again, slowly. Not nearly fast enough for a crash.

But it was only seven seconds before it drew to a gentle stop again. And this time, Pip heard the parking brake pull up.

They were here.

The second location.

It was too late. "I'm so sorry," Pip told the Ravi in her head. And: "I love you," just in case there was any way he could pass it on to the real one.

Car door opened. Car door closed.

Footsteps on gravel.

The terror was back, leaking out of the place at the back of her mind where she thought she'd locked it away.

Pip rounded into a ball, drew her knees up to her chest.

She waited.

The back door opened.

He was standing right there. But all Pip could see were his dark clothes, up to his chest.

A hand reached forward, pulled at the cover above her head, and it retracted, rolling itself up against the backseat.

Pip stared up at him.

A silhouette against the late-afternoon sun.

A monster in the daylight.

Pip blinked, her eyes readjusting to the glare.

Not a monster, just a man. A familiarity in the way he held his shoulders.

The DT Killer showed her his face. Showed her the glint in his smile.

It wasn't the face she thought she'd see.

It was Jason Bell.

TWENTY-SEVEN

Jason Bell was the DT Killer.

The thought was so loud in Pip's head, louder than the terror. But she didn't have time to think it again.

Jason bent down and grabbed her elbow. Pip recoiled, smelling the metallic tang of his sweat, staining the front of his shirt. She tried to swing her legs out to kick him away, but Jason must have read the thought in her eyes. He leaned down hard on her knees, pinning her legs there. With his other hand, he pulled her up to sitting.

Pip screamed, the sound of it stifled against the tape. Someone must hear her. Someone must be able to hear her.

"No one can hear you," Jason said then, as though he were right there too, implanted in her head alongside Ravi, who was now telling her to run. Run. Make a break for it.

Pip flicked her legs out and pushed off against her knuckles. She landed on her feet on the gravel and tried to take a step, but her ankles were bound too tight. She tipped forward.

Jason caught her. Righted her, gravel scuffing around them. He hooked his arm through one of hers, clenching it tight.

"There's a good girl," he said quietly, absently, as though he wasn't really seeing her at all. "Walk, or I'll have to carry you." He didn't say it loud, he didn't say it hard; he didn't have to. He was in control and he knew it. That's what all this was about.

He started walking and so did she, minuscule steps against the duct tape. It was slow-moving, and Pip used the time to look around her, study her surroundings.

There were trees. Off to the right and behind her. Encircling them was a tall metal fence painted a dark green. A gate right behind them that Jason must have opened when he'd first left the car. It was still open now, wide open. Taunting her.

Jason was leading her toward an industrial-looking building—iron-sheeting sides—but there was a separate brick building off to the left. Wait. Pip knew this place. She was sure of it. She took it all in again: the tall green metal fence, the trees, the buildings. And if that wasn't clear enough, there were five vans parked over there, the logo emblazoned on their sides. Pip had been here before. No, she hadn't. Not really. Only as a ghost, skulking up and down the road through a computer screen.

They were at Green Scene Ltd.

The complex off a tiny country road in the middle of nowhere in Weston. Jason was right; no one would hear her scream.

That didn't stop her from trying again, as they reached a metal door at the side of the building.

Jason smiled, flashed his teeth at her again.

"None of that," he said, fiddling with his front pocket. He pulled something out, sharp and shiny. It was an overloaded ring of keys, different shapes and sizes. He flicked through them, selected a long thin one with jagged teeth.

He muttered to himself, guiding the key toward the bulky silver lock in the middle of the door. His other arm loosened a little, the arm holding her there.

Pip took her chance.

She slammed her arm down against his and broke the hold.

Freedom. She was free.

But it didn't get her far.

She couldn't even take one step before the force of his hand pulled her back, holding her bound arms behind her like a leash.

"It's pointless," Jason said, turning his attention back to the lock. He didn't look angry; the expression in the curve of his mouth was closer to amusement. "You know as well as I do that that's pointless."

Pip did. *Less than one percent.*

The door unlocked with the sound of clanging metal and Jason pushed it inward. It screamed on its hinges.

"Come on."

He dragged Pip over the threshold. It was dark in here, full of tall, wiry shadows, just one small window high up on the right, barring most of the sunlight. Jason seemed to read her mind again, flicking a switch on the wall. The industrial lights blinked to life with a lazy buzz. The room was long and thin and cold. It looked like some kind of storeroom: tall metal shelving units down both walls, huge plastic vats stacked up and along the shelves with small faucets near the bottoms. Pip's eyes scanned across them: different types of weed killer and fertilizer. There were two sunken channels in the concrete floor under the shelves, running the length of the room.

Jason pulled her along by her arms, the heels of her sneakers dragging against the ground.

He dropped her.

Pip landed hard on the concrete, just in front of the right-hand shelves. She struggled up into a sitting position, watching as he stood over her. The breath in and out of her nose too loud and too fast, the sound reshaping in her mind into *DT, DT, DT.*

And here he was. Strange, really, that he looked just like a man. He'd been so much bigger in her nightmares.

Jason smiled to himself then, shaking his head at something funny.

He raised one finger at her, pacing toward a sign that read *Warning! Toxic Chemicals.* "That security alarm," he said, stifling the laugh.

“That security alarm you were so interested in?” He paused. “It was Tara Yates who set it off. Yes,” he added, studying her eyes. “You misread that one, didn’t you? It was Tara who set it off. She was tied up in here, in this very room.” He glanced around the storeroom, filling it with dark memories that Pip couldn’t see. “This is where they all were. Where they died. But Tara, she somehow managed to break free of the tape on her wrists when I left her. Was moving around and set off the alarm. I’d forgotten to disable it correctly, see.”

His face creased again, as though he were only talking about a small mistake, one that could be laughed off, shrugged off. The hairs rose up the back of Pip’s neck, watching him.

“All turned out fine. I reached her in time,” he said. “Had to rush the rest of it to get back to the dinner party, but it all turned out fine.”

Fine. The word that Pip used too. An empty word with all manner of dark things buried beneath it.

Pip tried to speak. She didn’t even know what she wanted to say, just that she wanted to try, before it was too late. She couldn’t get through the tape, but the formless sound of her voice was enough, reminded her that she was still there. Ravi was still there too, he told her gently. He’d stay with her until the end.

“What’s that?” Jason asked, still pacing back and forth. “Oh no. No, you don’t have to worry. I’ve learned from my mistake. The alarm is definitely disabled. So are the security cameras, inside and out. All of them are off, so you have nothing to worry about now.”

Pip made a sound in her throat.

“They’re off as long as I need them to be. All night. All weekend,” he said. “And no one will be coming here, not until Monday morning, so you don’t need to worry about that either. Just you and me. Oh, but let me have a little look here.”

Jason approached her. Pip pushed back against the shelves. He knelt at her side and studied the tape wrapped around her wrists and ankles.

He tutted to himself, fiddling with the binds. "No, that won't do. Far too loose. Was in a hurry to get you in the car. Going to have to redo them," he said, patting her lightly on the shoulder. "We don't want you doing a Tara, do we?"

Pip sniffed, gagging at the smell of his sweat. Too close.

Jason straightened up, grunting as he leaned on his knees. He walked past her, down the row of shelves. Pip turned her head to follow him with her eyes, but he was already rounding back into view, something new in his hands.

A roll of gray duct tape.

"Here we are," he said, bending to his knees again, pulling the end loose from the roll.

Pip couldn't see what he was doing behind her back, but his fingers touched hers and a shiver gushed up her spine, sickening and cold. She thought she might be sick, and if she was, she would choke on it, the same way Andie Bell had gone.

Andie flashed into her mind, her ghost sitting beside her, holding Pip's hand. Poor Andie. She'd known what her father was. Had to come home every day to a house where a monster lived. Died trying to get away from him, to protect her sister from him. And that's when two separate memories jumped like static across Pip's brain. Fusing, to become one. A hairbrush. But not just a hairbrush. The purple paddle hairbrush on Andie's desk—the one in the corner of the photos Pip and Ravi took—it had belonged to Melissa Denny, Jason's second victim. The trophy he took from her, to relive her death. He'd given it to his teenage daughter; probably got a dark thrill from watching her use it. Sick fuck.

The thought ended there, as a quick burst of pain shot up from her wrists. Jason had pulled off the tape, pulling hairs and skin with it. Freedom, again. Unbound. She should fight. Go for his neck. Dig her nails into his eyes. Pip grunted and she tried, but his grip was too tight.

"What did I say to you?" Jason said quietly, holding on to her squirming arms. He pulled them up, uncomfortably high behind her, and pulled them back, pressing the insides of her wrists against the front metal pole of the shelving unit.

The duct tape was sticky and cold as he wound it from one wrist, round the metal pole, and round the other wrist.

Pip concentrated, trying to push her hands as far out from each other as she could, so the tape wouldn't be so tight, so constricting. But Jason was holding them fast, going over the duct tape with another layer. And another. And another.

"There we go," he said, trying to shake her wrists, but they didn't budge. "Nice and secure. Won't be going anywhere, now, will you?"

The tape at her mouth swallowed another scream.

"Yes, I'm getting to those, don't worry," Jason said, shuffling toward her feet. "Always worrying. Always nagging, all of you. So loud."

He knelt on her legs to pin them down, and then wound a new length of duct tape around her ankles, over the first one. Tighter this time, going over it twice.

"That will do." He pivoted to look back at her. His eyes narrowed. "I normally give you one chance to speak now. To apologize, before . . ." He drew off, staring down at the roll of duct tape, running his finger tenderly around its edge. Jason leaned over and reached for her face. "Don't make me regret it," he said, tugging sharply at the tape across her cheeks, pulling it free of her mouth.

Pip sucked at the air, and it felt different through her mouth. More space, less terror.

She could scream now, if she wanted. Cry out for help. But what would be the point? No one could hear, and no help was coming. It was just the two of them.

Part of her wanted to look up at him and ask him: *Why?* But there was no why, Pip knew that. He wasn't Elliot Ward, or Becca, or Charlie

Green, where their whys pushed them out of the dark and into that confusing gray space. That human space of good intentions or bad choices or mistakes or accidents. She'd read the criminal profile and that told her all she needed to know. The DT Killer had no gray area and no why; that's exactly why it had seemed so right before. The perfect case: save herself to save herself. She wouldn't be saving anybody now, especially not herself. She'd lost, she was going to die, and there was no why, not to Jason Bell. Only why not. Pip and the five who came before her, they were somehow intolerable to him. That was all. Not murder in his eyes, but an extermination. Pip wouldn't get any more if she asked.

Another part of her, that thornier side where the rage hibernated, wanted to shout at him to go fuck himself, and keep shouting it until he was forced to kill her right here, right now.

Nothing she could say would stop him or hurt him. Nothing. Unless . . .

"She knew who you were," Pip said, her voice bruised and raw. "Andie. She knew you were the DT Killer. She saw you with Julia and she put it all together."

Pip watched as new creases formed around Jason's eyes, a twitch in his mouth.

"Yeah, she knew you were a killer. Months before she died. In fact, that's why she died. She was trying to get away from you." Pip took another gulp of unrestricted air. "Even before she found out who you were, I think she knew there was something wrong with you. That's why she never brought anyone round the house. She'd been saving up money for a year, to escape, to live somewhere else far away from you. She was going to wait for Becca to finish school, and then she was going to come back for Becca, take her with her. And once they were somewhere you couldn't find them, Andie was going to turn you in to the police. That was her plan. She hated you so much. So does

Becca. I don't think she knows who you really are, but she hates you too. I worked it out: that's why she chose to go to prison. It was to stay away from you."

Pip shot the words up at him, her voice hiding six bullets that would blow gaping holes in him. Narrowed her eyes to eviscerate him with her gaze. But he didn't fall down. He stood there, a strange expression on his face, eyes darting side to side as he took in what she just said.

He sighed.

"Well," he said, an affectation of sadness in his voice, "Andie shouldn't have done that. Got herself involved in my business; it wasn't her place. And now we both know why she died, then. Because she didn't listen." He tapped the side of his head by one ear, too hard. "I spent her whole life trying to teach her, but she never listened. Just like Phillipa and Melissa and Bethany and Julia and Tara. Too loud, all of you. Speaking out of turn. That's not how it's supposed to be. You're supposed to listen to me. That's all. Listen and do what you're told. How is that so hard?"

He fiddled agitatedly with the end of the duct tape.

"Andie." He said her name out loud, mostly to himself. "And you know, I even gave it all up for her. I had to, after she went missing. The police were too close, it was too much of a risk. I was done. I found someone who listened to me. I would have been done." He laughed, darkly, quietly, pointing at Pip with the roll of duct tape. "But then you came along, didn't you? And you were just so loud. Too loud. Meddling in everyone's business. In mine. I lost my second wife, the only woman who listened, because she listened to you instead. You were a test, just for me, and I knew I couldn't fail it. My last one. Far too loud to let it be. Seen, not heard; didn't your daddy ever teach you that?" He gritted his teeth. "And here you are, trying to interfere again with your last words, telling me about Andie. It doesn't hurt me, you know. You can't hurt me. It only proves I was right. About her. Becca too. All of you. Something badly wrong with all of you. Dangerous."

Pip couldn't speak. She didn't know how to, watching this man pacing up and down in front of her, raving. Spit flying from his mouth, veins branching out of his reddening neck.

"Oh." He drew up suddenly, his eyes widening with delight, a wicked smile on his face. "But I have something that will hurt you. Ha!" Jason clapped his hands loudly, and Pip flinched at the sound, hitting her head against the metal shelf. "Yes, one final lesson before you go. And now you'll understand how perfect this all was, how fitting. How it was always supposed to end this way. And I'll always get to remember the look on your face."

Pip stared up at him, confused. What lesson? What was he talking about?

"It was last year," Jason began, locking onto her eyes. "Near the end of October, I think. Becca wasn't listening to me again. Wasn't replying to me or answering my texts. So, I dropped round the house one afternoon, *my* house, though I was living with my other wife at the time, the one who listened. I brought a late lunch round for Becca and Dawn. And did they say thank you? Dawn did, Dawn has always been weak. But Becca was acting strange. Distant. I had words with her again, as we ate, about *listening,* but I could tell she was keeping something from me." He paused, licked his dry lips. "So, when I left, I didn't really leave; I stayed in my car down the road and watched the house. And, what do you know, little more than ten minutes later, Becca walks out of the house, and she has a dog on a leash. Her little secret. I didn't tell them they were allowed to get a dog. They never asked me. I didn't live there, but they still had to listen to me. You can just imagine how furious that made me. So I got out of the car and I followed Becca into the woods as she walked this new dog."

Pip's heart jumped, a cliff-drop down her ribs, landing hard in the pit of her stomach. No no no. Not this. Please don't go where she thought he was going.

Jason smirked, watching it play out on her face, enjoying every moment. "It was a golden retriever."

"No," Pip said quietly, the pain in her chest a physical ache.

"So, I'm watching Becca walk this dog," he continued. "And she lets him off the leash, gives him a pet, and then tells him to go home, which of course I thought was strange at the time. Proved to me even more that Becca did not deserve a dog, if she couldn't handle the responsibility. And then she starts throwing sticks for him, and he kept bringing them back. Then she throws one as far as she possibly can through the trees, and as the dog is running after it, Becca runs away. Back toward home. The dog can't find her. He's confused. So, of course, now I know Becca isn't ready for a dog, because she never asked me, because she doesn't listen. So, I approach this dog. Very friendly little thing."

"No," Pip said again, louder this time, trying to pull at her restraints.

"Becca wasn't ready and she hadn't listened to me. She had to learn her lesson." Jason smiled, feeding himself from the despair on Pip's face. "So, I walk this friendly dog down to the river."

"No!" Pip shouted.

"Yes!" he laughed, matching her. "I drowned your dog. Of course, I didn't know it was *your* dog back then. I did it to punish my daughter. And then you release your podcast, which caused all sorts of trouble for me, but you talked about your dog—Barney, wasn't it? You thought it was just an accident, and you didn't blame Becca for what happened. Well," he clapped his hands again, "it wasn't an accident. I killed your dog, Pip. See, destiny moves in mysterious ways, doesn't it? Binding us together all the way back then. And now you're here."

Pip blinked, and all the color leeched out of Jason, out of the room, replaced with red. Rage red. Violent red. Behind-her-eyes red. Blood-on-her-hands red. I'm-going-to-die red.

She screamed at him. A bottomless scream, raw and visceral. "Fuck you!" she screamed, angry, desperate tears falling into her open mouth. "Fuck you! Fuck you!"

"We've reached that point, have we?" Jason said, a shift in the way he held his face, in the curve of his eyes.

"Fuck you!" Pip's chest shuddered with the force of all her hate.

"OK, then."

Jason walked toward her, a ripping sound as he pulled a long length of duct tape from the roll.

Pip drew her legs into her chest, kicked out at him with her bound feet.

Jason sidestepped her easily. He knelt down beside her, slowly, assuredly.

"Never listen," he said, reaching out for her face.

Pip tried to pull away, pulled so hard she thought she might just leave her hands behind, tied to the shelves while she went free. Jason pushed one hand against her forehead, holding it fast against the metal pole.

Pip bucked. She tried to kick. Tried to thrash her head side to side.

Jason pressed the tape against her right ear. Looped it up over the crown of her head, back down, and pressed it into her other ear, stuck down under her chin.

More ripping. More tape.

"Fuck you!"

Jason shifted the angle, winding it horizontally across her chin, around the back of her head, sticking to her hair.

"Stop moving," he said, frustrated. "You're ruining it."

He wound the tape up over her chin, another row, catching her bottom lip.

"Never listen," Jason said, his eyes narrowed and concentrated.

"So now you can't listen. Or speak. Or even look at me. You don't deserve to."

The winding duct tape pressed her lips together, stealing her screams again. Up higher, tucked in under her nose.

Jason wound the tape round the back of her head again, shifting up to leave her nostrils clear. Panicked breaths in and out. Tape round and round and up the bridge of her nose, to the bottom of her eyes.

Jason shifted again, pulling the roll of tape up to cover the top of her head. Round and round. Working down her forehead. Down and round.

Tape over her eyebrows, sticking them down.

Round the back of her head again.

And there was only one thing left.

One final strip of her face.

Pip watched him do it. Watched him as he took her sight from her, as he'd taken the rest of her face, only closing her eyes at the very last moment before he pressed the tape over them.

Jason removed the pressure from her head, and she could move it again, but she could not see.

A ripping sound. The weight of his fingers at her temple as he stuck the end down.

It was complete. Her death mask.

Faceless.

Dark.

Quiet.

Disappeared.

TWENTY-EIGHT

Faceless. Dark. Quiet. Too quiet. Pip could no longer hear the hiss of Jason's breath, nor smell the metallic tang of his sweat as she breathed rattling breaths in and out of her nose. He must have moved away from her.

Pip stopped breathing, sounding out the room with her covered ears, feeling out the concrete around her with her doubled-up legs. She heard a scuffled footstep, far away from her, back toward the door he'd dragged her through.

She listened.

Metal clanging as a door opened. A shriek of old hinges. More footsteps, crunching on the gravel outside. Another shriek of the hinges and the door clicking shut. Silence, for a few in-and-out breaths, and then a much smaller sound: a key scraping against the lock. Another clunk.

Had he just left? He'd just left, hadn't he?

Pip strained, listening for the faint sounds of shoes and cascading gravel. A familiar sound: a car door slamming. The growl of an awakening engine and the wheels reversing away from her.

He was leaving. He was gone.

He'd left her here, locked her in, but Jason was leaving. DT was gone.

She sniffed. Wait. Maybe he wasn't gone. Maybe this was some kind of test, and he was sitting in the room with her still, watching her. Holding his breath so she couldn't hear him. Waiting for her to make any kind of wrong move. Hiding there in the dark underside of her eyelids, taped down.

Pip made a sound in her throat, testing it out. Her voice vibrated against the duct tape, tickling her lips. She groaned again, louder, trying to make sense of the impenetrable darkness around her. But she couldn't. She was helpless here, restrained to this tall metal shelving unit, her face disappeared, wrapped up in tape. Maybe he was still in the room with her; she couldn't rule it out. But she had heard the car, hadn't she? It couldn't have been anyone but Jason. And another memory, shaking loose from her broken-down brain: the typed words of a transcript. Lieutenant Nolan asking Billy Karras why he left his victims alone for a period of time, proved by wear and tear in the duct tape restraints. The DT Killer *did* leave. This was part of it, his routine, his MO. Jason was gone. But he would be back, and that's when Pip would die.

OK, she was alone, Pip settled on that, but she couldn't linger in that momentary relief. Now on to the next problem. The terror wasn't locked up, like she was, in the back of her head. It was everywhere. It was in her taped-down eyes and her taped-up ears. In every beat of her overused heart. In the raw skin of her wrists and the uncomfortable bend of her shoulders. In the pit of her stomach and the deep of her soul. Pure and visceral, fear as she'd never known it before. Inevitable. The segue between being alive and not.

Her breaths were coming shorter, too short, panicked spurts of in-and-out. Oh fuck. Her nose was blocking up, she could feel it, every breath rattling more than the last. She shouldn't have cried, she shouldn't have cried. The air was struggling, scraping its way through two tightening holes. Soon they would block up entirely and she would suffocate. That's how it would all end. Dead girl walking. Dead girl not breathing. At least that way DT wouldn't get to kill her, not *his* way, at least, with a blue rope around her neck. Maybe it was better this way, something out of his control and closer to hers. But, oh god, she didn't want to die. Pip forced the air in and out, feeling lightheaded, though she no longer had a head, just two shrinking nostrils.

A new chorus in her mind. *I'm going to die. I'm going to die. I'm going to die.*

"Hey, Sarge." Ravi was back, inside her head. Whispering into her taped-up ear.

"I'm going to die," she told him.

"I don't think so," he replied, and Pip knew he was saying it with the trace of a smile, a dimple carved into one cheek. "Just breathe. Slower than that, please."

"But look." She showed him the restraints: her ankles, her hands tied to a cold metal pole, the mask around her face.

Ravi already knew all that, he'd been there for it too. "I'm staying with you, until the very end," he promised, and Pip wanted to cry again but she couldn't, her eyes were forced shut. "You won't be alone, Pip."

"That helps," she told him.

"That's what I'm here for. Always. Team Ravi and Pip." He smiled behind her eyes. "And we made a good team, didn't we?"

"You did," she said.

"And you did too." He took her hand, bound behind her back. "Of course, I supplied all the devilish good looks," he laughed at his own joke, or hers, she supposed. "But you were always the brave one. Meticulous, annoyingly so. Determined to the point of recklessness. You always had a plan, no matter what."

"I didn't plan for this," Pip said. "I lost."

"That's OK, Sarge." He gave her hand a squeeze, her fingers starting to fizz from the awkward angle. "You just need a new plan. That's what you're good at. You're not going to die here. He's gone, and now you have time. Use that time. Come up with a plan. Wouldn't you like to see me again? See everyone you care about?"

"Yes," she told him.

"Then you better get started."

Better get started.

She took a deep breath, her airway clearer now. Ravi was right: she'd been given time and she had to use it. Because as soon as Jason Bell walked back through that door with the shrieking hinges, there was no longer a chance. None. She was dead. But this Pip, left alone and bound here to these metal shelves, she was only very likely dead. Not much of a chance, but more than near-future Pip had.

"OK," she said to Ravi, but really to herself. "A plan."

She couldn't see, but she could still check her surroundings. There hadn't been anything in her vicinity before DT taped over her sight, but maybe he'd left something nearby after the mask was done. Something she could use. Pip swiped her bound legs in an arc, to one side and the other, straining her arms to reach farther out. No, there was nothing here, just concrete and the dipped-down channel running beneath the shelves.

That's fine, she hadn't expected there to be anything, don't sink back down into despair. Ravi wouldn't let her, anyway. OK, so, she couldn't move, she was stuck here to these shelves. Was there anything there that could help her? Vats of weed killer and fertilizer that were useless to her, even if she could reach them. Fine, so what could she reach? Pip flexed her fingers, trying to bring the feeling back to them. Her arms were bent behind her back, pulled up higher than they should be. Her wrists were taped to the front metal pole of the shelving unit, just above the lowest shelf. She knew all that, had taken it in before her face was taken. Pip shifted her wrists against the tape and explored with two fingers. Yes, she felt the cold metal of the pole, and if she stretched her middle finger down, she could just feel the intersection of the shelf, where it attached to the pole.

That was it. All she could reach. All the help she had in the world.

"Maybe it's enough," Ravi said.

And maybe it was. Because somewhere, in that intersection between shelf and pole, there had to be a screw, to hold them together. And a screw could be freedom. Pip could use that screw. Pinch it between her thumb and finger and pierce holes in the tape at her wrists. Keep piercing and ripping until she could tear herself free.

OK, that was it. That was the plan. Get the screw from the shelf.

Pip had that feeling again, like there was a presence in the unknown around her. And not just the Ravi in her head. Something malignant and cold. But time didn't wait for anybody and it definitely wouldn't wait for her. So how was she going to get the screw?

Pip could only just touch the top of the shelf with one finger; she needed to somehow move her wrists lower, so she could reach the underside of the shelf. The duct tape was wrapped around her wrists, sticking them to this exact part of the pole. But if she shifted around, maybe, just maybe, she might get the tape to unstick from the metal. It was just on one side. Only an inch or two of contact. If she could unstick the tape there, then she could slide her hands up or down the pole. She'd struggled and she'd left herself a little room inside the tape, inside Jason's grip. She could do it. Pip knew she could.

She walked her legs in so she could push her weight back against the tape. Shoved her hands farther into the shelves, fingertips brushing the plastic edge of one of the vats. She pushed and she strained and she shifted and she could feel it give. Felt one side of the tape coming unstuck from the metal.

"Yes, keep going, Sarge," Ravi urged her on.

She pushed harder, she strained harder, the tape cutting into her skin. And slowly, slowly, the tape came free from the pole.

"Yes," she and Ravi hissed together.

They shouldn't have, because she wasn't free. Pip was still stuck to this pole, her wrists bound tight around it, still very likely dead.

But she had gained something: movement up and down between two shelves, her restraints sliding against the pole.

Pip wasted no more time, dropping her wrists as far as they could go, resting just above that lower shelf. She felt her way around the corner of the shelf with her fingers, and there, on the inside, she felt something: small and hard and metal. It must be the nut, secured to the end of the screw. Pip pressed her finger hard against it. She could feel the end of the screw, emerging from the nut. It wasn't as sharp as she'd like, but it would work. She could still use it to hack away at the duct tape.

Next step: remove the nut. It wasn't going to be easy, Pip realized, as she shifted her hands again. There was no way she could get either of her thumbs around that side of the pole; they were stuck here on the outside. She would have to use two of her fingers instead. Her right hand, obviously. It was stronger. She positioned her middle finger and forefinger around the nut, clamped them together, and tried to twist. Fuck, it was screwed on tight. And which was the right way to loosen it, anyway? Was it to the left, so *her* right?

"Don't panic, just try," Ravi told her. "Try until it gives."

Pip did try. And she tried. It wasn't working, it wouldn't budge. She was dead again.

She shifted and tried the other way, struggling with the angle. This would never work. She needed her thumbs: How could anyone do this without their thumbs? She pushed her fingers together around the metal and twisted. It hurt, right into the bones, and if she broke the fingers . . . well, she had more of them. The nut shifted. Barely, but it had shifted.

Pip paused to stretch out her aching fingers, to tell Ravi about it.

"Good, that's good," he said to her. "But you've got to keep going, you don't know how long he'll be gone."

It might have already been a half hour since Jason left, Pip had no way of knowing, and the terror moved time in strange ways. Lifetimes in seconds, and the other way around. The nut had hardly loosened at all; this was going to take a while and she couldn't lose focus.

She shifted her fingers again, clamped around the protruding metal nut, and pulled it round. It was stubborn, moving only after she'd given it everything, and hardly moving at that. Every time it gave, she had to reposition her fingers around it.

Shift. Clamp. Turn.

Shift. Clamp. Turn.

It was only a tiny movement, in one hand, and yet Pip could feel the sweat running down the insides of her arms, into the fabric of her hoodie. Sliding against the tape at her temples and her upper lip. How long had it been now? Minutes. More than five? More than ten? The nut was loosening, giving a little more each turn.

Shift. Clamp. Turn.

It must have made a full turn by now, growing looser against the screw, against her fingers. She could turn it in quarter circles now.

Half circles.

A full turn.

Another.

The nut came free of the screw, resting on the ends of her fingers.

"Yes," Ravi hissed in her head as Pip let the nut drop to the floor, a small tinkle of metal in the great, dark unknown.

Now to remove the screw and hack away the tape at her wrists. She was only likely dead now, not very. But she might live. She might just. Hope discoloring some of terror's dark edges.

"Careful," Ravi said to her as she felt for the end of the screw. Pip pushed it, driving it back through the hole. She had to push hard, the weight of the shelf and all those vats leaning down on the screw. She pushed again and the end disappeared inside the hole.

OK, breathe. She shifted her hands once more, reaching for the front side of the metal pole. This was better: she could use her thumb now. Pip felt for the protruding screw, found it with her finger, and hooked on, holding it between her finger and thumb.

Don't let go.

She tightened her grip and pulled out the screw, a grinding sound of metal on metal.

The shelf tilted forward, losing its front support.

Something hard and heavy slid down it, knocking into her shoulder.

Pip flinched.

Her grip loosened, just for a second.

The screw fell from her hand.

A small clatter of metal on concrete, bouncing once, twice, rolling away.

Away into the dark unknown.

TWENTY-NINE

Nononononononono.

Breaths rattled in and out of her nose, hissing against the edges of the tape.

Pip swiped with her legs, feeling out the unknown, this way and that. There was nothing around her but concrete. The screw was gone, out of reach. And she was dead again.

"I'm sorry," she told the Ravi in her head. "I tried. I really did. I wanted to see you again."

"It's OK, Sarge," he told her. "I'm not going anywhere. And neither are you. Plans change all the time. Think."

Think what? That had been her last chance, the last sliver of hope, and now the terror was feeding itself on that too.

Ravi sat with her, back-to-back, but he was actually the heavy vat of weed killer leaning against her, pushing down on the loose corner of the shelf. The metal groaned, bending out of shape.

Pip tried to take Ravi's hand behind her and felt the drooping corner of the shelf instead. Felt the tiniest gap between the lopsided shelf and the pole it was supposed to be attached to. Tiny. But enough to slide her fingernail through. And if it was big enough for that, then it was big enough for the width of the duct tape wrapped around her wrists.

Pip held her breath as she tried. Lowering her hands, forcing that empty side of tape through the gap. It caught on the shelf, so she shifted and jerked, and it came free. She slipped her binds below the shelf, and now she was attached only to the lowest part of the shelving unit. Just this small length of pole and the ground it rested on, that was all that was keeping her here now. If she could somehow raise the leg of the pole, she could slip her restraints down under the end and out.

She shuffled her bound feet, feeling around the area, careful to keep blocking the vat so it didn't fall. Her legs dipped down into the lowered channel running through the concrete floor. That was an idea. If she could drag the shelf forward to that gutter, there would be space beneath the pole leg for her to slip out. But how was she going to drag it? She was attached to it by the wrists, arms locked behind her. If she hadn't been able to fight off Jason Bell with her arms, there was no way she could lift this heavy shelving unit with them. She wasn't that strong, and if she was going to survive, she had to understand her limits. That wasn't her way out of here.

"So what is?" Ravi prompted.

One idea: the duct tape had snagged against the uneven shelf as she'd lowered her hands. If she kept passing the tape through that small gap, kept snagging, maybe it would start to tear small holes in her binds. But that would take a while, a while she'd already spent loosening the nut and removing the screw. DT could be on his way back at any time. Pip must have been alone for over an hour now, maybe more. Alone, even though Ravi was right here. Her thoughts in his voice. Her lifeline. Her cornerstone.

Time was a limitation. The strength of her arms another. What was left?

Her legs. Her legs were bound at the ankles, but they could move, as one. And unlike her arms, they were strong. She'd been running from monsters for months. If she was too weak to drag or lift the shelves, maybe she was strong enough to push them.

Pip explored the unknown with her legs again, stretching out to the back pole of the shelving unit. Through the fabric of her sneakers, she could feel that the back of the shelves wasn't against the wall—it stood a few inches in front of it, at least the width of her foot. Not a lot of room, but it was enough. If she could push the shelves back, they would overtip, landing against the wall. And the front legs would stick up, like an insect on its back. That was the plan. A good plan. And maybe she really would live to see everyone again.

Pip swung her legs forward and dug in her heels, using the lip of the gutter to push against. She propped up her shoulders against the front of the shelf, still blocking the nearest vat from sliding off.

She pushed down, into her heels, and raised herself from the floor.

"Come on," she told herself, and she didn't need to hear it in Ravi's voice anymore. Hers was enough. "Come on."

Pip screeched with the effort of it, the muffled sound filling up her death mask.

She threw her head back against the pole and pushed with it too.

Movement. She felt movement, or hope was only tricking her.

She shuffled one foot incrementally closer, and the other, and she drove them into the gutter, ramming her shoulders against the shelves. The muscles up the backs of her legs shuddered, and it felt like her stomach was tearing open. But she knew it was this or death, so she pushed and she pushed.

The shelves gave way.

They tipped back. The sound of metal meeting brick. A crash as the vat of weed killer finally slid free, cracking open against the concrete. Others sliding, thumping against the back wall. A sharp chemical smell, and something soaking into her leggings.

But none of that mattered.

Pip lowered her binds down the metal pole. And there, at its end, was freedom. It stood up only about an inch from the concrete, that's what it felt like, and that was more than enough. She slipped the tape over the end and she was free.

Free. But not all the way.

Pip shuffled away from the shelves, from the liquid pooling around her. She lay on her side, tucked her knees into her chest, and slipped her bound hands over her feet, arms now in front of her.

The tape came off easily, one hand slipping out of the space left by the pole, then freeing the other.

Her face. Her face next.

Blindly, she felt around her duct tape mask, searching for the end DT had left. There it was, by her temple. She pulled it, the tape undoing with a loud rip. It pulled at her skin, pulled out eyelashes and eyebrows, but Pip tore it off, hard and quick, and she opened her eyes. Blinked in the cold storeroom and the destruction of the shelves behind her. She kept going, pulling and tearing, and the pain was agonizing, her skin raw, but it was a good pain, because she was going to live. She held on to her hair to try to stop it from pulling out from the root, but small clumps of it came away with the tape.

Unwinding and unwinding.

Up her head, and down her nose. Her mouth came free and she breathed through it and breathed hard. Her chin. One ear. Then the other.

Pip dropped her unraveled mask to the floor. The duct tape long and meandering, scattered with hair and small spots of blood it had claimed from her.

DT had taken her face, but she had taken it back.

Pip leaned over and unraveled the tape still binding her ankles, then she stood up, her legs still shaking, almost buckling under her weight.

Now the room. Now she just had to get out of the room and she would be alive, as good as. She skittered over to the door, treading on something on the way. She glanced down: it was the screw she'd dropped. It had rolled almost all the way to the door through the unknown. Pip rammed the door handle down, knowing it was useless. She'd heard Jason lock her in. But there was a door down at the other end of the storeroom. It wouldn't lead outside, but it would lead somewhere.

Pip sprinted to it. She lost control as her sneakers scuffed on the concrete, skidding into a workbench beside the door. The workbench jumped, with a sound of colliding metal from a large toolbox on top. Pip righted herself and tried the door handle. It was also locked. Fuck. OK.

She returned to the other side, to her vat of weed killer, the dark liquid draining into the gutter like a cursed river. A bright line was reflected in the liquid, but it wasn't from the overhead lights. It was from the window, high up in front of her, letting in the last of evening light. Or the first of it. Pip didn't know the time. And her tipped-back shelves, they reached right up to the window, almost like a ladder.

The window was small, and it didn't look like it opened. But Pip could fit through it, she was sure she could. And if she couldn't, she would make herself fit. Climb through and drop down on the outside. She just needed something to break it with.

She checked around. Jason had left the roll of duct tape on the floor by the door. Beside it was a coiled length of blue rope. *The* blue rope, she realized with a shiver. The rope DT was going to use to kill her. *Was.* But would still, if he came back right now.

What else was in the room? Just her and lots of weed killer and fertilizer. Oh wait—her mind jumped back to the other side of the storeroom. There was a toolbox there.

She ran to the other side again, an ache in her ribs and a pain in her chest. There was a Post-it note stuck to the top of the toolbox. In slanting scribbles, it said: *J—Red team keep taking tools assigned to Blue team. So I'm leaving this in here for Rob to find.—L.*

Pip undid the clips and pulled open the lid. Inside was a jumble of screwdrivers and screws, a tape measure, pliers, a small drill, some kind of wrench. Pip dug her hand inside. And underneath it all was a hammer. A large one.

"Sorry, Blue team," she muttered, tightening her grip around the hammer, pulling it out.

Pip stood in front of the tipped-over shelves, *her* shelves, and looked back once more at the room where she'd known she would die. Where the others had died, all five of them. And then she climbed, balancing her feet on the lowest shelf like a rung, pulling herself up to the next level. There was still strength left in her legs, moving adrenaline-fast.

Feet planted on the top shelf, she crouched, balancing herself in front of the window. A hammer in her hand, and an unbroken window in front of her; Pip had been here before. Her arm knew what to do, it remembered, arching back to pick up momentum. Pip swung at the window and it cracked, a spiderweb splintering through the reinforced glass. She swung again, and the hammer went through, glass shattering around it. Shards still clung to the frame, but she knocked them out one by one so she wouldn't cut herself open. How far was it to the ground? Pip dropped the hammer through and watched it tumble to the gravel below. Not far. She should be fine if she bent her legs.

And now it was just her and a hole in the wall, and something was waiting on the other side. Not something. Everything. Life, normal life and Team Ravi and Pip and her parents and Josh and Cara and everyone. They might even be looking for her now, though she hadn't disappeared for long. Some parts of her might be gone, parts she might never get back, but she was still here. And she was coming home.

Pip gripped the window frame and pulled herself forward, sliding her legs out ahead of her. She held on as she dipped her shoulders and head and maneuvered them out too. She stared down at the gravel, at the hammer, and she let go.

Landed. Hard on her feet, the force ricocheting up her legs. A pain in her left knee. But she was free, she was alive. A breath came out too hard that it was almost a laugh. She'd done it. She'd survived.

Pip listened. The only sound was the wind in the trees, some of it finding the new holes in her too, blowing through her rib cage. Pip bent down and picked up her hammer, holding it at her side, just in case. But as she rounded the corner of the building, she could see that the complex was empty. Jason's car wasn't here and the gate was locked again. The metal fence at the front was high, too high, she'd never be able to climb it. But the back of the yard was bordered by woods, and the fence was unlikely to encircle those too.

New plan: she just had to follow the trees. Follow the trees, find a road, find a house, find someone, call the police. That was all. The easy parts left, just one foot in front of the other.

One foot in front of the other, the crunch of gravel. She walked past the parked vans, dumpsters and machines, trailers with ride-on mowers, and a small forklift. One foot in front of the other. Gravel became dirt became the crunch of dry grass. The sun was close to setting, burning through the clouds to watch over Pip. She was surviving, one foot in front of the other, that's all it took. Her sneakers and the grass crunching beneath them. She dropped the hammer, she was far enough away now, and carried on through the trees.

A new sound stopped her in her tracks.

The distant drone of a car engine. The slam of a car door far behind her. The shrieking of a gate.

Pip darted behind a tree and stared back into the complex.

Two yellow headlights, winking at her through the branches, as they pulled forward. Wheels on gravel.

It was DT. Jason Bell. He'd returned. He was back to kill her.

But he wouldn't find her there, only the parts she'd left behind. Pip was out, she'd escaped. All she had to do was find a house, find a person, call the police. The easy parts. She could do that. She turned, leaving the headlights in the unknown behind her. Moving on, picking up her pace. She just had to call the police and tell them everything: that DT had just tried to kill her and she knew who he was. She could even call Detective Hawkins directly; he'd understand.

She faltered, one foot hovering above the ground.

Wait.

Would he understand?

He never understood. Not any of it. And it wasn't even a question of understanding, it was a question of believing. He'd come right out and said it to her face, said gently but said all the same: that she was imagining it. She didn't have a stalker, she was just seeing things, seeing danger around every corner because of the trauma she'd lived through. Even though he'd been part of that trauma, because he hadn't believed her when she went to him about Jamie.

It was a repeating pattern. No, not a pattern, it was a circle. That's what this all was, everything winding up, coming full circle. The end was the beginning. Hawkins hadn't believed her before, twice, so why did she think he'd believe her now?

And the voice in her head wasn't Ravi anymore, it was Hawkins. Said gently, but said all the same. "The DT Killer is already in prison. He's been there for years. He confessed." That's what he'd say.

"Billy Karras isn't the DT Killer," Pip would counter. "It's Jason Bell."

Hawkins shook his head inside hers. "Jason Bell is a respectable man. A husband, a father. He's already been through so much, because of Andie. I've known him for years, we play tennis sometimes. He's a friend. Don't you think I'd know? He's not the DT Killer and he's not a danger to you, Pip. Are you still talking to someone? Are you getting help?"

"I'm asking you for help."

Asking him again and again, and when would she finally learn? Break the circle?

And if her worst fears were right, if the police didn't believe her, didn't arrest Jason, then what? DT would still be out there. Jason might take her again, or someone else. Take someone she cared about to punish her, because she was too loud and had to be silenced in some way. He'd get away with it. They always got away with it. Him. Max Hastings. Above the law because the law was wrong. A legion of dead girls and dead-eyed girls left behind them.

"They won't believe me," Pip told herself, in her own voice now. "They never believe us." Out loud so she would truly listen this time, understand. She was on her own. Charlie Green wasn't the one with all the answers; she was. She didn't need to hear it from him to know what to do this time.

Break the circle. It was hers to break, here and now. And there was only one way to do that.

Pip turned, grass bunching, clinging to the white soles of her shoes.

And she walked back.

Returned through the darkening trees. A glint of dying sunlight across the surface of the dropped hammer, showing her the way. She bent to pick it up, testing out her grip.

From grass, to dirt, to gravel, easing her steps, pressing her feet down with no sound. Maybe she was too loud for him, but he'd never hear her coming now.

Ahead, Jason was out of his car, walking up to the metal door he'd dragged her through, his steps disguising hers. Closer and closer. He stopped and she did too, waiting. Waiting.

Jason slid his hand down into his pocket, returning with the ring of keys. A rustle of tinkling metal and Pip took a few slow steps, hiding beneath the sound.

Jason found the right key, long and jagged. He pushed it into the lock, metal scraping metal, and Pip moved closer.

Break the circle. The end was the beginning and this was both, the origin. Finish it where it had all begun.

He twisted the key, and the door unlocked with a dark click, the sound echoing in Pip's chest.

Jason pushed open the door into the yellow-lit storeroom. He took one step over the threshold, looked up, then took one back, staring ahead. Taking in the scene: tipped-over shelves, smashed-open window, a river of spilled weed killer, lengths of unwound duct tape.

Pip was right behind him.

"What the—" he said.

Her arm knew what to do.

Pip pulled it back and swung the hammer.

It found the base of his skull.

A sickening crunch of metal on bone.

He staggered. He even dared to gasp.

Pip swung again.

A crack.

Jason dropped, falling forward onto the concrete, catching himself with one hand.

"Please—" he began.

Pip pulled her elbow back, a spray of blood hitting her in the face.

She leaned over him and swung again.

Again.

Again.

Again.

Again.

Again.

Again.

Until nothing moved. Not a twitch in his fingers, or a jerk in his legs. Only a new river, a red one, slowly leaking out of his undone head.

PART II

THIRTY

He was dead.

Jason Bell, the DT Killer: one and the same, and he was dead.

Pip didn't need to check the swell of his chest or feel for a pulse to know that. It was clear just looking at him, at what was left of his head.

She'd killed him. Broken the circle. He'd never hurt her and he'd never hurt anyone.

It wasn't real and she wasn't real, tucked against the wall by her overturned shelves, hugging her legs to her chest. Her warped reflection in the discarded hammer as she rocked back and forth. It was real, he was right there in front of her, and she was here. He was dead and she'd killed him.

How long had she been sitting there now, going backward and forward over this? What was she doing, waiting to see if he'd take a breath and stand back up? She didn't want that. It had been her or him. Not self-defense, but a choice, a choice she made. He was dead and that was good. Right. Supposed to be.

So, what was supposed to happen now?

There hadn't been a plan. Nothing beyond breaking the circle, beyond surviving, and killing him was how she survived. So, now that it was done, how did she keep on surviving? She repeated the question, asking the Ravi who lived in her head. Asking him for help because he was the only person she knew how to ask. But he'd gone quiet. No other people in there, just a ringing in her ears. Why had he left her? She still needed him.

But he wasn't the real Ravi, only her thoughts wrapped up in his voice, her lifeline at the very brink. But she wasn't at the brink anymore. She had lived, and she would see him again. And she needed to, right now. This was too much for her alone.

Pip picked herself up from the ground, trying not to look at the flecks of blood up her sleeves. And on her hands too. Real, this time. Earned. She wiped them off on her dark leggings.

She'd spotted it from across the room, a rectangular shape in Jason's back pocket. His iPhone, protruding out from the fabric. Pip approached, carefully, avoiding the red river reflecting the overhead lights. She didn't want to get any closer, scared that her proximity might somehow drag him back from death. But she had to. She needed his phone to call Ravi so he could come and tell her that everything would be OK, would be normal again, because they were a team.

She reached for the phone. *Wait, Pip, hold on a second. Think about this.* She paused. If she used Jason's phone to call Ravi, that would leave a trace, irrevocably tying Ravi to the scene. DT was a murderer but he was also a murdered man, and it didn't matter that he deserved it, the law didn't care about that. Someone would have to pay for his broken-open head. No. Pip couldn't have Ravi tied to the scene, to Jason, not in any way. That was unthinkable.

But she couldn't do this on her own, without him. That was unthinkable too. A loneliness too dark and deep.

Her legs felt weak as she stepped over Jason's body and stumbled outside onto the gravel. Fresh air. She breathed in the fresh air, but it was tainted somehow, by the metallic smell of blood.

She walked six, seven steps away, toward his car, but that smell, it followed her, held on to her. Pip turned to look at herself, her dark reflection in the window of the car. Her hair was matted and torn. Her face raw and inflamed from the tape. Her eyes far away and yet also right here. And those freckles there, they were new. Castoffs of Jason's blood.

Pip felt her vision dip in and out, knees buckling underneath her. She looked at herself and then looked into herself, through the dark of her eyes. And then past herself: there was something beyond the window drawing her eye, the late sun glinting against its surface, showing her the way again. It was her bag. Her bronze backpack, sitting on the back seat of Jason's car.

He'd taken it when he'd taken her.

It wasn't much, but it was hers, and it felt like an old friend.

Pip scrabbled for the door handle and pulled. It opened. Jason must have left the car unlocked, his keys still waiting there in the ignition. He had meant to finish it quickly, but Pip had finished it first.

She reached in and pulled out her bag, and she wanted to hug it to her chest, this part of her old self before she'd almost died. To borrow some of its life. But she couldn't do that, she'd get his blood on it. She lowered it to the gravel and undid the zipper. Everything was still here. Everything she'd packed when she'd left the house that afternoon: clothes for staying at Ravi's, her toothbrush, a water bottle, her wallet. She reached in and took a long draw from the water bottle, her mouth dried-out from all those taped-up screams. But if she drank any more, she'd be sick. She replaced the bottle and stared at the bag's contents.

Her phone wasn't here. She'd already known that, but hope had partially hidden the memory from her. Her phone was smashed, dropped and abandoned in the road down Cross Lane. There was no way Jason had brought it with him for that very same reason: an irrevocable link to the victim. He'd gotten away with this for a long time; he knew things like that, just as she knew them.

Pip almost sank to her knees, but a new thought caught her in time, and the sun again, glinting on something in the front passenger seat. Yes, the DT Killer did know things like that, that's why they'd never caught him. And that's why he must have used a burner phone to call his victims, otherwise his connection to the case would have been discovered right after the first victim. Pip knew this now because she could see it, right there. Discarded in the front passenger seat. A small boxy Nokia, like hers, the screen reflecting the last sun rays to catch her eye, showing her the way. Pip opened the car door and stared down at it. Jason Bell had a burner phone. Paid in cash, untraceable to her, or to Ravi, unless someone found the phone. But they wouldn't find it; she would destroy it after.

Pip reached down, her fingers alighting on its cool plastic edge. She pressed the middle button and the green backlit screen glared up at her. It still had battery. Pip glanced up and thanked the sun, almost crying with relief.

The numbers on the screen told her it was 6:47 p.m. That was it, that was all. She'd been in the trunk of that car for days, in that storeroom for months, trapped inside the tape for years, and yet it had all happened in less than three hours. Six forty-seven p.m.: a normal early evening in August, with a pink-tinged sun low in the sky and a chill in the breeze, and a dead body behind her.

Pip navigated through the menu to check the recent call list: at 3:51 p.m., this phone had received a call from No Caller ID, from her. And right before that, it had called Pip's number. She would have to destroy the phone anyway, because of that connection between her and the dead man on the floor over there. But this was it: her path to Ravi, to help.

Pip typed Ravi's number in the keypad, but her thumb hesitated over the call button. She backspaced and deleted it, replacing it with the landline for his house. That was better, less of a direct link to him, if they ever found the burner phone. They won't find the burner phone.

Pip clicked the green button and held the small phone to her ear.

It rang. Only through the phone this time. Three chimes and then a click. Rustling.

"Hello, Singh residence," said a bright, high voice. It was Ravi's mom.

"Hi, Nisha, it's Pip," she said, her voice rasping at the edges.

"Oh, there you are, Pip. Ravi's been looking for you. Over-worrying as usual, my little sensitive boy." She laughed. "I hear you're coming over for dinner tonight? Mohan's insisting we play Articulate; he's already reserved you for his team, apparently."

"Um." Pip cleared her throat. "I'm actually not sure I'm going to be able to make it tonight. Something's come up. I'm so sorry."

"Oh no, that's a shame. Are you OK, Pip? You sound a little strange."

"Ah, yeah, no, I'm fine. Just have a bit of a cold, that's all." She sniffed. "Um, is he there? Ravi?"

"Yes, yes, he is. Two seconds."

Pip heard her calling his name.

And in the background, she heard the distant sound of his voice. Pip sank down into the gravel, her eyes glazing. It wasn't so long ago she thought she'd never hear his voice again.

"It's Pip!" She heard Nisha shout, and Ravi's voice grew nearer: nearer and frantic.

Rustling as the phone changed hands.

"Pip?" he said down the line, like he didn't believe it. And Pip hesitated a moment, refilling herself with his voice, welcoming it home. She'd never take it for granted, never again. "Pip?" he said, louder.

"Y-yes, it's me. I'm here." It was hard to push the words out, around the lump in her throat.

"Oh my god," Ravi said, and she could hear him thundering up the stairs to his room. "Where the fuck have you been? I've been calling you for hours. Your phone's been going straight to voice mail. You were supposed to keep checking in." He sounded angry. "I called Nat and she said you didn't even go round there. I've just got back from yours, seeing if you were at home, and your car was at home but you weren't, so your parents are probably worried now because they thought you were with me. I was literally minutes from calling the police, Pip. Where the fuck have you been?"

He was angry, but Pip couldn't help smiling, holding the phone tighter to her ear, to bring him closer. She had disappeared and he had . . . he had looked for her.

"Pip?!"

She could imagine the look on his face: stern eyes and a cocked eyebrow, waiting for her to explain herself.

"I—I love you," she said, because she never said it enough and it was important. She didn't know when she'd last said it, and if she said it again, that wouldn't be the last time either. "I love you. I'm sorry."

Ravi hesitated, and his breath changed. "Pip," he said, the hard edge gone from his voice. "Are you OK? What is it? Something's wrong, I can tell. What's wrong?"

"I just didn't know when I last told you." She wiped her eyes. "It's important."

"Pip," he said, steadying her. "Where are you? Tell me where you are right now."

"Can you come here?" she asked. "I need you. I need help."

"Yes," he said firmly. "I will come right now. Just tell me where you are. What's happened? Is it something to do with DT? Do you know who he is?"

Pip stared back at Jason's feet, hanging out the doorway. She sniffed and she focused, turning back.

"It's . . . I'm at Green Scene. Jason Bell's company, in Weston. Do you know where it is?"

"Why are you there?" His voice higher now, confused.

"Just—Ravi, I don't know how long the battery lasts on this phone. Do you know where it is?"

"What phone are you using?"

"Ravi!"

"Yes, yes," he said, shouting now too, though he didn't know why. "I know where it is, I can look it up."

"No no no," Pip said quickly. She needed him to understand without her saying it. Not on the phone. "No, Ravi, you can't use your phone to get here. You need to leave your phone at home, OK? Do not bring it with you. Do not bring it."

"Pip, wh—"

"You have to leave your phone at home. Look at the way on Google Maps now, but do not type Green Scene into your search browser, whatever you do. Just search on the map."

"Pip, what's going—"

She interrupted him, something else occurring to her. "No, wait. Ravi, you can't drive on any highways. Not any. You have to take the back roads, small roads only. Highways have traffic cams. You can't be seen on any traffic cams. Residential and back roads only. Ravi, do you understand?" Her voice was urgent now, the shock gone, left behind in that room with the dead body.

She heard the click of his trackpad in the background.

"Yes," he said. "I'm just looking now. Yep, that way. Up Brookside, toward New Canaan," he muttered under his breath. "Avoid Route 15, take these residential roads instead. Then . . . Yeah," he said to her. "Yeah, I can find it. I'll write all this down. Back roads only, leave phone at home. I've got it."

"Good," she said, exhaling, and even the effort of that made her feel weak, sinking farther into the gravel.

"Are you OK?" he said, taking charge again, because that's what teammates did. "Are you in danger?"

"No," she said quietly. "Not anymore. Not really."

Did he know? Could he hear it in her voice, raw and scratchy, marked forever by the last three hours?

"OK, hold tight. I'm on my way, Pip. I'll be there in twenty minutes."

"No, wait, don't speed, you can't get—"

But he was already gone, three loud beeps in her ear. He was gone, but he was on his way.

"I love you," she said to the empty phone, because she never wanted there to be a last time again.

Another crunch of gravel. Step after step after step. Pacing up and down, counting her steps, to count the seconds, to count the minutes. And though she told herself not to look, her eyes always found their way back to the body, convincing herself each time that he had shifted. He hadn't; he was dead.

Pacing up and down, the early stirrings of a plan seeding in her brain, now that the shock had passed. But it was missing something. It was missing Ravi. She needed him, the team, their back-and-forth that always showed her the right way, the middle road between her and him.

Headlights broke open the deepening sky, a car pulling into the drive just before the Green Scene gate, hanging wide open. Pip held up her hand to shield her eyes from the glare of the low sun, and then she waved for Ravi to stop. The car stopped in front of the gate, and the headlights blinked out.

The car door opened and a Ravi-shaped silhouette stepped out. He didn't even wait to shut the door, running over to her, scattering gravel.

Pip stopped and studied him, like it was the very first time again. Something tightened in her gut, another thing loosening in her chest, releasing, breaking open. He'd promised she would see him again, and here he was, getting closer and closer.

Pip held up her hand again to keep him back from her. "Did you leave your phone at home?" she said, voice quavering.

"Yes," Ravi said, his eyes wide with fear. Widening farther as he studied her in return. "You're hurt," he said, moving forward. "What happened?"

Pip stepped away from him. "Don't touch me," she said. "It's . . .

I'm fine. It's not my blood. Not most of it. It's . . ." She forgot what she was trying to say.

Ravi steadied his face, held up his hands to steady her too. "Pip, look at me," he said calmly, though she could tell he was anything but. "Tell me what happened. What are you doing here?"

Pip glanced behind her, at Jason's feet hanging out the doorway.

Ravi must have followed her eyes.

"Fuck, who is— Are they OK—"

"He's dead," Pip said, turning back. "It's Jason Bell. It was Jason Bell, he was the DT Killer."

Ravi blinked for a moment, shuffling through her words, trying to find the sense in them.

"He's . . . What? How did he . . ." Ravi shook his head. "How do you know?"

Pip couldn't tell which answer he needed to hear first. "How do I know he was the DT Killer? Because he took me. Abducted me from Cross Lane, tied me up in the trunk of his car. Brought me here. Wrapped my face up in duct tape, bound me to a shelf. Exactly like he did to the rest of them. They died here. And he was going to kill me." It didn't sound real, now that she was saying it out loud. Like all of that had happened to a different person, separate from her. "He was going to kill me, Ravi." Her voice snagged in her worn-out throat. "I thought I was dead and . . . and I didn't know if I'd ever see you again, see anyone. And I thought about you finding out I was dead and—"

"Hey, hey, hey," he said quickly, taking one careful step toward her. "You're OK, Pip. I'm here, OK? I'm here now." He glanced back over at Jason's body, eyes lingering too long. "Fuck," he hissed. "Fuck, fuck, fuck. I can't believe it. You shouldn't have been out on your own. I shouldn't have let you be out on your own. Fuck," he said again, hitting his palm against his forehead. "Fuck. Are you OK? Did he hurt you?"

"No, I'm . . . I'm fine," she said, that small, cavernous word again, hiding all sorts of dark things. "Just from the tape. I'm fine."

"So how did . . . ?" Ravi began, his eyes abandoning her again, slipping back over to the dead man twelve feet away.

"He left me. Tied up." Pip sniffed. "I don't know where we he went, or for how long. But I managed to push over the shelves, get free, and take off the tape. There's a window, I broke out of it. And—"

"OK, OK." He cut her off. "OK, that's OK, Pip. It's going to be OK. Fuck," he said again, more to himself than to her. "Whatever you did, it was in self-defense, OK? Self-defense. He was going to kill you so you had to kill him. That's what this is. Self-defense, and that's OK, Pip. We just need to call the police, OK? Tell them what happened, what he did to you and that it was self-defense."

Pip shook her head.

"No?" Ravi lowered his eyebrows. "What do you mean *no,* Pip? We have to call the police. There's a dead man on the ground over there."

"It wasn't self-defense," she said quietly. "I had escaped. I was free. I could have walked away. But I saw him return, and I went back. I killed him, Ravi. Snuck up behind him and hit him with a hammer. I chose to kill him. It wasn't self-defense. I had a choice."

Ravi was shaking his head now; he still couldn't see it, the full picture. "No, no, no. He was going to kill you, that's why you killed him. That's self-defense, Pip. It's OK."

"I killed him."

"Because he was going to kill you," Ravi said, his voice rising.

"How do you know that?" Pip said. She had to make him see, make him see that *self-defense* wasn't an option here, as she'd already realized, pacing up and down.

"How do I know that?" Ravi asked, incredulous. "Because he took you. Because he's the DT Killer."

"The DT Killer has been in prison for more than six years," Pip said, not in her own voice. "He confessed. There have been no killings since."

"What? B-but—"

"He pleaded guilty in court. There was evidence. Forensic and circumstantial. The DT Killer is already in prison. So why did I kill this man?"

Ravi's eyes narrowed in confusion. "Because he was the real DT Killer!"

"The DT Killer is already in prison," Pip repeated, watching his eyes, waiting for him to understand. "Jason Bell was a respectable man. A managing director of a midsize company, and no one has a bad word to say about him. Acquaintances—friends, even—with Detective Richard Hawkins. Jason has already been through a tragedy, a tragedy—you might argue—that I made much worse. So, why did I have a fixation on Jason Bell? Why was I trespassing on his private property on a Saturday evening? Why did I sneak up behind him and hit him with a hammer? Not just once. I don't know how many times. Go look at him, Ravi. Go look. I didn't just kill him. 'Overkill,' that's the term, isn't it? And that is incompatible with self-defense. So, why did I kill this nice, respectable man?"

"Because he was the DT Killer?" Ravi said, less certain now.

"The DT Killer is already in prison. He confessed," she said, and she saw the shift in Ravi's eyes as he understood what she was telling him.

"That's what you think the police will say."

"It doesn't matter what the truth is," Pip said. "What matters is a narrative they will find acceptable. Believable. And they won't believe my narrative. What evidence do I have other than my word? Jason got away with this for years. There might not *be* any evidence that he was DT." She deflated. "I don't trust them, Ravi. I trusted the police before and they've let me down every single time. If we call them, the most likely outcome is that I'm going away for the rest of my life for murder.

Hawkins already thinks I'm unhinged. And maybe I am. I killed him, Ravi. I knew what I was doing. And I don't even think I regret it."

"Because he was going to kill you. Because he's a monster," Ravi said, reaching for her hand, before remembering the blood and letting his arm fall to his side. "The world is better off without him. Safer."

"It is," she agreed, looking back again, checking Jason hadn't moved, wasn't listening in. "But no one else will understand that."

"Well, what the fuck are we going to do?" Ravi asked, shifting his weight from foot to foot, a quiver in his lip. "You can't go down for murder. That's not fair, that's not what this was. You . . . I don't know if we can say it was the right thing, but it wasn't wrong. It's not like what he did to those women. He deserved it. And I don't want to lose you. I can't lose you. That's your whole life, Pip. Our whole life."

"I know," she said, a new kind of terror making its home in her head. But there was something else there too, keeping it back. A plan. They just needed a plan.

"Can't we go to the police and explain th—" Ravi drew off, chewing his lip, another glance at those disembodied feet. He was silent for a moment, and another, eyes flickering, his mind busy behind them. "We can't go to the police. They got it wrong with Sal, didn't they? And Jamie Reynolds. And do I trust a jury of twelve peers with your life? Like the jury that decided Max Hastings was innocent? No, no way. Not you, you're too important."

Pip wished she could take his hand, feel his warmth on her skin as their fingers intertwined in the way that they did. Team Ravi and Pip. Home. They looked into each other's eyes, a silent conversation in their shifting glances. Ravi finally blinked.

"So what do we . . . how would we get away with this?" he said, the question almost ridiculous enough for a smile. How to get away with murder. "Just, theoretically. Do we . . . I don't know, bury him somewhere so no one ever finds him?"

Pip shook her head. "No. They always find them eventually. Like

Andie." She took a deep breath. "I've studied a lot of murder cases, as have you, listened to hundreds of true crime podcasts. There's only one way to get away with it."

"Which is?"

"To not leave any evidence and to not be here at the time of death. To have an ironclad alibi somewhere far away during the time-of-death window."

"But, you *were* here?" Ravi stared at her. "What time did it . . . what time did you . . . ?"

Pip checked the time on Jason's burner phone. "I think it was around six-thirty that it happened. So, coming up to an hour ago now."

"Whose phone is that?" Ravi nodded to it. "You didn't call me from *his* phone, did you?"

"No, no, it's a burner phone. Not mine, it's his, Jason's, but it . . ." Her voice escaped from her as she saw the question forming in Ravi's eyes. And Pip knew, she'd finally have to tell him. They had bigger secrets now, no room for this anymore. "I have a burner phone I never told you about. At home."

There was movement in Ravi's lips, almost close to a smile. "I always said you'd end up with your own burner phone," he said. "Wh-why do you have one?"

"I have six, actually," Pip sighed, and somehow this felt harder to say than telling him that she'd killed a man. "It's, um . . . I haven't been coping well, with what happened to Stanley. I said I was fine, but I wasn't fine. I'm sorry. I, um, I've been buying Xanax from Luke Eaton, after the doctor wouldn't prescribe me any more. I just wanted to be able to sleep. I'm sorry." She dropped his gaze, staring down at her sneakers. There were flecks of blood on those too.

Ravi looked hurt, taken aback. "I'm sorry too," he said quietly. "I knew you weren't fine, but I didn't know what to do about it. I thought you just needed time, change of scenery." He sighed. "You should have told me, Pip. I don't care what it is, whatever it is." He glanced quickly over at Jason's body. "But no secrets between us, OK? We're a team. We're a team, you and me, and we will fix this. Together. I promise we're going to get through this."

Pip wanted to fall into him, let him wrap her up in his arms and disappear down into them. But she couldn't. Her body, her clothes, were a crime scene, and she couldn't contaminate him. It was like he knew, somehow, had read it in her eyes. He stepped forward and reached out, carefully stroking one finger under her chin, in a place without blood, and it was just the same.

"So, if he died at six-thirty p.m.," Ravi said, locking back onto her eyes, "how do we give you an ironclad alibi for six-thirty p.m., when you were here?"

"We can't, not that way," she said, looking inside, into that growing idea in her head. It should be impossible, but maybe . . . maybe it wasn't. "But I was thinking, when I was waiting for you, I was thinking about it. Time of death is an estimate, and the medical examiner uses three main factors in that estimation: rigor mortis—that's how the muscles stiffen after death; livor mortis—that's when the blood pools inside the body; and body temperature. Those are the three factors they use to narrow down the time of death. And so, I was thinking, if we can manipulate those three factors, if we can delay them, we can make the medical examiner think he died hours after he did. And in *that* time window, you and I can have solid alibis, separately, with people and cameras and an undeniable evidence trail."

Ravi considered for a moment, chewing on his bottom lip.

"How would we manipulate those factors?" he said, eyes ahead, skimming over dead Jason and back.

"Temperature," Pip said. "Temperature is the main one. Colder temperatures slow the onset of rigor mortis, and lividity—that's the blood pooling. But also, with lividity, if you turn the body before the blood has settled, it will resettle. And if you could turn the body a few times, you could buy yourself hours there, alongside cooling the body."

Ravi nodded, turning his head, studying their surroundings. "How could we cool his body, though? I suppose it's too much to ask for Jason Bell to have owned a fridge-freezer company instead."

"The problem is body temperature, though. If we keep him cool to delay rigor and lividity, his body temperature will also drop. He will be too cold, and the plan won't work. So we would have to cool him down, and then warm him up again."

"Right," Ravi said with a disbelieving sniff. "So, we've just got to put him in a freezer and then stick him in a microwave. Fuck, I can't believe we are even talking about this. This is crazy. This is crazy, Pip."

"Not a freezer," Pip said, following Ravi's lead, looking at the Green Scene complex with new eyes. "That's too cold. More like a fridge temperature. And then, of course, after we've warmed him up again, we will have to make sure his body is found only a few hours later, by the police and the medical examiner. Otherwise none of this will work. We need him to be warm and stiff when they find him, and his skin still blanchable—that means the pooled blood moves when you press the skin. If that's the early morning, then they should think he died six to eight hours before then."

"Will it work?"

Pip shrugged, a near-laugh in her throat. Ravi was right: this was crazy. But she was alive, she was alive, and she was very nearly not. At least this was better than that. "I don't know, I've never killed someone and gotten away with murder before." She sniffed. "But it should work. The science works. I did a lot of research when I was looking at that Jane Doe case. If we can do all that—cool him down, turn him a couple of times, and then heat him back up—it should work. It will look like he died more like, I don't know, nine o'clock, ten o'clock. And we will both be somewhere else by then. Ironclad."

"OK." Ravi nodded. "OK, that sounds, well, it sounds crazy, but I think we can do it. I think we might actually be able to do this. It's a good thing you're such an expert in murder."

Pip pulled a face at him.

"No, I mean, like, from studying it, not killing people. I hope this is the first and last time." Ravi tried and failed at a smile, shifting on his feet. "One thing, though: say we're actually going to try to pull this off, and we want them to find his body so this time-of-death manipulation works. Well, they're going to know that *someone* killed him. And they will look for a killer until they find one. That's what the police do, Pip. They'll have to have a killer."

Pip tilted her head, studied Ravi's eyes, her reflection captured inside them. This was why she needed him; he pushed her forward or reined her back when she didn't know she needed it. He was right. This would never work. They could shift the time of death and make sure they were far away from here in that time frame, but the police would still need a killer. They would look until they found one, and if she and Ravi made even one mistake, then . . .

"You're right." She nodded, her hand moving out to take his, before she remembered. "It won't work. They need a killer. Someone has to have killed Jason Bell. Someone else."

"OK, so . . ." Ravi began, talking them back to square one, but Pip's mind wandered away from him, flipped over to show her all those things at the very back. The things she hid away: the terror, the shame, the blood on her hands, the red, red, violent red thoughts, and one face hanging there, angular and pale.

"I know," Pip said, cutting Ravi off. "I know who the killer is. I know who's going to have killed Jason Bell."

"What?" Ravi stared at her. "Who?"

It was inevitable. Full circle. The end was the beginning and the beginning was the end. Back to the very start, to the origin, to set it all right.

"Max Hastings," she said.

THIRTY-ONE

Twelve minutes.

Twelve minutes was all it took. Pip knew because she'd checked the time on the burner phone as she and Ravi talked it through. She thought it would have taken much longer, it *should* have taken much longer, a plan to set someone up for murder. Agonizing hours and a cascade of details, tiny yet critical. That's what you'd think, what Pip would've thought. But twelve minutes and they were done. Ideas back and forth, picking holes in them and plugging the gaps when they found them. Who and where and when. Pip didn't want to involve anyone else, but Ravi made her see it couldn't be done, not without help. The entire thing almost unraveled until Ravi came up with the cell phone tower idea, from a case he was working on at his internship, and Pip knew exactly what call to make. Twelve minutes, and there the plan was, like a physical thing between them. Precious and solid and clear and binding. They could never go back from this, go back to who they were before. It would be difficult, and it would be tight; they could make no wrong turns, no delays. No room for error.

But the plan worked, in theory. How to get away with murder.

Jason Bell was dead, but he wasn't dead yet—he would be in a few hours. And Max Hastings would be the one who killed him. Finally locked away, where he belonged.

"They deserve it," Pip said, standing back. "They both deserve it, don't they?" It was too late for Jason, but Max . . . She hated him, down to the very core of who she was, but was that blinding her, leading her?

"Yes," he reassured her, though she knew he hated him just as much. "They've hurt people. Jason killed five women; he would have killed you. He started everything that led to Andie and Sal dying. So did Max. Max will carry on hurting people if we do nothing. We know that. They deserve this, both of them." He gently tapped his finger in that safe space under her chin, pulling her face up to look at him. "It's a choice between you or Max, and I choose you. I'm not losing you."

And Pip didn't say but she couldn't help thinking of Elliot Ward, who'd made a choice exactly like this, making Sal a killer to save himself and his daughters. And there Pip was too, in that messy, confusing gray area, dragging Ravi in with her. The end and the beginning.

"OK." She nodded, talking herself back into it. The plan was binding and they were in it now, and time was not on their side. "A few things still left to work out, but the most important is the—"

"Refrigerating and heating up the dead body," Ravi finished the sentence for her, glancing again at those abandoned feet. He still hadn't seen the body up close, seen what Pip had done to Jason. Pip hoped Ravi wouldn't change his mind when he did, wouldn't look at her any differently. He pointed to the brick building behind them, separate from the corrugated-iron building with the chemical storeroom off its side. "That building there looks more like an office building, where the office staff works. There's probably a kitchen in there, right? With a fridge and a freezer?"

"Yeah, there probably is." Pip nodded. "But not human-sized."

Ravi blew out a mouthful of air, his face tight and tense. "Again, why couldn't Jason Bell have owned a meat-processing factory with giant refrigerators?"

"Let's go have a look around," Pip said, turning back to the open metal door, and Jason's feet lying across the threshold. "We have his keys." She nodded at them, still in the lock where Jason had left them.

"He's the owner, he must have a key to every door here. And he told me the alarms were disabled everywhere, and the security cameras. He told me he had all weekend, if he wanted it. So we should be fine."

"Yeah, good idea," Ravi said, but he didn't take a step forward, because stepping toward that door also meant stepping toward the dead body.

Pip went first, holding her breath as she walked over, eyes stalling on Jason's broken-open head. She blinked, dragging her gaze away, and pulled the heavy ring of keys out of the door. "We need to make sure we remember everything we've touched—I've touched—so we can wipe it down later," she said, cradling the keys in her hand. "Come on, this way."

Pip stepped over Jason, avoiding the halo of blood around his head. Ravi followed close behind, and Pip saw his eyes lingering, blinking hard as though he might wish it all away.

A small cough as he picked up his pace behind her.

They didn't say anything. What was there to say?

It took a few attempts for Pip to find the right key for the door at the end of the storeroom, by the workbench. She pushed it open into a dark and cavernous room.

Ravi pulled his sleeve up over his fingers and flicked on the light switch.

The room came into view in flickers, as the overhead lights settled into their buzzy glow. This building must have once been a barn, Pip realized, staring up into its impossibly high ceiling. And laid out before them were rows and rows and rows of machines. Lawn mowers, weed trimmers, leaf blowers, machines she didn't even understand, and tables with smaller tools, like hedge cutters. Over on the right were large machines Pip assumed must be ride-on mowers, covered with black tarps. There were shelves with more metal tools, glinting in the light, and red plastic gas cans, and bags of soil.

Pip turned to Ravi, his eyes taking in the room, feverish and fast.

"What's that?" He pointed to a bright orange machine, tall, with a funnel-shaped top.

"I think that's a shredder," she said. "Or a wood-chipper, whatever it's called. Branches go in and it shreds them to tiny little pieces."

Ravi pursed his lips to one side, like he was considering something.

"No," Pip said firmly, knowing exactly what it was.

"I didn't say anything," he countered. "But there are clearly no giant fridges in here, are there?"

"But"—Pip's gaze alighted on the rows and rows of mowers—"lawn mowers run on gas, don't they?"

Ravi eyes picked up hers, widened in recognition. "Ah, for the fire," he said.

"Even better," Pip added. "Gasoline doesn't just burn. It explodes."

"Good, that's good," Ravi nodded. "But that's the very last step, and we have a long night ahead of us before then. All of it's pointless if we can't work out how to cool him down."

"And warm him up," Pip said, and she felt it catching from the look in Ravi's eyes. Despair. The plan might be over before it began. Her life in the balance, and the scales were tipping away from them. *Come on, think.* What could they use? There had to be something.

"Let's check the office building," Ravi said, taking charge, leading Pip away from the regimented lines of mowers, back through the chemical storeroom, picking their way through the spilled weed killer and the spilled blood. Around the dead body, more dead each time, treading around him with featherlight steps, like this was just a childhood game.

Pip glanced back at the storeroom, at the coils of duct tape with tufts of her hair and spots of her blood. "My DNA is all over this room," she said. "I'll take the duct tape with me, dispose of it with my clothes. But we're going to have to clean those shelves too. Clean it all before we burn it."

"Yes," Ravi said, taking the ring of keys from her. "And these," he jangled them. "There should be cleaning supplies in the office, I'd guess."

Pip caught sight of herself again, reflected in the window of Jason's car as they passed. Her eyes too dark, the pupils overgrown, eating away at the thinning border of hazel. She shouldn't stare too long, in case her reflection stayed in Jason's window, forever leaving a mark of her there. That's when she remembered.

"Fuck," she said, and Ravi's footsteps crunched to a halt.

"What?" he said, joining her reflection in the window, his eyes too big and too dark too.

"My DNA. It's all over the trunk of his car too."

"That's OK, we can deal with that as well," Ravi's reflection said, and Pip saw the mirror version of him reach for her hand too, before he remembered and pulled back.

"No, I mean it's *all over* the trunk," she said, panic rising again. "Hair, skin. My fingerprints, which the police already have on file. I left as much as I could. I thought I was going to die and I was trying to help. Leave a trail of evidence so you could find him, catch him."

A new look in Ravi's eyes, desolate and quiet, and a quiver in his lip like he was trying not to cry. "You must have been so scared," he said quietly.

"I was," she said. And as scary as this was, the plan, and what would happen if they failed, nothing came close to the terror she'd felt in that trunk or in that storeroom, taped up in her death mask. Its traces still there, all over her skin, in the craters of her eyes.

"We will fix it, OK?" he said loudly, speaking over the tremor in his voice. "We will deal with the car later, when we're back. First we need to find something to—"

"Cool him down." Pip sounded out the words, staring beyond herself, into the inside of Jason's car. "Cool him down and then heat him up," she said, her eyes circling the control panel beside the steering wheel. The idea started small, as a simple *what if,* then kept growing and growing, gorging itself on Pip's attention until it was all she could think of. "Oh my god," she hissed, and again, louder: "Oh my god!"

"What?" Ravi asked, instinctively checking over his shoulders.

"The car!" Pip turned to him. "The car *is* our fridge. This is a new-ish car, expensive SUV, how cold do you think the AC gets?"

The idea pulled in Ravi too, she could see it in his eyes, something close to excitement. "Pretty cold," he said. "On the coldest setting, full blast from all the vents, enclosed space. Yeah, pretty fucking cold," he said with a near-smile.

"A standard fridge is about forty degrees; you think we can get it to that?"

"How do you know what a standard fridge temperature is?" he asked.

"Ravi, I know things. How do you not know by now that I know things?"

"Well," Ravi glanced up at the sky, at the setting sun. "It's kinda chilly out tonight. Can't be more than sixty degrees outside, sixty-five at most. So, if we just need the car to cool by twenty degrees or so . . . yeah, yeah, I'd say that's feasible."

A shift in Pip's rib cage, a feeling like relief that opened out her chest, gave her a little more space to breathe. They could do this. They might actually do this. Play god. Bring a man back to life for a few hours, so another could kill him.

"And," she said, "when we get back here later—"

"—turn on the heaters to the hottest setting, full blast." Ravi took over the sentence for her, speaking fast.

"Bring his body temperature back up," Pip finished it.

Ravi nodded, eyes darting left to right as he ran it through his head again. "Yes. This is going to work, Pip. You're going to be OK."

She might, she just might. But they hadn't even started yet, and time was ticking away from them.

"Remember the last time we did this?" Ravi asked her, pulling on the pair of work gloves he'd found in the office building, in a closet full of spare uniform parts bearing the company logo.

"Moved a dead body?" Pip asked, clapping her gloves together, small clumps of mud disintegrating into dust before her eyes.

"No, we haven't actually done that before," Ravi sniffed. "I meant, the last time we wore gardening gloves to commit a crime. Breaking and entering into the Bells' house, *his* house." He nodded back in the direction of the chemical storeroom. "That, er . . ." He drew off.

"Don't," Pip told him, giving him a stern look.

"What?"

"You were going to make a 'that escalated quickly' joke, Ravi. I can always tell."

"Ah, I forgot," he said. "You *know* things."

She did. And she knew that humor was Ravi's tic, his way of coping.

"OK, let's do this," she said.

She crouched and pulled up one edge of the tarp covering the oversized mower. The black plastic crinkled as she threw it up and over the machine, Ravi dragging it off from the other side. It came free, and Ravi folded it up roughly in his arms.

Pip guided him out of the large room, back into the chemical storeroom, the weed killer fumes still strong, a headache starting to make itself known.

Ravi laid the tarp out over the concrete, beside Jason's body, avoiding the blood.

Pip could read the tension in the way he held his mouth, that far-away look she was sure she had too.

"Don't look at him, Ravi," she said. "You don't have to look at him."

Ravi stepped toward her, as though to help her with the next part.

"No," she said, sending him away. "You don't touch him. You don't touch anything unless you have to. I don't want any traces of you here."

That would be far worse than the unthinkable. If she went down for murder, but if Ravi went down with her. No, this could not touch him, and so he could not touch the scene. If they failed, it would all be on her; that was the deal. Ravi knew nothing. Saw nothing. Did nothing.

Pip bent to her knees on the other side of Jason, and slowly she reached out, gripping onto his shoulder and his arm. He wasn't stiff yet, but rigor would start to set in soon.

She leaned forward and pushed, rolling Jason and his broken-open head onto his front. His face was untouched. Pale and slack, but he almost looked like he could be sleeping. Pip reset her grip and rolled him again, facedown on the edge of the tarp, and again, faceup in the middle.

"OK," she said, pulling up one side of the tarp and wrapping it over him. Ravi did the same on the other side.

Jason was gone, tidied away. The remnants of the DT Killer; just a dark red puddle and a rolled-up tarp.

"He needs to be lying on his back in the car, for the lividity," Pip said, positioning herself where Jason's shoulders should be. "And then when we come back, we turn him onto his front. The blood will resettle, make it look like those hours never happened."

"Yeah, OK." Ravi nodded, bending down and gripping onto Jason's ankles through the tarp. "One, two, three, lift."

He was heavy, too heavy, Pip's grip under his shoulders awkward through the sheet of plastic. But together they had him, walking slowly out the metal door, Ravi moving backward, glancing down to check he wasn't trekking through the blood.

The gentle hum of an engine greeted them outside. They already had Jason's car up and running, the air-conditioning on the coldest setting, every vent in the car opened fully. Doors closed to keep in the chill. Ravi had found some ice packs in the freezer in the office building, presumably for workplace accidents. But now they were scattered around the inside of the car, close to the vents, cooling it even more.

"I'll get the door," Ravi said, leaning down to place Jason's feet gently on the gravel. Pip stuck her leg forward, buttressed against Jason's back to take some of the weight.

Ravi opened the door to the backseat.

"Already pretty cold in there," he said, returning to the other end of Jason and picking him up with a grunt.

Carefully, half steps at a time, they maneuvered the rolled-up tarp through the car door, dropping Jason onto the backseat and sliding him through.

It was already cold in here, like leaning inside a fridge, and Pip could see the foggy billows of her breath in front of her as she tried to push Jason farther in. His head, his undone head, wouldn't fit inside.

"Hold on," Pip said, running round the back of the car to open the other door. She reached through the opening at the end of the tarp, gripped Jason's ankles, and pushed them up to bend his knees, using the extra room to drag him all the way in. Holding him in position as she slowly closed the door, the sound of his feet knocking against it, like he was trying to kick his way free.

Ravi closed the door on the other side and stepped back, clapped his hands with a tense outward breath.

"And it will keep running for hours, while we're gone?" Pip checked again.

"Yeah, he has almost a full tank. It will keep going, long as we need it to," Ravi replied.

"Good, that's good," she said, another word she knew to be meaningless. "So, now we go. Back home. The plan."

"The plan," Ravi parroted her. "Feels scary, leaving it like this, invisible traces of you all over it."

"I know," she said. "But it's secure; no one is coming here. Jason said so himself. He planned to kill me here, and he had all night, all weekend. No cameras, or alarms. So we have the same. Everything will be the same when we get back. And then we remove those traces, plant new ones." She glanced through the car window, at the rolled-up black tarp and the dead man inside who wasn't dead yet. Not if everything worked out.

Ravi removed his gloves. "You taking your backpack?"

"Yes," Pip said, pulling her gloves off too, placing them and Ravi's pair inside her unzipped bag. Her duct tape binds were in here too, removed from the storeroom: ankles, wrists, unwound mask with her ripped-out hair.

"And you have everything in there, everything you came with?"

"Yes, it's all in here," she said, zipping it up. "Everything I packed in it this afternoon. Now the gloves, the used duct tape. Jason's burner phone. I've left nothing behind."

"And the hammer?" Ravi asked.

"That can stay here." She straightened up, shouldering the bag. "We can clean my prints off it later. Max will need a murder weapon too."

"OK," Ravi said, taking the lead, heading toward his car abandoned by the open Green Scene gate. "Let's go home."

THIRTY-TWO

One last check.

Ravi leaned in close across the parking brake, studying her, his breath sweet but sharp on her face.

"There's still some on your face that's dried. And on your hands." He glanced down. "And there are spots on your hoodie. You'll have to get upstairs quickly, before they see you."

Pip nodded. "Yeah, I can do that," she said.

She'd laid her spare T-shirt out on the seat so no blood would transfer onto Ravi's car. And she'd used her spare pair of underwear, pouring a little water from her bottle, to try to wipe the blood from her face and her hands while Ravi drove the back roads. It would have to do.

Pip pushed open the car door with her elbow and stepped out, leaning back in to stuff the T-shirt she'd sat on into her bag too, zipping it up. House keys in the other hand.

"Are you sure?" Ravi asked her again.

"Yes," she told him. They'd gone over the plan again. Over and over in the car. "I can do this part on my own. Well, you know what I mean."

"I can help," Ravi said, a hint of desperation in his voice.

Pip looked at him, took in every inch and left none behind. "You've already helped, Ravi, more than you know. You helped me stay alive in there. You came to get me. I can do this part alone. What will help me is you being safe. That's what I want. I don't want any of this to come back on you, if it goes wrong."

"I know, but—"

Pip cut him off. "So, you're going to go establish your alibi now, for the whole evening. In case our timing doesn't work out and we don't delay the time of death by enough. What are you going to do?" She wanted to hear him say it again: airtight, ironclad.

"I'm going home to grab my phone, then driving to Stamford to pick up my cousin Rahul," Ravi said, staring ahead. "Use the highways, so the traffic cams pick me up. Going to take out some cash from an ATM, so the camera there also gets me. Then we're going to go to IHOP, or another chain, and order food, pay with my card. Be loud, draw attention to us, so people remember us being there. Take photos and videos on my phone, showing us there. Make a call too, probably to Mom to tell her what time I'll be home. I'm going to text you and ask you how your evening is going because I don't know you lost your phone yet and we haven't seen each other all day." He took a quick breather. "Then we'll go to that bar where all my cousin's friends hang out, lots of witnesses. Stay until eleven-thirty. Then I drop Rahul home, and I drive back, fill up with gas on the way, so another security camera gets me. Go home, pretend to go to bed."

"Good, yes," Pip said, glancing at the clock on the car's dashboard. It had just turned 8:10 p.m. "Meet me at midnight?"

"Meet you at midnight. And you'll call me?" he asked. "From your burner phone, if anything goes wrong."

"It won't go wrong," Pip answered, trying to convince him with her eyes.

"Be careful," he said, tightening his grip on the wheel, a substitute for her hand. "I love you."

"I love you," she said, another last time. But it wouldn't be the last; she'd see him in a few hours.

Pip closed the door and waved to Ravi as he turned on his blinker and peeled off down the road. She took one deep breath to prepare herself, and then she turned and walked up her driveway to the front door.

She saw her family through the front window, the frames of the TV dancing across their faces. She watched them for a moment, from out here in the twilight. Josh was folded up on the rug in his pajamas, awkward and small, playing with his Lego. Her dad was laughing at something on TV, and Pip could feel its vibrations even out here. Her mom tutted, slapped a hand against his chest, and Pip heard her say, "Oh, Victor, that's not funny."

"It's always funny when people fall over," came his booming reply.

Pip felt her eyes prickle, a catch in her throat. She thought she'd never see them again. Never smile with them, or cry, or laugh, never grow old as her parents grew older, their traditions becoming hers, like the way her dad made mashed potatoes, or the way her mom decorated the tree at Christmas. Never see Josh grow into a man, or know what his forever-voice sounded like, or what made him happy. All those moments, a lifetime of them, big and small. Pip had lost them, and now she hadn't. Not if she could pull this off.

Pip cleared her throat, dislodging the lump, and unlocked the front door as quietly as she could.

She crept inside, shutting the door behind her with a barely audible click, hoping the noise of an audience clapping from the TV would cover it. Keys gripped too hard in her fist so they wouldn't make a sound.

Slowly, carefully, holding her breath, she passed the living room doorway, glancing at the backs of their heads against the sofa. Her dad moved and Pip's heart dropped, freezing her to the spot. No, it was OK, he was just shifting his position, placing his arm around her mom's shoulders.

Up the stairs, quiet, quieter. The third stair creaked under her weight.

“Pip?! Is that you?” her mom called, shuffling on the sofa to turn around.

“Yeah!” Pip called back, bounding up the stairs quickly before her mom got a good look. “It’s me! Sorry, I’m just desperate to pee.”

“We have a bathroom downstairs, you know,” her dad shouted as she rounded the top of the stairs into the hallway. “Unless by *pee,* you really mean a p—”

“Thought you were staying at Ravi’s?” Her mom now.

“Two minutes!” Pip shouted in response, running straight for the bathroom, closing the door behind her, locking it. She’d have to clean that door handle too.

That was close. But they were acting normally; they hadn’t seen anything, not the flecks of blood, or her ripped-up hair, or the raw skin on her face. And those were Pip’s first tasks.

She pulled her hoodie off over her head, shutting her mouth and shutting her eyes, so none of the drying blood would stray inside. She dropped it carefully, inside out on the tiles. She kicked off her sneakers, and her socks, then peeled off her dark leggings. She couldn’t see any blood against the material, but she knew it was there, hiding somewhere in the fibers. And then her sports bra, a small, rusted stain near the middle where some of the blood had transferred through her hoodie. She left the clothes in a pile and turned on the shower.

Warm. Hot. Hotter. So hot that it hurt to step inside under the stream. But it needed to be hot, to feel like it was scouring away the top layer of her skin. How else would she ever feel clean of DT? She scrubbed at herself with shower gel, watching as the pinkish blood-dyed water ran off her legs, between her toes and down the drain. She scrubbed and scrubbed again, finishing off the half-full shower gel, cleaning under her fingernails too. She washed her hair, three separate times, the strands feeling thinner, more brittle now. Shampoo stinging the graze on her cheekbone.

When she finally felt clean enough, Pip stepped out into a towel, leaving the water running for a while longer, to wash away any residue of blood on the shower floor. She'd clean that later too.

With the towel tucked under her armpits, she grabbed the flip-lid trash can nestled beside the toilet and pulled out the plastic bucket liner from inside. There were just two empty toilet paper rolls in it, and Pip removed these, stacking them on the windowsill instead. In the cabinet under the sink she found the toilet bleach, unscrewed the lid, and poured some into the plastic bucket. More. All of it. She straightened up and filled the bucket halfway with warm water from the faucet, diluting the bleach, the smell strong and noxious.

She'd have to make two journeys to her bedroom, but her family were all downstairs, it should be clear. Pip hoisted the bucket, heavy now, holding it with one arm against her chest as she unlocked the bathroom door. She staggered out, across the landing, and into her bedroom, placing the bucket down in the middle, water sloshing dangerously close to the rim.

More eerie sounds of a TV audience applauding her as Pip returned to the bathroom, grabbing the pile of bloodied clothes and her backpack.

"Pip?" came her mom's voice from the stairs.

Fuck.

"Just showered! I'll be down in a minute!" Pip called back, hurrying into her room and closing the door behind her.

She dropped the clothes beside the bucket, and then, on her knees, she turned to the discarded pile, and gently, one by one, lowered them into the bleach mixture, stuffing them down. Her sneakers too, bobbing half-in at the top.

From her backpack, she added the lengths of duct tape that had bound her face and her hands and her ankles, pushing them down into the diluted bleach. She pulled out Jason's burner phone, sliding the back off to remove the SIM card. She snapped the little card in half and dropped the disassembled phone into the water. Then the underwear she'd used to wipe the blood from her face, and the spare T-shirt she'd sat on. Finally, the branded Green Scene gloves she and Ravi had used—perhaps most incriminating—she pushed them right to the bottom. The bleach would deal with the visible bloodstains and probably the dye of the fabrics too, but it was just a precaution: everything in here would be gone forever by this time tomorrow. Another job for later.

For now, Pip dragged the bucket across the carpet and hid it inside her closet, poking her sneakers back in. The smell of bleach was strong, but no one would be coming into her bedroom.

Pip dried herself and dressed, in a black hoodie and black leggings, and then turned to the mirror to deal with her face. Her hair hung down in feeble, wet strands, her scalp too sore to run a brush through. She could see a small bald patch on the crown of her head, where she'd ripped out her hair with the tape. She'd have to cover it. Pip dragged her fingers through and secured her hair into a high ponytail, tight and uncomfortable. She layered two more hair ties on her wrist for later, when she and Ravi returned to Green Scene. Her face still looked raw and blotchy, and then slightly sickly as she piled foundation on to cover it. Concealer on the worst parts. She looked pale and the texture of her skin looked rough, peeling in places, but it would do.

She emptied her backpack to repack it, checking off items from the mental list she and Ravi had assembled, seared into her brain like a mantra. Two beanies, five pairs of socks. Three of the burner phones from her desk drawer, all powered on. The small pile of cash she kept in that secret compartment too, taking it all just in case. In the pocket of her smartest jacket, hanging in her closet over the bucket of bleach, she found the embossed card she hadn't touched since that mediation meeting, and placed it carefully in the front pocket of her bag. Darting quietly into her mom and dad's bathroom, she grabbed a handful of the latex gloves her mom used to dye her hair, at least three pairs each. She repacked her wallet on top of everything, checking her debit card was inside; she would need it for her alibi. And her car keys.

That was it, everything from upstairs. She ran through it again, double-checking she had everything needed for the plan. There were a few more items to get from downstairs, somehow avoiding the watchful gaze of her family, and a younger brother who made everyone's business his own.

"Hey," she said breathlessly, skipping down the stairs. "Just had to shower because I'm heading out and went on a run earlier." The lie came out too fast, she needed to slow it down, remember to breathe.

Her mom turned her head against the backrest of the sofa, looking at her. "I thought you were going to Ravi's for dinner and staying over."

"A sleepover," Joshua's voice added, though Pip couldn't see him through the couch.

"Change of plans," she said, with a shrug. "Ravi had to go see his cousin, so I'm hanging out with Cara instead."

"No one asked me about any sleepover," added her dad.

Pip's mom narrowed her eyes, studying her face. Could she see, could she tell what was hiding just beneath the makeup? Or was there something different in Pip's eyes, that haunted faraway look? She'd left the house still her mom's little girl, and she'd returned as someone who knew what it was to die violently, to cross over that line and somehow come back from it. And not only that: she was a killer now. Had that changed her, in her mother's eyes? In her own? Reshaped her?

"You haven't had an argument, have you?" she asked.

"What?" Pip said, confused. "Me and Ravi? No, we're fine." She attempted a lighthearted sniff, dismissing the idea. How she wished for anything as normal, as quiet, as an argument with her boyfriend. "I'm just grabbing a snack from the kitchen, then heading out."

"OK, sweetie," her mom said, like she didn't believe her. But that was fine; if her mom wanted to believe she and Ravi had had an argument, that was fine. Good, even. Far better than anything near the truth: that Pip had murdered a serial killer and was now, at this very moment, heading out to frame a rapist for the crime she'd committed.

In the kitchen, Pip opened the wide drawer at the top of the island, the drawer where her mom kept the foil and baking paper, and the plastic sandwich bags. Pip grabbed four of the resealable sandwich bags, and two of the larger plastic freezer bags, stuffing them on top of her backpack. From the bits-and-pieces drawer on the other side of the kitchen, Pip retrieved the candlelighter and packed it too.

And now for the last item on the list, which wasn't really a specific item, more a problem to be dealt with. Pip thought inspiration would have struck her by now, but she was coming up empty. The Hastings family had fitted two security cameras to either side of their front door, since Pip vandalized their house months ago, after the verdict. She needed something to *deal* with those cameras, but what?

Pip opened the door into the garage, the air cold in here, almost nice against her skin, still adrenaline-hot. She surveyed the room, her eyes flicking over her parents' bikes, to her dad's tool kit, to the mirrored dresser that her mom kept insisting they'd find room for. What could Pip use to disable those cameras? Her eyes lingered over her dad's tool kit, pulling her over, across the room. She opened the lid and looked inside. There was a small hammer lying on top. She supposed she could sneak up and break the cameras, but that would make a sound, might alert Max inside. Or those wire cutters, if the cameras had exposed wiring. But she'd been hoping for something less permanent, something that better fit with the narrative.

Her eyes caught on something else, head-height on the shelf

above the toolbox, staring at her in that way inanimate objects sometimes did. Pip's breath caught in her throat and she sighed, because it was perfect.

A near-full roll of gray duct tape.

That was exactly what she needed.

"Fucking duct tape," Pip muttered to herself, grabbing it and shoving it inside her bag.

She left the garage and froze in the doorway. Her dad was in the kitchen, half-inside the fridge, picking at the leftovers and watching her.

"What are you doing in there?" he asked, lines crisscrossing his forehead.

"Oh, um . . . looking for my blue Converse," Pip said, thinking on her feet. "What are you doing in there?"

"They're in the rack by the door," he said, indicating down the hall with his head. "I'm just getting your mother a glass of wine."

"Oh, and the wine's kept under that plate of chicken?" Pip said, walking past, shouldering her bag.

"Yes. I'll have to heroically eat my way to it," he replied. "What time will you be home?"

"Eleven-thirty-ish," Pip said, calling bye to her mom and Josh, her mom telling her not to stay out too late because they were heading to Adventureland in the morning, and a small whoop of excitement from Josh. Pip said she wouldn't, the normalness of the scene like a punch in her gut, doubling her over, making it hard to even look at her family. Would she ever belong in a scene like this again, after what she did? Normal was all she'd wanted, what all of this was for, but was it now out of reach forever? It definitely would be if she went down for Jason's murder.

Pip closed the front door behind her and exhaled. She didn't have time for these questions; she needed to focus. There was a body fifteen miles away, and she was in a race against it.

It was eight twenty-seven p.m. now, already behind schedule.

Pip unlocked her car and climbed inside, placing the backpack on the passenger seat. She turned the key in the ignition and pulled away, her leg shaking against the pedal, stage one complete behind her.

On to the next.

THIRTY-THREE

The dark red door peeled open in front of Pip, the shadow of a face in the small crack.

"I told you already," said the shadow, registering who it was at the door. "I don't have them yet."

Luke Eaton pulled the door fully open, dark hallway behind him, the streetlights outside illuminating the tattoos that climbed his neck like a net holding his flesh together.

"Doesn't matter how many times you text, from how many different phones, I don't have it," he said, a hint of impatience in his voice. "And you aren't supposed to just show up like—"

"Give me the stronger stuff," Pip said, cutting him off.

"What?" He stared at her, one hand running through his close-shaved head.

"The stronger stuff," Pip repeated. "The Rohypnol. I need it. Now." Her face was blank, like a shield, or a mask, the girl back from the dead hiding behind it. But her hands might give her away, fidgeting nervously in the pocket of her hoodie. If he didn't have it, if he'd already sold his whole stash to Max Hastings himself, then it was all over. Not one part of the plan could fail or it all did, a stack of cards precariously balanced on her back. And her whole life was right there, in Luke's gray-tattooed hands.

"Huh?" he said, studying her, but he wouldn't get through the mask. "You sure?"

Pip's shoulders relaxed, the cards still balanced. He must have it, then.

"Yes," she said, harder than she meant, the word hissing against her teeth. "Yes, I need it. I need . . . I have to sleep tonight. I have to be able to sleep." She sniffed, wiped her nose on her sleeve.

"Yeah." Luke eyed her. "You don't look great. It's more expensive than your usual, though."

"I don't care, however much it is. I need it." Pip pulled out the small stack of notes from her hoodie pocket. She had a hundred dollars here, and she folded all of them into Luke's outstretched hand. "Whatever this will get me," she said. "As much."

Luke looked down at the money folded into his hand, a muscle twitching in his cheek as he chewed on some unknown thought. Pip watched him, urging him on, planting invisible marionette strings inside his head, pulling on them like her life depended on it.

"OK, stay there," he said, pushing the door almost closed, his bare footsteps carrying him away down the dark hallway.

The relief was bright but short-lived. Pip still had a long night ahead of her, and a thousand chances for something to go wrong. She might be alive, but tonight she was fighting for her life all the same, just as hard as she had while wrapped up in that tape.

"Here," Luke said, returning, opening the door to only a sliver again, eyes glinting behind it. He held out a paper bag through the gap and Pip took it from him.

She opened it and glanced inside: two small clear baggies with four of those moss-green pills inside.

"Thank you," Pip said, scrunching up the bag and stuffing it into her pocket.

"Yeah, OK," Luke said stepping away. But before the door closed, he came back, face hanging in the gap. "Sorry about the other day. Didn't see you on the crossing there."

Pip nodded at him, arranging her mouth in a closed-lip smile to give none of herself away. "That's OK, I'm sure you didn't mean to."

"Yeah." Luke nodded, sucking on his teeth. "Um, listen. Don't take too much of that, OK? It's a lot stronger than what you're used to. One will be enough to knock you out."

"Got it, thanks," she said, catching the look on his face, almost like he was concerned about her. The most unlikely of places for it, the most unlikely of people. She really must look terrible.

Pip heard the door closing gently behind her as she made her way back to her car, walking past Luke's bright white BMW, her reflection following her in its dark windows.

Inside the car, she removed the paper bag from her pocket. Pulled out the clear plastic bags and looked at them in the glow from the streetlights. Eight pills, each inscribed with *1mg* on one side. Luke said one would be enough to knock her out, but she wasn't the one who needed to be unconscious. And she had to make sure it worked, quickly, but not enough to cause an overdose. That would make her a two-time killer in the same day.

Pip opened both of the small bags and pulled out two of the pills from one of them. She dropped one pill into the other bag, five in there now. Then she snapped the last pill in two, dropping one half into each bag. Two and a half milligrams. She didn't know what she was doing, but that seemed like it would do it.

Pip replaced the baggie with more pills into the paper bag and stuffed it into her backpack. She'd get rid of them later, along with everything else. Didn't trust herself to keep them.

But the other bag, with two and a half, she made sure the top was sealed up tight, and then she dropped the bag into the footwell, just in front of the pedals. Pip guided her foot over the bag and pressed down against the pills with her heel, hearing them crack. She ground her heel down hard, working at every lump, pushing and grinding until they were crushed.

She picked up the bag and held it in front of her eyes. The pills were gone, replaced by a fine green dust. Pip shook it to make sure there were no remaining chunks.

"Good," she said under her breath, tucking the bag of powder into her pocket and patting it to know it was still there.

Pip started the car, her headlights scaring away the growing darkness outside, but not the other kind that lived in her head.

It was 8:33 p.m., now 8:34, and still three more houses in Fairview to visit tonight.

THIRTY-FOUR

The Reynoldses' house on Cedar Way looked like a face. Pip had always thought so, ever since she was little. It still did now, as she walked up the path toward its toothy front door, windows staring down at her. The steadfast guardian of the family inside. The house shouldn't let her in, it should turn her away. But the people inside wouldn't, Pip knew it in her gut.

She knocked, hard, watching the outline of someone approach through the stained glass of the door.

"Hell—Oh, hi, Pip," Jamie said, a wide smile stretching onto his face as he pulled the door open. "Didn't know you were coming round. The three of us were just going to order pizza, if you want to join?"

Pip's voice stalled in her throat. She didn't know how to begin, but she didn't have to, because Nat appeared in the hallway behind Jamie, the ceiling lights gliding off her white-blond hair, making it glow.

"Pip," she said, walking over, slotting in beside Jamie. "Are you OK? Ravi called me a while ago and said he couldn't get hold of you. He said you were coming round to my house to talk to me about something, but you never showed." Her eyes narrowed, flicking across Pip's face. Nat might see behind the mask; she'd had to learn to wear one herself. "Are you OK?" she asked again, confusion making way for concern.

"Um . . . ," Pip said, her voice still gravelly and raw in her throat. "I—"

"Oh hey, Pip," said a new voice, one she knew well. Connor had emerged from the kitchen, eyes flicking from the gathering at the door and down to his phone. "We were just going to order pizza if—"

"Connor, shush." Jamie cut him off, and Pip could see the same look in his eyes as Nat's. They knew. They could tell. They could read it on her face. "What's wrong?" he asked her. "Are you OK?"

Connor sidled in behind, staring at her too.

"Um." Pip took a breath to steady herself. "No. No, I'm not OK."

"What's—" Nat began.

"Something's happened. Something bad," Pip said, glancing down and noticing that her fingers were shaking. They were clean, but blood was leaking out the ends, and she didn't know if it was Stanley's or Jason Bell's or her own. She hid them inside her pocket, alongside the bag of powder and one burner phone. "And . . . I need to ask you for help. All of you. And you can say no, you can say no to me and I promise I will understand."

"Yeah, anything," Connor said, his eyes picking up on her fear, darkening with it.

"No, Connor, wait," Pip said, glancing between the three of them. Three of the people she'd thought would look for her if she disappeared. Three people she'd been with through the fire and back. And she realized, then, that those same people, the ones who would look for you when you disappeared, they were the same people you could turn to if you needed to get away with murder. "You can't say yes yet, because you don't . . . you don't . . ." She paused. "I need to ask you for your help, but you can never ask me why, or what happened. And I can never tell you."

They all stared at her.

"Never," Pip reiterated. "You have to have plausible deniability. You can never know why. But it's . . . it's something I think we all want.

Make someone pay, get what they deserved all along. But you can never know, you can never . . ."

Nat stepped forward, over the threshold, and placed her hand on Pip's shoulder, her grip tight and warm and quieting.

"Pip," she said, gently, eyes hooking on. "Do you need us to call the police?"

"No." Pip sniffed. "Not the police. Ever."

"What do you mean, make someone pay?" Connor asked. "Do you mean Max? Max Hastings?"

Nat stiffened, passing it down through the bone in Pip's shoulder.

Pip lifted her head and nodded, ever so slightly.

"Put him away. Forever," she whispered, pulling out one hand and resting it on top of Nat's, stealing its warmth. "If it works. But you can never know, I can't tell you, and you can never tell anyone—"

"I'll do it," Jamie said, his face hardening, a determined set to his jaw. "I'll do it, whatever it is. You saved me, Pip. You saved me, so I'll save you. I don't need to know why. Only that you need my help, and you have it. Anything to put him away." His gaze softened as his eyes moved from Pip to the back of Nat's head.

"Yes." Connor nodded, dark blond hair falling into his freckled face. A face she'd watch grow up, shifting with the years, just as he had with her. "Me too. You were there when I needed you." He stretched out his angular arms in an awkward shrug. "Of course I'll help."

Pip felt her eyes filling up as she glanced between the Reynolds brothers. Two faces she'd known as far as memory would take her, two players in the history of who she was. Part of her wished they'd said no, for their own sakes. But she'd make sure they were safe. The plan would work, and if it didn't, she would be the only one to pay. Her silent promise to them all. This never happened; Pip never stood at their door and asked them for help. None of them were here right now.

Pip's gaze trailed over to Nat, seeing her own face reflected in the brilliant blue orbs of Nat's eyes. Nat was the one who truly mattered. They hadn't believed her as many times as they hadn't believed Pip; that unthinkable violence of not-believing. They shared that darkness, and Pip had taken on Nat's scream that day, the day of the verdict, as though it were hers, binding them together. They looked at each other, past the masks.

"Will this get you into trouble?" Nat asked.

"I'm already in trouble," Pip replied quietly.

Nat breathed in, slowly. She let go of Pip's shoulder and took her hand instead, gripping hard, fingers interlocked in hers.

"What do you need us to do?" she said.

THIRTY-FIVE

Courtland. One of those roads in Fairview Pip couldn't extricate from herself, from who she'd become, mapped inside her in place of an artery. Back here once more, like it was something inevitable, this very journey inscribed within her too.

Pip glanced up, the Hastings house coming into view up ahead on the right. Here it had all started, a branch of beginnings all those years ago. Five teenagers one night—Sal Singh, Naomi Ward, and Max Hastings among them. An alibi Sal always had, snatched away from him by his friends, because of Elliot Ward. And here Pip would end it all.

She checked back over her shoulder, at the three of them sitting inside Jamie's car, parked farther down the street. Her car was nestled behind it. She saw Nat nodding to her from the darkness of the passenger seat, and that gave her the courage to carry on.

Pip held on to the straps of her backpack and crossed the street. She stopped at the outer fence around Max's front drive, peeking through the branches of a tree. Max's car was the only one in the drive, as she'd known it would be. His parents were at their second house in Santa Barbara, because of the *emotional distress* Pip had caused them. And—if she was right—Max should have returned from his evening run around eight, if he'd been on one. Turned out all those months of running into each other wasn't for nothing after all.

Max was alone inside, and he had no idea she was coming for him.

But she'd told him. She'd warned him all those months ago. *Rapist. I will get you.*

Pip focused her eyes on the front door, picking out the security cameras mounted on the walls on either side. They were small, pointed diagonally down to face the path up to the front door. They might not be real cameras, might just be for show, but Pip had to assume they were real. And that was OK, because they had a clear blind side: up against the house approaching from the other end. A blind side she would disappear right into.

Pip patted her pocket, checked the duct tape was there, as well as the burner phone, the bag of powder, and one set of latex gloves. Then she placed her hands over the top rail of the outer fence, waist-high, and swung her legs over the top. She landed silently in the grass on the other side, just another shadow among the branches. Keeping to the right-hand perimeter of the front yard, up against a hedgerow, she skirted toward the house. Toward the corner, and one of the windows she'd smashed open months ago.

The room beyond was dark, some kind of office, but she could see through an open door, into the hallway where the lights were on.

Keeping herself flat against the wall of the house, Pip sidled up behind the unsuspecting camera. She glanced up, positioned almost underneath it. Reaching into her pocket, she removed the duct tape and found its ragged end. She pulled a length of tape from the roll and ripped it free. Pip stretched to full height, on her toes, arm snaking up beneath the camera, the tape ready and poised against her fingers. She pressed it over and around the glass, fully covering the lens. Another piece of tape to be sure it was all blocked.

One down, one to go. But she couldn't walk over to it, right into its view. She left the same way she'd come, back along the house and the hedgerow, vaulting the fence where it hid beneath the tree. Walked down the sidewalk with her head down, hood up, to the other side of the house. An opening in the fence between two shrubs. Pip climbed over and in, creeping up the outer edge of the other side of the house. Sidled in across the front. Ripped more tape free, reached up, and covered the camera.

She exhaled. OK, the cameras were disabled, and they wouldn't have caught a trace of the one disabling them. Because it was Max, not her. Max was the one who covered the cameras.

Pip returned to the outer corner of the house and carried on around its side, walking carefully up to a glowing window near the back. She ducked and peered inside.

The room was bright, lit up by yellow spotlights on the ceiling. But there was another light, flickering blue, clashing against the yellow. Pip's eyes found the source: the huge TV mounted against the back wall. And in front of the TV, his messy blond hair visible over the arm of the sofa, was Max Hastings. A controller in his raised hands as he thumbed one button over and over, a gun firing on-screen. Feet up on the oak coffee table, beside the obnoxious blue water bottle he took with him everywhere.

Max shuffled and Pip dropped to the grass, her head below the window. She took two deep breaths, leaning against the bricks, crushing her bag between them. This was the part Ravi had been most worried about, that any number of small factors could send the plan spinning off course, out of her control, that he should be there to help.

But Max was here, and so was his blue water bottle. And if Pip could get inside, that's all she needed. He'd never even know.

Pip wouldn't have long to work out how to break in. Minutes, if that. She'd told Nat to buy her as much time as she could, but even two minutes was optimistic. Jamie had volunteered for the distraction at first, said he'd be able to keep Max at the door long enough. They'd been at school together, Jamie could find something to say, but Nat had shaken her head at them both, stepped forward.

"Put him away forever, you said?" Nat had asked her.

"Thirty to life," Pip replied.

"Well, then this is my last chance to say goodbye. I'll do the distraction," she'd said, teeth gritted and determined.

The same look was on Pip's face now, as she reached into her pocket, fingers closing around the slippery latex gloves. She pulled them out and pulled them on, stretching her fingers down to the very ends. The burner phone next, with a new number saved. The number of the other burner phone she'd just given to Jamie and Connor.

Ready, she typed slowly, the gloves tripping up her fingers.

It was only a few seconds until she heard the sound of a car door slamming in the distance.

Nat was on her way.

Any second that doorbell would ring. And everything, the entire plan, Pip's life, depended on the next ninety seconds.

The shrill sound of a doorbell, a scream by the time it reached Pip's ears.

Go.

THIRTY-SIX

Breath-fogged glass and a getaway heart, escaping her chest.

Pip's eyes at the bottom of the window, watching as Max paused the video game.

He stood up, dropped the controller on the sofa. Stretched his arms over his head, then wiped his hands on his running shorts.

He turned away.

Headed toward the hallway.

Now.

Pip was numb and she was flying.

Feet carrying her round the back of the house.

She heard the doorbell, pressed twice again.

A muffled shout from inside, Max's voice. "I'm coming, I'm coming!"

More windows at the back. Damn, they were all closed. Pip had hoped at least one would be open—it was summer, after all. But there was an unwelcome chill to the evening and hope wasn't on her side. Pip would break a window if she had to; undo the catch and climb through. Pray he wouldn't hear, that he wouldn't go into that room until it was too late. But a broken window didn't fit the narrative as well.

How long had it been now? Had Max already opened the door, shocked to see Nat da Silva standing in the dark outside?

Stop. Stop thinking and move.

Pip ran across the back of the house, keeping low.

There was a patio up ahead, with a folded-up sunshade and a covered-up table. Leading out to it was a wide set of patio doors, small squares of glass in a white painted frame. There was no light leaking out of them, but as Pip approached, the moon lit her way this time, taking over from the sun, showing her a large dining room inside. And the door that must connect it to the living room was closed, yellow lines of light around its border.

Her breaths were adrenaline-fast, and each one hurt.

Pip hurried up to the patio doors. Through the glass, she could see the door handle inside, and a set of keys in the lock. This was it. Her way in. She just had to break that one small pane of glass and she could reach inside to unlock the door. It wasn't perfect, but it would do.

Quickly.

She braced one hand against the handle, readying the elbow on her other arm. But before she could ram it forward, into the glass, her other hand gave way. The handle pushed down, under her weight. And then—to her shock—it opened outward as she pulled.

The door was already unlocked.

It shouldn't be unlocked; the plan had counted on an open window, not an open door. But maybe Max didn't fear the danger lurking outside in the night, because he already was the danger. Plain-sight danger, not the dark-of-night kind. Or maybe he was just forgetful. Pip didn't pause, didn't stop to question it anymore, sliding through the gap and shut the patio door quietly behind her.

She was inside.

How long had that taken? She needed more time. How much longer could Nat distract him for?

Pip could hear their voices now, carrying through the house. She couldn't make out the words, not until she opened the dining room door and crept through into the living room.

The room was open-plan, leading out onto the hallway. Pip glanced over, and Max was right over there, standing at the front door with his back to her. Beyond him, Pip could just make out the halo of Nat's white hair.

"I don't understand why you're here," she heard Max say, his voice quieter than usual, unsure.

"Just wanted to talk to you," Nat said.

Pip held her breath and stepped forward. Slow, silent. Her eyes shifted, away from Max to his blue water bottle, waiting on the coffee table ahead.

"Kind of feel like I shouldn't talk to you, not without a lawyer present," replied Max.

"And doesn't that say everything?" Nat said with a sniff.

There was still water in the bottle, almost a third. Pip had hoped for more, but that would do. It should be tasteless. Her feet moved from polished wood to the huge over-patterned rug in the center of the room. There were no shadows to disappear into, nothing to hide behind. The room was bright and if Max looked back now, he'd see her.

"So, what did you want to say?" Max coughed lightly, and Pip halted, checking over her shoulder.

"Wanted to talk to you about this libel suit you're filing against Pip."

Pip crept forward, testing out each step before she leaned into it, in case one of the floorboards creaked.

She reached the edge of the large corner sofa and ducked beneath it, crawling forward, toward the bottle. The controller and Max's phone lying abandoned on the seat of the sofa.

"What about it?" asked Max.

Pip reached out with her gloved hand, fingers wrapping around the sturdy plastic of the bottle. Its spout was already up and waiting, globs of his spit resting on top.

"Why are you doing it?" Nat said.

Pip unscrewed the top of the bottle, round and round.

"I have to," said Max. "She spread lies about me to a significant number of people. Damaged my reputation."

The top of the bottle came free, attached to a long plastic straw.

"Reputation," Nat laughed darkly.

Pip rested the bottle top on the table, a few drops of water falling from the straw onto the rug below.

"Yes, my reputation."

She reached into her pocket, pulled out the sealed plastic bag with the green powder. Holding the bottle in the crook of her elbow, Pip peeled open the baggie.

"Except they weren't lies, you know that. For fuck's sake, Max, she has a recording of you admitting it. What you did to Becca Bell. And me. And all the others. We know."

Pip tipped the bag over the opening of the bottle. The green powder made a gentle hiss as it slid down, landing in the water.

"That recording was fabricated. I would never say that."

Green dust clung to the inner walls of the bottle, sinking down through the water.

"Have you said that so many times you're even starting to believe it yourself?" Nat asked him.

Pip swirled the water inside the bottle, picking up the dregs. Gently. A small splashing sound of water crashing on water.

"Look, I really don't have time for this."

Pip froze.

She couldn't see beyond the sofa. Was it over? Was Max shutting the door? Would he catch her right here, crouched on his rug, his water bottle in her hands?

A sound. Shuffling. And then something harder, like wood crashing up against something.

"But I'm not finished," Nat said, louder now. Much louder. Was it a signal to Pip? Get out of there now, she couldn't keep him any longer.

Pip gave the bottle one last shake. The powder was dissolving, cloudy in the water, but Max wouldn't be able to tell, not through the dark blue plastic. She picked up the top and screwed it back on.

"What are you doing?" Max said, his voice rising too. Pip flinched. But, no, he wasn't talking to her. He was still over there, talking to Nat. "What do you want?"

Nat coughed, a harsh, unnatural sound. That was a signal, Pip was sure.

She placed the bottle back on the coffee table, exactly where she'd found it, and she turned. Crawling back the way she'd come.

"I wanted to tell you . . ."

"Yes?" Max snapped, impatient.

Past the edge of the sofa, and Pip straightened up. She looked at them, Nat's foot over the threshold, blocking the front door.

"That if you take it to trial, this libel case against Pip, I will be there, every day."

Pip crept, one foot in front of the other, bag shuffling against her shoulders. Too loud. She looked across, her eyes meeting Nat's over Max's shoulder.

"I will testify against you. So will the others, I'm sure."

Pip shifted her gaze, focusing on the closed door into the dining room ahead of her. Max wouldn't go in there, she was sure. She could wait him out in there, or outside.

"You won't get away a second time. I promise. We will get you."

More scuffling. Fabric on fabric. Then a thump.

Someone roared.

Max.

Pip wouldn't make it. Too far. She darted right instead, to a slatted door fitted under the grand staircase. She opened it and swung herself inside, falling back into the small space, between a vacuum cleaner and a mop. She leaned up and pulled the closet door closed.

It slammed. Loudly.

No, that wasn't her door.

That was the front door.

The slam echoing down the polished hall.

No, that wasn't an echo, those were feet.

Max's.

Slapping against the wooden floorboards, a person-shaped blur passing through the slats in front of her.

He stopped, right outside, and Pip didn't breathe.

THIRTY-SEVEN

Pip still didn't breathe.

She pushed her eyes up against the closet door, adjusting to the checkerboard view beyond.

Outside, Max swayed on his feet for a moment. Then he stumbled past her, holding one hand to his face. Up to his eye.

Pip exhaled, carefully, breath bouncing back into her face. Nat must have hit him. That was the thump Pip heard. Not part of the plan, but it had worked. Bought Pip enough time to hide in this closet.

Max hadn't seen her; he didn't know anyone was inside. The drugs were in place, dissolved in his blue water bottle. She'd made it. The part where Ravi was scared it would all fall apart. She'd just about held it together.

And now, Pip waited.

Max moved away from her, past the living room, toward an archway into the kitchen. Pip heard clattering, Max swearing to himself under his breath, and another slamming door. He returned a minute later, clutching something up to his eye.

Pip shifted to get a better view as Max padded over to the sofa. Something green and plastic; maybe a pack of frozen peas. Good. Pip hoped Nat hadn't held back. Although, now Max would have a black eye to explain, to fit into the narrative. But maybe that wasn't a bad thing, maybe that worked even better. A fight, between Max and Jason Bell. Jason punched him and Max walked away, returned with a hammer, sneaking up behind him. Yes, the bruise blossoming on Max's face could bend to fit right into the story Pip was creating for that not-yet-dead man fifteen miles away.

Max slumped down into his place on the sofa. Pip could no longer see his face, just a striped view of the back of his head. A grunt, a shuffling sound as he must have rearranged the peas. His head moved as he leaned forward.

Pip couldn't see. She couldn't see from here if he was drinking the water.

But she could hear it. That obnoxious sucking sound from the spout, filling the silent house, cutting right through her.

Pip pushed up onto her feet, quietly, quietly, her bag snagging on the top of the vacuum cleaner. She unhooked it and straightened up, looking through the slats again. Now she could see him, from this height. One hand on the frozen peas over his eye, the other clutched around his bottle. At least four large sips before he put it back down. That wasn't enough. He had to drink all of it, most of it.

She pulled out the burner phone from the front pocket of her hoodie. It was 8:57 p.m. Fuck, almost nine already. Pip thought they could buy at least three hours with Jason's body. Which meant she only had a half hour until the time-of-death window might open. She was supposed to start establishing her alibi in forty-five minutes.

And yet, there was nothing she could do now. All she could do was wait. Watch Max from her hiding place. Try to play god, using that dark place in her mind to make him sit forward and drink more.

Max didn't listen. He leaned forward, but only to place his phone on the coffee table. Then he picked up his controller and unpaused his game. Gunshots. A lot, but Pip heard only six, striking her through the chest, Stanley's blood creeping over her hands in the dark closet. Stanley's, not Jason's. She could tell the difference somehow.

Max took another sip at 9:00 exactly.

Two more at 9:03.

Went to the downstairs bathroom at 9:05. It was right next to Pip's closet, and she could hear everything. He didn't flush, and she didn't breathe.

Another sip at 9:06 as he returned to the sofa, a sucking, rattling sound from the spout. He put down the water bottle, and then picked it back up again, getting to his feet. What was he doing? Where was he taking it? Pip couldn't see, shifting her head to peer through the slats.

He wandered through the archway into the kitchen. Pip heard the sounds of a running faucet. Max appeared again, the blue bottle in his hand. Twisting his wrist as he screwed the top back on. He'd just refilled the bottle. He must have drunk it all, or at least he'd gotten close enough to the bottom to need to fill up.

The drugs were gone. Inside him now.

Max stumbled, tripping over his own bare foot. He stood there for a moment, blinking down at his feet, like he was confused, a deepening red mark under one eye.

The pills must already be starting to take effect. Some had been in his system for more than ten minutes now. How long would it be until he passed out?

Max took a tentative step, swaying slightly, and then another quick one, hurrying over to the sofa. He lowered himself down, took another sip of water. He was feeling dizzy, Pip could tell. She'd had that same feeling last year, sitting across from Becca in the Bells' kitchen, though she'd been given more than two and a half milligrams. The exhaustion, like her body was starting to separate from her mind. Soon his legs wouldn't be able to hold him up.

Pip wondered what he was thinking right now, as he unpaused the game and started shooting again, taking cover behind a dilapidated wall. Maybe he was thinking his light-headedness had come from the blow to his head, from Nat's fist. Maybe he was feeling tired, and as he felt sleep dragging him in, closer and closer, he'd tell himself he just needed to sleep it off. He'd never know, never suspect, that as soon as he fell asleep, he would be out of the house, killing a man.

Max's head lowered against the arm of the sofa, resting on the frozen peas. Pip couldn't see his face, couldn't see his eyes. But they must still be open, because he was still shooting.

But his on-screen character was moving sluggishly too, the violent world spinning around him in dizzying circles as Max started to lose control of his thumbs.

Pip watched, eyes flicking between the two.

Waiting. Waiting.

She glanced down at the time, the minutes running away from her.

And when she looked back up, neither of them was moving. Not Max, stretched out on the sofa, head up on the arm. And not his character on-screen, standing still in the middle of a battlefield, life bar draining as he took hit after hit.

You're dead, the game told him, fading to a loading screen.

And Max didn't react, didn't move at all.

He must have passed out, right? He must be unconscious. It was 9:17 p.m. now, twenty minutes after he'd first started drinking the spiked water.

Pip didn't know. And she didn't know how she could know for certain, trapped back here in the under-stairs closet. If she left her hiding place and he wasn't asleep, the plan was finished, and so was she.

Gently, Pip pushed the slatted door of the closet, opening it just a few inches. She glanced around her, looking for something, something small, to test it out. Her eyes landed on the plug for the vacuum cleaner, its long wire wound around the machine. That would do. Pip unwound some of the cable, to give herself some slack, ready to reel it back in and close the door if Max reacted at all.

She threw the plug out of the closet, toward the living room. It clattered, bounding three times against the floorboards before it reached the end of its wired leash.

Nothing.

Max didn't stir at all, lying deadly still on the sofa.

He was out.

Pip pulled the vacuum plug back in, the plastic hissing loudly against the floor, and still Max didn't move. She rewound the wire, and then left her closet, closing it behind her.

She knew he was out, but she trod carefully anyway, creeping one foot in front of the other, toward the large rug, toward the sofa, toward him. As she neared, she could now see his face, cheek crushed up against the hard end of the couch, his breaths deep and whistling. At least he was breathing—that was good.

Pip approached the coffee table, the hairs rising up the back of her neck. She felt like he was watching her somehow, even though his eyelids were heavy and closed, the beginnings of a bruise around one. He looked helpless, lying there behind her, his face almost child-like, innocent. People always looked innocent when they slept; pure, removed from the world and its wrongs. But Max was not innocent, not even close. How many girls had he looked at like this, laid out helpless before him? Had he ever felt guilty, like Pip almost did now? No, he hadn't, he was a taker, through and through. Born wrong, bred wrong, it didn't matter which.

And Pip knew, as her eyes trailed away from him, that this wasn't just about her own survival. She knew herself well enough by now. Had reckoned with that dark place in her mind long enough.

This was also revenge.

This town wasn't big enough for the both of them. This world wasn't. One of them had to go, and Pip was going to give one hell of a fight.

She reached forward, wrapping her gloved fingers around Max's phone. It lit up as she picked it up, telling her that it was 9:19 now, and she better hurry up.

The symbol at the top told her that the battery had at least half of its charge left. Good, that should be enough.

Pip stepped away from Max, behind the sofa. She flicked the side button to switch his phone onto silent and then she bent to her knees, removing her backpack. She reached inside and retrieved one of the small, clear sandwich bags, swapping it with the empty baggie from her pocket and the roll of duct tape.

She opened the sandwich bag and dropped Max's phone inside, sealing the top after it. She straightened up, her knees clicking at her, and turned toward the front door. She left her backpack behind her on the floor; she wasn't finished here yet, she'd be back in a minute. But first she needed to pass off Max's phone to Jamie and Connor.

She passed a sideboard in the hallway, a wooden bowl on top with a collection of coins and keys. Pip rifled through until she found an Audi key ring and pulled it free. These must be Max's car keys, the house keys attached too. Pip would need these as well.

Keys in one hand, bagged-up phone in the other, Pip pulled open the Hastingses' front door and stepped outside into the cool evening, shutting the door gently behind her. She walked down the front path, glancing quickly at the duct-taped cameras. She could see them, but they couldn't see her.

Down Courtland, to the dark waiting shape of Jamie's car.

The passenger-side door opened and Nat poked her head out.

"All OK?" she asked, and the relief in her eyes was evident.

"Y-yeah, fine," Pip said, taken aback. "What are you still doing here, Nat? You were supposed to leave straight after, go to your brother's house to establish an alibi."

"I wasn't going to leave you alone in there with *him,*" Nat said firmly. "Not until I knew you were safe."

Pip nodded. She understood. Even though she wouldn't have been alone—Jamie and Connor were right here—she understood.

"All good?" Connor asked her from the backseat.

"Yeah, he's out," said Pip.

"Sorry, I had to hit him." Nat looked up at her. "He was trying to push me out and shut the door, and I could still see you there behind him, so I just—"

"No, that's fine," Pip cut across her. "Might actually work out for the better, even."

"And it felt good." Nat smiled. "Wanted to do that for a long time."

"But you need to get to your brother's now," Pip said, her voice hardening. "Unlikely anyone will believe Max when he says you went over for a *chat,* but I want you to be as secure as possible."

"I'll be fine," Nat replied. "Dan will be on his fifth beer already. I'll tell him it's eight-forty-five, he won't know the difference. Kim and the baby are at her mom's."

"OK." Pip shifted her focus to Jamie behind the steering wheel. She leaned across Nat to hand him Max's bagged-up phone. Jamie took it and gave her a small nod, placing it down on his lap. "I've put it on silent already," she said. "Battery looks good."

Jamie nodded again. "I've plugged the location into the GPS," he said, indicating the car's in-built system. "We'll find it. Green Scene Limited. Back roads only."

"And your phones are off?" Pip asked.

"Phones off."

"Connor?" She turned to him.

"Yes," he said, eyes glowing from the dark backseat. "Turned it off back at home. We won't turn them back on again, not until we're clear."

"Good." Pip exhaled. "So, when you get there, you'll see that the gate is open. Do not go inside, you understand? You must not go inside. Promise me."

"No, we won't," Connor said. A small glance between the brothers.

"Promise," Jamie added.

"Don't even look through the gate, just pull up outside, off the road," Pip said. "Leave Max's phone in the bag, don't touch it, whatever you do. There are some rocks, big rocks, on the grass, lining the small drive up to the gate. Leave the phone in the bag behind the first big rock. Just put the bag there and leave."

"Pip, we've got it," Jamie said.

"Sorry, I just . . . it can't go wrong. Not one part can go wrong."

"It won't," Jamie said softly, kindly, calming her spiking nerves. "We've got you."

"Have you worked out where you're going after?" she asked.

"Yes," Connor said, leaning forward into the yellow glow of the light by the rearview mirror. "There's this late-night Marvel movie festival thing at one of the movie theaters in Norwalk. We'll go there. Turn our phones on when we get to the parking lot. Make a couple of calls and texts while we're there. Cameras everywhere. We'll be fine."

"OK." Pip nodded. "Good, yeah, that's a good idea, Connor."

He smiled weakly at her, and she could tell he was scared. Scared because he could tell that something terrible had happened, and he'd never know what he'd been a part of. Though they could guess, they'd probably guess when the news got out. But as long as it was never said out loud, as long as they didn't truly know, beyond any doubt. Connor didn't need to be scared; if anything went wrong, Pip would bring it all down on her. The rest of them would be safe. They were just at a late-night showing at the movie theater; they knew nothing. She tried to tell him all of that with her eyes.

"And you'll call me, from the burner, once you're clear of Green Scene?" Pip said. "Drive for at least five minutes and then call me from the burner to tell me Max's phone is in place."

"Yes, yes, we will," Connor said, waving the burner phone she'd given them.

"OK, I think we're all set." Pip stepped back from the car.

"We'll drop Nat at her brother's and then we'll go straight there," Jamie said, starting the car, the engine cutting through the quiet night.

"Good luck," Nat said, holding Pip's eyes for a lingering second before she closed the door.

Headlights on and Pip shielded her eyes from the glare as she backed up, watching them drive away. But only for a moment. She didn't have time to dwell or time to doubt, or time to wonder if she was dragging everyone she cared about down with her. Time wasn't something she had.

She hurried back up the sidewalk, up the front path to the Hastingses' house. She tried two keys before she found the one that unlocked the front door, pushing it open quietly. Max was passed out, but she didn't want to push her luck.

She left the car keys on the floor of the hall, near her backpack, so she wouldn't forget them on her way out. Her mind was scattering, pushed out of place by Jamie's kindness and Nat's concern and Connor's fear, but she needed to focus again. The plan was working and it pulled up a new list in her mind now. The list she and Ravi had worked out of everything she needed to take from Max's house.

Three things.

Pip headed up the staircase, rounding the corner into the hallway upstairs and across into Max's bedroom. Pip knew which one it was. She'd been here before, back when she first found out Andie Bell had been selling drugs. It didn't look any different: the same maroon bedspread, the same piles of discarded clothes.

She also knew that behind that *Reservoir Dogs* poster, pinned up on the bulletin board, was a photo of Andie Bell. A topless photo Andie had left in Elliot Ward's classroom, that Max had found and kept all this time.

It made Pip feel sick, knowing it was there, and part of her wanted to rip the hidden photo down, carry Andie safely home with her along with her ghost. Andie had suffered enough at the hands of violent men. But she couldn't do that. Max couldn't know anyone had been here.

Pip turned her attention to the white laundry basket, overflowing, its lid balanced precariously on top. She pushed the lid off and rummaged through Max's dirty clothes, glad for the gloves covering her hands. About halfway down she found something that would do. A dark gray hoodie with a zipper, creased and crinkled. Pip chucked it out, onto Max's bed, then repacked the too-full laundry basket the same way she'd found it.

Next, she headed toward his built-in closet. Shoes. She needed a pair of his shoes. Preferably ones with a unique tread pattern. Pip opened the doors and stared inside, eyes falling to the very bottom and the chaotic jumble of shoes that greeted her there. She bent down and reached in toward the back. If the shoes were at the back, that likely meant Max didn't wear them as often. Pip discounted one pair of dark running shoes, their soles rubbed flat and smooth with age. She found another nearby, a white sneaker and turned it over, her eyes following the hectic zigzagged lines of its soles. Yes, that would make for some good tracks, and these weren't the shoes he used on his daily runs. She fished through the pile of mismatched shoes, searching for the pair, fishing it out from a tangle of laces.

She straightened up, about to close the closet doors, when something else caught her eye. A dark green baseball cap with a white check mark balanced on top of the hangers. *Yes, that might come in handy too, thank you, Max,* she thought, mentally adding it to the list as she grabbed it.

With the gray hoodie, the white sneakers, and the cap bundled in her arms, she made her way downstairs, stepping in between Max's deep-sleep breaths. She laid the pile of clothes down beside her backpack.

One last thing, and then she was out of here. The thing she was most afraid to do.

She reached in and pulled out another resealable sandwich bag.

Pip held her breath, though she didn't need to. If Max could hear anything, it would be the sound of her heart throwing itself around her ribs. How long could it keep going at this rate before it gave up and gave out? She walked up silently behind him, to the other side of the sofa, where his head lay, and listened to the sound of his breaths as they rattled his top lip.

Pip edged closer and then crouched, cursing her ankle as the bone clicked, echoing in the quiet room. She opened the sandwich bag and held it up beneath Max's head. With her other gloved hand, she drew her thumb and forefinger close and then gently, slowly, she pushed them through Max's hair, toward his scalp. There was only so gentle she could be, pulling hairs out of his head, but that's what she had to do. She couldn't cut them out; she needed the root and skin cells attached to the hair, carrying his DNA. Carefully, she pinched her finger and thumb together around a small clump of his dark blond hair.

She jerked her hand back.

Max sniffed. A heavy breath and a stuttering in his chest. But he didn't move.

Pip could feel her wild heartbeat, even through the backs of her teeth, as she studied the hairs snagged between her fingers. Long, wavy, a few visible bulbs of skin at the root. There weren't many, but they would have to do. She didn't want to risk trying again.

She lowered her fingers into the sandwich bag and rubbed them together, the blond hairs floating down into the clear bag, almost invisible. A couple still clung to the latex glove. She wiped those off against the sofa, sealed the bag, and stepped away.

Back in the hall, she packed Max's hoodie away into the large plastic freezer bag, his shoes and his cap into another, before stuffing them all into the main body of her backpack. It was full now, the zipper struggling to fasten, but that was OK, she had everything she needed. She tucked the bag with Max's hair into the front pocket instead, and then hoisted it all up onto her shoulders.

She flicked off the light in the living room before she left, unsure why she did. The yellow lights, harsh as they were, wouldn't be enough to pull Max out of unconsciousness. But she didn't want to take the chance; he still had to be like this when she got back in a few hours. Pip trusted the pills, as Max had surely done himself countless times in his life, but she didn't trust anything that much. Not even herself.

Pip scooped up the keys from the floor and walked out, pulling the front door closed behind her. She pressed a button on the fob and the taillights blinked on Max's black car, telling her that it was unlocked. She opened the driver's-side door, dropped the keys on the seat, and then shut it again, leaving the car behind her as she walked down the drive and down the street.

She pulled off the latex gloves. They were stuck fast to the sweat on her hands—sweat or Stanley's blood, it was too dark to tell now—and she had to use her teeth to rip them free. The evening air felt cold and too solid on the bare skin of her fingers as she stuffed the used gloves in her pocket.

Her car was waiting for her just ahead. Waiting for her and the next step of the plan.

Her alibi.

THIRTY-EIGHT

"Why, hello, quelle surprise, what are you doing here, muchacha?"

The smile dropped out of Cara's face a moment later, as she opened the door fully, the light from the hallway lighting up Pip's eyes. She could tell. Pip knew she would be able to tell. Not just a friend, more like a sister. Something was off in Pip's eyes, behind them, this long, horrific day imprinted in them somehow, and of course Cara knew. But she could never know. Not all of it. Just like the others. Ignorance kept them safe from her.

"What's wrong?" Cara said, her voice dropping an octave. "What's happened?"

Pip's lower lip trembled, but she held it in.

"I—I, um . . . ," she started shakily. Torn between needing Cara and needing to keep her safe, safe from her. Between her old, normal life—standing right in front of her, blinking—and whatever was left to her now. "I need your help. You don't have to say yes, you can tell me to go away, but—"

"Of course," Cara cut her off, reaching for her shoulder and guiding her through the door. "Come in." They paused in the hallway, the look in Cara's eyes as serious as Pip had ever seen them. "What's happened?" she asked. "Is Ravi OK?"

Pip shook her head, sniffed. "Yeah, no, Ravi's fine. It has nothing to do with him."

"Your family?"

"No, it's . . . they're all OK," Pip said. "I just, I need to ask you to help me with something, but you can never know why. You can never ask me, and I can never tell you."

The background sounds of a TV cut out, shuffling footsteps drawing their way. Oh fuck, Steph wasn't here, was she? Nonono. No one else could know about this, just those people, the ones who would have looked for Pip when she disappeared.

It wasn't Steph. Naomi appeared in the hallway, a hand raised in a small wave.

Pip didn't think she'd be here, she hadn't planned on Naomi being here. But it was OK, now that she thought about it: Naomi was one of them, intertwined in this same full circle. If Cara was a sister, then Naomi was too. And Pip couldn't not involve her now, the plan shifting and adapting to take in one more person.

Cara hadn't seen her sister.

"What the fuck are you talking about, Pip?" she said urgently.

"I just said, I can't tell you. I can never tell you."

They were interrupted, not by Naomi, but by a high-pitched, eight-bit ringtone coming from Pip's front pocket.

Her eyes widened, and so did Cara's.

"Sorry, I have to take this," Pip said, reaching for the burner phone to accept the call. She turned her back on Cara and lifted the small phone to her ear.

"Hey," she said.

"Hey, it's me," said Connor's voice on the other end.

"Everything OK?" Pip asked him, and she could hear Naomi behind her, asking Cara what the fuck was going on.

"Yes. All good," Connor said, slightly breathless. "Jamie's driving us to Norwalk now. The phone is in place, behind that first rock. We didn't go in the gate, didn't even look. All good."

"Thank you," Pip said, her chest releasing slightly. "Thank you, Co—" She almost said his name, stopping herself before it was too late with a glance up at Cara and Naomi. They shouldn't know who else was involved, that kept them safer. All of them. "This is the last time we talk about this. It never happened, understand? Never mention it, not on the phone, not in texts, not even to each other. Never."

"I know, bu—"

Pip spoke over him.

"I'm going to hang up now. And I want you to destroy that phone. Snap it in half, and the SIM card too. Then dump it in a public garbage can."

"Yeah, yeah, OK, we will," Connor said, and then to his brother: "Jamie, she's telling us to break the phone, throw it in the trash while we're out."

She heard Jamie's distant voice over the sound of moving wheels.

"Consider it done."

"I have to go now," Pip said. "Bye." *Bye.* Such a normal word for such an un-normal conversation.

Pip cut off the call and lowered the phone, turning slowly to look at Cara and Naomi, gathered behind her, an identical look of confusion and fear in their eyes.

"What the fuck?" Cara said. "What's going on? Who were you talking to? What phone is that?"

Pip sighed. There was a time she'd told Cara everything, every mundane detail of her day, and now she could tell her nothing. Nothing except her part. A wedge between them that had never been there before. Solid, unspeakable.

"I can't tell you that," Pip said.

"Pip, are you OK?" Naomi stepped in now. "You're scaring us."

"Sorry, I—" Pip's voice croaked away from her. She couldn't do this now. She wanted to explain, but the plan wouldn't let her. She had to make another call. Right now. "I'll explain in a minute, as much as I can, but first I need to call someone else. Can I use your landline?"

Cara blinked at her, Naomi's eyebrows drawing down to eclipse her eyes.

"I'm confused," Cara said.

"It'll be two minutes, then I'll explain. Can I use the phone?"

They nodded, slow and unsure.

Pip hurried past them to the kitchen, hearing their steps as they followed her in here. She dropped her backpack onto one of the dining chairs and unzipped the front pocket, pulling out Christopher Epps's business card. She grabbed the Wards' landline handset and typed in his cell phone number, memorizing three digits at a time.

Cara and Naomi were watching her as she raised the phone, ringing in her ears.

A crackling sound down the line, someone clearing their throat.

"Hello?" Epps said, an uncertainty in his tone, the uncertainty of an unknown number at night.

"Hi, Christopher Epps?" Pip said, ironing out the rasp in her voice. "It's me, Pip Fitz-Amobi."

"Oh." He sounded surprised. "Oh," he said it again, reclaiming control, another clearing of his throat. "Right."

"Sorry," Pip said, "I know it's a Saturday evening, and it's getting late. But when you gave me your card, you said to call anytime."

"Yes, I did say that, didn't I?" Epps said. "So, what can I do for you, Miss Fitz-Amobi?"

"Well." Pip coughed lightly. "I did what you said to me after the mediation meeting. Went away and thought about it for a couple of weeks, when things weren't so *emotional*."

"Right? And have you come to any conclusions?"

"Yes," Pip said, hating what she was about to say, imagining the triumphant look on Epps's arrogant face. But he had no idea what the real reason for this call was. "So, I've thought about it, a lot, and I think you're right that it's in everyone's best interest to avoid a court case. So, I think I'm going to take the deal you offered. The seven thousand dollars damages."

"That's very good to hear, Miss Fitz-Amobi. But it wasn't just the seven thousand, remember?" Epps said, overenunciating his words like he was talking to a small child. "The most important part of the deal was the public apology and a statement issued, recanting the libelous claims, and explaining that the voice recording you posted was fabricated. My client won't accept any deal without those."

"Yes," Pip said, gritting her teeth. "I remember, thank you. I'll do all of that. The money, the public apology, recant the statement and the voice recording. I'll do it all. I just want this to be over now."

She heard a satisfied sniff down the line. "Well, I have to say, I think you're making the correct decision here. This works out the best for everyone involved. Thank you for being so mature about it."

Pip's grip tightened around the phone, cutting into her hand, red flashing behind her eyes until she blinked it away. "No, sure, and thank you for talking some sense into me," she said, recoiling at her own voice. "So, I guess you can now tell Max that I accept the deal."

"Yes, I will," Epps said. "He will be very pleased to hear it. And on Monday, I shall give your lawyer a call and get everything rolling. Sound good?"

"Sounds good," Pip said; a meaningless word, just as empty as "fine."

"All right, well you have a good evening, now, Miss Fitz-Amobi."

"You too."

The line cut out. She imagined Epps, beyond the beeps of the dead tone, miles away, now scrolling through his phone to find another number. Because he wasn't just the family lawyer; he was a family friend. And he was going to do exactly what Pip wanted him to.

"Have you lost your mind?" Cara stared at her, eyes stretched too wide. The face had grown around them, but they were the same eyes of the nervous six-year-old she'd been when they first met. "Why the fuck did you just accept that deal? What the hell is going on?"

"I know, I know," Pip said, hands up either side of her, in surrender. "I know none of this makes any sense. Something happened, and I'm in trouble, but there's a way out of it. All I can tell you is what I need you to do. For your own safety."

"What happened?" Cara said, desperation stretching her voice.

"She can't tell us," Naomi said, turning to her sister, her eyes reshaping with understanding. "She can't tell us because she wants us to have plausible deniability."

Cara turned back to Pip. "S-something bad?" she asked.

Pip nodded.

"But it's going to be OK, I can make it OK, I can fix it. I just need your help with this part. Will you help me?"

A clicking sound in Cara's throat. "Of course I'll help you," she said quietly. "You know I'd kill for you. But—"

"It's nothing bad," Pip cut her off, glancing down at the burner phone. "Look it's just turned nine-forty-three p.m. See?" she said, showing them the time. "Don't look at me, look at the time, Cara. See? You never have to lie, ever. All that's happened is I came over a few minutes ago, made that call to Max's lawyer from your landline, because I lost my phone."

"You lost your phone?" Cara said.

"That's not the something bad," Pip replied.

"Yeah, no shit," Cara said through a nervous laugh.

"What do you need us to do?" Naomi asked, lips folded in a determined line. "If it has anything to do with Max Hastings, you know I'm in."

Pip didn't answer that, didn't want them to know more than they had to. But she was glad Naomi was here with them. It felt right somehow. Full circle.

"You just need to come with me. In the car. Be with me for a couple of hours, so I'm with you guys and not anywhere else."

They understood, or close to it, Pip could tell from the shift in their faces.

"An alibi." Cara spoke the unspoken thing.

Pip tilted her head up and down, the tiniest of movements, not quite a nod.

"You never have to lie," she said. "About any of it, any of the details, ever. All you ever need to say, need to know, is exactly what we're going to do. You're not doing anything wrong, anything illegal. You're hanging out with your friend, that's all, and that's all you know. It's nine-forty-four and you just need to come with me."

Cara nodded, and the look in her eyes was different now, sadder. It still looked like fear, but not for herself. For the friend standing in front of her, unraveling. The friend she'd known twice as long as she hadn't. Friends who would die for each other, kill for each other, and Pip would be the first one to lean on that.

"Where are we going?" Naomi asked.

Pip exhaled and gave them a strained smile. She rezipped her bag and threw it over her shoulders.

"We're going to McDonald's," she said.

THIRTY-NINE

They didn't talk much during the drive. Didn't know what to say, what they were allowed to say, or even how much to move. Cara sat in the passenger seat, her hands tucked in between her legs, shoulders arched and stiff, taking up as little space as she could.

Naomi was in the back, sitting up too straight, her back not even touching the seat. Pip glanced in the rearview mirror and saw streaks of headlights and streetlights striped over Naomi's face, bringing life back into her eyes.

Pip concentrated on the road instead of the silence. She was on I-95, southbound, trying to hit as many traffic cameras as possible. This time she wanted them to see her; that was the whole point. Airtight, ironclad. If it came to it, the police could follow the route Pip and her car had taken, through the eyes of all these cameras, retrace her steps. Proof she was right here and not somewhere else, killing a man.

"How's Steph?" Pip said when the quiet in the car got a little too loud. She'd turned the radio off a while ago; it was too eerie, too aggressively normal in what was the most un-normal drive the three of them would ever take.

"Um." Cara gave a small cough, watching out the window. "Yeah, she's good." That was it, silence again. Well, what had Pip expected, involving them in this? Asking too much of them.

Pip's eyes drew up, catching sight of the McDonald's logo on the sign up ahead, her headlights lighting up the golden *M* until it glowed. It was in Darien Service Plaza, that's why she and Ravi had picked it. Cameras everywhere.

Pip exited the highway and pulled into the service plaza, into the huge parking lot that was still heaving with people and cars, even though it had just passed ten.

She rolled forward, waiting for a space near the front, right by the huge gray-and-white building. Pulled in, turned off the car.

The silence was even louder now that the engine wasn't hiding it. Saved by a group of men, clearly drunk, squawking as they stumbled in front of the car and through the entrance doors into the well-lit building.

"Started early," Cara said, nodding at the group, reaching out across the silence.

Pip grabbed at it, with both hands.

"Sounds like my kind of night out," she said. "In bed by eleven."

"My kind of night out too," Cara said, turning around, a small smile on her face. "If it ends in fries."

Pip laughed then, a guttural, hollow laugh that split open into a cough. She was so glad they were here with her, even though she hated herself for having to ask. "I'm sorry for this," she said, staring forward at the other groups of people. People on long trips away, or long trips home, or not-very-long trips either way. People on family visits with small, sleepy children, or nights out, or even nights in, picking up food on the way. Normal people living their normal lives. And then the three of them in this car.

"Don't be," Naomi spoke up now, resting a hand on Pip's shoulder. "You'd do it for us."

And Naomi was right: she would, and she had. She'd kept the secret of the hit-and-run Naomi had been involved in. Pip had found another way to clear Sal's name so Cara didn't lose her father and her sister at the same time. But that didn't make her feel any better about what she'd asked of them now. The kind of favor you hoped would never need returning.

But hadn't Pip realized yet? Everything was returning, that full circle, dragging them all back around again.

"Exactly," Cara said, pressing her finger lightly to the badly covered graze on Pip's cheekbone, as though touching it would tell her what had happened, the thing she'd never know for sure. "We just want you to be OK. Just tell us what to do. Lead the way and tell us what to do."

"That's the thing," Pip said. "We don't need to do anything, really. Just act normal. Happy." She sniffed. "Like something bad hasn't happened."

"Our dad killed your boyfriend's older brother and kept a girl in his attic for five years," Cara said quickly with a glance back at Naomi. "You have yourself two experts at acting normal."

"At your service," Naomi added.

"Thank you," Pip said, knowing deep down how inadequate those two words were. "Let's go."

Pip opened the door and stepped out, taking the backpack that Cara was handing across to her. She shouldered it and looked around. There was a tall streetlight behind her, lighting up the parking lot with an industrial yellow glow. Halfway up the pole, Pip could see two dark cameras, one pointed their way. Pip made sure to look up, study the stars for a second, so the camera could capture her face. A million, million lights in the gaping blackness of the sky.

"OK," Naomi said, shutting the back door and gathering her cardigan around herself.

Pip locked the car and they walked together, the three of them, through the automatic doors and into the service plaza.

It still had that buzz, that same energy all rest stops had: that clash of those too heavy-eyed and those too wired, the *nearly-there*s and the *just-begun*s. Pip wasn't either of them. The end wasn't in sight yet, this long night would be longer still, but she was past the middle of the plan, leaving the checked boxes behind in the back of her mind. Burying them deep. She just had to keep going. One foot in front of the other. Two hours until she had to meet Ravi.

"This way," she said, leading Cara and Naomi over to the McDonald's at the back end of the cavernous building.

The drunk men were already there, at a table in the middle. Still squawking, but around mouthfuls of fries now.

Pip picked a booth close to them, but not too close, dumping her bag down on one chair. She opened it to pull out her wallet, and then zipped it back up before Naomi and Cara saw anything they shouldn't.

"Sit," Pip said to them, smiling for the cameras that she couldn't see but knew would be here somewhere. Cara and Naomi slid themselves along the shiny, plastic-covered booth, the material screaming against their clothes. "I'll get the food. What do you guys want to eat?"

The sisters looked at each other.

"Well, we already ate dinner, at home," Cara said tentatively.

Pip nodded. "So, just fries for you, Naomi. I don't think there's a vegetarian option, sorry. And chicken nuggets for Cara, of course, don't even need to ask. Cokes?"

They nodded.

"OK, perfect. Be back in a sec."

Pip strolled past the table of drunk men, wallet swinging from her hand, up to the counter. There was a line, three people in front of her. Pip stared ahead, clocking the security cameras posted on the ceiling behind the registers. She sidestepped a few inches so they had a good view of her, waiting in line. She tried to act normal, natural, like she didn't know she was being watched. And she couldn't help but wonder if that's what normal was for her now: an act. A lie.

Pip stuttered when it was her turn at the front, smiling at the cashier to cover the hesitation. She didn't want to eat, just as much as

Cara and Naomi didn't. But it didn't matter what she wanted. This was all a show, a performance for the cameras, a believable narrative in the traces she was leaving behind.

"Hi." She smiled, recovering. "Can I please have two chicken nugget meals, both with Cokes. And a large fries and . . . um, another Coke, please."

"Yep, sure," the cashier said, plugging something into the screen in front of him. "Want any sauces with that?"

"Um . . . just ketchup, please."

"Sure," he said, scratching his head beneath his cap. "Is that everything?"

Pip nodded, trying not to glance up at the camera behind the cashier's head as he called the order to a colleague. Because she would be looking directly into the eyes of the detective who might be watching this footage in the weeks to come, daring them not to believe her this time. It would likely be Hawkins, wouldn't it? Jason was from Fairview, so his murder would probably be dealt with by the Fairview Police Department. A new game with new players: her against Detective Hawkins, and Max Hastings was her offering.

"Hello?" The cashier stared at her, narrowing his eyes. "I said that comes to sixteen dollars, forty-seven cents"

"Sorry." Pip unzipped her wallet.

"Paying by card?" he asked.

"Yes," she said, almost too forceful, straying out of character for a moment. Of course she had to pay by card: she had to leave an indisputable trace of her being here at this time. She pulled out her debit card and tapped it against the contactless card reader. It beeped and the cashier handed her a receipt. She should keep that too, she thought, folding it neatly and tucking it inside her wallet.

"It'll just be a minute," the cashier said, gesturing her aside so he could take the order of the man standing behind her.

Pip stood off to the side, leaning against the backlit menu, still in sight of the cameras. She arranged her face for Hawkins, slack and unthinking, but really she was thinking about him studying the position of her feet, the arch of her shoulders, and the look in her eyes. She tried not to fiddle too much as she waited, in case he thought she looked nervous. She wasn't nervous; she was just here to eat some junk food with her friends. She glanced over to Cara and Naomi and gave them a small wave. See, Hawkins? Just getting food with her friends, nothing to see here.

Someone handed Pip her order and she thanked them, smiling for the cameras, for Hawkins. She gripped the three paper bags in one hand and balanced the cardboard tray of drinks on the other, walking carefully back to their table.

"Here we go." Pip passed the drink tray to Cara and slid the food bags across the table. "That's you, Naomi," she said, handing her the one at the front.

"Thanks," Naomi said, hesitating to open it. "So"—she broke off, studying Pip's eyes for answers—"we just eat and talk?"

"Exactly." Pip grinned back, with a small laugh, as though Naomi had said something funny. "We just eat and talk." She unrolled her paper bag and reached inside, pulling out her box of nuggets and her fries, a few lying abandoned and soggy at the bottom of the bag. "Oh, I've got the ketchups," she said, passing one each to Naomi and Cara.

Cara took the small packet from her, staring down at Pip's outstretched arm, her sleeve sliding back toward her elbow.

"What happened to your wrists?" she asked quietly, uncertainly, her eyes on the raw, ragged skin the duct tape had left behind. "And your face?"

Pip cleared her throat, pulling the sleeve back down over her hand. "We don't talk about that," she said, avoiding Cara's eyes. "We talk about everything except that."

"But if someone hurt you, we can—" Cara began, but it was Naomi who cut her off this time.

"Cara, could you go grab us some straws?" she asked, an older-sister edge to her voice.

Cara's gaze flicked between the two of them. Pip nodded.

"OK," she said, pushing up from the booth and over to a counter a few tables away with a straw dispenser and napkins. She returned with a few of each.

"Thanks," Pip said, piercing the straw through the lid of her Coke, taking a sip. It burned in her throat, in the gouges left by her screams.

She picked up one nugget. She didn't want to eat it, she couldn't eat, but she put it in her mouth and chewed all the same. The texture felt rubbery, her tongue coating itself with saliva. She forced it down, noticing that Cara hadn't started her own food, was staring too hard at Pip.

"It's just," Cara said, voice dipping into whispers, "if someone hurt you, I would kill th—"

Pip choked, swallowing the regurgitated food back down. "So, Cara," she said when she recovered. "Have you and Steph decided where you're going on your travels? I know you said you really wanted to do Thailand?"

Cara checked with Naomi before answering. "Um, yeah," she said, finally opening her box of nuggets, dipping one into the ketchup. "Yeah. We want to do Thailand, do our scuba diving there, I think. Steph really wants to go to Australia too, maybe do some kind of tour."

"That sounds amazing," Pip said, turning to her fries instead, forcing a few down. "You'll remember to pack sunscreen, won't you?"

Cara sniffed. "Such a Pip thing to say."

"Well"—Pip smiled—"I'm still me." She hoped that was true.

"You're not going to do skydiving or bungee jumping, are you?" Naomi said, stuffing in a few more fries, chewing uncomfortably. "Dad would freak out if he knew you were throwing yourself off a bridge or out of a plane."

"Yeah, I don't know." Cara shook her head, staring down at her own hands. "I'm sorry, this is just really strange, I don't—"

"You're doing really well," Pip said, taking a sip of Coke to force down another bite. "Really well."

"I want to help, though."

"This *is* helping." Pip locked her eyes on Cara's, trying to tell her with her mind. They were saving her life right now. They were sitting in a rest stop McDonald's forcing down fries, having a stilted, awkward conversation, but really they were saving her life.

There was a crash behind Pip. She whipped her head around, saw one of the drunk men had tripped over a chair, knocked it to the ground. But that's not what the sound was by the time it reached Pip's ears. And she was surprised, in a way, that the sound wasn't the crack of Jason Bell's skull breaking open. It was still a gunshot, blowing an unfixable hole through Stanley Forbes's chest. Staining the sweat on her hands a deep, deep, violent red.

"Pip?" Cara called her back. "Are you OK?"

"Yes." She sniffed, wiping her hands on a spare napkin. "Fine. Fine. You know what?" She leaned forward, pointed at Cara's phone lying facedown on the table. "We should take some pictures. Videos too."

"Of what?"

"Of us," Pip said. "Hanging out, looking normal. The metadata will have a record of the time and be geo-tagged. Come on."

Pip got up from her chair and moved over to the booth, sidling in beside Cara. She picked up Cara's phone and flicked it onto the camera. "Smile," she said, holding the camera out to take a selfie of the three of them, Naomi holding up her McDonald's cup in a mock-cheers.

"Yeah, that was good, Naomi," Pip said, studying the photo. She could tell the smiles weren't real, none of them. But Hawkins wouldn't.

Pip had another idea, the hairs rising up her arms as she realized where it had come from. She might just be putting one foot in front of the other, getting through the plan, but her steps weren't in a line. They were curving back on themselves, right to the start of everything.

"Naomi," she said, holding up the camera again, "in the next one, can you be looking down at your phone, angling the screen this way, so we can see it in the photo. On the lock screen, so it displays the time."

Both of them stared at her for a second, eyes flickering with recognition. And maybe they could feel it too, that all-seeing circle reeling them back along. They knew where the idea came from too. It was exactly how Pip had worked out that Sal Singh's friends had taken his alibi away from him. A photo taken by Sal, and in the background had been an eighteen-year-old Naomi, looking down at her phone's lock screen, the time on it giving everything away. Proving that Sal had been there, long after his friends originally said he left. Proving that he had never had enough time to kill Andie Bell.

"Y-yeah," Naomi said shakily. "Good idea."

Pip watched the three of them in the front-facing camera of Cara's phone, waiting for Naomi to get her positioning right, lining up the shot. She took the photo. Shifted her smile and her eyes and took another, Cara fidgeting beside her.

"Good," she said, studying it, her eyes drawn to the little white numbers on Naomi's home screen, telling them the photo had been taken at 10:51 p.m. exactly. The numbers that had helped her crack a case once before, and now they were helping her make one. Concrete evidence. Try not believing that, Hawkins.

They took more photos. Videos too. Naomi filming Cara as she attempted to see how many fries she could fit in her mouth at once, spitting them into the trash while the table of drunk men cheered her on. Cara zooming in on Pip's face while she sipped her Coke, zooming and zooming, until the shot was only of Pip's nostril, while she innocently asked: "Are you filming me?" A line they had prepared.

It was a performance. Hollow, orchestrated. A show for Detective Hawkins days from now. Weeks, even.

Pip forced down another chicken nugget, her gut protesting, foaming and simmering. And then she felt it, that metallic coating at the back of her tongue.

"Excuse me," she said, standing up abruptly, the others looking up at her. "Gotta pee."

Pip hurried across the concourse, her sneakers shrieking against the just-mopped tiles as she headed toward the restrooms.

She pushed through the door, almost crashing into someone drying their hands.

"Sorry," Pip just about managed to say, but it was coming, it was coming. Rising up her throat.

She darted into a stall, slamming the door behind her but no time to lock it.

She dropped to her knees and leaned over the toilet just in time.

She vomited. A shudder down to the very deepest parts of her as she vomited again. Her body convulsing, trying to rid itself of all that darkness. But didn't it know, that was all inside her head? She threw up again, undigested bits of food, and again, until it was just discolored water. Until she was empty, retching with nothing more to come, but the darkness remained.

Pip sat back beside the toilet, wiping her mouth with the back of her hand. She pulled the flush and sat there for a moment, breathing hard, her neck resting against the cool tile of the bathroom wall. Sweat trickled down her temples and the insides of her arms. Someone tried to push into her stall, but Pip kicked it shut with one foot.

She shouldn't stay in here too long. She had to hold it together. If she broke down then the plan did too, and she wouldn't survive it. Just a few more hours, a few more boxes to check off in her head, and then she would be clear. Safe. *Get up,* she told herself, and the Ravi inside her head said it too, so she had to listen.

Pip pushed up to her feet, shakily, and pulled open the stall. Two women around her mom's age stared at her as she walked over to the sink to wash her hands. Wash her face too, but not too hard that it cleared away the foundation covering the tape marks beneath. She swilled cold water around in her mouth and spat it out. Took one tentative sip.

Their stares hardened, disgust in the way they held their upper lips.

"Too many Jägerbombs," Pip said, shrugging at them. "You've got lipstick on your teeth," she told one of the women before leaving the bathroom.

"All right?" Naomi asked her as she sat back down.

"Yeah." Pip nodded, but her eyes were still watering. "No more for me." She pushed the food away and reached for Cara's phone to check the time. It was 11:21 p.m. They should probably leave in the next ten minutes. "How about a McFlurry before we go?" she said, thinking of that final charge on her card, another bread crumb in the trail she was leaving for Hawkins.

"I really couldn't eat anything else." Cara shook her head. "I'll be sick."

"Two McFlurries coming up." Pip stood, grabbing her wallet. She added, under her breath: "To go. Or to go in the trash when I drop you home."

She waited in line again, shuffling forward a few steps at a time. She ordered the ice creams, told the cashier she didn't care which flavor. She tapped her card to pay for them, that beep reassuring her. The machine was on her side, telling the world that she'd been right here, until past eleven-thirty. Machines didn't lie, only people did.

"Here we are," Pip said, passing the too-cold McFlurries into their hands, glad to be away from the sickly-sweet smell. "Let's go."

They didn't talk much on the way back either, driving the same route in reverse. Pip wasn't there with them anymore, she'd moved forward in time, back to Green Scene Ltd. and the river of blood on the concrete. Working through everything she and Ravi still had to do. Memorizing the steps, so nothing was forgotten. Nothing could be forgotten.

"Bye," she said, almost laughing at how ridiculous and small the word sounded, as Cara and Naomi stepped out of her car, untouched ice creams still clutched in their hands. "Thank you. I . . . I can never thank you enough for . . . but we can never talk about it again. Never mention it. And remember, you don't need to lie. I came here, made one phone call, then we drove to McDonald's, and I dropped you home after, at"—Pip checked the time on the dashboard—"eleven fifty-one p.m. That's all you know. That's all you say, if anyone ever asks you."

They nodded. They got it now.

"Will you be OK?" Cara asked, her hand hesitating on the passenger door.

"I think so. I hope so." The truth was, there were still so many things that could go wrong, then all of this would have been for nothing, and Pip would never be OK again. But she couldn't tell them that.

Cara was still hesitating, waiting for a firmer answer, but Pip couldn't give her one. She must have realized, reaching back inside to give Pip's hand a squeeze before closing the door and walking away.

The sisters watched as Pip reversed out of their drive, one final wave.

OK. Pip nodded, turning down the hill. Alibi: done.

She followed the moon and the plan, and in that moment, they were one and the same, taking her back home and to Ravi.

FORTY

Her parents were already in bed by the time Pip got home, waiting up for her. Well, one half of them was.

"I said don't be too late," her mom hissed, squinting through the weak light given off by her bedside lamp. "We're up at eight for Adventureland."

"It's only just past midnight," Pip said, shrugging from their doorway. "Apparently late nights are a lot later than that at college. I'm in training."

Her dad grunted from his half sleep, book open and cradled on his chest.

"Oh, and just so you know, I lost my phone earlier," Pip whispered.

"What? When?" her mom said, trying and failing to keep her voice down.

Another grunt of agreement from her dad, no idea what it was he was agreeing with.

"On my run, I think," Pip said. "Must have bounced out of my pocket and I didn't realize. I'll replace it next week, don't worry."

"You need to be more careful with your things," her mom sighed.

Well, Pip was going to lose or break a lot more than just her phone tonight.

"Yeah, I know. Adulting," she said. "Training for that too. Anyway, I'm going to bed now. Night."

"Good night, sweetie," her mom said, an accompanying grunt from her dad.

Pip closed their door gently, and as she walked across the landing, she could hear her mom telling her dad to put the book down if he was already asleep, for God's sake.

Pip stepped inside her bedroom, shutting the door behind her. Loudly—not loud enough to wake up an already grumpy Josh, but loud enough that her mom could hear her settling in for the night.

It smelled like bleach in here, and Pip checked inside her closet, bending down to look into the bucket. Floating lumps of clothing and duct tape. She prodded her sneakers back down, farther into the liquid. The blue markings on their sides had begun to bleach to white, disappearing against the material. As had the bloodstains on the toes.

Good. Everything was going to plan. Except, not quite. She was already late for meeting Ravi. She hoped he wasn't sitting there, panicking, although she knew him better than hope. Pip just had to wait a few minutes more. For her mom to fall asleep.

She double-checked everything in her backpack again, repacking the items in the order she thought she'd need them. She looped another hair tie around her ponytail, tying it into a loose bun, and then pulled one of the beanies over her head to secure it all, tucking in any stray strands of hair. Then she pulled on her backpack and waited by her bedroom door. Cracking it open, moving it a half inch at a time so it made no noise, Pip peeked her head out and stared down the landing. Watching the weak yellow light in the gap beneath her parents' door, cast from her mom's bedside lamp. She could already hear the soft rumbling of her dad's snores, using the in-and-out to measure the time slipping away from her.

The light cut out, leaving only darkness behind, and Pip gave it a few minutes more. Then she closed her bedroom door and walked across the hall, steps careful and quiet. Down the stairs, remembering this time to step over the one that creaked, third up from the bottom.

Out the front door into the cold again, leaning into the door slowly, so the only sound it made was the click of the lock sliding into the mechanism. Her mom was a heavy sleeper anyway, had to be, considering the grunting, snoring man she slept next to.

Pip walked down her drive, past her parked car, and onto Thatcher Road, turning right. Even though it was late, and dark, and she was walking alone, she didn't feel afraid. Or if she did, it was a dull kind of afraid, an ordinary kind of fear, near-unremarkable when placed beside that terror she'd felt just hours ago, its mark still all over her.

Pip spotted the car first: a black Audi, waiting on the corner, the intersection where Pip's road met Max's road.

Ravi must have seen her, the headlights in Max's car blinking on, carving two white funnels through the black of midnight. Past midnight. Quite-a-lot-past-midnight. Ravi would have been panicking about the time, she was sure, but she was here now.

Pip used her sleeve to open the door and dropped into the passenger seat.

"It's eighteen minutes past." Ravi turned to her, eyes wide with dread, just as she thought they'd be. "I've been waiting. I thought something bad had happened to you."

"Sorry," she said, using her sleeve to close the door again. "Nothing bad. Just running a bit late."

"'A bit late' is like six minutes," he said, eyes refusing to back down. "That's how late I was; took longer to walk through the woods to Max's house than I thought. Eighteen minutes is *a lot* late."

"How did everything go with you?" Pip asked, leaning forward to press her forehead against his, in the way he always did to her. To take on half her headaches, or half her nerves, he said. And here, Pip took on half his fear, because it was the ordinary kind, and she could handle it.

It worked, Ravi's face relaxing a little as she pulled away.

"Yeah," he said. "Yeah, everything's good on my end. Went to the ATM, and the gas station. Paid for everything on my card. Yeah, good. Rahul commented that I seemed distracted, but he just thought I'd had an argument with you or something. All fine. Mom and Dad think I'm asleep. What about your end? How did everything go?"

She nodded. "I don't know how, but everything went OK, somehow. Got everything I needed from Max's. Did you pick up the car OK?"

"Clearly," he said, indicating around the dark car with his eyes. "Of course, he has a fucking nice car too. It seemed quiet inside the house still. Dark. Did it take him long to pass out?"

"Fifteen, twenty minutes," she replied. "Nat had to hit him to buy me more time, but I think that will work better with the narrative."

Ravi thought about that for a moment. "Yes, and maybe Max will think that's why he has a giant headache in the morning. And his phone?"

"Connor and Jamie planted it around nine-thirty-ish, nine-forty. I made the call to Epps right after."

"And your alibi?" he asked.

"I'm covered. From nine forty-one to just after midnight, lots of cameras. Mom heard me go to bed."

Ravi nodded to himself, staring through the windshield at the air floating through the piercing headlights. "Let's hope we've managed to push the time-of-death by three hours at least, then."

"Speaking of," Pip said, reaching into her backpack, "we need to get back quickly and turn him again. He's already been on one side a while." She pulled out a handful of latex gloves, passing a pair over to Ravi, as well as her other beanie.

"Thanks," he said, pulling the hat on, Pip helping him to tuck in any stray hairs. Then he removed the purple mittens he'd already been wearing, stretching his hands inside the clear gloves. "These were all I could find at home. My mom's." He passed the purple mittens to Pip, who shoved them into her backpack. "Guess I know what I'm getting her for her next birthday." He started the car, the engine humming quietly, vibrating under Pip's legs. "Back roads?" he said.

"Back roads," Pip replied. "Let's go."

FORTY-ONE

The gates of Green Scene Ltd. glared at them, open but not welcoming, throwing the harsh light of the headlights back in their eyes.

Ravi pulled up just outside them, flicking the car off, and when it was quiet, they could hear the sound of another engine idling through the night. Jason Bell's car up ahead, beyond the gates, keeping their body cold for them.

Pip stepped out, shutting the door behind her, the sound like a clap of thunder in the night. But if no one could hear her screams, no one would hear that either.

"Hold on," she told Ravi as he climbed out and headed toward the open gate. "The phone," she reminded him, walking along the boulders that lined the drive, connecting road to gate. She stopped at the large rock closest to the road and stepped around it, crouching low. A sigh of relief. There, waiting for her, was Max's phone in the sealed-up sandwich bag.

Pip said another thank you in her head, sent it Jamie and Connor's way, as she reached down and picked up the phone. Through her gloves, and the plastic bag, she pressed the side button and the lock screen lit up. Her eyes jumped across it, the white light so bright that Pip saw a ghostly silver halo around it, creeping toward her like a fog. And maybe it was: there were many ghosts here now, Jason added to the five women he'd killed, and the ghost of Pip herself, untethered from time, stalking up and down the road on a computer screen. Pip narrowed her eyes and looked beyond the bright light.

"Yes," she hissed, turning to give Ravi a gloved thumbs-up.

"What've we got?" he asked, hurrying over.

"One missed call from Christopher Epps at nine forty-six. A missed call from 'Mommy' at nine-fifty-seven, and another at ten-oh-nine. And, finally, one from Dad at ten-forty-eight."

"Perfect." Ravi's mouth stretched into a smile, teeth glowing in the night.

"Perfect," Pip agreed, sliding the bagged-up phone safely inside her backpack.

They thought they were calling Max to tell him the good news, that Pip would be accepting the deal and recanting her statement. But that wasn't what they'd done; they'd fallen right into the trap Pip and Ravi had planned for them. Those calls to Max's phone had routed through the local cell phone tower here. Which meant they placed Max, and his phone, right here at a crime scene, where the police would find a dead man. At the crime scene, right in the middle of the manipulated time-of-death window.

Because Max Hastings killed Jason Bell, not Pip. And his parents and his lawyer had just helped her pull it off.

Pip stood up and Ravi reached for her hand, intertwined his fingers through hers, the plastic gloves snagging together. He gave it a squeeze.

"Almost there, Sarge," he said, pressing his lips into her eyebrow, sore from where the tape had ripped it. "Last push."

Pip inspected his hat, made sure none of his long, dark hair was poking through.

Ravi dropped her hand to clap his together. "OK, let's do it," he said.

They walked through the gates, their steps crunching alternately in the gravel. Heading for the deep red eyes glowing in the night: the taillights of Jason's car, and the quiet sigh of the running engine.

Pip stared at her reflection in the rear passenger window again, this long night etched all over her face, and she opened the door.

It was cold inside, very cold, her fingers prickling with it through the gloves as they crossed the threshold. She leaned inside and could even see her own breath, fogging out in front.

Ravi opened the back door opposite her.

"Fuck, it's freezing," he said, bending down and readying his arms, grabbing Jason's ankles through the black tarp. He glanced up, watching as Pip positioned her hands under Jason's shoulders. "Ready?" he asked. "Three, two, one, go."

They lifted him up and then Pip raised one knee to brace the body, her foot on the seat.

"OK," she said, her arms weaker now, struggling with the weight, but the promise of survival kept them going. Gently, using her knee to guide them, they twisted the roll of tarp, flipping the body over and then resting him back down on the seat. Facedown again, the same way he had died.

"How's he looking?" Ravi asked as Pip unwrapped one side of the tarp, trying to ignore the mess of the back of Jason's head. She felt detached from the person who had done that, separate somehow, because she'd lived a hundred lifetimes in the hours since. Pip prodded his neck, feeling the muscles beneath his skin, moving down his shoulders over his bloodstained shirt.

"Rigor has started," she said. "It begins in the jaw and neck, but it hasn't gotten much farther than that."

Ravi stared at her, a question in his eyes.

"That's good," Pip said, answering the unasked thing. "That means we managed to delay the onset . . . by quite a lot. It hasn't even reached his lower arms yet. Rigor mortis is normally complete within six to twelve hours. He died over six hours ago now, and it's still only in the upper part of his body. That's good," she said, trying to convince herself as much as Ravi.

"OK, good," Ravi said, the word escaping his mouth as a wisp of cloud in the cold air. "And the other thing?"

"Lividity," Pip said. She gritted her teeth and unwrapped a little more of the tarp. She leaned forward and carefully peeled up the back of Jason's shirt by an inch, peering in closer at the skin underneath.

It looked bruised, a mottled, purple-red tinge from the blood that had pooled inside.

"Yeah, it's started," Pip said, stepping one leg inside the footwell of the car to get closer. She reached over and pressed her gloved thumb into the skin of Jason's back. When she pulled it away, the mark of her thumb stayed behind, one small, white half circle, an island surrounded by discolored skin. "Yes, it's not fixed. Still blanchable."

"Which means . . . ?"

"Which means that now we've flipped him, the blood will move again, start to settle on the other side. Make it look like he hasn't already been lying in this position for almost five hours. Buy us time."

"Thanks, gravity," Ravi said with a thoughtful nod. "The real MVP."

"Right, well." Pip ducked her head and moved back out the car door. "Now those two processes are really going to kick into high gear because it's time to—"

"Microwave him."

"Will you stop saying 'microwave him'?"

"Just supplying the comic relief," Ravi said seriously, holding up his gloved hands. "That's my job in the team."

"You undersell yourself," Pip said, and then pointed to the ice packs dotted around the inside of the car. "Can you grab those?"

Ravi did, collecting them in his arms. "Still frozen solid. We got it really cold in here."

"Yeah, we did well," Pip said, moving to the front of the car and opening the driver's-side door.

"Just going to take these back." Ravi gestured at the ice packs.

"OK, rinse them off, in case they smell like—you know," Pip called. "Oh, and Ravi, see if you can find cleaning supplies in there. Antibacterial spray, some cloths. A broom, maybe, so we can do a sweep for any hairs."

"Yeah, I'll have a look," he said, running off toward the office building, kicking up the gravel around him.

Pip lowered herself into the driver's seat, a glance over her shoulder at Jason Bell, keeping her eyes on him. Alone again. Just the two of them in this small, confined space. And even though he was dead, Pip didn't trust him not to grab her when her back was turned. *Don't be silly.* He was dead, six hours dead, even though he only looked like he'd been gone for two. Dead, and helpless, not that he ever deserved any help.

"Don't try to make me feel bad for you," Pip told him quietly, turning away to study the buttons and dials on the control panel. "You evil piece of shit."

She grabbed the dial—currently on the coldest setting—and turned it all the way to the other side, the notch pointing to a bright-red triangle. The system was already on the highest number, a five, the incoming air hissing loudly through the vents. Pip held her gloved hand out in front of one and kept it there as the air went from cool to warm to hot. Like a hair dryer held close to her fingers. This wasn't an exact science; she didn't know by how much this would be able to raise Jason's body temperature. But the air felt hot enough to her, and they had some time to heat him up while they dealt with the rest of the scene. But not too long, because the heat would start to accelerate the rigor and the livor mortis. It was a balancing act between the three factors.

"Happy heating," Pip said, stepping out of the car, shutting the door behind her. She closed the other doors too, sealing Jason back up inside the warming car, his temporary tomb.

A rattling sound behind her. Footsteps.

Pip turned, a gasp ready in her throat. But it was only Ravi, returning from the office.

She told him off with her eyes.

"Sorry," he said. "Look what I found." In one hand he was holding a reusable Walmart bag filled with assorted antibacterial-spray bottles, bleach, and dusting cloths. On top of the pile was a wrapped-up extension cord, black and industrial. And in his other arm, clasped in the nook of his elbow and draped around his neck, was a vacuum cleaner. Red, with two googly eyes stuck to it, just above the hose. "I found a friend," he said, giving the machine a little shake, making it say hello. The printed brand name along the bottom looked like a toothy smile.

"Yes, I can see that," Pip said.

"And this long-ass extension cord, so we can go over any places you were, in case any hairs are left behind. The trunk too." He nodded at Jason's car.

"Yeah," Pip said, unnerved by the innocent smile on the vacuum cleaner's face, a forever-grin, just as happy to help them clear up a crime scene. "I'm afraid he's stolen your job, though."

"What, the comic relief?" Ravi asked. "That's fine, he's better suited to it, and I'm in more of a leadership role anyway. Co-CEO of Team Ravi and Pip."

"Ravi?"

"Yeah, right, sorry, nervous rambling. Still not used to seeing a dead body up close. Let's get going."

They started in the chemical storeroom, carefully stepping over and around the pool of blood. They didn't need to clean that, they would leave the blood there, untouched; Max had to have killed Jason somewhere, after all. And they needed the blood as a signal, to tell the first people on the scene that something bad—very bad—had happened here, so they'd look for a body, and find it, while Jason was still warm and stiff. That was important.

Ravi plugged the extension cord into an outlet in the larger storage room—where the machines were kept—and started vacuuming. He went over and over the places Pip pointed out to him. Everywhere she'd been dragged, everywhere she'd walked and run in a blind panic. Everywhere he'd been, too. Careful to keep a margin around the spot where Jason died, and the river of blood.

Pip worked on the shelves, a spray bottle in one hand, a cloth in the other. She went up and down the upturned shelves, the metal poles, spraying and wiping everywhere she'd touched or brushed up against. Every side, every angle. Finding the screw and nut she'd removed from the shelf and wiping those down too. Her fingerprints were already on file; she couldn't leave even a partial behind.

She climbed up the collapsed shelves again like a ladder, painstakingly wiping anywhere she might have touched—the lip of the metal shelves, the plastic vats of weed killer and fertilizer. Up to the wall and around the smashed window, even polishing the pieces of jagged glass left in the frame, in case she'd touched those.

Clambering back down carefully, avoiding Ravi as he vacuumed back and forth, and over to the toolbox on the workbench at the far end. Pip removed everything from inside it; she could have touched anything as her hand burrowed through. One by one she wiped down every single tool, even the individual drill heads and fittings. She used up one of the spray bottles and had to fetch another, carrying on. She'd touched the Post-it note about the Blue team's tools; she remembered doing it. She peeled the note off, crumpled it, and shoved it in the front pocket of her backpack to take home.

The blood had almost dried on the hammer as Pip picked it up from its resting place, clumps of Jason's hair stuck in the gore. Pip left that end as it was, wiping up and down the handle, again and again, removing any traces of herself. Replacing it close to the river of blood, staging it.

Door handles, locks, Jason's large ring of Green Scene keys, light switches, the cupboard in the office building that Ravi touched. All of it, wiped and wiped again. Once more over the shelves to be sure.

When Pip finally looked up, checking off another box in her head, she checked the time on the burner phone. It had just ticked past 2:30 a.m.; they'd been cleaning for close to two hours, and Pip was warm with sweat inside her hoodie.

"I think I'm done," Ravi said, reemerging from the larger storeroom, an empty gas can in his hands.

"Yeah." Pip nodded, slightly breathless. "Just the car to do. Mostly the trunk. And his car keys. But it's been almost two hours now," she said, glancing through the open storeroom door, back into the dark night. "I think it's time."

"To take him out?" Ravi checked.

Pip could tell he'd been about to make an oven-ready type joke but had reconsidered.

"Yes. We're going to flip him again, but I don't want the rigor to be too advanced, he needs to still be stiff when they find him. I feel like it must be over a hundred degrees in there now, maybe even higher. Hopefully it's brought his temperature back up to somewhere in the low nineties. He'll start to cool again once he's outside, one and a half degrees every hour until he reaches ambient temperature."

"Explain that to me in 'getting away with murder' terms?" Ravi said, fiddling with the top of the gas can.

"Well, if he's found and the ME initially examines him at the scene around six a.m.—in three and a half hours' time—working the one-and-a-half-degree rule backward, it should show that he died at more like nine o'clock, ten o'clock. The rate of rigor and lividity should support that too."

"OK," Ravi said. "Let's take him out, then."

He followed her outside to Jason's car, peering in the window.

"Hold on." Pip dropped to her knees beside her open backpack. "I need the things I took from Max's."

She pulled out the freezer bag containing Max's gray hoodie, and the one with his white sneakers and cap. Ravi reached for the bag with the shoes.

"What are you doing?" Pip said, harder than she meant to, making him flinch and retract his hand.

"Putting on Max's shoes?" he said uncertainly. "I thought we wanted to leave track marks through the mud, where we dump the body. The tread pattern of the shoes."

"Yes, we do," Pip said, pulling something else out of her bag. The five balled-up pairs of socks. "That's why I brought these. I'm putting on the sneakers. I'm dragging him out there." She untied her Converse and started pulling on the socks, a pair at a time, padding out her feet.

"I can help," Ravi said, watching her.

"No, you can't." Pip slid her first bulked-up foot into Max's sneaker, doing the laces up tight. "There can only be one set of tracks. Just Max's. And you're not dumping the body, I'm not letting you do that. It should be me. I killed him, I got us into this." She tied the second shoe and stood up, testing out her grip against the gravel. Her feet budged a little up and down as she stepped, but it would be fine.

"I mean, *you* didn't get us into this, *he* did," Ravi said, gesturing with his thumb back toward Jason's body. "You sure you can do it?"

"If Max can drag Jason's body through the trees, then so can I." Pip unsealed the bag with Max's hoodie and pulled it on over her own. Ravi helped her, careful not to disturb the hat covering her head, making sure she left none of her hairs behind on its collar.

"You're good," Ravi said, taking a step back to look at her. "I can at least help you get him out of the car."

Yes, he could at least help with that. Pip nodded, walking over to the back door of the car, on the side where Jason's head was. Ravi looped around her to the other side.

They opened the doors at the same time.

"Whoa," Ravi said, doubling back. "It's getting hot in here."

"Don't!" Pip said firmly, across the backseat.

"What?" He glared at her, over the tarp. "I wasn't going to sing the song. Even I know when it's stepping over a line."

"Sure."

"What I meant is that it's really hot in here," he said. "Higher than a hundred, I'd say. That was almost opening-the-oven-and-the-heat-slaps-you-in-the-face hot."

"Right." Pip sniffed. "You push him this way, I'll drag him out."

Pip managed to pull him out of the car using Ravi's momentum from the other side. Jason's tarp-wrapped feet landed on the gravel with a crash.

"Got him?" Ravi asked, coming around.

"Yeah." Pip laid him gently down. She stepped back to her backpack, opened the front pocket, and pulled out the sandwich bag with the small clump of Max's hair sealed inside. "Need this," she explained to Ravi, shoving it in the front pocket of Max's hoodie.

"You gonna keep him in the tarp?" Ravi watched her as she returned to the body, struggling to pick Jason up beneath the shoulders again, his arms now stiff and unyielding.

"Yeah, he can stay in the tarp," Pip said, grunting with the effort as she tried to drag Jason's trailing feet through the stones, glad the tarp was there so Jason's facedown dead face wasn't watching her as she did. "Max could have tried to cover him too."

Pip took a step back and she hauled.

She tried to not think about what she was doing. Building a barrier inside her mind, a fence to keep it out. It was just one of the boxes to check, that's what she told herself. Focus on that. Just a task to check off in the plan, like all the plans she'd ever made, even the small ones, even the mundane. This was no different.

Except it was, that dark voice reminded her, the one that hid at the back beside the shame, unpicking her barrier piece by piece. Because it was late at night, in that in-between time when too-late became too-early, and Pip Fitz-Amobi was dragging a dead body.

FORTY-TWO

Dead Jason was heavy and Pip's progress was slow, her mind trying to distance itself from the thing in her hands, from her hands themselves.

It was a little easier as she moved from small stones to grass, checking behind her every two steps so she didn't trip.

Ravi remained behind on the gravel. "I'll start on the trunk of the car, then," he said. "Vacuum every inch."

"Wipe down the plastic sides too," Pip called, the breath struggling in her chest. "I touched those."

He shot her a thumbs-up and turned away.

Pip leaned Jason against her leg for a moment, to take the weight, give her arms a break. The muscles in her shoulders were already screaming. But she had to keep going. This was her job, her burden.

She dragged him to the trees, Max's sneakers crunching in the dry mud. Pip laid him down for two minutes, stretched out her aching arms, moved her head from side to side to crack her neck. Stared up at the moon to ask it what the fuck she was doing. Then she picked him up again.

Hauled him between those trees and around that one. Leaves bunching up around Jason's feet as he dragged them with him, collecting them for his final resting place.

Pip didn't go in far. She didn't need to. They were about fifty feet into the woodland, where the trees started to bunch close together, barring the way. A distant hum of Ravi and the vacuum. Pip checked behind her, spotting the trunk of a larger tree, old and gnarled. That would do.

She dragged Jason around that tree, and then laid him down. The plastic tarp rustled and the grass whispered dark threats to Pip as he settled into the ground, facedown in the tarp.

She bent to one side of him and pushed, rolling his stiffening body over. Now he was faceup, and the blood inside would settle along his back once again.

The tarp shifted slightly as she'd flipped him over, one corner slipping down to show her his dead face one last time. To etch that image into the underside of her eyelids forever, a new horror waiting for her in the dark whenever she blinked. Jason Bell. The Stratford Strangler. The DT Killer. The monster who had chased Andie Bell away, creating this jagged circle, this awful carousel they were all stuck on.

But at least Pip was still alive, to be haunted by his face. If it were the other way around, as it should have been, Jason wouldn't have cared enough to be haunted by hers. He'd tried to take it away from her. He would have enjoyed seeing her like this, face wrapped up in tape, skin mottling to the color of bruise, body hard like it was made from concrete and not flesh. A wrapped-up doll, and a trophy to always remember how the sight of dead-her had made him feel. Elated. Excited. Powerful.

So, yes, Pip would remember his dead face, and she would be glad to. Because it meant she didn't have to be afraid of him anymore. She had won and he was dead, and the sight of it, the proof, that was her trophy, whether she wanted it or not.

She unfolded that same side of tarp, uncovering half of him, from his face to his legs, and pulled out the sandwich bag from Max's pocket.

She pulled open the seal and dipped her gloved hands inside, pinching some of the dark blond hairs. Crouching low, she dropped them, sprinkled them over Jason's shirt, two tucked under his collar. His dead hand was rigid and wouldn't open, but Pip slid a couple hairs in through the gap between his thumb and forefinger, coming to rest against his palm. There were only a few left in the bag now, the weak moonlight showed her. She pulled out just one more, tucking it in under the nail of Jason's right thumb.

She straightened up, resealing the bag to put it away. She studied him, creating the scene in that dark place in her mind, bringing the plan to life behind her eyes. They'd tussled, fought. Knocked over a row of shelves in the storeroom. Jason had punched Max in the face, giving him a black eye, maybe pulling some of his hair out at the same time. Look, there it was, stuck under one nail, and in the creases of his fingers, snagging on his clothes. Max had walked away angry and come back even angrier, creeping up on Jason in the storeroom, a hammer gripped in his hand. Undone Jason's head. A rage kill. Heat of the moment. Calmed down and realized what he'd done. Covered him and dragged him through the trees. Should have covered your hair, Max, while you were attempting to clear up a murder scene. He'd managed to clear up his prints from the weapon, and the room he killed Jason in, but he'd forgotten about his hair, hadn't he? Too fair, too fine to see it. Too panicked after killing a man.

Pip flicked the tarp back over Jason with her shoe. Max's shoe. Max would have made some effort to cover the body, at least, to hide it. But not too well, and not too far, because Pip wanted the police to find Jason right away, on their first search of the property.

She walked around Jason, pressing the zigzag imprint of Max's shoes into the soft mud around him, old rotten leaves bunching around the shoeprints.

Shouldn't have worn a pair of sneakers with such a unique tread pattern, either, should you, Max? And you certainly shouldn't have left your phone on while you were here, killing a man and cleaning up after yourself.

Pip turned and walked away. Dead Jason didn't call her back as she left him, laying another set of Max's tracks, back through the trees and grass, onto the gravel.

She walked through the door into the chemical storeroom, kicking mud from Max's shoes over the concrete.

"Hey, I just vacuumed in there," Ravi said with mock annoyance, a hidden smile on his face, standing in the doorway at the other end. Trying to calm her, Pip knew, make her feel normal again after what she'd just done. But she was too focused to break her chain of thought, following the unchecked boxes in her head, not many left now.

"Max brought it in, on his way back from dumping the body," she said quietly, her voice trancelike, stepping forward. Closer and closer to that river of drying blood. She planted one heel and laid down the toe of the shoe, pressing it into the blood.

"What are you doing?" Ravi said.

"Max accidentally stepped in the blood on his way back in," she answered, crouching down and dabbing the end of Max's sleeve in the river too, coming away with a small red swipe against the gray. "And he got some on his clothes. He'll try to wash this stain off at home, but he won't do a very good job."

She pulled out the sandwich bag again and scraped out the last remaining hairs, dropping them into the pool of sticky, drying blood.

Pip carried on toward Ravi, Max's left shoe leaving a tacky red zig-zag mark on the concrete, fading by the third step.

"OK, OK," Ravi said gently. "Can I have Pip back now? Not Max Hastings."

Pip shook him out of her head, breaking her faraway stare, softening her eyes as she glanced across at Ravi. "Yeah, done," she said.

"Right. I've done the trunk. Vacuumed it like four times. Did the ceiling too, and that pullout cover thing. Wiped down all the plastic parts with antibacterial spray. Turned the car off and wiped his keys too. And I've put the cleaning supplies and vacuum cleaner back where I found them. The cloths we used are in your backpack. Should have removed all traces of you. Of us."

Pip nodded. "Fire will do the rest."

"Speaking of." Ravi finally showed her what was in his hands: the gas can. He shook it to show her it was half-full. "I've managed to siphon gas out of the lawn mowers. I found this little tube thing on the shelves. You just insert it into the tank, blow into it, and the gas starts running out."

"We'll have to dispose of that tube then," Pip said, creating another item on the list in her head.

"Yeah, I thought you could do it the same way as your clothes. How much more do you think we'll need?" he asked, shaking the can again.

Pip thought about it. "Maybe three."

"That's what I was thinking. Come on, there's loads in those ride-on mowers."

Ravi led her back into the huge storeroom, the machines winking under the buzzy industrial lights. He walked them over to a mower and Pip helped him as he guided the small tube into the tank, creating a seal around the opening with his gloved hand before blowing into the tube.

A strong smell of gasoline as the yellowy-brown liquid flowed through the tube, tinkling into the gas can Pip held. When it was filled, they moved on to another can and another mower.

Pip started to feel dizzy from the fumes, from the lack of sleep, from her trip to and back from death, she wasn't sure which. It was the fumes that ignited, she knew, not the liquid, and if those were inside her then maybe she'd burn up too.

"Nearly there," Ravi said, to her or to the gas can, she couldn't quite tell.

He stood up and clapped his hands when the third can was near-full. "Need something to start the fires with too, something that will catch."

Pip looked around the cavernous room, scanning the shelves.

"Here," she said, walking over to a cardboard box filled with small plastic plant pots. She ripped several lengths of cardboard away, stuffing them in Max's pocket.

"Perfect," Ravi said, picking up two gas cans so she only had to carry one. It felt heavier than it should, the weight of the dead body still in her muscles somehow.

"We should lead the fire in here too," Pip said, dousing a row of still-full mowers in the gasoline, pouring a trail behind her as they walked back toward the chemical storeroom. "We want things to go *boom*. Blow out the windows to cover up the one I broke."

"Lots of things to go *boom* in here," Ravi said, flicking the lights off with his elbow as he followed her. He tilted one of his cans, pouring a thick trail of gas alongside Pip's as they stepped together. She doused the workbench and Ravi continued on to the shelving unit, lifting the can high to splash gasoline all over it, spattering against the plastic vats and dripping down the metal shelves.

They coated the room, the walls, the floor, a new river along the concrete, beside the weed killer in the gutter. Pip's can was almost empty, the final drops splattering out onto the ground as she avoided the pool of blood; they didn't want that to burn. The fire was to bring the police here, the blood was to send them out to Jason. That's how this night would finally end, in fire and blood, and a sweep of the trees to find what Pip had left for them.

Ravi finished his can too, threw it behind his shoulder back into the room.

Pip stepped outside and let the night breeze play across her face, breathing it in until she felt steady again. She didn't, not until Ravi was standing beside her, holding her gloved hand in his, that small gesture anchoring her. The final gas can was in his other hand.

There was a question in his eyes and Pip nodded.

Ravi turned to Jason's SUV. He started in the trunk, soaking the carpet floor and the plastic sides. Over the retractable cover and on to the soft material of the ceiling. Covering the backseats and the footwells, and into the front too. He left the can on the backseat where Jason had laid, some gas still sloshing around inside it.

Boom, he mimed with his hands.

Pip had pulled on Max's baseball cap now, over the beanie she already wore, so it would never touch her, never pick up a trace. And one last thing from the backpack before she pulled the straps over her shoulders: in went the rubber tube that Ravi had pressed his mouth to, out came the lighter that her mom used to light their Autumn Spice candle every evening.

Pip readied the lighter in her hand, pulling out the strips of cardboard.

She clicked it, and a small bluish flame emerged at the end. Pip held it to the corner of the cardboard, waiting for it to catch. She let the fire grow, whispering to it, welcoming it to the world.

"Step back," she told Ravi as she leaned forward and threw it into the trunk of Jason's car.

A whirl of bright yellow flames erupted with a loud roar, growing and spreading, licking out toward her face.

Hot, so incredibly hot, drying out her eyes, cleaving at her throat.

"Nothing cleans like fire," Pip said, handing the lighter and another strip of cardboard to Ravi as he walked back toward the storeroom.

The click of the lighter, the flame eating up the cardboard, adolescent and slow. Until Ravi threw it onto their new river, and that small flame exploded into an inferno, high and angry. The screaming of ghosts as it melted plastic and began to twist metal.

"I've always secretly wanted to set fire to something," Ravi said, returning to her, retaking her hand, fingers fusing together as the gravel crunched under their feet and the flames flickered at their backs.

"Well," Pip said, her voice rough and scorched, "arson is another crime we can check off the list tonight."

"Think we've probably got a full house by now," he replied. "Bingo."

They walked toward Max's car.

Back out the waiting gates of Green Scene Ltd., those spiked metal posts like an open jaw, spitting them out as its body withered and burned.

Pip blinked as they stepped through, picturing these gates in a few hours, yellow-and-black crime-scene tape wrapped across them, barring the way, the buzz of murmured voices and police radios in the smoky aftermath. A body bag and the squeaking wheels of a gurney.

Follow the fire, follow the blood, follow her story. That's all they had to do. It was out of her hands now.

Their fingers broke apart as Pip dropped into the driver's seat and shut herself in. Ravi opened the back door, climbing inside and lying down across the footwell, to hide. He couldn't be seen. They were taking the highway back to Fairview, through as many traffic cameras as they could. Because it wasn't Pip driving, it was Max this time, driving home after breaking a man's head open and setting fire to the scene. Here he was, in his hoodie and his hat, if any of those cameras had a view through the windows. Pressing his shoes into the pedals, leaving behind traces of blood.

Max started the engine and reversed. Pulling away just as the explosions began behind them. Those rows and rows of mowers blowing up, firing into the night like gunshots. Six holes in Stanley's chest.

A yellow flare that set the sky ablaze, growing smaller and smaller in the rearview mirror. *Someone would hear that,* Pip told herself as Max drove, another blast cracking the earth around them, much louder than a thousand screams. A billowing column of smoke smothering the low moon.

FORTY-THREE

Max Hastings got home at 3:27 a.m. after killing Jason Bell.

Pip pulled up into the drive outside the Hastings house, parking the car exactly where it had been before, at the beginning of the night. She switched off the engine; the headlights blinked off and the darkness crept in.

Ravi pulled himself up from the backseat, stretched out his neck. "Glad the gas light came on, just to give this night one last jolt of adrenaline. Really needed one last hit."

"Yeah." Pip exhaled. "That was a fun little plot twist."

They couldn't have stopped to fill up the car, of course; they were supposed to be Max Hastings, and gas stations were covered in security cameras. But they'd made it home—Pip's eyes constantly flicking to the warning light—and now it didn't matter anymore.

"I should go in alone," Pip said, grabbing her backpack and pulling out the car keys. "Be quick and quiet as possible. I don't know how deep he'll still be. You can walk home."

"I'll wait," Ravi said, climbing out the door and carefully pushing it shut. "Make sure you're OK."

Pip stepped out, studied his face in the darkness, a streak of red in his eyes as she blipped the fob to lock Max's car.

"He's unconscious," she said.

"He's still a rapist," Ravi replied. "I'll wait. Go on, get it done."

"OK."

Pip moved silently up to the front door, a glance at the taped-up cameras on either side. She slid the house key into the lock and stepped inside the dark, sleeping house.

She could hear Max's breaths from the sofa, deep and rattling, stepping forward with each in-and-out, hiding her steps beneath the sound. She wiped the car keys on Max's hoodie; neither of them had touched them with their bare hands, but she wanted to be sure.

Upstairs first, her steps light and cautious, trekking mud from the crime scene into the carpet. She flicked on the light in Max's bedroom and dropped her bag to the floor, removing Max's cap from her head and peeling his hoodie away from the one she was wearing underneath, careful not to dislodge her beanie. Pip checked the gray material for any of her dark hairs that might have caught. It was clear.

She studied the sleeves to find the one with the bloodstain. Moved silently across the landing to the bathroom. Light on. Faucet on. Dipped the bloody sleeve under the water, rubbed at it with her gloved fingers until the blood faded to a muted brown mark. She took it back to his bedroom, over to the laundry basket where she'd found it. Pushed aside the towering pile of clothes and dumped the gray hoodie in, shoving it down to the very bottom.

She untied Max's shoes, her own feet looking oversized and ridiculous in their five extra pairs of socks. The zigzag soles of his sneakers were still caked in mud, clumps falling away as Pip placed them at the very back of his closet, building up another pile of shoes around them, to hide them. From Max, not from the people who really mattered, the forensics team.

She put the cap back where she'd found it, balanced atop the hangers, and then closed the closet. She returned to her bag, putting her own shoes back on, and reached inside for the sandwich bag with Max's phone. Crept back down the stairs with it gripped in hand.

Pip shuffled down the hallway, closer to him, closer, when all she wanted was to recoil, hide, in case two bright eyes snapped open in the middle of that angular face. The face of a killer: that's what everyone had to believe.

One more step and she caught sight of Max over the back of the sofa, in the exact same position she'd left him more than six hours ago. Cheek crushed against the arm of the sofa and a thawed bag of peas, a string of saliva connecting him to it. Bruise darkening around his eye. Breaths so deep they shuddered his entire body.

He was out cold still. Pip checked, nudging the sofa, ready to duck if he stirred. He didn't.

She stepped forward and slid his phone out of the sandwich bag, back onto the coffee table. She picked up his blue water bottle, took it over to the dark kitchen to wash it out several times and refill it, so there were no traces, no dregs of the drugs along the bottom.

She placed it back on the coffee table, spout open, her eyes snapping to Max's face as he took a particularly heavy, shaking breath, sounding almost like a sigh.

"Yeah," Pip whispered, looking down at him. Max Hastings. Her cornerstone. The upturned mirror by which she defined herself, everything he was and everything she wasn't. "It sucks when someone puts something in your drink and then ruins your life, huh?"

She walked away and back out into the night, hiding her eyes from the too-bright stars.

"You good?" Ravi asked her.

A sound escaped her, a punch of breath that was almost a laugh. She knew what he'd meant, but the question hit deeper, reverberating around her gut, tucking itself in. No, she wasn't good. She could never be again after today.

"I'm tired," she said, her lower lip quaking. She shook it off, retook control. Couldn't give in yet. Not done, but so close now. "Fine," she said. "Just got to remove the tape from the cameras."

Ravi waited down the road while she did it. The same way she'd placed the duct tape earlier, sidling up against the front of the house, pulling it off, looping around the back of the house this time to remove the other. But it wasn't her doing that, of course, it was Max Hastings. And this was the very last time she had to be him. She didn't like it there, in his head, or him in hers. He wasn't welcome there.

Pip clambered over the front fence and found Ravi on the moonlit street. Neither of them had left her yet, the moon still showing her the way.

They finally pulled off their latex gloves, the skin on both their hands wrinkled and damp as Pip slid her fingers in between his, where they belonged, hoping they still did. Ravi walked her home, and they didn't speak, they just held hands, like they'd given everything already and there were no words left. Only three of them, the only three that mattered as Ravi said goodbye at her front drive.

His arms wrapped around her, too tight, like his holding her was the only thing stopping her from disappearing. Because she already had once today—she'd disappeared, and she'd said her final goodbyes to him. Pip burrowed her face into the place where his neck met his shoulder, warm, even when it had no reason to be.

"I love you," she said.

"I love you," he said back.

Pip kept those words close, forced the Ravi in her head to echo them as she silently unlocked her front door and crept inside.

Up the stairs, over the creaky one, back into her bedroom and the smell of bleach.

The first thing she did was cry.

Dropped onto her bed and wrapped a pillow around her face, taking it away just as DT had. Silent, aching sobs that retched, tearing at her throat, unpicking threads in her chest, leaving them unraveled and bare.

She cried and she let herself cry, a few minutes to grieve for the girl she could never be again.

And then she pushed herself up, and pushed herself back together, because she wasn't finished yet. An exhaustion like she'd never known before, stumbling across her carpet like a dead girl walking.

She carried the bucket with the bleach mixture carefully out of her room, stepping with the loud outward breaths of her dad down the hall, disguising her movements beneath them. Into the bathroom and the shower, slowly tipping the mixture out and down the drain. The clothes and tape left behind were sodden, white bleach marks starting to leach the color out of them.

Pip took the bucket and everything inside back to her room, pushing her door close-to but not clicking it shut; she'd be in and out over the next few hours.

From her backpack, she laid out one of the larger plastic freezer bags—now empty—to protect the carpet and tipped out the wet, bleached things from the bucket. On top of those she added everything else from her backpack that she needed to dispose of. Destroy and get rid of, so they could never be tied back to her. She knew just how to do it.

From the top drawer of her desk, she pulled out a pair of large scissors, sliding her fingers in through the red plastic handle. She stood over the pile and surveyed it all, creating new columns of boxes to check off in her head. Small, manageable tasks, one at a time.

☐ Sports bra	☐ Green Scene gloves x 2	☐ Spare underwear
☐ Leggings	☐ Used latex gloves x 3	☐ Spare t-shirt
☐ Hoodie	☐ Nisha Singh's mittens	☐ Duct tape
☐ Sneakers	☐ Cleaning cloths	☐ Burner phone
☐ Rubber tube	☐ Rohypnol pills	☐ Jason's burner phone

She started with the first item, picking up the sloppy, stained-white mess of the sports bra she'd been wearing, the rusted blood-stain gone to the naked eye, but there would always be traces of it.

"Was my favorite sports bra, you fucker," she muttered to herself as she took the scissors to them, cutting the stretchy material into small strips, and then into smaller squares. She did the same to her leggings, and her hoodie, and all the clothes that had come into contact with Jason Bell or his blood. The cleaning cloths too. Cutting and snipping, and as she did, imagining a scene fifteen miles away, the fire department arriving at an out-of-control fire at a medium-sized grounds-maintenance and cleaning company, summoned by a call from a concerned neighbor, not close enough to hear screams but close enough to hear the sound of explosions in the night, wondering if they were fireworks.

A wet pile building up in front of her, mismatched squares of material.

The gloves next, cutting the latex ones into two-inch pieces. The material of the Green Scene work gloves was thicker, harder to cut, but Pip persisted, making sure to decimate the logo. Ravi's mom's mittens too, not tied to the crime scene, but Ravi had worn them when picking up Max's car, and there might be fibers left inside; they had to be destroyed too. No room for errors or mistakes, even a microscopic one could mean the undoing of the plan and the undoing of Pip.

She cut the duct tape into two-inch pieces, finding where the gap in her left eyebrow had come from, the small hairs stuck into the tape that had wrapped her face. And finally, she snipped the rubber tube into tiny pieces. She pushed the sneakers and the two burner phones aside; she'd have to get rid of those some other way.

But the rest of it, this pile in front of her, it was all going one place: down the toilet.

Thank fuck for central sewage systems. As long as she didn't block the pipes in the house—and she'd cut the pieces small to make sure that didn't happen—everything here, all of this incriminating evidence, would end up at a public sewage-treatment center, no possible way to ever trace it back to her, or to this house. Not that they would ever be found anyway; people flushed all sorts of things. It would all be filtered out of the sewage and end up in some landfill somewhere, or even incinerated. As close to disappearing as it was possible to get. No traces. Airtight, ironclad. It never happened.

Pip grabbed the clear bag of the remaining Rohypnol pills first; she didn't like the way they were looking at her, and she didn't trust herself around them. She grabbed a small handful of cut-up material too and, treading quietly, she walked across to the bathroom, lowered her hands into the toilet bowl and dropped it all in.

She flushed and watched it disappear, the pills the last thing to be sucked away by the whirlpool.

The toilet bowl refilled as normal. Good. She shouldn't try to push it, keep it to a small handful each time, and leave several minutes between every flush, so there was no buildup anywhere in the pipes.

Pip quickly worked it out in her head. She had this toilet here, in the upstairs family bathroom, and the one downstairs near the front door. Two toilets, small handfuls, that large pile of evidence. This was going to take a while. But she had to be done before her family woke up. On the flip side, she couldn't let her exhaustion make her rush, take too much at a time and cause a blockage in the pipes.

Pip went back for a second handful, sharing it between her cupped hands as she crept down the stairs—skipped the third step—and flushed it down the toilet.

Alternating trips, to the upstairs bathroom and downstairs, leaving enough time between each to refill. Doubting herself every time she flushed, that brief second of panic when it seemed like the toilet wasn't refilling and oh shit she must have blocked it, she was finished, it was over, but the water always came back.

She wondered if the fire department had called the police in as soon as they saw the burnt-out car and smelled the accelerant. It was a clear case of arson. Or would they wait until they had the fire under control and could see the bloody concrete floor in the ruined building?

Another handful. Another flush. Pip resting her mind in the repetition, just letting her hands do all the work for her, all the thinking. Up and down, to the pile and out.

At six a.m., her mind stirred back to life behind her dried-out eyes, wondering if the police were now just arriving at the smoky scene, nodding as the firefighters pointed out the obvious signs of foul play. It was clear someone had been badly hurt here, maybe even killed. "Look, that hammer, we think that might have been the weapon." Were they starting their searches of the surrounding area? It wouldn't take long for them to find the tarp, and the dead man inside it.

Would a detective be called to the scene then? Would it be Hawkins, disturbed from his Sunday sleep-in, pulling on his dark green jacket while he made a call to the crime-scene technicians and told them to meet him there right away?

Down the stairs. Flush. Up the stairs. Handful.

"Secure the crime scene," Hawkins would be barking, the too-early-morning chill biting at his face and his eyes. "Where's the ME? No one else goes near the body until I have photographs and a cast of those footwear impressions."

Flush.

Time had positioned itself, halfway between six and seven. The medical examiner should be at the scene now, wearing a plastic forensics suit. Which would they do first? Take the temperature of the body? Feel his muscles for the state of rigor? Press their thumb into the skin of Jason's back to see if the skin discoloration was still blanchable? Warm, stiff, blanchable: Pip repeated it in her head like a mantra. *Warm. Stiff. Blanchable.*

Were they right now, at this very second, doing those tests, working out the possible time frame in which this man died? Making initial observations, taking photographs? Hawkins watching it all from a distance. Was it happening right now? Fifteen miles away and the person it all came down to, the one who decided whether Pip got to live or whether she didn't.

Down the stairs. Flush.

Had they worked out who the dead man was yet? Detective Hawkins knew him—acquaintances, friends—he should recognize his face. When would he tell Dawn Bell? When would he call Becca?

Pip's fingers scrabbled against the clear plastic bag on the carpet. This was it, there were just four pieces left. One that looked like it was once part of her leggings, two pieces of latex glove, and a swatch of her hoodie.

Pip straightened up and took a ceremonial breath before she flushed, watching that very last swirl of the water, taking everything away, disappearing it.

It was all gone.

It had never happened.

Pip stripped off her clothes and showered again. There was nothing on her skin, but it still felt unclean, marked in some way. She put her black hoodie and leggings at the top of her laundry basket; there shouldn't be anything incriminating on them, but she should still wash them on high, to be sure.

She pulled on a pair of pajamas and rolled herself up in her comforter, shivering beneath it.

She couldn't close her eyes. It was all she wanted to do, but she knew she couldn't, because any second now . . .

Pip heard the sounds of the alarm from her parents' bedroom, that squawking birdsong that was meant to be gentle, but it wasn't because her mom had the volume on her phone too loud. Pip thought it sounded like the end of the world, a swarm of headless pigeons throwing themselves against the window.

It was seven-forty-five a.m. Far too early for a Sunday. But Pip's parents had promised to take Joshua to Adventureland.

Pip would not be going to Adventureland.

She couldn't, because she'd spent all night throwing up and sitting on the toilet. Alternating between the two as her stomach cramped and shuddered. Flushing a hundred times and ending up right back there, leaning over the toilet. That's why the bucket was in her room, why it smelled of bleach. She'd tried to drown the vomit smell out of it.

Pip heard murmuring down the hall as her mom woke up Josh, a small yap of excitement from him as he remembered the reason for the early morning. Voices back and forth, the sound of her dad rolling out of bed, that loud sigh he did as he stretched.

A gentle rap of knuckles on Pip's door.

"Come in," Pip said, her voice scratchy and foul. She didn't even need to try to sound sick; she sounded broken. Was she broken? She thought she already had been before the longest day had begun.

Her mom poked her head inside and her face wrinkled up immediately.

"Smells like bleach in here," she said, confused, her eyes circling the bucket positioned by Pip's bed. "Oh no, honey, are you sick? Josh said he heard the toilet flushing throughout the night?"

"Been puking since about two a.m." Pip sniffed. "And the other thing. Sorry, I was trying not to wake anyone. Brought the bucket in here, but it smelled like puke so I cleaned it with toilet bleach."

"Oh no, sweetie." Her mom came over to sit on her bed, pressed the back of her hand against Pip's forehead.

Pip almost broke right there and then, at her touch. At the devastating normality of this scene. At a mother who didn't know how close she'd come to losing her daughter. And maybe she still would, if the plan went wrong, if the numbers the medical examiner was telling

Hawkins right now weren't what she needed them to be. If she'd overlooked something that the autopsy would find.

"You do feel warm. You think it's a bug?" she said, her voice as soft as her touch, and Pip was so glad to be alive to hear it again.

"Maybe. Or maybe something I ate."

"What did you eat?"

"McDonald's," Pip said with a closed-mouth smile.

Her mom widened her eyes in a *there you go.* She glanced behind her, at the door. "I told Josh we'd go to Adventureland today," she said, uncertainly.

"You guys should still go," Pip said. *Please go.*

"But you're not well," her mom said. "I should stay and take care of you."

Pip shook her head. "Honestly, I haven't thrown up in a while now. I think it's over. I just want to get some sleep. Really. I want you guys to go." She watched her mom's eyes flicker as she considered. "And just think about how annoying Josh will be if you don't go."

Her mom smiled, tapped Pip under the chin, and Pip hoped she hadn't felt the way it had quivered. "Can't argue with you there. You sure you'll be OK, though? Maybe I can get Ravi to come check in on you."

"Mom, really, I'm OK. I'm just going to sleep. Day-sleeping. Practicing for college."

"OK. Well, let me at least get you a glass of water."

Her dad had to come in as well, of course, after being told she wasn't well and not coming.

"Oh no, not my little pickle," he said, sitting beside her and making the entire bed sink, Pip almost rolling onto his lap because there was no strength left in her. "You look terrible. Soldier down?"

"Soldier down," she replied.

"Drink lots of water," he said. "Plain food only, even though it pains me to say that. Plain toast, rice."

"Yeah, I know, Dad."

"OK. Mom says you lost your phone, and apparently you told me that last night, but I remember no such thing. I'll call the landline in a few hours, check you're still alive."

He was about to walk out her door.

"Wait!" Pip sat up, scrabbling against the comforter. He hesitated at the threshold. "Love you, Dad," she said quietly, because she couldn't remember the last time she'd said it, and she was still alive.

A grin broke across his face.

"What do you want from me?" he laughed. "My wallet's in the other room."

"No, nothing," she said. "I was just saying."

"Ah, well, I'll just say it too, then. Love you, pickle."

Pip waited until they left, the sound of the car peeling up the drive, cracking the curtains to watch as they drove away.

Then, with the very last of her strength, she pushed herself up and stumbled across the room, feet dragging beneath her. Picked up the damp sneakers she'd hidden back in her backpack, and the two burner phones.

Three boxes left to check; she could do this, crawling toward that finish line, the Ravi in her head telling her that she could make it. She slipped the back cover off her burner phone. Pulled out the battery and the SIM card. Snapped the small plastic card between her thumbs, through the middle of the chip, just as she'd done with Jason's. Carried it all downstairs.

Into the garage, to her dad's tool kit. She replaced his duct tape roll with another "Fucking duct tape" under her breath. Then she picked up his drill, pressing the trigger to watch the head spin for a moment, twisting the particles of air. She drove it through the small Nokia phone that used to live in her drawer, right through the screen, shattering it, black plastic scattering around the new hole. And again, to the phone that had belonged to the DT Killer.

One black garbage bag for the sneakers, tied up tight. Another for the SIM cards and batteries. Another for the small smashed-up burner phones.

Pip grabbed her jacket, hanging on the rack by the front door, slipped on her mom's shoes, even though they didn't fit.

It was still early; hardly anyone was out and about town yet. Pip stumbled down the road with the garbage bags in one hand, holding the jacket tight around her with the other. She could see Mrs. Yardley up ahead, walking their dog. Pip turned the other way.

The moon was gone, the sun trapped behind the clouds, so Pip had to guide herself, but there was something wrong with her eyes, the world moving strangely around her, stuttering, like it hadn't loaded completely.

So tired. Her body close to giving up on her. She couldn't really pick up her feet, only shuffle, tripping on the edges of the sidewalk.

Up on West Way, Pip picked a random house: number thirteen. On second thought, maybe it wasn't so random. To the garbage cans at the end of their drive, the one for general waste. Pip opened it and checked there were already garbage bags inside. Then she pulled the top one out, a waft of something rotten, and placed the bag with the sneakers underneath, burying it under the other trash.

To Monroe, the road where Howie Bowers had lived. Pip walked up to his house, though it could no longer be his house, and she opened the garbage can, shoving in the bag holding the SIM cards and batteries.

The last bag, the Nokia 8210 and some other kind of Nokia, with holes drilled through their middles, Pip put that in the garbage can outside that nice house on Weevil Road, the one with the red tree in the front yard that Pip liked.

She smiled up at that tree as she checked off the final box in her head. The entire night of them, done, now falling to pieces inside her mind.

The garbage was collected on Tuesdays. Pip knew that because every Monday evening her mom would call through the house: "Oh Victor, you've forgotten to take the garbage cans out!"

In two days, the burner phones and those sneakers would find themselves on the way to a landfill, disappeared along with everything else.

She was free of them, and she was done.

Pip returned home, tripping through the front door as her legs tried to give out under her. She was shaking now, shaking and shivering and maybe this is just what bodies did, in the aftermath of a night like that, destroyed by the adrenaline that had kept them going when they most needed to.

But there was no more doing. No more going.

Pip fell across her bed, too weak to even get her head to the pillows. Here would do, here was comfortable and safe and still.

The plan was over, for now. On pause.

There wasn't anything more Pip could do. In fact, she was supposed to do nothing, live life as though she had just gone out for junk food with her friends and then to bed, nothing else. Call Ravi from the landline later to tell him about her lost cell phone, so there was a record of that conversation, because of course she hadn't seen him. Go replace the phone on Monday.

Just live. And wait.

No googling his name. No driving by the house just to see. No impatiently refreshing the news sites. That's what a killer would do, and Pip couldn't be one of those.

The news would come in its own time. Jason Bell found dead. Homicide.

Until then, she just had to live, see if she remembered how to.

Her eyes fell closed, breaths deepening in her hollowed-out chest, as a new darkness crept in, disappearing her.

Pip finally slept.

FORTY-FOUR

Pip waited.

The raw skin started to heal on her face and around her wrists, and she waited.

It didn't come on Monday, Pip sitting on the sofa while the nightly news was on, her mom shouting over it to remind her dad to take the trash out.

It didn't come Tuesday either. Pip had MSNBC on in the background all day while she set up her replacement phone. Nothing. No bodies found. Kept it on even when Ravi came round in the evening, talking with haunted looks in their eyes and brief touches of their hands because they couldn't use words. Not until they were behind the closed door of her bedroom.

Had they not found him? That was impossible: the fire, the blood. Surely employees at Green Scene must know, they must have been told something was wrong, why they couldn't go in to work, the fire, the crime scene. Pip could just look them up—

No. She couldn't look anything up. That would leave a trace, a trail.

She just had to wait, fight that impulse to know. It would get her caught.

Sleep was difficult; what had she expected? She had nothing to take, and maybe she needed it even more now, because every time she closed her eyes she was scared they'd never reopen again, that they were taped down, and so was her mouth when she tried to breathe. Gunshot heartbeats. It was only the exhaustion that ever settled her.

"Hello, sleepy," Pip's mom said to her Wednesday morning, as she made her way unsteadily downstairs, skipping the third one down out of habit now. "Couple of my showings canceled this morning, so I've made us coffee and breakfast."

Pancakes.

Pip sat at the kitchen island and took a deep sip of her coffee, too hot in her still-ragged throat.

"I'm going to miss you when you go off to college, you know," her mom said, sitting across from her.

"You'll still see me all the time," Pip said around a mouthful—not hungry, but she wanted to make her mom happy.

"I know, but it's not quite the same, is it? So grown-up now, time goes like that." She snapped her fingers, glancing down at her phone as it pinged from its place on the counter. "That's weird," she said, picking it up. "Siobhan from work just texted me, telling me to put on the news."

Pip's chest closed around her heart, filling her head with the sound of cracking ribs. Her neck too cold, her face too warm. This was it, wasn't it? What else could Siobhan mean? She kept her face neutral, digging her fork through the pancakes to have something to do with her hands. "Why?" she said casually, watching her mom's downturned face.

"She just said put it on, I don't know. Maybe something's happened at the school." Her mom dropped from the chair and hurried out into the living room.

Pip waited for one moment, then two, trying to breathe down the panic rising up inside. This was it, the moment it all became real, and not real; she had to put on a show and do it right, perform for her life. She put down her fork and followed her mom.

The remote was already in her mom's hands, the TV ticking on. Straight on MSNBC, where Pip had left it last night.

A newscaster, cut in half by the scrolling text at the bottom.

Breaking News.

A crease in her brow as she spoke to the camera.

". . . in Connecticut, a town that has had more than its fair share of tragedy. Six years ago, two teenagers—Andie Bell and Sal Singh—died in what has since become one of the most talked-about true crime cases in the country. And earlier this year, a man confirmed to have been Child Brunswick, who had been living in Fairview under the name Stanley Forbes, was shot and killed. The suspect, Charlie Green, was only arrested and charged last week. And here we are now, this same small town in the news again with confirmation today from local police that resident Jason Bell, the father of Andie Bell, has been found dead."

A gasp from her mom, mouth open in horror. Pip mirrored the look on her face, shared it with her.

"Police are treating his death as suspicious and gave a statement outside Fairview Police Station a short while ago."

The shot cut away from the newsroom to a bright outside scene with a gray sky and a graying building behind that Pip knew too well. The bad, bad place.

A podium had been set up in the parking lot, a microphone reaching out the top, swaying slightly in the wind.

He was standing behind it, clean shirt, crisp suit jacket, his green padded one clearly deemed inappropriate for press conferences.

Detective Hawkins cleared his throat. "Today we sadly confirm that Jason Bell, aged forty-eight, a resident of Fairview, was found dead early Sunday morning. His body was found at his place of work, at a company he owned based in Weston. We are investigating Jason's death as a homicide, and I cannot comment any further on the details of the case, as this investigation is still in the early stages. We are appealing for any witnesses who were in the area south of Devil's Den Nature Preserve late Saturday evening, particularly in the vicinity of Woodside Lane, and may have seen anything suspicious."

No witnesses, Pip thought, telling him with her eyes through the glass of the TV screen. No one near to hear her screams. And that other thing: late Saturday evening, that's what he'd said, wasn't it? But what time did that mean? That could mean anything, really, from seven, or maybe even earlier, depending on who you asked. The term was too loose, too vague. She still couldn't know if they'd pulled it off.

"Any questions?" Hawkins paused, looked past the camera. "Yes," he pointed at someone.

A voice off-screen: "How was he killed?"

Hawkins stretched out his face. "You know I cannot tell you that. It's an active investigation."

Hammer to the head, Pip answered in her mind. *Hit at least nine times. Overkill. An angry, angry death.*

"This is awful," her mom said, hands clasped around her face.

Pip nodded.

A different voice behind the camera: "Has this got any connection with the death of his daughter Andie?"

Hawkins studied the man for a second. "Andie Bell died tragically more than six years ago, and her case was brought to resolution last year. I was personally in charge of the investigation when she went missing. I have a connection with the Bell family, and I promise I will find out what happened to Jason—who killed him. Thank you."

Hawkins stepped back from the podium with a curt wave of his hand, the shot cutting back to the newsroom.

"Terrible, terrible," Pip's mom said, shaking her head. "I can't believe it. That poor family. Jason Bell dead. Murdered." She turned to look at Pip, hardening her face. "No," she said firmly, raising one finger.

Pip didn't know what she'd done wrong with her face. Jason Bell deserved to be dead, but her mom couldn't tell that from her face, right? "What?" she asked her.

"I can tell exactly what that glint in your eye is, Pip. You are *not* getting obsessed with this. You are *not* going to start looking into this."

Pip looked back at the TV and shrugged.

Except that's exactly what she was going to do.

It's what she would do, if this really were the first time she was hearing about it. This is what she did: investigate. Drawn to dead people, missing people, chasing the why and how. It was expected, normal. And Pip had to act normal, in the way people expected.

The final part of the plan was kicking in, rehashed over and over in tense whispers with Ravi last night. Interfere, but don't interfere too much. Guide, don't lead.

The police had their killer. They just had to know where to look for him.

Pip could give them a nudge in the right direction, to find the person behind all that evidence she'd left for them. She had the perfect, expected, normal way to do it. Her podcast.

A Good Girl's Guide to Murder Season 3: Who Killed Jason Bell?

And she knew exactly who to interview first.

FORTY-FIVE

Pip's face in the near-dark, underlit by the ghostly glow of her laptop, shadows like bruises around her eyes. A voice in her ears, Jackie from the café, and her own, in an interview recorded yesterday, Cara murmuring in the background. It went perfectly: Pip pushing her just the right amount, to get her to say what she needed her to say, sentences dancing around each other and silences that were full of meaning. The way Jackie's voice hissed between her teeth as she spoke Max's name, the hairs rising up the back of Pip's neck.

She listened to it again, in the dead of night, an old pair of white earphones plugged into her laptop. Josh must have stolen her black headphones again to play *FIFA,* but that was OK; he could take whatever he wanted from her. Just a week ago she thought she'd never see him again, thought she'd become the ghost he tried not to think about. He could take whatever he wanted, and Pip would love him back twice as hard.

She studied the spiking blue lines on her audio software, the erratic picture of her own voice, firm when it needed to be, quiet when it should, up and down, mountains and valleys. She isolated a clip and copied it into a new file.

Pip imagined Hawkins listening to these same words in a couple of days, imagined him snapping to attention, pushing out of his chair as this out-of-time Pip pulled the strings. The same Pip he'd find grinning in the security footage from McDonald's if he ever needed to look. Pip couldn't include Max's name—Hawkins would have to go find it himself—but she was showing him exactly where to look.

Follow the trail, Hawkins. The path of least resistance was right here, he just had to follow it, as he had once followed it to Sal Singh. Pip was making it so easy for him. All he had to do was follow, step into the world she was creating just for him.

File Name:

Teaser for AGGGTM Season 3: Who Killed Jason Bell?.wav

[Jingle plays]

[Insert clip]

NEWSCASTER: *Fairview [. . .] a town that has had more than its fair share of tragedy [. . .] confirmation today from local police that resident Jason Bell, the father of Andie Bell, has been found dead [. . .] police are treating his death as suspicious [. . .]*

[End clip]

[Insert sound file of police siren]

PIP: Hi, my name is Pip Fitz-Amobi, and I live in a small town. Over six years ago, two teenagers were killed in this small town. A few months ago, a man was shot dead in this small town. There's that saying, isn't there? That things always come in threes, even murder. One small town and this week we learned that someone else is dead.

[Insert clip]

DETECTIVE HAWKINS: *Jason Bell [. . .] a resident of Fairview, was found dead early Sunday morning [. . .]*

[End clip]

PIP: Jason Bell, the father of Andie and Becca Bell, was found dead at his place of work in a nearby town last week.

[Insert clip]

DETECTIVE HAWKINS: *We are investigating Jason's death as a homicide [. . .]*

[End clip]

PIP: It wasn't an accident, or a natural death. Someone killed him, but beyond that, very few details of the case are as yet known. It appears the murder took place on the evening of August fifteenth, judging by information police have released when appealing for witnesses in the area. Jason was found at his place of work, a grounds-maintenance and cleaning company he owned called Green Scene and Clean Scene Limited. That's it. We might not know much, except one thing: there's a killer out there, and someone needs to catch them. Join us for a new season as we attempt to piece together this case alongside the active police investigation. Someone killed him, so someone wanted him dead, and there must be a trail somewhere. People talk in a small town. And there's been a lot of talk over the last week—the town is practically cracking open with whispered secrets and furtive glances. Most isn't worth listening to, but there is some that cannot be ignored.

[Insert clip]

PIP: Hi, Jackie. So just to introduce you, you're the owner of an independent café in Fairview, on Main Street.

JACKIE: Yes, that's me.

[. . .]

PIP: Can you tell me what happened?

JACKIE: Well, Jason Bell was here a few weeks ago, standing in line to order his coffee. He came in quite a bit. And there was someone in line in front of him, it was *[—-BEEEEEEEP—-]* [. . .] Jason shoved him back, spilled his coffee [. . .] told him to stay out of his way.

PIP: A physical altercation, would you say?

JACKIE: Yes, it was quite violent, quite angry, I'd say. [. . .] Very clear that they disliked each other.

PIP: And you said this was just two weeks before Jason was killed?

JACKIE: Yes.

PIP: Are you suggesting that *[BEEP]* might be the one who killed him?

JACKIE: No, I . . . no, of course not. It's just that I think there was already animosity between them.

PIP: Bad blood?

JACKIE: Yeah [. . .] because of what *[BEEP]* did to Jason's daughter Becca. Even though he wasn't convicted. I'm sure that gave Jason plenty of reason to hate him.

[End clip]

PIP: I don't know about you, but there's already one name on my Persons of Interest list. All of this and more coming up in episode one. Join us soon for season three of *A Good Girl's Guide to Murder: Who Killed Jason Bell?*

[Insert clip]

DETECTIVE HAWKINS: *I promise I will find out what happened to Jason—who killed him.*

[End clip]

PIP: So do I.

[Jingle plays]

FORTY-SIX

It started with a phone call.

"Hi, Pip, it's Detective Hawkins here. I wonder if you have time to come down to the station today for a little chat?"

"Sure," Pip had told him. "What's this about?"

"It's about that podcast trailer you posted a couple of days ago, about the Jason Bell case. I just have a few questions for you, that's all. It's a voluntary interview."

She pretended to think about it. "OK. I can be there in an hour?"

The hour was gone now and here she was, standing outside the bad, bad place. The graying building of Fairview Police Station, a gun going off in her heart and her hands slick with sweat and Stanley's blood. Pip locked her car and wiped her red hands off on her jeans.

She'd called Ravi to tell him where she was going. He hadn't said much, other than the word "fuck" over and over again, but Pip told him it was OK, not to panic. This was to be expected; she was indirectly involved in the case, either through her interview with Jackie or through her phone call to Max's lawyer that night. That's all this would be about, and Pip knew exactly how to play her part. She was on the outskirts of this murder, that's all, a peripheral player. Hawkins wanted information from her.

And she wanted some from him in return. This could be it: the answer to the question she couldn't shake, the lurking undertow to every waking thought. The moment Pip learned whether they'd managed to pull it off or not, whether their time-of-death trick had worked. If it had, she was free. She'd survived. She was never there and she hadn't killed Jason Bell. If it hadn't worked . . . well, not worth thinking about that quite yet. She locked that trailing thought in the dark place at the back of her mind and walked through the sliding automatic doors.

"Hello, Pip." Eliza, the detention officer, gave her a strained smile from behind the front desk. "It's all go here, I'm afraid," she said, her hands fidgeting a pile of papers.

"Detective Hawkins called me, asked me to come in for a chat," Pip replied, digging her hands into her back pockets so Eliza wouldn't see how they shook. *Calm down. Need to calm down.* She could crumble inside, but she couldn't let it show.

"Oh, right." Eliza stepped back. "I'll just go tell him you're here, then."

Pip waited.

She watched as an officer she knew, Soraya, hurried through reception, stopping only briefly to swap quick *hello*s and *how are you*s. Pip wasn't covered in blood this time, not the kind you could see, anyway.

As Soraya walked through the locked door at the back, someone else came through from the other way. Detective Hawkins, his limp hair pushed back, his face paler than usual, grayer, as though he'd spent too much time in this building and its color was leaching into him too, claiming him.

He can't have slept much since Jason's body was found.

"Hi, Pip." He beckoned her over and she followed.

Down that same corridor, from the bad, bad place to the worse, worse place. Treading in her own out-of-time footsteps again. But this one, this Pip, she was the one in control, not that scared girl who'd just seen death for the first time. And she might be following Hawkins now, into Interview Room 3, but really he was following her.

"Please, have a seat." Hawkins gestured her into a chair, taking his own. There was an open box on the floor beside him, a pile of files inside, and a tape recorder waiting on the metal table.

Pip sat on the edge of her seat and nodded, waiting for him to begin.

He didn't, though. He just watched her and the darting of her eyes.

"So," Pip said, clearing her throat. "What did you want to ask me about?"

Hawkins leaned forward in his chair, reaching for the tape recorder, the bones in his neck clicking. "You understand that even though this is voluntary, and we just want you to help us with our inquiries, I still need to record our conversation?" His eyes searched her face.

Yes, she understood that. If they seriously considered she had something to do with it, she would have been arrested and read her Miranda rights. This was standard practice. But there was a strange look in his eyes, like he wanted her to be afraid. She wasn't, she was in charge here. She nodded.

Hawkins pressed a button. "This is Detective Hawkins interviewing Pippa Fitz-Amobi. The time is eleven-thirty-one a.m. on Tuesday, the twenty-fifth of August. This is a voluntary interview in relation to our inquiry into the death of Jason Bell and you can leave at any time, do you understand?"

"Yes," Pip said, directing her voice toward the recording device.

Hawkins sat back, his chair creaking. "So," he said, "I heard the trailer for the new season of your podcast, as did hundreds of thousands of other people."

Pip shrugged. "I thought you could use some help on this case. Considering you needed me to solve two of your previous cases for you. Is that why you asked for a chat today? Need my help? Want to give me an exclusive for the podcast?"

"No, Pip." The air whistled through his teeth. "I don't need your help. This is an active investigation, a homicide. You know you cannot be interfering and posting important information online. That's not how justice works. The journalistic standards apply to you too. One might even see this as contempt."

"I haven't posted any 'important information' yet. It was just a trailer," she said. "I don't know any details of the case yet, other than what you said in the press conference."

"You released an interview with a"—Hawkins glanced down at his notes—"Jackie Miller, speculating about who might have killed Jason Bell," he said, widening his eyes as though he'd scored a point against her.

"Not the whole interview," Pip said, "just the most interesting clips. And I didn't name the person we spoke about. I know that might prejudice any potential future trial. I do know what I'm doing."

"I'd say the context made it pretty obvious who you were talking about," Hawkins said, reaching down for the box of files beside him. He rerighted himself, a small pile of papers clutched in one hand. "After I heard your trailer, I spoke to Jackie myself, as part of our inquiries." He shook the pages at her, and Pip recognized an interview transcript. He placed the transcript down on the metal table, flicked through it. *"I think there was a certain amount of bad blood between Max Hastings and Jason Bell,"* he read aloud. *"You hear these things around town, especially when you own a café on Main Street. . . . Jason must have hated Max for what he did to Becca, and how it was connected to Andie dying. . . . Certainly seemed like Max didn't like Jason either . . . A lot of anger there. It was pretty violent. I've never had a situation like that between two customers. And, as Pip said, isn't it concerning that that was just two weeks before Jason was murdered?"* Hawkins finished reading, closed the transcript, and looked up at Pip.

"I would say it's a fairly standard first step in an investigation," Pip said, not dropping his eyes, she wouldn't be the first to look away. "Finding out if anything unusual happened recently in the victim's life, identifying anyone who had any ill will toward him, potential persons of interest. A violent incident leading up to his murder, interviewing a witness. Sorry if I beat you to it."

"Max Hastings," Hawkins said, his tongue hissing three times as it tripped over the name.

"Seems like he's not very popular in town," Pip said. "Has a lot of enemies. And apparently Jason Bell was one of them."

"A lot of enemies." Hawkins repeated her words, hardening his gaze. "Would you call yourself one of his enemies?"

"I mean"—Pip stretched out her face—"he's a serial rapist who walked free, hurt some of the people I care about most. Yes, I hate him. But I don't know if I have the honor of being *his* worst enemy."

"He's suing you, isn't he?" Hawkins picked up a pen, tapped it against his teeth. "For defamation, for a statement and an audio clip that you posted to social media the day the verdict was read in his sexual assault trial."

"Yes, he was going to," Pip replied. "As I said, great guy. We're actually settling out of court, though."

"Interesting," Hawkins said.

"Is it?"

"Well." He clicked the pen in his hand, in and out, and all Pip heard was *DT DT DT.* "From what I know of your character, Pip, from our handful of interactions, I'd say I'm surprised you've decided to settle, to pay up. You strike me as the type who would fight to the very end."

"Normally I am." Pip nodded. "But, see, I think I've lost my trust in the courts, in the justice system, criminal or civil. And I'm tired. Want to put it all behind me, start fresh at college."

"So, when was it you came to this decision, to settle?"

"Recently," Pip said. "Weekend before last."

Hawkins nodded to himself, pulling another piece of paper from a file at the top of the box. "I spoke with a Christopher Epps, the attorney representing Max Hastings in this defamation matter, and he told me that you called him at nine-forty-one p.m. on Saturday, the fifteenth of August. He says that's when you told him you wanted to accept a deal he had offered you a few weeks prior?"

Pip nodded.

"Strange time to call him, don't you think? That late on a Saturday evening?"

"Not really," she said. "He told me to call him anytime. I'd been thinking about it all day and finally made the decision. I didn't see a reason to delay any further. For all I knew, he was going to file the lawsuit first thing Monday morning."

Hawkins nodded along with her words, making a note on the page that Pip couldn't read upside down.

"Why are you asking me about a conversation I had with Max Hastings's lawyer?" she asked, wrinkling her eyes in confusion. "Does that mean you *have* started to look into Max as a person of interest?"

Hawkins didn't say anything, but Pip didn't need him to. She knew. Hawkins wouldn't know about Pip's call with Epps if he didn't first know about Epps's call to Max just a few minutes later. And the only way he'd know about that was if he'd already looked into Max's telephone records. He probably hadn't even needed a warrant; Max probably gave up his phone voluntarily, on Epps's advice, thinking he had nothing to hide.

Hawkins could already place Max at the scene at the time Epps had called him and the later calls from his mom and dad; surely that was probable cause to get a search warrant of Max's house, his car? To take samples of his DNA to test against those they found at the scene? Unless the time Max was there didn't match Jason's time of death. That last unknown.

Pip tried not to let it cloud her face, staring ahead at Hawkins, a hint of interest in her narrowed eyes, but not too much.

"How well did you know Jason Bell?" Hawkins asked, folding his arms across his chest.

"Not as well as you did," she said. "I knew a lot about him, rather than knowing him, if that makes sense. We'd never really had a full conversation, but, of course, when I was looking into what happened to Andie, I did a lot of looking into his life. Our paths have crossed but we didn't really *know* each other."

"And yet you seem determined to find out who killed him, for your podcast?"

"It's what I do," Pip said. "Didn't have to know him well to think he deserves justice. Cases in Fairview don't seem to get solved until I get involved."

Hawkins laughed, a bark across the table, running his hand over his stubble.

"You know, Jason complained to me after you released the first season of your podcast. Said he was being harassed, by the press, online. Would you think it's fair to say he didn't like you? Because of that."

"I have no idea," Pip said, "and I'm not sure how that's relevant. Even if he didn't like me, he still deserves justice, and I'll help in any way I can."

"So, have you had any recent contact with Jason Bell?" Hawkins asked.

"Recent?" Pip looked up at the ceiling, as though searching through her memory. Of course she didn't have to look far; it had only been ten days since she'd dragged his body through the trees. And before that, she'd knocked on Jason's door to ask him about Green Scene and the DT Killer. But Hawkins could never know about that conversation. Pip was already connected to the case indirectly, twice. Recent contact with Jason was far too risky, might even give them probable cause to get a warrant for her DNA sample, especially with the way Hawkins was looking at her now, studying her. "No. Haven't spoken to him, let alone seen him around town in, well, it must be months," she said. "I think the last time our paths crossed would have been at the six-year memorial for Andie and Sal, remember? You were there. The night Jamie Reynolds went missing."

"So that's the last time you remember coming across Jason?" Hawkins asked. "Back at the end of April?"

"Correct."

Another note on the lined paper in front of him, the pen scratching, the sound traveling all the way up the back of her neck. What was he writing about? And in that moment, Pip couldn't shake this uncanny feeling, that it wasn't Hawkins sitting across from her, questioning her. It was herself, from a year ago. The seventeen-year-old who thought the truth was the only thing that mattered, no matter the context, no mind to that suffocating gray area. The truth was the goal and the journey, just as it was for Detective Hawkins. That's who was sitting across from her: her old self set against whoever she'd become now. And this new person, she had to win.

"The phone number you used to call Christopher Epps," Hawkins said, running his finger down a printed sheet of paper, "that's not your cell phone number. Or your home phone number."

"No," Pip said. "I called him from the landline at my friend's house."

"Why is that?"

"That's where I was," Pip said, "and I'd lost my phone earlier that day, my cell phone, that is."

Hawkins leaned forward, his lips in a tight fold as he considered what she just said. "You lost your cell phone that day? On Saturday the fifteenth?"

Pip nodded, and then said "Yes" for the recorder, prompted by Hawkins's eyes. "I went jogging in the afternoon, and I think it must have bounced out of my pocket. I couldn't find it. I've replaced it now."

Another note on the page, another shiver up Pip's spine. What was he writing about? She was supposed to be in control; she should know.

"Pip." Hawkins paused, his eyes circling her face. "Can you tell me where you were between nine-thirty p.m. and midnight on Saturday, the fifteenth of August?"

And there it was. The last unknown.

Something released in Pip's chest, a little more breathing room around her gun-beat heart. A lightening in her shoulders, a loosening in her clenched jaw. Blood on her hands that was only sweat.

They'd done it.

It was over.

She kept her face neutral, but there was a fizzing by the sides of her mouth, an invisible smile and a silent sigh.

He was asking her where she was between nine-thirty p.m. and midnight because that was the estimated time of death. They'd done it. They'd pushed it back by more than three hours and she was safe. She'd survived. And Ravi, and everyone she'd turned to for help, they would be OK too. Because Pip couldn't possibly have killed Jason Bell; she'd been somewhere else entirely.

She couldn't be too eager to tell him, or too rehearsed.

"That's the night Jason Bell was killed?" she asked, checking.

"Yes, it was."

"Erm, well, I went over to my friend's house—"

"Which friend?"

"Cara Ward, and Naomi Ward," Pip said, watching as he took note. "They live on Hillside. That's where I was when I made the phone call to Christopher Epps at . . . what time did you say?"

"Nine-forty-one p.m.," Hawkins said, the answer ready on the tip of his tongue.

"Right, nine-forty-ish. And I arrived at their house several minutes before then, so I guess at nine-thirty I would have been driving to theirs, across town."

"OK," he said, "and how long were you at the Wards' house?"

"Not long," Pip said.

"No?" He studied her.

"No, we were only there for a little while before we decided we were all hungry. So I drove the three of us to go get some food."

Hawkins scribbled something else. "Food?" he said. "Where did you go?"

"To McDonald's," Pip said with a small shameful smile, dipping her head. "The one in Darien Service Plaza, off I-95."

"The service plaza?" He chewed his pen. "Was that the closest place you could have gotten food?"

"Well, it was the closest McDonald's that we knew would definitely be open."

"Which rest stop? Southbound? Northbound?"

"South."

"And what time did you arrive?"

"Um . . ." Pip thought about it. "I wasn't really keeping track of the time, especially as I didn't have a phone, but if we left not long after my phone call to Epps, then we must have gotten there just after ten-ish."

"And you said you drove? In your car?" he asked.

"Yep."

"What kind of car do you have?"

Pip sniffed. "It's a VW Beetle. Gray."

"License plate number?"

She recited it to him, watching as he noted it down and underlined it.

"So you arrived at McDonald's around ten-ish," he said. "Isn't that a little late for dinner?"

Pip shrugged. "Still a teenager, what can I say?"

"Had you been drinking?" he asked her.

"No," she said firmly, "because that would have been a crime."

"That it would," he said, eyes flicking back down his page of notes. "And how long were you at this McDonald's for?"

"Yeah, a while," Pip said. "We got our meals and we sat there for like an hour and a half-ish, I'd guess. Then I went up and got us a couple of ice creams for the journey back. I could check on my banking app what time that was; I paid for the food."

Hawkins shook his head slightly. He didn't need to see it on her phone; he had his own ways of verifying her alibi. And there he would see her on the footage, clear as day, standing in line, avoiding eye contact with the camera. Two separate payments made by her card. Airtight, Hawkins.

"All right. So you think you left McDonald's around eleven-thirty?"

"That would be my best guess, yes," she said. "Without checking."

"And where did you go from there?"

"Well, home," she said, lowering her eyebrows because the answer was too obvious. "I drove us back to Fairview, dropped the Ward sisters home, and then I drove back to my house."

"What time did you get back to your house?"

"Again, I wasn't really keeping an eye on the time, especially because I didn't have my phone," she said. "But when I got in, my mom was still waiting up in bed for me, and it must have been after twelve because she made some comment about it being after midnight. We were getting up early the next morning, see."

"And then?" He glanced up.

"And then I went to bed. To sleep."

Covered, for the entire time-of-death window. Pip could see it playing out in the new lines wrinkling across Hawkins's forehead. Of course, she could be lying; maybe that's what he was thinking. He'd have to check. But she wasn't lying, not about this part, and all the evidence was there, just waiting for him.

Hawkins exhaled, running his eyes down his page again, something troubling him, Pip could see it in his eyes. "Interview paused at eleven-forty-three." He clicked stop on the machine. "I'm just going to grab a coffee," he said, rising from his chair, gathering up the files. "Would you like one?"

No, she didn't. She felt sick on the comedown from the adrenaline, her gut finally untwisting now she knew she'd survived, she'd won, that Max had killed Jason and it couldn't possibly have been her. But it hadn't untwisted all the way; it was that look in his eyes she couldn't work out. Hawkins was waiting for an answer.

"Yes, please," she said, even though she didn't want to. "Milk, no sugar." An innocent person would take the coffee, someone who had nothing to hide, nothing to worry about.

"Two minutes." Hawkins smiled at her, shuffling out the door. It clicked shut behind him, and Pip listened to the muffled clip of his shoes, carrying him down the hall. Maybe he was going to get coffee, but he was probably also handing that new information off to another officer, directing them to start looking into her alibi.

She exhaled, slumped in her chair. She didn't have to perform just now, no one was watching. Part of her wanted to cup her hands over her face and cry into them. Bawl. Scream. Laugh. Because she was free and it was over. She could lock that terror away and never let it out again. And maybe one day, years from now, she'd even forget about it, or life would have dulled its edges, made her forget the feeling of almost dying. Only a good life would do that, she thought. A normal one. And maybe, maybe, that's what she'd have. Maybe she'd just earned it back.

Pip's phone vibrated in her pocket, against her leg. She pulled it out and looked at the screen.

A text from Ravi:

How's your day going?

They had to be careful texting each other; that left a permanent record. Most of their texts were in code now, unassuming, or simply arranging a time to speak. *How's your day going?* really meant *What's happening, did it work?* Not to any outside eyes, but a secret language they were working out together, like the million small ways they had of saying *I love you.*

Pip flicked through the keyboard onto the emojis. She swiped through until she found the thumbs-up symbol and she sent that, just that. Her day was going well, thanks, was what it could mean. But really what it meant was: *We did it. We're in the clear.* Ravi would understand that. He'd be blinking at his screen right now, and then letting out a long breath, the relief a physical sensation, unraveling inside him, changing the way he sat in his chair, the shape of his bones, the feel of his skin. They were safe, they were free, they were never there.

Pip slipped her phone away as the door into the interview room clattered open, Hawkins walking in back-first to push the door, his hands filled with two cups.

"Here." He passed one over to her.

"Thank you," she said, cupping it between her hands, forcing down a small sip. Too bitter, too hot, but she smiled at him in thanks anyway.

Hawkins didn't take a sip. He put his cup down on the table and pushed it away from him. Reached out and pressed a button on the tape recorder.

"Interview commenced at"—he pulled up his sleeve to glance at his watch—"eleven-forty-eight."

He watched Pip for a second and she watched him. What more did he have to ask her? She'd explained her call to Epps and she'd given him her alibi—what else could he need to know from her? Pip couldn't think. Had she missed something? No, everything had gone to plan, she couldn't have missed something. *Don't panic, just sip, listen, and react.* But first she had to wipe her hands because Stanley's blood was back.

"So," Hawkins said suddenly, tapping one hand against the table. "This podcast, this investigation, you're planning to carry on with it?"

"Kind of see it as my duty," Pip said. "And, like you said, once I've started something, I like to see it through to the end. Stubborn like that."

"You know you cannot publicly post anything that would hamper our investigation?" he said.

"Yes, I do know that. And I won't. I don't know anything. Vague theories and background are all I've got at the moment. I've recently learned a lesson about online defamation, so I won't post anything without 'allegedly' or 'according to a source.' And if I do find anything concrete, I'd come to you first anyway."

"Oh," Hawkins said. "Well, I appreciate that. So, with this podcast, how do you record your interviews?"

Why did he need to know that? Or was this just idle chitchat while he waited on something? What—for a colleague to look into her alibi? Surely that would take hours.

"Just this audio software," Pip said. "Or if it's a phone call, I have an app that can do it."

"And do you use microphones, say, if you were recording someone face to face?"

"Yes." Pip nodded. "Microphones that plug in by USB to my laptop."

"Oh, that's very clever," he said.

Pip nodded. "Bit more compact than this guy," she said, gesturing her head toward the tape recorder.

"Yes," Hawkins laughed. "Quite. And do you have to wear headphones when you're interviewing someone? Listen through those while you record?"

"Well," Pip said, "yes, I put on my headphones at the start to check the levels, see whether they are too close to the microphone or there's background noise. But I don't usually need to wear them throughout an interview."

"Oh, I see," he said. "And do they need to be specialist headphones, for that purpose? My nephew wants to start a podcast, see, and he's got a birthday coming up."

"Oh right." Pip smiled. "Um, no, mine aren't specialist. Just some big noise-canceling ones that go over your ears."

"And can you use them for everyday use too?" Hawkins asked. "Listening to music, or podcasts, even?"

"Yeah, I do that," she said, trying to understand the look in Hawkins's eyes. Why were they talking about this? "Mine connect by Bluetooth to my phone. Good for music when you're running or walking."

"Ah, so good for everyday use, then?"

"Yep." Pip nodded slowly.

"Would you say you use them daily? Don't want to get him something he won't use, especially if they're expensive."

"Yeah, I use them all the time."

"Ah great." Hawkins smiled. "Do you know what brand yours are? I've had a look on Amazon and some are ridiculously expensive."

"Mine are Sony," she said.

Hawkins nodded, a shift in his eyes, almost a flicker.

"Black?" he asked.

"Y-yes," Pip said, her voice catching in her throat as her mind doubled back, trying to understand what was going on here. Why she had a sinking feeling in her gut; what had it realized that she hadn't?

"*A Good Girl's Guide to Murder,*" Hawkins said, running one hand up his sleeve, fidgeting. "That's the name of your podcast, isn't it?"

"Yes."

"Good name," he said.

"It has pizzazz," Pip replied.

"You know, there's just one other thing I wanted to ask you." Hawkins sat back, one hand crawling down toward the outside pocket of his jacket. "You said you haven't had any contact with Jason Bell. Not since the memorial in April, right?"

Pip hesitated. "Right."

A twitch in Hawkins's cheek as he dropped her eyes, glancing down at his fingers as they dug inside his pocket, bulky with something Pip finally noticed. "Explain to me, then, why your headphones, the ones you use on a daily basis, were found inside the home of a murdered man you've had no contact with in months?"

He pulled something out. A clear bag with a red strip at the top reading *Evidence.* And inside the bag were Pip's headphones. Undeniably them: the *AGGGTM* sticker Ravi had had made for her wrapped around one side.

They were hers.

Found at Jason Bell's house.

And Hawkins had just made her admit it on tape.

FORTY-SEVEN

The shock didn't last long, not before the panic set in. Curdling in her stomach, rising up her spine, quick as insect legs or a dead man's fingers.

Pip stared at her headphones in the evidence bag and she didn't understand. No, that couldn't be right. She'd seen them in the last week, hadn't she? When she was working on the audio of Jackie's interview. No, no, she hadn't been able to find them; she thought Josh had borrowed them again.

No, the last time she'd had them was . . . *that* day. She'd taken them off, put them in her backpack before knocking on Nat's door. But then Jason grabbed her.

"Are these yours?" Hawkins asked, his gaze a physical sensation on her face, an itch she couldn't ignore, watching her for any giveaway. She couldn't give him one.

"They look similar," Pip said, speaking slowly, assuredly over the panic and her hummingbird heart. "Can I see them closer?"

Hawkins slid the evidence bag across the table, and Pip stared down at the headphones, pretending to study them while she bought herself time to think.

Jason had had her backpack in his car. She'd checked before she and Ravi left the scene and she thought she had everything she'd packed that afternoon. She did, except the headphones. She hadn't been thinking about them because they'd gone in after. But where, when . . .

No. That sick fuck.

Jason must have taken them out. When he left her there, wrapped up in tape, he went home. He looked through her bag. He found the headphones and he took them. Because they were his trophy. The symbol for his sixth victim. The thing he would clutch close to relive the thrill of killing her. Her headphones were his trophy. That's why he took them.

That sick fuck.

Hawkins cleared his throat.

Pip glanced up at him. How should she play this? How could she play this? Was there any play left to make? He'd caught her in a lie, a direct link to the victim.

Fuck.

Fuck.

Fuck.

"Yes," she said, quietly. "Those are mine, of course. The sticker."

Hawkins nodded, and now Pip understood that look in his eyes and she hated him for it. He'd trapped her. He'd caught her. Spun a web she couldn't see until it was wrapped around her, cutting off her air. Not free, not safe, not free.

"And why did a forensics team find your headphones inside Jason Bell's house?"

"I—I," Pip stuttered. "I honestly cannot tell you. I don't know. Where were they?"

"In his bedroom," Hawkins said. "Top drawer of his bedside table."

"I don't understand," Pip said, and that wasn't true because she knew exactly why they were there, how they got there. But she couldn't find any other words because her mind was busy, the plan shattering into a million pieces, cascading behind her eyes.

"You said you use your headphones daily? 'All the time,'" he quoted her. "Yet you haven't had contact with Jason Bell since April. So how did your headphones get there?"

"I don't know," she said, shuffling in her seat. No, don't shuffle, that makes you look guilty. Stay still, stare back. "I use them all the time, but I haven't seen them lately—"

"Define 'lately'?"

"I don't know, maybe a week or more," she said. "Maybe I left them somewhere. . . . I can't really remember."

"No?" Hawkins said lightly.

"No." Pip stared him down, but her eyes were weaker than his. Blood on her hands, gun in her heart, bile at the back of her throat and a cage tightening around her, squeezing the skin on her arms. Biting, like the duct tape had. "I'm as confused as you are."

"You have no explanation?" Hawkins said.

"No, none," Pip said. "I didn't realize they were missing."

"So, they can't have been gone long?" he asked. "Maybe nine or ten days? Could you have lost them on the same day you lost your phone?"

Pip knew then. He didn't believe her. He wouldn't follow the path she'd created for him. She wasn't a peripheral outsider to the case anymore—there was a direct line between her and Jason. Hawkins had found her, the real her, not the one she'd planted for him to find. He'd won.

"I really don't know," Pip said, and the terror was back, that cliff edge inside her own head, breaths coming faster, throat narrowing. "I guess I can ask my family, see if they remember when they last saw me with the headphones. But I can't think how this happened."

"Right," Hawkins said.

She needed to leave, get out before the panic took over her face and she couldn't hide it anymore. She had to leave, and she could—this interview was voluntary. They couldn't arrest her. Not yet. The headphones were only circumstantial; they'd need more.

"In fact, I probably need to get going. My mom's taking me shopping for college supplies in a bit. I'm going this weekend and, unlike me, I'm not organized. I'll ask my family if they remember when I last had those headphones, and I'll get back to you on that."

She stood up.

"Interview terminated eleven-fifty-seven." Hawkins clicked stop on the tape and stood as well, picking up the evidence bag. "I'll walk you out," he said.

"No," Pip said from the door, "no, don't worry. Been here enough times, I know the way."

Back out into that corridor, in the bad, bad place, blood on her hands, blood on her hands, blood on her face and everywhere, marking her out in red as she stumbled outside.

Flipped her laptop over. Panicked fingers, almost dropped it. A screwdriver from her dad's tool kit. Pip could remove the hard drive, she knew exactly how, put it in the microwave and watch it explode. If they got a warrant and took her computer, they couldn't see that she'd been looking into Green Scene before Jason died, or Andie's second email account, or any connection to Jason or the DT Killer. The time of death was nine-thirty to midnight and she had an alibi, she had an alibi, the headphones were just circumstantial and she had an alibi.

She got one screw out before she realized the truth, before it crashed into her, solid and indisputable, stuck through the middle of her chest. She was in denial but the voice at the back of her mind knew, guided her out, slowly, slowly.

It was over.

Pip dropped everything and cried into her hands. But her

alibi—the plan had worked, one last part of her protested. No, no. She couldn't think like that anymore, she couldn't fight, she couldn't see this through to the end. She could have, if it were just her, but she wasn't the only one at risk here. Ravi, and Cara and Naomi, and Jamie and Connor and Nat. They'd helped her because she'd asked, because they loved her and she loved them.

And there it was. She loved them, a simple and powerful truth. Pip loved them all and she couldn't let them fall when she did.

That was the promise.

And if this was it, the beginning of the end, there was only one way Pip knew to protect them all now. She had to make sure they were removed from the narrative before it was uncovered. She had to create a new one, a new story, a new plan.

It hurt to even think of it, to know what it meant for her and the life she'd never live.

She had to confess.

FORTY-EIGHT

"No, you're fucking not," Ravi said to her, his voice cracking down the line, his breath fast and panicked.

Pip gripped the phone too hard against her ear. One of her burner phones; she didn't trust her real phone for this conversation. All those traces, those ties to Ravi.

"I have to," she said, picturing the look in his eyes, staring off into that middle space as the world fell down around them.

"I asked you multiple times," he said, a flash of anger now, crackling in his voice. "I said, 'Did you check you had everything in your bag?' I said that, Pip! I said did you check!"

"I know, I'm sorry, I thought I did." She blinked, tears pooling at the crack in her mouth, her gut twisting to hear him like this. "I forgot about them. It's my fault. It's all my fault. That's why I have to confess, so it's only me—"

"But you have an alibi," he said, and he was trying not to cry now, Pip could tell. "The pathologist thinks Jason died between nine-thirty and twelve and you're covered for that whole time. It's not over, Pip. The headphones are circumstantial, we can think of something."

"It's a direct link between me and Jason," she said.

"We can think of something," Ravi said louder, speaking over her. "Come up with a new plan. That's what you do, what we do."

"Hawkins caught me in a lie, Ravi. He caught me in a lie and that and the headphones give him probable cause. That means they can probably get a warrant to collect my DNA, if they want to. And if we accidentally left any hairs, anything behind at the scene, then it's over. The plan only worked if there was never a connection to me, only indirectly through my call to Epps that night, and the podcast. It's over."

"It isn't over!" he shouted, and he was scared, Pip could feel it through the phone, catching her too, burrowing under her skin like a living thing. "You're giving up."

"I know," she said, closing her eyes. "I am giving up. Because I can't have you go down with me. Or the Reynoldses or the Wards or Nat. That was the deal. If it went wrong, I was the only one who would take the fall. It went wrong, Ravi. I'm sorry."

"It hasn't gone wrong." She heard shuffling down the line, the sound of his fist punching against a pillow. "It worked. It fucking worked and you have an alibi. How can you confess when you were somewhere else at the time?"

"I'll tell them what I did with the car AC, the same trick, it just didn't work as well. Your alibi covers you from eight-fifteen that night, so maybe I tell them I killed him at around eight; that leaves you totally in the clear. I put him in the car and I went to fake my alibi with Cara and Naomi. They didn't know anything. They're innocent." Pip wiped her eyes. "They'll stop looking if I do this. A confession is the single most prejudicial piece of evidence—we know that from Billy Karras. They won't need to keep looking. I'll tell Hawkins who Jason was, what he was going to do to me. I don't think they'll believe me, unless there's any evidence Jason was DT, but maybe there is, somewhere. There are the trophies. Self-defense is out the window, especially with the whole elaborate scheme to cover it up, but maybe a good lawyer would be able to argue the charge down from murder to voluntary manslaughter and I ca—"

"No!" Ravi said, desperate and angry. "You'll be in prison for decades, maybe your whole life. I won't let that happen. Max killed

Jason, not you. There is so much more evidence that points to him than you. We can do this, Pip. It can still be OK."

It hurt too much to hear him like this. How was she going to be able to say goodbye when he was actually right there in front of her? Her ribs closed in on her heart, squeezing until it gave out, thinking about not being able to see him every day ever again, only twice-a-month visits across a cold metal table, guards watching to make sure they didn't touch. That wasn't a life, not one she wanted for herself or for him.

Pip didn't know what to say. She couldn't fix this.

"I don't want you to," Ravi said quietly. "I don't want you to go."

"If it's a choice between me and you, I choose you," Pip whispered.

"But I choose you too," Ravi said.

"I'll come over to say goodbye before I go." She sniffed. "I'm going to go downstairs and have one last normal family dinner. Say goodbye to them, even though they won't know. Just one last bit of normal. And then I'll come say goodbye to you. Then I go."

Silence.

"OK," Ravi finally said, his voice thicker now, and something else in it that Pip didn't recognize.

"I love you," she said.

The phone clicked off, dead tone ringing in her ears.

FORTY-NINE

"Joshua, eat your peas."

Pip smiled as she watched her dad speaking in his mock-warning voice, opening his eyes comically wide.

"I just don't like them today," Josh complained, pushing them around his plate, kicking his feet out against Pip's knees under the table. Normally she'd tell him to stop, but this time she didn't mind. This time was the last, in an hour full of lasts, and Pip wouldn't take any of them for granted. Study them, sear them into her brain to make the memories last decades. She'd need them in there.

"That's because *I* made them," her mom said, "and I don't add a pound of butter," with a sharp look across at her dad.

"You know," Pip said to Josh, ignoring her own plate, "peas are meant to make you better at soccer."

"No, they aren't," Josh said in his *I'm ten not stupid* voice.

"I don't know, Josh," her dad said thoughtfully. "Remember how your sister knows everything. And I mean *everything.*"

"Hmm." Josh glanced at the ceiling, considering that. Shifted his gaze to Pip, studying her just as hard back, for very different reasons. "She does know quite a lot of things, I'll give you that, Dad."

Well, she thought she did, from useless facts to how to get away with murder. But she'd been wrong, and one small mistake had brought it all crashing down. Pip wondered how her family would talk about her years from now. Would her dad still brag about her, tell everyone there's nothing his pickle doesn't know? Or would she become a hushed-up topic, one that didn't carry beyond these four walls? A shameful secret, locked up as a ghost bound to the house? Would Josh make up excuses when they were visiting her, so he wouldn't have to tell his friends what she was? Maybe he'd even pretend he never had a sister. Pip wouldn't blame him, if that's what he had to do.

"But it still doesn't mean I like these peas," Josh carried on.

Pip's mom smiled with exasperation, sharing a look across the table at Pip, one that clearly said just: *Boys, hey?*

Pip blinked back at her. *Tell me about it.*

"Pip's going to miss my cooking anyway, won't you?" her mom asked. "When she goes off to college."

"Yep." Pip nodded, fighting the lump in her throat. "I'll miss a lot of things."

"But you'll miss your fabulous daddy the most, won't you?" her dad said, winking across the table.

Pip smiled, and she could feel her eyes prickling, glazing. "He is very fabulous," she said, picking up her fork and glancing down to hide her eyes.

A normal, family dinner, except it wasn't. But none of them knew it was really a goodbye. Pip had been so lucky. Why hadn't she stopped to think about that before? She should have thought it every single day. And now she had to give it all up. All of them. She didn't want to. She didn't want this. She wanted to fight against this, rage against this. It wasn't fair. But it was the right thing to do. Pip didn't know any more about good or bad or right or wrong; those words were meaningless and empty, but she knew this was what she had to do. Max Hastings would still be free, but so would everyone else she cared about. A compromise, a trade.

Pip's mom was busy listing off all the things they had to get sorted before this Sunday, all the things they still needed to buy.

"You still haven't bought new bedsheets."

"I can take old bedsheets, it's fine," Pip said. She didn't like this conversation, planning for a future that would never happen.

"I'm surprised you haven't started packing, that's all," she said. "Normally you're so organized."

"I've been busy," Pip said, and now she was the one pushing peas around her plate.

"With this new podcast?" her dad asked. "Terrible, isn't it, what happened to Jason."

"Yeah, it's terrible," Pip said quietly.

"What exactly happened to him?" Josh's ears perked up.

"Nothing," Pip's mom said pointedly, and that was it, it was over; her mom was picking up the empty and near-empty plates and carrying them off to the counter. Dishwasher sighing as it was opened.

Pip stood up and she wasn't sure what to do. She wanted to hug them close to her and cry, but she couldn't because then she'd have to tell them, tell them the terrible thing she'd done. But how could she leave, how could she say goodbye without that? Maybe just one, maybe just Josh.

She caught him as he climbed down from his chair, wrapping him in a quick hug, disguised as a wrestle, carrying him through and chucking him onto the sofa.

"Get off me," he giggled, kicking out at her.

Pip grabbed her jacket, forcing herself to walk away from them, otherwise she might just never go. She headed toward the front door. Was this the last time she'd ever walk through it? Would she be a woman in her forties, her fifties, the next time she was here? The lines on her face all from that one night, etched into her forever. Or would she never come home again?

"Bye," she called, her voice catching in her throat, a black hole in her chest that might never go away.

"Where are you off to?" Her mom poked her head out of the kitchen. "A podcast thing?"

"Yeah." Pip shrugged, sliding her feet into her shoes, not looking back at her mom because it hurt too much.

She dragged herself toward the door. *Don't look back, don't look back.* She opened it.

"I love you all," she shouted, loud, louder than she meant to because it covered the cracks in her voice. She shut the door behind her, the slam cutting her off, severing her from them. Just in time too, because she was crying now, heaving sobs that made it hard to breathe as she unlocked her car and sat inside.

She bawled into her hands. For a count of three. Just a count of three. And then she had to go. To Ravi. She was broken now, but this next goodbye would shatter her.

She started the car and she drove, thinking of all the people she couldn't say goodbye to: Cara, Nat, the Reynolds brothers, Naomi. But they'd understand, they'd understand why she couldn't.

Pip drove down Main Street, veering off the road down Gravelly Way, toward Ravi. Toward the goodbye she'd never wanted to make. She pulled up outside the Singhs' house, remembering that naive girl who'd knocked on this door so long ago, introducing herself by telling Ravi she didn't think his brother was a killer. So different from the person standing here now, and yet they'd always share one thing: Ravi. He was her best thing, this girl and the one before.

But something was wrong, Pip could tell already. There were no cars in the drive. Not Ravi's, not his parents' cars. She knocked anyway. Putting her ear to the glass to listen. Nothing. She knocked again, and again, ramming her fist against the wood until it hurt, invisible blood dripping from her knuckles.

She held open the mail slot and called his name. Reaching for him, in every corner and crack. He wasn't here. She'd told him she was coming; why wasn't he here?

Had that been it, on the phone? No last goodbye, face-to-face, eye-to-eye? No tucking her face into that place where his neck met his shoulder, her home. No holding on to him and refusing to let go, to disappear.

Pip needed that. She needed that moment to keep her going. But maybe Ravi didn't. He was angry at her. And the last she would hear of him before all their conversations were from a prepaid prison phone was that strange "OK," and the final click as he'd let her go. Ravi was ready, and so she had to be too.

It couldn't wait. She had to tell Hawkins tonight, now, before they dug too far and found any link to those who had helped Pip that night. A confession was how she saved them from her, how she saved Ravi, even if he hated her for it.

"Bye," Pip said to the empty house, leaving it behind her, her chest shuddering as she climbed back into her car. Peeling away, both the car and her.

She turned back on Main Street, driving south toward the police station, leaving Fairview, her part of Fairview, behind her in the rearview mirror, and part of her wanted to go back and stay there forever with her people, the ones she could count on her fingers, and the other part wanted to burn it down behind her. Watch it die in flames.

She felt numb inside now and she thanked that black hole in her chest for taking the pain too, letting the numbness spread as she drove toward the police station and the bad, bad place. She was just this journey, she didn't think about what came after, she was just this car and these two yellow headlights, carving up the darkening sky.

Pip followed the road, over the bridge, dark trees pressing in around her as she focused on the turn up ahead, the road that would lead her to the station, to the end. Headlights were coming toward her, on the other side of the road, passing by with a small *shush*. There was another set, down the road, but something was wrong. They were flashing quickly at her, flickering in her eyes so the world disappeared in between. The car was getting closer, closer. A horn pressed in a three-part pattern: *long-short-long.*

Ravi.

That was Ravi's car, Pip realized as it passed her and she scanned the last three numbers of the license plate in her mirror.

He was slowing down behind her, swinging dangerously across the road to turn.

What was he doing? What was he doing *here*?

Pip turned on her signal and pulled off the road, onto a drive that led up to a locked gate, blocking her from the old half-torn-down gas station. Her headlights lit up red, dripping graffiti against the dilapidated white building as she pulled open the door and stepped out.

Ravi's car was pulling in behind her now. Pip held her sleeve up to her eyes against the glare of his headlights, to wipe her rubbed-red eyes.

He had barely stopped the car before he jumped out.

It was just the two of them, no one else around except the *shushing* of a passing car, too fast to pay them any mind. Just them and the moon, and the run-down building behind. Face to face, eye to eye.

"What are you doing?" Pip shouted across the dark wind.

"What are you doing?" Ravi shouted back.

"I'm going to the police station," she said, confused as Ravi started shaking his head, stepping toward her.

"No, you're not," he said, his voice deep, taking on the wind.

The hairs rose up Pip's arms.

"Yes, I am," she said, and she was pleading, that's what that sound was. Please, this was already the hardest thing. Although at least now she had seen him before.

"No, you're not," Ravi said, louder now, still shaking his head. "I've just come from there."

Pip froze, trying to understand his face.

"What do you mean, you've just come from there?"

"I've just been at the station, talking to Hawkins," he said, yelling over the sound of another passing car.

"What?!" Pip stared at him, and the black hole in her chest gave everything back: the panic, the terror, the dread, the pain, the shiver up her back. "What are you talking about?"

"It's going to be OK," Ravi said to her. "You're not confessing. You didn't kill Jason." He swallowed. "I've fixed it."

"You what?!"

The gun went off in her chest six times.

"I fixed it," he said. "I told Hawkins it was me—the headphones."

"No no no no." Pip stepped back. "No, Ravi! What have you done?"

"It's OK, it's going to be OK." Ravi walked forward, reached for her.

Pip batted his hand away. "What did you do?" she said, her throat tightening around her words, breaking them in half. "What exactly did you say to him?"

"I told him that I borrow your headphones all the time, sometimes without you knowing. That I must have had them with me when I went round to the Bells' house to see Jason one evening a couple weeks ago. The twelfth, I said. Accidentally left the headphones there."

"Why the fuck would you have gone round to see Jason?" Pip whisper-shouted, and her mind was reeling away from him, pushing her feet back, almost against the gate. *No, no, no, what had he done?*

"Because I was talking to Jason about an idea I had, to set up some kind of scholarship scheme in Andie's and Sal's names, a charity thing. I went to discuss ideas with Jason, showed him some printouts, and that's when the headphones must have fallen out of my bag. We were in the living room, sitting on the sofas."

"No, no, no," Pip said quietly.

"Jason liked the idea but said he didn't have time to be involved. That's how we left things, but I must have also left the headphones there. I'm guessing Jason later found them and didn't realize they belonged to me. That's what I said to Hawkins."

Pip clamped her hands to her ears, like she could make this go away if she couldn't hear him anymore.

"No," she said quietly, the word just a vibration against the back of her teeth.

Ravi finally reached her. He pulled her arms away from her face, held her hands in his. Grip tight, like he was anchoring her to him. "It's OK, I fixed it. The plan is still in play. You didn't kill Jason. Max did. There's no direct link to you anymore. You haven't had contact with Jason since April, and Hawkins didn't catch you in a lie. It was me; I left your headphones there. You knew nothing about it. You told me about your interview today, and that's when I realized it was me who had had contact with Jason, who left the headphones there. So I went down to the station to clear things up. That's what happened. Hawkins believed me, he will believe me. He asked me where I was on the evening of the fifteenth and I told him: I was in Stamford with my cousin, listed all the places I went. Got home just before midnight. Airtight, ironclad, just like we planned. And no connection to you. It's going to be OK."

"I didn't want you to do that, Ravi," she cried. "I didn't want you to ever talk to him, ever to have to use your alibi."

"But you're safe," he said, eyes flashing at her in the dark. "Now you don't have to go."

"But *you* aren't!" she said. "You've just directly implicated yourself in the whole thing. Before we could keep you separate, you were separate from it all, but now . . . What if Dawn Bell was home on the twelfth? What if she tells them you're lying?"

"I can't lose you," Ravi said. "I wasn't going to let you do this. I sat on my bed after you called and I did that thing I do when I'm nervous or scared or unsure about something. I asked myself, *What would Pip do? What would she do in this situation?* So, that's what I did. I came up with a plan. Was it reckless? Probably. Bravery to the point of stupidity, that's you. But I thought it through and I didn't overthink it. I acted, like you do. It's what you would have done, Pip." He breathed, shoulders rising and falling with it. "It's what you would have done, and you would have done it for me, you know you would. We're a team, remember? You and me. And no one's taking you away from me, not even you."

"Fuck!" Pip shouted into the wind, because he was right and he was wrong and she was happy and she was devastated.

"It's going to be OK." Ravi wrapped her up into him, inside his jacket, warm even when he had no business being so. "It was my choice and I chose you. You're not going anywhere," he said, his breath in her hair, along her scalp.

Pip held on, watching the road over Ravi's shoulder. Blinking slowly, the black hole in her chest trying to catch up. She didn't have to go. She didn't have to be that woman in her fifties, looking up at her old family home after decades, thinking it was somehow smaller than she remembered it, because she had forgotten it, or it had forgotten her. She didn't have to watch everyone she cared about live a life without her, catching her up across a metal table every few weeks, visits growing fewer and further between as their lives got in the way and her edges got fainter and fainter until she disappeared at last.

A life, a real one, a normal one: it was still possible. Ravi had saved her, he had, and by doing so he had damned himself.

Now there was no choice, no backing down.

She had to bare her teeth and see this through to the end.

No doubt.

No mercy.

Blood on her hands and a gun in her heart and the plan.

Four corners. She and Ravi standing in one. The DT Killer in another. Max Hastings opposite them, and Detective Hawkins opposite him.

One last fight, somewhere in the middle, and they had to win. They had to, now that Ravi was on the line too.

Pip pushed herself into him, closer, harder, her ear to his chest to listen to his heart, because she was still here, and she still could.

She closed her eyes and made a new silent promise to him, because he had chosen her and she had chosen him: they were going to get away with it.

FIFTY

The town buzzed with talk, fizzled with it. The hushed kind, but the kind of hush meant to be overheard, particularly loud in Pip's ears.

Isn't it just terrible?

—Gail Yardley, walking her dog

There's something very wrong with this town. I can't wait to leave.

—Adam Clark, near the train station

Have there been any arrests yet? Your cousin knows someone at the police, doesn't he?

—Mrs. Morgan, outside the library

Dawn Bell came into the store last week and she doesn't seem too upset. You don't think she had anything to do with it?

—Leslie, from the Stop & Shop

Pip had two hushed conversations of her own, not out in the open for everyone to hear. Behind closed doors and whispered all the same.

The first was with Nat, on the Wednesday, both sitting on Pip's bed.

"Someone from the police called me. A Detective Hawkins. In relation to their inquiries into the death of Jason Bell. He asked me if I'd knocked on Max Hastings's door on the night of the fifteenth. If I'd hit him in the face."

"And?" Pip asked.

"I told him I had no idea what he was talking about, and why on earth he would insinuate that I would willingly go to the house of someone who assaulted me, put myself in a situation where I was alone with him."

"Good, that's good."

"I told him I was at my brother's house from around eight that night. Dan was already drunk and basically asleep on the sofa, so he will verify that too."

"Good." It was good. That meant Hawkins must have interviewed Max at least once already, probably again after securing his cell phone data, asking once more for him to explain his whereabouts on the evening Jason died. Max told him he was home alone all night, fell asleep early, and that Nat da Silva had knocked on his door. But Hawkins already had the data from his phone, could see that Max wasn't at home, could see the calls that pinged a cell tower placing him at the scene, and now he'd caught Max in a lie, several of them.

There was another unsaid thing hovering between Pip and Nat. And that was a dead Jason Bell. Nat could never ask and Pip could never tell, but Nat must know, the look in her eyes told Pip that. And yet she didn't look away, she didn't, she held Pip's eyes and Pip held hers and though it could never be said, it was understood. Max killed Jason, not her. Another secret bond that held the two of them together.

Her second conversation was with Cara, the next day, sitting at the table in the Wards' kitchen after Pip had received a text: *can you come over?*

"The detective, he asked me and Naomi where we were on the night of the fifteenth, if we were with you. So, we told him yes, and what times we left and arrived, where we went. That it was just a normal night, and we were hungry, that was it. Showed him the photos and videos on my phone too. He asked me to send them in."

"Thank you," Pip said, the words inadequate and frail. There was that same look in Cara's eyes too. She must have known, when the news broke about Jason; what else could it be? She and Naomi must have looked at each other and known, whether they said it out loud or not. But there was something unshakable in Cara's eyes too, a trust between them, and even if this tested it, it had not broken it. Cara Ward, more a sister than a friend, her constant, her crutch, and that familiar look on her face helped loosen the knot in Pip's gut. She didn't know if she could have taken it, if Cara had looked at her any differently.

And that was another good thing. Hawkins was now looking into her alibi, verifying it. He'd checked with the witnesses, and he must be following up, requesting the traffic camera footage, searching for the journey her car had made that night. Maybe he'd already seen the tapes from McDonald's, seen the charges on her card and the times they were made. See, Hawkins, she was exactly where she said she was, miles and miles away at the time Jason was killed.

Another conversation—which was probably more of an argument than a conversation—with her parents:

"What do you mean you're not going on Sunday?" Her mom gaped.

"I mean I'm not going. I can skip the first week of college, classes don't actually start until the week after. I can't go yet, I have to see this through. I'm on to something here."

Her dad, who rarely shouted, had shouted. For hours. This was, apparently, the worst thing she'd ever done to him.

"I think they need me, to find the killer for them, and you're saying a week of getting drunk is more important than that?"

A glare in answer.

"If I miss anything, I'll catch up. I always do. Please trust me. I need you to trust me."

Just as Ravi had trusted her, and she couldn't leave town without knowing they'd done it. No mercy, no holding back, this was the final fight. Pip had given the police everything: she'd placed Max at the scene during the time-of-death window using the cell phone tower, she'd left Max's hair at the scene, his shoeprints, traffic cam footage of his car driving away after burning it down, blood on the sleeve of his hoodie at his house, and in the mud caked under his shoes. Maybe they hadn't found all that yet, but she was about to give them something else too: episode 1. Tie the narrative together, the motive. The background of this town, what happened to Andie, to Becca. Bad blood between two men, an altercation confirmed by witnesses, a hint at wounded pride, at a fight that maybe went too far. Security cameras at this individual's home that would surely back him up if he had nothing to hide. The interview with Jackie had already gone some of the way, but Pip had to take it one step further.

The worst they could do was tell her to take it down, tell her to stop interfering, but the damage would already be done, the seed planted. She couldn't name the suspect and she wouldn't have to; Hawkins would know who she was talking about, and this was just for him. He was the only listener who mattered. Build the case against Max for him so he'd never try to build one against her.

41:29 MB of 41:29 MB uploaded

A Good Girl's Guide to Murder: Who Killed Jason Bell?

Season 3 Episode 1 successfully uploaded to SoundCloud.

FIFTY-ONE

Another game, another race, between her heart and the pounding of her sneakers pattering out of time. Pip filled herself with the sound, just one foot in front of the other, to take herself out of her head. Maybe, if she ran fast enough, she might even sleep tonight. She was supposed to have been in a new bed tonight, in a new city, but Fairview wouldn't let her go just yet.

She shouldn't have been looking down at her feet, she should have been watching where she was going. She hadn't thought about it, hadn't needed to think; it was just one of her regular routes, her circuit. One road flowing into another, and her mindlessly following.

It wasn't until she heard the commotion of voices and vehicles that she glanced up and realized where she was running to. Courtland, about halfway up, on the way to the Hastings house.

The house was just up there, but there was something new that didn't belong, catching her eye. Parked outside the house, jutting out onto the road, were three police cars and two marked trucks with blue lines along their sides.

Pip kept going, her eyes dragging her closer and closer, until she could see a gathering of people moving in and out of the front door. Dressed in white plastic suits that covered the bottoms of their feet to the tops of their heads. Masks across their faces and blue latex gloves for hands. One carrying a large brown paper bag out of the house and into the waiting van, followed by another.

A forensics team.

A forensics team searching Max's house.

Pip slowed to a stop, her heart winning out against her feet, throwing itself against her ribs as she watched the orderly chaos of the plastic-wrapped people. She wasn't the only one. Neighbors were standing at the edges of their drives, eyes wide, murmuring behind their hands to each other. A white van was parked on the other side of the street and milling around it were more people, one taking photographs of the scene, another man with a large camera propped on one shoulder, pointing it across the road.

This was it. This was it. She couldn't smile, she couldn't cry, she couldn't let any reaction play out on her face other than faint curiosity, but this was it. The beginning of the end. Her heart beat back that black hole in her chest as she watched.

A uniformed officer was standing beside one of the police cars, talking with two people, a man and a woman. The man was spraying clipped, heated words at the officer, his voice carrying on the wind. They were Max's parents, back from Santa Barbara, huddled with their deep, expensive tans. Pip searched him out, but Max wasn't here. Neither was Detective Hawkins.

"Ridiculous!" Max's dad shouted, pulling his phone out, his movements rough and angry.

"Mr. Hastings, you have already been shown the signed search warrant. It shouldn't be too much longer, if you could just calm down."

Mr. Hastings spun on his heels, ramming the phone up to his ear.

"Epps!" he barked down into it.

The officer was pivoting too, keeping his eye on Mr. Hastings. Pip turned before he could see her down the street, her hair whipping out behind her, shoes scraping on the pavement.

The officer might recognize her and she shouldn't be seen here. Keep herself on the periphery.

She picked up her heels and started running, back the way she'd come. Another game, another race, and she was winning now.

It wouldn't be long, it couldn't be. They'd issued a search warrant for the house. They'd comb through it and they'd find that blood-stained hoodie and the sneakers with the zigzag soles in Max's room; maybe Pip had even seen them being carried out, inside two of those large brown bags. If they had a warrant to search the house, it was likely they also had one to take DNA samples from Max, see if he was a match for those blond hairs found in dead Jason's hand and in his river of blood. Maybe that's where Max was right now.

She rounded the corner, her eyes no longer on her feet but on the gray churning sky. The results of the DNA testing could take several days to come through from the lab, verifying the blood on Max's clothes and the hairs found on Jason's body. But once they did, Hawkins would have no choice. The evidence was overwhelming. Pieces shifting on a board, players staring out at each other from their own corners.

Pip picked up her pace, faster and harder, and she could feel it, the end, catching up behind her.

New message

From mariakarras61@hotmail.com 11:39 a.m.

To AGGGTMpodcast@gmail.com

Subject: some news!

Hi Pippa,

I hope you are keeping well! I see from the episode you just released that you have found the case for your third season, or rather it found you. Such a tragedy, and poor Mr. Bell! I really hope you find who did this to him.

I understand totally why this case had to take priority over looking into Billy and the DT Killer case, but I had some news this morning and I thought you would like to know. Apparently, Billy's case is under review! There is some new evidence that has come to light, I don't know all the details yet, but it sounds like it's big—new DNA or fingerprint evidence. That's why everyone is suddenly taking an interest. I wonder if they've finally identified the unknown fingerprint that was found on Melissa Denny, the second victim.

These things take time, I'm sure, but a lawyer from The Innocence Project has been in touch with Billy about filing a writ of habeus corpus to try to overturn his conviction. So, it seems as though the police may think they've found the real DT Killer, or at least they've found enough evidence to start looking into whether Billy was wrongfully convicted.

Anyway, all very exciting here and I will of course keep you updated. I may even have my boy home for Christmas, who knows!

Thank you for believing in me and Billy.

Best wishes,
Maria Karras

FIFTY-TWO

Pip stroked her finger down the computer screen, stalling over the last line of the email.

Thank you for believing in me and Billy.

She had believed in them, because Pip was supposed to be the sixth victim of the DT Killer and, in a way, she always would be. From the moment Jason grabbed her, there was no doubt that an innocent man was sitting in prison. But *the plan* had forgotten Billy. Survival had taken over, survival and revenge, and protecting Ravi and the others from the plan. But Billy needed to be saved from Jason Bell as much as she did, and Pip had left him behind, made him secondary. She could have done something, couldn't she? The plan only worked if she didn't know Jason Bell was the DT Killer, had nothing to do with him, but she could have thought of something.

Another realization, stone-cold and stone-hard in her gut: Pip thought there wouldn't be any significant evidence that Jason Bell was the DT Killer. Which meant two things: she was always going to leave Billy Karras behind, save herself, and bury him away at the back of her mind. And the second: none of this had to happen. Maybe Pip could have kept walking through those trees, Jason's car pulling up to Green Scene behind her. She could have kept going, found a road, found a house, found a person and a phone. Maybe Hawkins wouldn't have believed her still, but he might have looked into it. Maybe he would have found the same evidence they'd found now to back up her word, acted before Jason had a chance to act again. Jason behind bars and Billy free, on the strength of Pip's firsthand account.

But that's not what happened. A fork in a path she hadn't taken.

Pip had made a different choice, standing in the shadows of those trees. It wasn't an accident, or instinct, or fight or flight. She saw both paths and she'd made a choice. She went back.

And maybe that other Pip in that other life would say she'd made the right choice. She'd trusted in those who'd never trusted in her and it had worked out. Saved herself to save herself; maybe she was already fixed, Team Ravi and Pip moving on, living a normal life. But this Pip could also say hers was the right choice. Dead was the only way she could be sure the DT Killer would never hurt anyone again. And on this path, Max Hastings was going to go down too. Two birds, one stone. Two monsters and a ring of dead and dead-eyed girls of their making. One dead, one locked away for thirty to life, if it worked. Gone. Disappeared, and no one left to look for them. Maybe this way was better, who could say?

Anyway, there was something Pip could do now to rewrite that mistake, to un-forget Billy Karras. His mom was probably right; when they'd processed Jason's body and entered his fingerprint information into the database, it had pinged with that remaining question mark from the DT Killer case. Maybe other DNA hits to the DT Killer crime scenes that they'd previously written off. And there were the trophies. Pip had found three of them herself now, two more by looking at an old, printed photo of the Bell family, one she'd had pinned on her murder board a year ago. A gold necklace with a coin pendant that had belonged to Phillipa Brockfield, wrapped around Dawn Bell's neck. Two glints of light by Becca's ears: rose-gold earrings with pale green stones. The same earrings she still wore now. They belonged to Julia Hunter. Pip wished she could get a message to Becca somehow, tell her everything that happened, tell her about those earrings, because DT still had a hold over her as long as they were in her ears. Reliving the moment he'd killed these women whenever he saw his wife and his daughters.

The police had searched Jason's house; if they'd found and collected Pip's headphones, maybe they'd found the trophies from the other victims. Andie's purple hairbrush, the necklace Dawn wore, Bethany Ingham's Casio watch, Tara Yates's key rings.

And if they hadn't yet found the trophies, Pip could lead Hawkins to them, she just had to show him this photo.

Not only that, she had Andie's secret email account and that unsent draft. That email—Andie's words that weren't her last but felt like it—would be the nail in Jason Bell's coffin. Lead the police to Andie's connection with HH too. Pip would need to change the password on the account to something less conspicuous than her temporary *DTKiller6.* She did that now, swapping it out for *TeamAndieAndBecca;* she thought Andie would like that best.

The police might have a fingerprint, but Pip could give them everything else, shore up the case against Jason Bell to beyond reasonable doubt. So when Billy's conviction was overturned, they wouldn't have to take it to a retrial with this new exculpatory evidence, but they'd dismiss the charges outright. Let Billy finally go home. Pip owed him that much.

And if everyone knew who Jason Bell really was, Pip would no longer have to listen to people say how fucking awful it was that someone killed him.

Pip practiced in the mirror, her voice dry and unused all day. "Hi, Detective Hawkins, sorry, I know you must be extraordinarily busy. It's just . . . well, as you know, I've been looking into Jason Bell's background as part of my research into who might have killed him. Looking into his company, personal relationships, et cetera. And, I don't know"—she paused, an apologetic look on her face, teeth gritted—"I've found some troubling connections to another case. I didn't want to bother you with them, but I really think you should take a look."

The duct tape and rope taken from Green Scene Ltd., and the company's connection with the dump sites. The recording of her old interview with Jess Walker about a security alarm set off on the premises on the same night Tara Yates and Andie died. The username for Andie's secret second email address, and the just-reset password. A photo of the school planner on Andie's desk, the purple paddle hairbrush beside it. And this family photo, with the necklace and the earrings.

"Becca's still wearing them. I know because I've been visiting her. Maybe it's just me, but don't these look just like the earrings the DT Killer took from Julia Hunter as a trophy?"

The voice in her head that sounded like Ravi told her not to. The real one would probably agree, that she should try not to bring any more attention to herself. But Pip had to do this, for Billy, for his mom, and so that the other Pip in that other life—the one who made the other choice—wasn't right.

Pip collected everything she needed to free a man, and she left.

That same journey again, to the Fairview Police Station, but this time Pip completed it. And there was no black hole in her chest anymore, only determination, only rage and fear and determination. Her final chance to set everything right. Save Billy, take on Hawkins, take down Jason Bell and Max Hastings, save Ravi, save herself, live a normal life. The end was the beginning and both were running out.

She pulled into an empty space in the parking lot, checked her eyes in the rearview mirror, and opened the door.

Pip shouldered her backpack with everything inside and slammed the door, the sound clapping through the quiet Thursday afternoon.

But it wasn't quiet, not anymore, as Pip walked up to the brick building and the bad, bad place. A rush of tires on concrete behind her, lots of them, peeling to a stop.

Pip stopped short of the automatic doors, looked over her shoulder.

Three cars had just pulled up outside the entrance. A white-and-black squad car in front, followed by an unmarked SUV and another squad car at the rear.

Two uniformed officers who Pip didn't know climbed out of the first vehicle, one speaking into the radio clipped to his shoulder. The doors of the squad car at the back opened, and out stepped officers Daniel da Silva and Soraya Bouzidi. Daniel's mouth tensed in a grim line as he caught Pip's eye.

The driver's-side door of the unmarked black car opened, and Detective Hawkins emerged, his green padded jacket zipped up to his neck. He didn't notice Pip standing there, twenty feet from him, as he stepped to the back door of his car, opened it, and leaned in.

Pip saw his legs first, then his feet swinging out onto the concrete, then his hands, cuffed in front of him as Hawkins pulled him out of the car.

Max Hastings.

Max Hastings under arrest.

"I'm telling you, you've made a huge mistake," he said to Hawkins. His voice was shaking, and in that moment Pip couldn't tell whether it was with rage or fear. She hoped it was the latter. "I had nothing to do with this, I don't understand—"

Max cut off, his pale eyes trailing toward the police station, finding Pip standing there, latching on. His breathing grew heavier, his eyes widening, darkening.

Hawkins didn't notice, gesturing for Soraya and one of the other officers to come over.

They didn't see it coming. Pip didn't see it coming. In one quick, shuddering movement, Max wrenched his arm free of Hawkins, shoving him to the ground. He broke away, flying across the parking lot, too fast she didn't have time to blink.

Max collided into Pip, cuffed hands against her neck, shoving her backward into the brick building. Her head connected with a crack.

Shouts and scuffles behind, but Pip could only see one thing: the flash of Max's eyes, inches from hers. His hands tightened around her neck, the points of his fingers burning through her skin.

He bared his teeth and she bared hers back.

"You did this!" he screamed in her face, spit flying. "You did this somehow!"

He pushed harder, grating Pip's head against the brick.

She didn't fight him off; her hands were free but she didn't push him away. She flashed her eyes back and whispered quietly, so only Max could hear:

"You're lucky I didn't put you in the ground too."

Max roared at her, the scream of a cornered animal, his face patchy and red, ugly veins sticking out by his eyes. "You fucking bitch!" he screamed, slamming her head just as Hawkins and Daniel caught up behind, dragging him off her. A scuffle, Max down on the ground kicking out at them as the other officers rushed over.

"She did this!" Max screamed. "I didn't do it. I didn't do anything. I'm innocent!"

Pip felt the back of her head: no blood. No blood on her hands.

"I didn't do it!"

They hauled him up to his feet again.

Max threw his head in her direction, and for a fleeting moment he looked just as he should: eyes narrow and violent, mouth gaping open hideous and wide, face inflamed and misshapen. There he was, the danger, ripped of all pretense, all disguise.

"She did this somehow!" he screamed. "She did! She's fucking crazy!"

"Get him inside!" Detective Hawkins shouted over Max, directing Soraya and the other two officers as they half dragged, half carried a writhing Max through the automatic doors into the station. Before he followed them in, Hawkins turned back to Pip, pointing at her. "You OK?" he asked, out of breath.

"Fine." She nodded.

"OK." He nodded too, then hurried inside the building, following the sound of Max's wild screams.

Someone sniffed behind her and Pip wheeled around, snapping her eyes to them. It was Daniel da Silva, righting his uniform, ruffled and askew where Max had pulled at it.

"Sorry," he said breathily. "You all right? Looked like he got you pretty hard there?"

"Yeah, no, fine," she said. "Just a bump on the head, it'll be fine. My dad says I have a few too many brain cells anyway, could afford to lose a few."

"Right." Dan sniffed with a small, sad smile.

"Max Hastings," Pip said quietly, a question hiding behind his name.

"Yeah," Dan said.

"They charging him?" she asked, both of them watching the entrance doors, the muffled sounds of Max's voice filtering through. "With murder?"

Daniel nodded.

Something had been pressing down on Pip, a shadow heavy on her shoulders, constricting her chest. But as she watched Daniel's head move up and down, it finally let her go, it released her. They were charging Max with Jason's murder. Her heart beat wing-fast against her ribs, but it wasn't the terror, it was something else, something closer to hope.

It was over, she had won. Four against four and here she was, still standing.

"Piece of shit," Dan hissed, pulling Pip back into the moment, here at the bad, bad place, watching those doors. "Don't tell anyone I said that, but . . . Jason Bell was like a father to me, and *he*"—Daniel broke off, staring at the glass doors that had swallowed Max whole—"he . . ." Daniel wiped at his eyes, coughed into his fist.

"I'm sorry," Pip said, and it wasn't a lie. She wasn't sorry that Jason was dead, not one bit, not sorry that she had killed him, but she did feel sorry for Daniel. Pip had thought him capable of violence three separate times now, convinced beyond a doubt he had to have been the DT Killer. He wasn't, he was just another one of those souls floating out in that expanse of gray area, in the wrong places at the wrong times. And another realization, hard and cold as they always seemed to be these days: Jason Bell had used Daniel. He was the reason Dan joined the police force at all; Jason convinced him to do it, supported him through training. Becca had told Pip all this last year, and now she saw it for what it really was. It wasn't because Jason saw Daniel as the son he'd never had. No, it was because he wanted a way to get information on the DT Killer case. An in with the police and the investigation. And all of Daniel's red-flag questions about DT had really been Jason's. His interest in the case, through Daniel. That's what it was, that's what Andie had meant when she said her dad was "practically one of them." He'd used him. Jason Bell hadn't been like a father to Daniel, just as he wasn't a father to Andie and Becca.

Pip could tell Daniel. She could warn him about the information that might come out about Jason soon, his links to the DT Killer. But she looked at the sad smile on his face, the red skin by his eyes, and she couldn't, she didn't want to be the one to take that away from him. She'd taken enough.

"Yeah," Daniel said absently, watching the entrance as someone walked through it, the doors hissing against their frames.

It was Detective Hawkins. "Daniel," he said, "could you . . . ?" He gestured back toward the station with his thumb.

"Yes sir," Daniel said with a quick shake of his head, picking up his feet and disappearing inside through the automatic doors.

Hawkins walked over to her.

"You OK?" he asked again. "Do I need to call in any medical assistance? Your head . . . ?" He narrowed his eyes at her.

"No, it's fine. I'm fine," she insisted.

"I'm sorry." He coughed awkwardly. "That was my fault. He wasn't resisting before then, I didn't expect him to . . . I should have been paying attention. My fault."

"That's OK." Pip gave him a tense closed-mouth smile. "No worries."

The silence between them was thick and teeming.

"What are you doing here?" Hawkins asked her.

"Oh, I came to talk to you. About something."

"Right?" He looked at her.

"I know you're busy, clearly." She glanced at the doors into the station. "But I think we should talk inside. I have some things I need to show you, something I've found in my research. It's important, I think."

Hawkins's eyes alighted on hers. Pip stared back; she wouldn't be the one to break it.

"Yeah, sure, OK," he said, looking quickly behind him. "Can you give me ten minutes?"

"Yes, that's fine," she said. "I'll wait out here."

Hawkins bowed his head as he turned away from her.

"So he did it, then?" Pip directed the question to the back of Hawkins's head. "Max killed Jason Bell?"

He halted, turned back around, his polished black shoes hissing against the concrete.

A small movement of his head, not quite a nod. "The evidence is overwhelming," he said. His eyes flicked back to hers, circling, like he was studying her for a reaction. She didn't give him one, her face stayed the same. What was he expecting her to do: smile? Remind him that she had been right from the start, ahead of him once again?

"That's good, then," she said. "The evidence, I mean. No doubt . . ."

"There'll be a press conference, later today," he said.

"OK."

Hawkins sniffed. "I need to . . ." He took one step back toward the automatic doors, tripping the sensors.

"Sure, I'll wait out here," she said.

Hawkins took another step, then paused, shaking his head with a tiny outward laugh.

"I suppose if you were ever involved in anything like this," he said, the after-laugh smile still on his face, "you'd know exactly how to get away with it."

He watched her and something fell, down into Pip's stomach, but it kept going, further and further, dragging her down with it. Hairs standing up across the back of her neck.

A flicker of a smile on her face, to match his. "Well," she said with a shrug, "I have listened to a lot of true crime podcasts."

"Right," Hawkins laughed quickly, looking down at his shoes again. "Right," with a nod, "I'll come find you when I'm done."

He walked back inside the station and Pip watched him go, and was that the hiss of the closing doors or was the sound coming from inside her own head?

FIFTY-THREE

His voice was all Pip heard, for the second night in a row, staring up at the dark shadows on her ceiling, molding them into shapes with her mind while Hawkins spoke. Eyes wide open, so they couldn't be taped shut. The gun firing in her heart.

I suppose if you were ever involved in anything like this, you'd know exactly how to get away with it.

In her head, Pip lifted and dipped the words, just as he had, laid the same pressure on the same syllables.

Hawkins hadn't brought it up again, when he and Pip sat in Interview Room 1 and she showed him her research into Jason, handed over the photos and the login details for Andie's email account. He told her, indirectly, that they had already found this connection to the DT Killer and it was being looked into, but that her information was helpful, thank you. He'd shaken her hand before seeing her out. Had his hand lingered over hers just a little too long, though? Like he was trying to feel for something?

Pip tried the sentence out again, filling herself with his voice, analyzing it from every angle, staring into every gap and intake of breath.

It was a joke, on the surface, that was all. But he hadn't said it like that. More stuttering, more uncertain, breathy from the laugh to take the sting out of it.

He knew.

No, he couldn't know. They had their killer. He had no evidence and she had an alibi.

OK, well, if he didn't know, then there was a small part of him, tiny, minuscule, even, the part he might lock away at the back of his mind, and that part had its doubts. It was ridiculous, it was nonsensical, Pip had an ironclad alibi somewhere else and the case against Max was strong. But was it too strong—just a little too easy and a little too clumsy? asked the small voice in the back of his head. A lingering suspicion he didn't know he could trust. That's what he'd been studying her eyes for, searching for traces of that doubt.

Max had been arrested and charged and the police were reinvestigating the DT Killer case. Billy Karras would be released. Pip had survived. She was free and safe, and so was everyone she cared about. Ravi had laughed and cried and held her too tight when she told him. But . . . but if that was winning, why did it not feel like it? Why was she still sinking?

I'll come find you when I'm done, the Hawkins in her head told her. She knew what he'd meant at the time, that he would come get her for their talk when he was finished processing Max. But that's not what he meant in this echo in her head. It was a promise. A threat. *I'll come find you when I'm done.*

He knew or he didn't, he suspected or he didn't, he thought and he overthought, and he shook it off and he came back to it. It didn't matter which; somewhere, somehow, the idea was in his head, however small, however ridiculous and irrational. It was there. Hawkins had let her in for one second and she'd seen it planted there.

She and Hawkins, the last ones standing, staring at each other from their opposite corners. He hadn't picked up on the truth before, with Sal Singh and Andie Bell, or with Jamie Reynolds's disappearance. But Pip had grown and changed, and maybe Hawkins had too. And that one thought, that one small doubt hiding at the back of his head, was her undoing.

Pip cried and she cried until she was empty, because she knew. She couldn't rest, she couldn't have her normal life back, the one thing she wanted above all else. The one thing all of this had been for. That was it, the price she'd have to pay. She spent hours talking it through with herself, running scenarios, asking *if*s and *when*s, and she only saw one way through this, one way to keep everyone safe from her. One more plan.

She knew what had to be done. But it might just kill her to do it.

FIFTY-FOUR

The sun lit up his eyes as he glanced back at her, dappled through the rising trees. Or maybe it was the other way, Pip wondered, maybe Ravi's eyes lit up the sun. A crooked smile creased his face.

"Sarge?" Ravi said lightly, trampling the early fallen leaves of Lodge Wood, the sound crisp and fresh, sounding like home, and beginnings and endings.

"Sorry." Pip caught up to him, stepping in time with his feet. "What did you say?"

"I said . . ." He drew out the word, nudging her in the ribs. "What time are your parents taking you tomorrow?" He waited. "To Columbia?" he reminded her. "Hello? Is anyone there?"

"Oh, um, early, I think," Pip said, shaking her head, bringing herself back. "Probably leave by ten."

She didn't know how to do it, how to say it, how to even begin. There weren't words for this, a pain that hummed through every part of her, stuck through her chest as her ribs caved in around it. Cracking bones and blood-wet hands, and a hurt that was worse than all of that.

"Cool," Ravi said. "I'll come round before, help your dad load up the car."

Pip's lip threatened to go, her throat tightened, cutting her off. Ravi didn't see, picking their way through the woods, off the path.

Exploring, he'd said, the two of them, Team Ravi and Pip, off in the wild.

"When should I come visit?" he said, ducking under a branch, holding it up for her without looking back. "Originally it was meant to be next weekend, so what about the weekend after? We could go out for dinner or something."

She couldn't, she couldn't do it. And she couldn't take another step after him.

Her eyes spilled over, fast and hard, a knot in her chest that would never go.

"Ravi," she said quietly.

He heard it in her voice. He whipped around, his eyes wide, eyebrows lowered.

"Hey, hey." He came back, sliding his hands up her arms. "What is it? What's wrong?" He pulled her into him, wrapped her in his arms, one hand on the back of her head, holding her to his chest.

"No." Pip twisted away, stepping back from him, and her body felt like it was peeling away from her, back to him, choosing him over her. "Ravi, it's . . . You can't come tomorrow morning to help load up the car. You can't come visit me. You can't, we can't . . ." Her voice cracked, broken in half by the shudder in her chest.

"Pip, what are you—"

"This is the last time," she said. "This is the last time we can see each other."

The wind played through the trees, blowing her hair across her face, strands sticking to the tears.

The light was gone from Ravi's eyes, now darkened by fear.

"What are you talking about? No, it's not," he said, his voice growing, fighting the whistling of the trees.

"It's the only way," Pip said. "The only way to keep you safe from me."

"I don't need to be safe from you," he said. "It's over. We did it. Max has been charged. We're free."

"We aren't," she cried. "Hawkins knows, or he suspects. What he said to me outside the station. The idea is there, in his head."

"So?" Ravi said, angry now. "It doesn't matter. They've charged Max; they have all the evidence. There's none against you. Hawkins can think whatever he wants, it doesn't matter."

"It does."

"Why?" he shouted, voice desperate and clawing. "Why does it matter?"

"Because." Pip's voice picked up too, thick with tears. "Because it isn't over. We didn't think it through all the way to the very end. There has to be a trial first, Ravi. A jury of twelve peers has to find Max guilty beyond a reasonable doubt. And if they do, then it will be over, truly over, and we'll be free. Hawkins won't have a reason to keep looking. It's near impossible to overturn a conviction once it's made; just look at the statistics, at Billy Karras. That's when we're free."

"Yes, and that's going to happen," he said.

"We can't know that." She sniffed, wiping her face on her sleeve. "He got away with it once before. And what if the jury finds him not guilty? What happens then? The case returns to the police to be reinvestigated. They have to have a killer. And who do you think will be the very first person Detective Hawkins looks into if Max is found to be innocent? It will be me, Ravi, he'll come for me, and everyone who helped me. Because that's the truth and that's his job."

"No!" Ravi shouted.

"Yes." Pip's breath stuttered. "If the trial doesn't go the right way, I'm going down. And I'm not having you go down with me, or any of the others."

"That's not your choice!" he said, his voice catching, eyes glazing.

"Yes, it is. You went to Hawkins about the headphones, which ties you into everything. But I know how to get you out."

"No, Pip, I'm not listening." He dropped his eyes.

"If the verdict is not guilty, if the police ever come back to talk to you about it, you tell them I made you do it."

"No."

"Under duress. I threatened you. I made you take the fall for the headphones to save me. You suspected what I'd done to Jason. You were scared for your life."

"No, Pip. Stop talking!"

"You did it under duress, Ravi," she pleaded. "That's the phrase you have to use. Under duress. You were afraid for your life if you didn't do what I said."

"No! No one will believe that!"

"Make them!" she shouted back. "You have to make them believe it."

"No." Tears overran his eyes, catching at the crack in his lips. "I don't want to. I don't want this."

"You tell them we haven't had any contact since I left for college. It will be the truth. You got away from me. We haven't spoken, haven't seen each other, no communication. But you were still scared what would happen if you told the police the truth. What I would do to you."

"Shut up, Pip. Stop it," he cried, cupping his hands over his face.

"We can't see each other. We can't have any contact at all, otherwise the duress angle won't work, the police will check our phone records. You're afraid of me, that's what it has to look like. So we can't be together anymore," she said, and the thing stuck through her chest cracked open, a thousand cuts.

"No." Ravi sobbed into his hands. "No, this can't be it. There must be something we can . . ." His hands dropped to his sides, a glint of hope in his eyes. "We can get married."

"What?"

"We can get married," he said, taking a shuddering sniff and a step toward her. "Spousal privilege. We can't be made to give evidence against each other if we are co-accused. We could get married."

"No."

"We can," he said, the hope growing in his eyes. "We could do that."

"No."

"Why not?!" he said, the desperation back in his voice, the hope gone in a blink.

"Because you didn't kill a man, Ravi. I did!" Pip took his hand, slid her fingers through his in the way they always belonged, gripping tight. "That won't save you from this, that just ties you to me and whatever happens to me. If it gets to that point, they might not need our testimony to put us both away. That is unacceptable. Do you think Sal would want this for you? Do you think he'd want everyone to think you'd played a part in killing someone, just like they thought of him?"

"Stop it," he said, squeezing her hand too hard. "Stop trying to make me—"

"It's not just from you." She spoke across him, squeezing back. "It's everyone. Cara, Nat, Connor, I have to cut myself off from everyone I care about, everyone who helped me. To protect them. Even my family; I can't have the police thinking they aided or abetted me in any way, I can't have that. I need to go away from everyone, on my own. Cut off from everyone, until the trial. And even after, if the jury—"

"No," he said, but the fight was gone from his voice now, the tears falling faster.

"I'm a ticking time bomb, Ravi. I can't have the people I love near me when it goes off. Especially not you."

"*If* it goes off," he said.

"If," she agreed, reaching up to catch one of his tears. "Until the trial. And if it goes our way, if the jury finds Max guilty, then I can get it all back. My life. My family. You. We can find each other again, I promise. If that's still what you want."

Ravi pressed his cheek into her hand.

"That could be months and months from now," he said. "Years, even. It's a murder case—they can take years to go to trial."

"Then that's how long I have to wait," Pip cried. "And if, after the wait, the jury finds him not guilty, you tell Hawkins you did it under duress. You weren't ever at the scene, you didn't know for sure I'd killed Jason, but I made you tell him about the headphones. I made you. Say it, Ravi."

"Under duress," he said quietly, his face breaking in half. "I don't want this." He sobbed, his hand shaking in hers. "I don't want to lose you. I don't care, I don't care what happens, I don't want to not see you again, not speak to you. I don't want to wait for the trial. I love you. I can't . . . I can't. You're my Pip and I'm your Ravi. We're a team. I don't want this."

Pip folded herself into him, tucking her face into that place it used to belong at the base of his neck. Her home, but it couldn't be, not anymore. His head fell against her shoulder and she held it there, her hand running through the back of his hair, slipping through her fingers.

"I don't want this either," she said, and it hurt so much she didn't think she could breathe. Nothing would heal this. Not time. Not space. Nothing. "I love you so much," she whispered. "That's why I have to do this, why I have to go and not come back. You would do it for me," she said. "You know you would." An echo of Ravi's words when he'd saved her, just as he'd saved her back in that storeroom, without knowing it. Now Pip had to save him back; that was her choice. And she knew, without a shadow of a doubt, that it was the right one to make. Maybe the other choices she'd made hadn't been, maybe every decision up to this point had been wrong or bad, untraveled paths and other lives. This choice was the worst of them all, hurt the most, but it was right, it was good.

Ravi bawled into her shoulder and Pip stroked his hair, silent tears rolling down her cheeks.

"I should go," she said eventually.

"No! No!" Ravi grabbed her tighter, wouldn't let her go, burying his face in her coat. "No, don't go," he begged her. "Please don't leave me. Please don't go."

But one of them had to be the first to leave. The first to take that last look. The first one to say it for the final time.

It had to be her.

Pip unwrapped herself from him, let him go. She pushed up onto her toes, pressed her forehead against his, in the way he always did to her. She wished she could take half of it from him, the hurt. Take half of everything bad, leave room for some good.

"I love you," she said, stepping back.

"I love you."

She looked into his eyes and he looked back into hers.

Pip turned, and she walked away.

Ravi broke behind her, crying out into the trees, the wind carrying his sobs over to her, trying to pull her back. She kept going. Ten steps. Eleven. Her foot hesitated on the next step. She couldn't. She couldn't do this. This couldn't be the last time. Pip looked back, over her shoulder, through the trees. Ravi was on his knees in the leaves, face hidden, bawling into his hands. It hurt more than anything, to see him that way, and her chest opened up, reaching out to him, trying to drive her back. Hold him, take the hurt away and let him take hers.

She wanted to go back. She wanted to run to him, fall into him, be Team Ravi and Pip and nothing more. Tell him she loved him in all those secret ways they had, hear him speak all those names he had for her in his butter-soft voice. But she couldn't, that wasn't fair. He couldn't be her person and she couldn't be his, right now. Pip had to be the strong one, the one to walk away when neither of them wanted to. The one who chose.

Pip looked at him one last time, then she tore her eyes away, stared ahead. The way forward was blurry, her eyes filling, tears streaming down her face. Maybe she'd see him again, maybe she wouldn't, but she couldn't look back again, she couldn't or she wouldn't have the strength to go.

She walked away, a howl on the wind that could have been Ravi or the trees, she was too far to know. She left, and she didn't look back.

FIFTY-FIVE

Day eighty-nine.

Pip counted them, every single day, marking them off in her mind.

An early December day in New York and the sun was already fading from the sky, staining it the pink of washed blood.

Pip gathered her coat around her and pushed on, walking the streets, block after block, again and again. In eleven days she'd be here again and it would be one hundred days since. It felt like longer.

No trial date set yet; in fact, she'd heard nothing for a while. Only something small yesterday: Maria Karras emailed her a photo of a grinning Billy decorating a Christmas tree, wearing a garish red sweater covered in reindeer. Pip had smiled back at him through the screen. Day thirty-one: that's when they'd released Billy Karras, all charges dropped.

Day thirty-three had been the day the news broke about Jason Bell being the DT Killer.

"Hey, isn't that the guy from your town?" someone had asked her in the common room of their dorms, the news on the TV in the background. Most people didn't talk to Pip, she kept herself to herself, but really she was keeping herself away from everyone else.

"Yeah, it is," Pip had said, turning up the sound.

Jason Bell hadn't just been the DT Killer, he'd also been the South Shore Stalker, a rapist who'd operated in that area of the city from

1992 to 1996, connected by DNA evidence. Pip worked it out: 1996 was the year Andie Bell had been born. Jason stopped when his first daughter was born and they'd moved from New York to Fairview. The DT Killer claimed his first victim when Andie was fifteen, when she'd first started to look like the woman she might become. Maybe that's why her father had done it. He stopped when she died, well, almost, but no one else would ever know about his sixth victim. Andie's entire life had been bookended by the monster living in her home, by his violence. She hadn't survived him, but Pip had, and Andie could come with her, wherever she went.

Pip turned the corner, cars shushing past her, readjusting her book-heavy backpack on her shoulders. Her phone buzzed in her coat pocket. Pip pulled it out and stared down at the screen.

Her dad was calling.

A knot in her gut and a hole in her heart. Pip pressed the side button to ignore the call, let it ring out in her pocket. She'd text him tomorrow, say sorry she'd missed his call, she'd been busy, maybe tell him she'd been in the library. Increase the gaps between every phone call until they were long, long stretches, weeks between, then months. Texts unread and unanswered. She'd have to think of something for Christmas, like she had for Thanksgiving, some reason she couldn't go back to town. Pip knew it would break their hearts, it was breaking hers, but this was the only way. Separation. *She* was the danger, and she had to keep them away from her, in case any of it rubbed off on them.

Day eighty-nine. Pip was only three months into her exile, her purgatory, walking these busy, regimented streets over and over, round and round. She walked every day, and she made promises. That's what she did. Promises of how she would be different, how she would be better, how she would deserve her life back and everyone in it.

She would never complain ever again about taking Josh to one of his soccer games, and she'd answer his every curiosity, big or small. Be his big sister, his teacher, the person he could look up to, until the day when he outgrew her and she looked up to him instead.

She'd be kinder to her mom, who had only ever wanted the best for her. Pip should have listened more, she should have understood. Pip had taken her for granted: her strength, the roll of her eyes, and the reason for her pancakes, and she'd never do that again. They were a team, they had been from the start, from her very first breath, and if Pip could have her life back, they would be a team again, until her mom's last. Holding hands, old skin on older skin.

Her dad. What she wouldn't give to hear his easy laugh again, hear him call her his pickle. She would thank him every day, for choosing her and her mom, for everything he'd ever taught her. Tell him all the ways she was like him and so glad for it, how he'd shaped the person she'd become. She just had to become that person again. And if she could, maybe it would happen one day, her dad's arm in hers as he walked her down that aisle, stopping halfway to tell her how proud he was.

Her friends. She'd always ask them how they were before they could ask her. She wouldn't let anything get in the way, wouldn't need them to be understanding because she would be instead. Laugh with Cara until it hurt during phone calls that lasted three hours, Connor's bad puns and awkward arms, Jamie's kind smile and big heart, Nat's strength that she'd always admired so much, Naomi who'd been a big sister to her when Pip needed one most.

And Becca Bell, Pip made a promise to her: she would tell Becca everything when they were both free. Pip had had to cut her off too, missed visits, missed phone calls. But prison wasn't Becca's cage, her father had been her cage. He was gone now, but Becca deserved to know everything, about her dad and how he died, about Max, and the part Pip had played. But mostly she deserved to know about Andie. Her big sister who'd known about the monster in their house and did all she could to save Becca from him. She deserved to read Andie's email and know how much she was loved, that those cruel things Andie said to her in her final moments were really her sister trying to protect her. Andie was terrified that one day their father would kill them both, and maybe she was scared that that would be the thing that made him snap. Pip would tell her all of it. Becca deserved to know that, in another life, she and Andie would have escaped their father, together.

Promises and promises.

Pip would earn them all back, if she got the chance.

It wasn't Max's trial she was waiting for, not really. It was hers. Her final judgment. The jury wouldn't only decide Max's fate, they would decide hers, whether she could have her life back and everyone in it.

Especially *him*.

She still spoke to Ravi every day. Not the real one—the one who lived in her head. She spoke to him when she was scared or unsure, asked him what he would do if he were there. He sat beside her when she was lonely, and she was always lonely, looking at old photos on her phone. He told her goodnight and kept her company in the dark while she learned how to sleep again. Pip wasn't sure anymore if she was getting the timbre of his voice quite right, the exact way he had leaned into his words, whether they lilted or tilted. How had he said "Sarge" again? Had his voice dipped up or dipped down? She had to remember, she had to hold on, preserve him.

She thought about Ravi every day, almost every moment of every day, eighty-nine days full of moments. What he was thinking, what he was doing, whether he'd like the sandwich she'd just eaten—the answer was always yes—whether he was OK, whether he missed her as much as she missed him. Whether that absence had grown into resentment.

She hoped that whatever he was doing, he would learn to be happy again. If that meant waiting for her, waiting for the trial, or if that meant waiting to find someone else, Pip would understand. It broke her heart to think of him doing that crooked smile for anyone else, making up new nicknames, new invisible ways of saying "I love you," but that was his choice. All Pip wanted to know was that he was happy, that there was good in his life again, that was all. Her freedom for his, and it was a choice she would make over and over again.

And if he did wait, if he did wait for her and the verdict went their way, Pip would work every day to be the kind of person who deserved Ravi Singh.

"You old softie," he said in her ear, and Pip smiled, a breath of laughter.

There was another sound, hiding beneath her breath, a faint whine, high and reeling, growing closer and closer.

A siren.

More than one.

Screaming up and down, clashing together.

Pip whipped her head around. There were three police squad cars at the end of the street, overtaking traffic, speeding toward her.

Louder.

Louder.

Blue and red lights spiraling, breaking up the twilight, flashing in her eyes and lighting up the road.

Pip turned away and shut her eyes, screwed them tight.

This was it. They'd found her. Hawkins had worked it out. It was over. They'd come for her.

She stood there and held her breath.

Louder.

Closing in.

Three.

Two.

One.

A scream in her ears. A rush of wind through her hair as the cars streamed past, one after the other, their sirens fading as they carried on down the street away from her. Left her behind on the sidewalk.

Pip peeled her eyes open, carefully, slowly.

They were gone. Their sirens dwindling to a whine again, then a hum, then nothing.

Not for her.

Not today.

One day they might be for her, but not today, day eighty-nine.

Pip nodded, picked up her feet.

"Just got to keep going," she told Ravi, and everyone else who lived in her head. "Keep going."

Her judgment day would come, but for now, Pip walked and she promised. That's all. One foot in front of the other, even if she had to drag them, even when that hole in her heart felt too big to keep standing. She walked and she promised and he was with her, Ravi's fingers slotting in between hers in the way they used to fit, fingertips in the dips of his knuckles. The way they might again. Just one foot in front of the other, that was all. Pip didn't know what was waiting for her at the end, she couldn't see that far, and the light was failing, night drawing in, but maybe, just maybe, it would be something good.

1 YEAR, 7 MONTHS, AND 28 DAYS LATER
DAY 694

3 minutes after the verdict was read in State of Connecticut vs. Max Hastings:

Hey Sarge, remember me?

...

THE END

ACKNOWLEDGMENTS

As ever, the first thanks must go to my agent, Sam Copeland. Thank you for being the best sounding board/agony aunt/bad cop/good cop. This all started with me pitching you *girl does school project about old murder case* back in June 2016, and look where we are now! *A whole-ass trilogy* is the technical term. But there wouldn't even be one book if you hadn't taken a chance on me back then and told me to write this idea, so thank you! (Although let's not give you ALL the credit—though I'm sure you'd love to take it!)

Next, I want to thank booksellers, who do such a fantastic job of getting books into the hands of readers and have continued to do so despite the incredible challenges of this past year. I am so so grateful to you for your enduring enthusiasm and dedication to books and reading, and for the huge part you have all played in the success of the AGGGTM series. To the bloggers, too, who dedicate so much of their time to posting reviews or shouting about books they have enjoyed. I could never thank you enough for all the love you have shown the AGGGTM series, and I am so looking forward to seeing your reactions to *As Good As Dead.*

To everyone at Delacorte Press who worked tirelessly to help turn my Word documents into actual, physical books. It takes a village. Thank you to Kelsey Horton for so expertly navigating this huge book with me and for understanding exactly what I wanted it to do. And again for guiding me through my fake-American-ness and all the ensuing hilarity that comes from "translating" UK to US English. Thank you so much to Beverly Horowitz for all your guidance and hard work overseeing this series from the very beginning, and for all the incredible opportunities you have given me. Thank you to Colleen Fellingham, Tamar Schwartz, and Marla Garfield for helping me whip this manuscript into shape. Thank you, as always, to the genius Casey Moses for the incredible cover design and for so expertly bringing to life my unhelpful suggestion of "duct tape—but make it creepy." And to Christine Blackburne for your superb photography once again. I think this is the best cover of the series—it's so dark and fitting for this finale and I couldn't have asked for a better cover. I hope no one looks at duct tape the same way again. Thank you to Caitlin Whalen, Emma Benshoff, Jenn Inzetta, Lili Feinberg, and everyone in the publicity and marketing teams for all your incredible hard work in making sure people hear about these books and are excited about them—I am eternally grateful. And to Victoria Rodriguez for being the most amazing advocate for YA books. Thank you to the sales team for all you do to get these books out into the world, and a massive thanks to Nick Martorelli and the audiobook team for making my words sounds so cool and professional! A special thank-you to Priscilla Coleman again for your fantastic artwork, and for bringing the DT Killer to life so expertly in the police composite sketch.

After the last year we have had, it would seem a glaring omission for me to not express my overwhelming gratitude and admiration to all NHS workers (in the UK—where I live). Your everyday heroism and bravery during the Covid-19 pandemic at times made my contribution to society feel very small (typing away made-up stories about made-up people), but I want to thank you for being so inspiring and compassionate, and for looking after us all during this horrific year. You truly are heroes, and the National Health Service is an incredible privilege that we should protect at all costs.

Thank you to my writer friends, as always, for helping me navigate the tricky waters of publishing, especially during these lockdown releases. And for Zoom game sessions so I could virtually escape my flat and my deadlines (temporarily). Thank you to my Flower Huns for keeping me sane (remotely) during the pandemic. I look back fondly on those weekly quizzes. I can't wait to do more IRL playing this year—although no more quizzes, yeah?

Thank you to my mum and dad as always for their unwavering support and for believing in me when no one else did. I think you probably knew I was going to be a writer from a young age, but thank you for fostering my love of stories by letting me have a childhood full of books, and video games, and TV, and films. Not a second of it was wasted. Also thank you, Dad, for your first reader comments, and for understanding the book perfectly. And thanks, Mum, for telling Dad that you "felt sick" when reading the book—that's when I knew it was doing exactly what I wanted it to do!

Thank you to my sisters, Amy and Olivia, for their constant support, and for showing me just how important sisters are. Pip has had to find her own sisters (Cara, Naomi, Nat, and Becca), but I was lucky enough to have two from the very start. I'm sure your influence will be all over every example of sibling banter/bickering I ever write, so thank you for that!

To my nephew, George, who says I am his favorite author, despite being ten-plus years too young to read my books: top marks for you! To my new niece, Kaci, for supplying the cuteness to keep me going during a dreadful year of deadlines, and for also being a badass pandemic baby. And especially to my niece Danielle, who is *almost* old enough to read these books now. Several years ago, when Danielle was about nine years old, she was studying creative writing at school, and she told me that all the best stories end in a *dot dot dot* . . . Well, Danielle, I have finished my first-ever trilogy with a *dot dot dot*—I hope you're proud (and I hope you're right!).

Thank you to Peter, Gaye, and Katie Collis as ever for being my early readers and for being the best second family one could ask for.

To Ben, who is *my* cornerstone, my forever partner-in-crime. Without you, none of this would have been possible and Pip would never have seen the light of day, let alone made it to the end of book three. Thank you.

After writing a series that is so heavily influenced by true crime, it would seem strange for me to end without one comment on the criminal justice system and the areas in which it fails us. I feel a helpless despair when I look at the statistics of rape and sexual assault in this country (and I'm sure the case is much the same in the US) and the abysmal rate of reporting and conviction. Something isn't right here. I hope the books themselves do the talking for me on this front. I think it's clear that parts of these stories come from an angry place, both personal anger at the times when I have been harassed and not believed, and frustration at a system of justice that sometimes doesn't feel very just.

Finally, to end on a lighter note, I want to thank all of you who have followed me through every page right to the end of book three. Thank you for trusting me, and I hope you found the ending you were looking for. I certainly did.

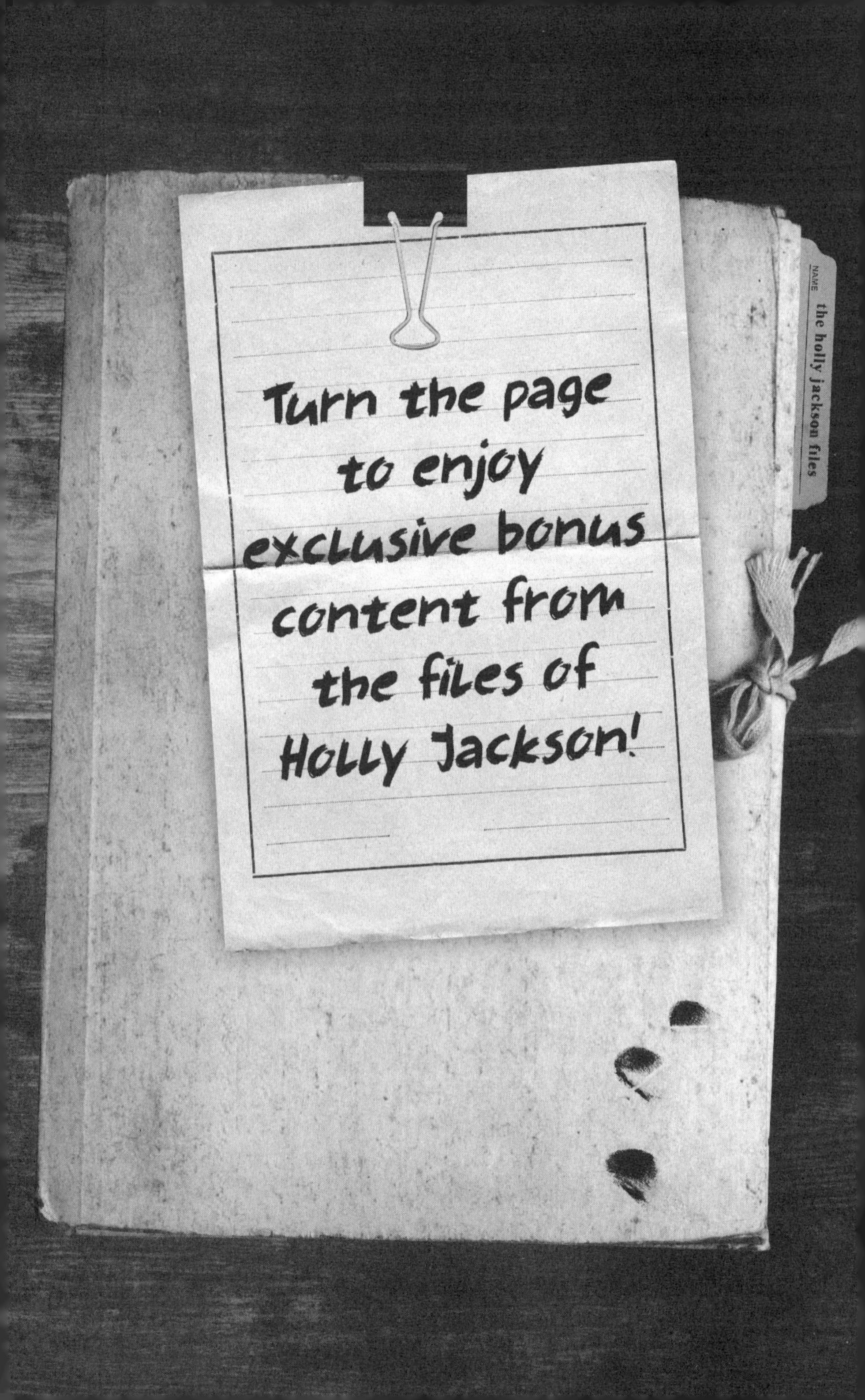
Turn the page to enjoy exclusive bonus content from the files of Holly Jackson!
NAME
the holly jackson files

for saving space
could have
just 'dead pigeons'
dead girl walking
chalk writing —
delete chalk
lines.
could
save
space?

ACT 1

1. Pip: dealing with PTSD, the libel case (setting up Max as her main antagonist), and self-medicating to cope.

2. Fixated on the idea that one more case (without moral grey area or ambiguity) will fix her and then she can get her normal life back. 'Just one more case,' like 'just one more pill' – destructive addiction. Researching the Jane Doe case to fill this hole + body decomposition

3. With the inciting incident of the second pigeon in the same place, and a message online from the same anon, it becomes clear that Pip has a stalker, and not just an online one.

4. Pip starts to look into her stalker, seeing patterns that must be from the same person. She starts to assemble the spreadsheet of connected events + chalk lines start to appear.

5. She got exactly what she wanted: 'one more case,' where the participant is clearly, without doubt bad. The stalker can only have bad intentions for harassing her. Opportunity has presented her the exact kind of case she needed, and this time she is the subject. Not only that, having a stalker is an obstacle to a normal life, so she will have to deal with this anyway to achieve her need.

6. But actually, having a stalker could be very dangerous. Escalating stalking behaviours – more chalk lines and maybe the 'Dead Girl Walking' writing on the road. Also, the stalker is a barrier to her returning to her normal life, which is her main need. So, it's now an obstacle she has to deal with. Stalking behaviours increasing in severity – makes spreadsheet and graph. One particular event – DGW, makes her think she might be in danger actually. This is when she makes first appeal to police.

7. Fails to convince the police that she has a stalker that might be a threat. She has a list of enemies. Hawkins sees it as harmless prank, no real threat to life – no proof of chalk lines and the writing might not have been for her. Patronises Pip – sends her further down her fatal flaw – justice only outside of law.

8. Now is paranoid too, and thinks she is in danger, though she can't convince police. Knows she is truly on her own in these matters now.

Big Shock moment.

Could Jason Bell have killed Barney? Becca let him go - Jason was walking in the area, saw the dog + drowned it

- went round for dinner with Becca - sensed she was keeping something from him - stayed + watched - saw her go on dog walk. He didn't give permission for them to get a dog - so he drowned him.

ACT 2

Now paranoid about a stalker she can't convince police is a threat, on top of all other problems.

Her need is the same: one more case to fix herself and save her soul. The desire has shifted now though, to a case that found her instead: her stalker This person must be objectively bad, so if she can find and catch them, maybe she can go back to normal.

She googles her stalking behaviours and comes across an article for the DT Killer which lists the same things. Starts to think that, somehow, her stalker is connected to the DT Killer.

Pip starts to research the DT Killer, reads profile, articles and contacts the Karras family. Reads the false confession transcript which convinces her – he seems innocent, which means *her stalker might not just be emulating the DT killer to fuck with her, they might actually BE the DT killer. Karras family invoke her help in proving son's innocence. She asks to speak to Jason Bell as Billy worked at his company.*

Stalking increases – first phone call.

This case is turning even more into exactly what she wanted. If her stalker is the DT Killer, then objectively he is a monster, and if she can find him and put him away (and free Billy) she will have done an objectively good thing – no ambiguity. This will definitely fix her, as the stakes are now raised. She talks to victims of the DT killer, and HH. HH makes the connection back to Andie and the secret email which Pip reads. Dan da Silva – beard. Second stalker phone call. Pip installs CallTrapper on her phone, Pip talks to police who investigated DT, who mentions a cop from Amersham asking questions a lot. It's looking like it could be Dan da Silva (or Max/ Luke if it's just a copy-cat). Charlie green in caught – possible moment of saving grace denied. Maybe she is on her way to talk to Kim da Silva, when her phone rings. She is about to identify both her stalker and the real DT Killer.

BUT, she is abducted before she does. A very heavy price. In the trunk of the car, she believes she is about to die – leaves DNA. Jason ties her up with Duct Tape at Green Scene, small killer confession. He wraps her face in DT and leaves saying he will be back soon. Pip thinks there is no hope – she is tied up fast and cannot get out. She will die.

She manages to escape from the DT and escape the room. She is free and alive – the normal life that *she just gave up hope on is back within her grasp.*

But . . .

She sees Jason return, and because of her fatal flaw (no trust police, justice can only exist outside the law), she makes the irrevocable decision to go back and kill Jason. She is changed – life can never be the same now, though she doesn't fully grasp that yet.

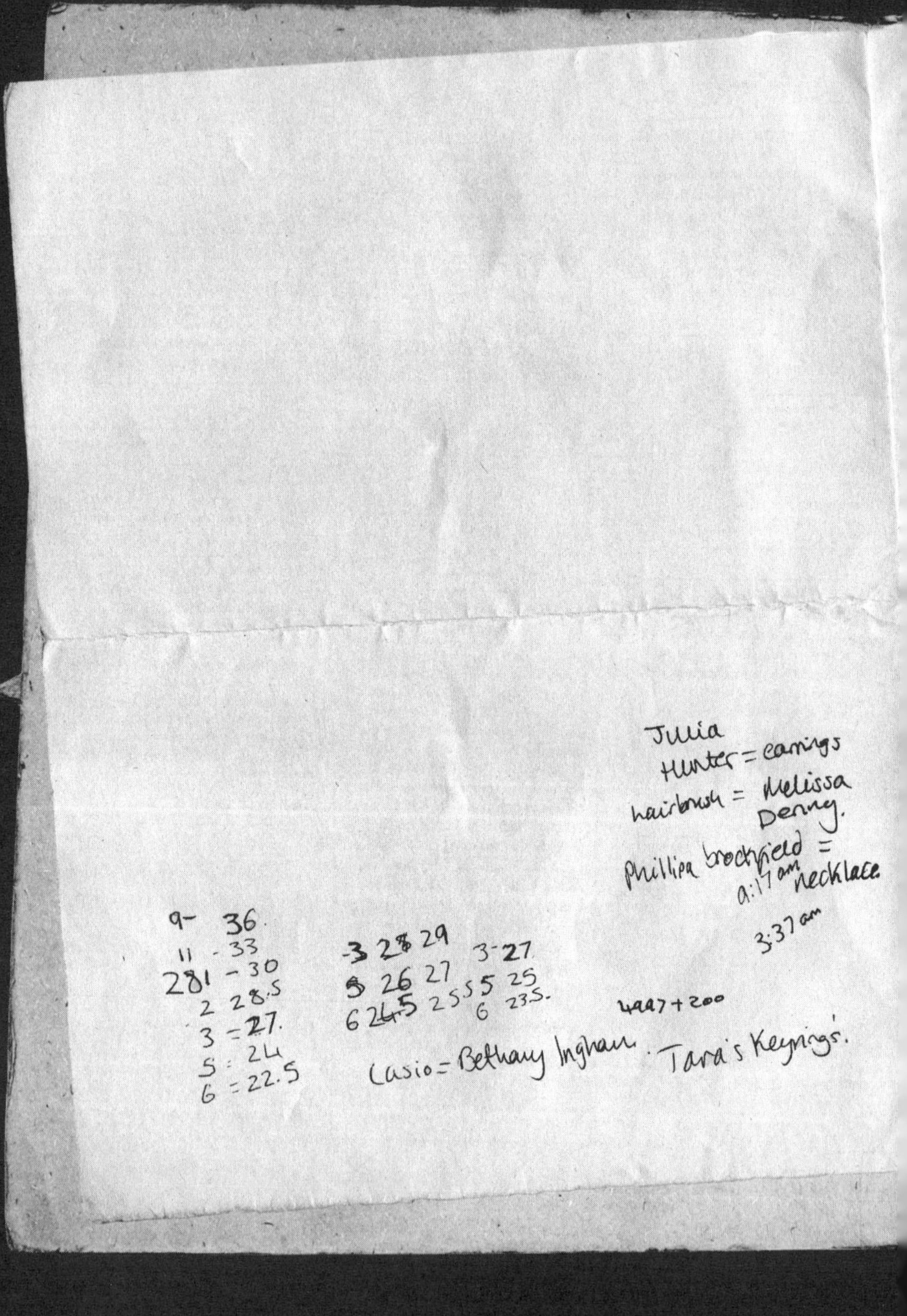
Julia
Hunter = earrings
hairbrush = Melissa
Denny.
Phillipa brockfield =
necklace.
9:17 am
3:37 am
9- 36.
11 - 33
281 - 30
2 28.5
3 = 27.
5 : 24
6 = 22.5
3 28 29
5 26 27
6 24.5 25.5
3- 27.
5 25
6 23.5.
4997 + 200
Casio = Bethany Ingham.
Tara's Keyrings.

US version
August 10th

Monday 3rd September
wed
Friday
sunday = chalk lines.

10th Monday, Tuesday
~~wed~~
Thurs
Friday.
Sat.
Sunday

17th Monday pdf
Tuesday
wed
Thurs
Friday: DI Wolum
22 Saturday
Sunday = body fare.

29th
Sat. = Becca
Sun
Agenty
tower

Tues = Hawkins.

ACT 3

May have to shift it by 1 week

Ravi surgar version

Midpoint: she has just killed Jason Bell. She has killed someone and this is her new normal.

Her need is the same (case with unambiguous bad people punished) but the outside goal has shifted. She has killed Jason Bell, but now (to keep her normal life) she has to get away with it. There is only one way to do this: set Max up for the murder. And it would kill 2 birds with one stone in terms of her goal. 2 bad men go down, one innocent free, and she can go back to normal life.

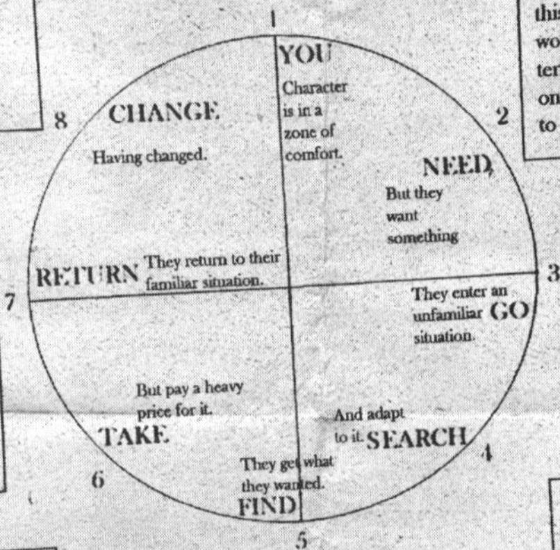

Having to stage the scene and come up with the intricate plan to set Max up. There is no room for error. But as Pip has studied so many crimes, now she is on the other side (the killer, not the detective) she thinks she knows exactly how to get away with it.

The Frame- up plan, and all its stages: dealing with the body to manipulate the time of death estimate, drugging Max to get the evidence she needs to set him up, involving allies, setting up her air tight alibi. Returning to the scene to set everything and dump Jason and then set the fire so the body is found soon. The next day disposing of clothes and trainers (hearing about the murder on the news), first interview with Becca and first release of podcast, trying to steer it towards Max.

When Pip is called in for her first police interview about it – because of the late call to the lawyer which seemed out of character and is the very call they've found on Max's records that place him at the scene. During the course of this interview, Hawkins asks her for where she was during (9:30 pm – 1 am) so this is the point where Pip knows the plan has worked and they have been successful. The time of death has been manipulated, and she and Ravi have solid alibis for that time. She gives Hawkins her alibi info, and he checks up on it. In the meantime, she does more to ensure that the police are looking at Max as suspect: interview with café owner. And maybe hints about Jason Bell being linked to DT. It all seems to be going well until...

Pip is asked to come in for a second police interview. Here Hawkins entraps her in several lies and then drops the bomb – her headphones were found in Jason's bedside table, creating a direct connection between her and the victim, though she claimed no contact. It's all over. Dark night of the soul. Pip talks to Ravi, and she knows the only way forward is to confess now, and hope that they will go less hard on her, maybe a lighter sentence if she can convince of self-defence – though the efforts to cover up will work against this.

The final meal. Pip wants one more slice of normality with her family before she confesses and is locked away. But when she goes to the police station, Ravi comes out and tells her he has fixed it, made a reason why her headphones were there, without connection to her.

Pip is distraught now that Ravi has implicated himself in the crime so directly. Now she has no choice: they have to get away with it now to save Ravi. Even more determined to do whatever it takes to make sure Max goes down: for Ravi's sake.

Exile is
start of december.
Then 1 year 7 month 6 days later
4 minutes after.

ACT 4

Has made promises about how she will be different to earn her life back. To deserve Ravi. She serves her penance for almost 2 years. She has changed.

At the very end we get a glimmer of hope that it has all worked out and she can have her life back.

Even more desperate to get away with it now and be successful in setting up Max.

Her need is the same: one more case to fix herself and save her soul. The desire has shifted now though, to setting up Max for the murder so she and Ravi can get away with it. Pip is maybe starting to realise that she will never obtain her 'need', having a normal life may no longer be possible.

One last slight obstacle. Max's house is being searched by forensic teams, but some people are questioning that they don't think it can be Max – maybe her mum/dad say this/ Hawkins/ someone on reddit. nd gets her to reveal the

So to double down on this and convince everyone Max is guilty, Pip forces Max's mum into an interview where she manipulates her into revealing the blocked cameras which looks very bad for Max. Additionally she speaks to Daniel da Silva in a way to steer him towards Jason Bell being the DT killer. His small chance at a redemption here. (She had been laying hints before with HH and Becca Bell).

Pip and Ravi go to the police station with 'proof' she has uncovered during her investigation of Jason Bell being the DT Killer – Andie's secret email address, the Green Scene links (crime scene and weapons), and the trophies taken of victims: Photo of Andie's hairbrush, Becca's earrings. While they are there, Max is brought in in handcuffs. He has been arrested. They did it, they won. He breaks free and attacks Pip saying she must have set him up. Pip says: You're lucky I didn't put you in the ground too. Max is lead off and Pip talks to Hawkins. He confirms that yes, Max will be charged for the first-degree murder of Jason Bell. SUCCESS. Pip has achieved her goal and the Plot is done.

But...

Hawkins makes a loaded comment to her, something like: I suppose if you were ever involved in something like this, you'd know exactly what to do to get away with it. Pip: I have listened to a lot of podcasts. But, inside, she knows this is catastrophic. Despite all the evidence to Max, Hawkins still has lingering suspicions about her. Now Pip knows for sure: until there is a guilty verdict at a trial, this might all still unravel with her head on the block. This is when she realizes that she can no longer have her normal life, in order to protect it and her allies. She has to distance herself from everyone, especially Ravi. Have the break-up scene with the duress plan.

Pip is in exile / purgatory. It has been months – no contact with Ravi or allies, lessening contact with family. No friends at uni. Complete isolation while awaiting trial. Makes promises of how she will change to deserve her normal life, if she is lucky enough to get it back.

feb = 17
July 2012 =18
feb= 2010.

Published by Delacorte Press, an imprint of Random House Children's Books,
a division of Penguin Random House LLC, New York.

Here and not. Red and black. One moment there, another gone. Her face in the glass. Disappearing in the light of oncoming headlights, reappearing in the dark of outside. Gone again. The window kept her face for its own. Good, it could keep it. Back, the window didn't want it either.

Red's reflection stared through her, but the glass and the darkness didn't get her quite right, blurring the details. The main features were there: the too-pale glow of her skin and the wide-set dark blue eyes that weren't hers alone. *You look so much alike,* she used to hear, more than she cared to. Now she didn't care to hear it at all, even think it. So, she looked away from her face, their face, ignoring them both. But it was harder to ignore something when you were trying.

Red shifted her gaze, looking instead at the cars in the lane beside and below. Something wasn't right; the cars seemed too small from up here at her window, but Red didn't feel any bigger. She watched a blue sedan edging forward to pass, and she helped it along with her eyes, pushing them ahead. There you go, bud. Ahead of this thirty-one-foot-long metal can, speeding down the highway. Which was strange when you thought about it; that you traveled *down* a highway when *high* was right there in the name.

"Red?" The voice opposite interrupted her thoughts of lowways and highways. Maddy was looking at her through the dimmed inside lights, skin screwed up around her sandy-brown eyes. She gave a small kick under the table, jabbing Red in the shin. "Did you just forget we were in the middle of playing a game?"

"No," Red said, but yes, yes she had. What had they been playing again?

"Twenty Questions," Maddy said, reading Red's mind. Well, they had known each other all their lives; Red had only gotten a seven-month head start and she hadn't done a lot with it. Maybe Maddy had learned to read her mind in all that time, more than seventeen years. Red really hoped not. There were things in there no one else could ever see. No one. Not even Maddy. Especially not Maddy.

"Yeah, I know," Red said, her eyes wandering to the other side of the RV, to the outside door and the sofa bed—currently sofa—where she and Maddy would sleep tonight. Red couldn't remember; which side of the bed did Maddy like again? Because she couldn't sleep if she wasn't on the left side, and just as she was trying to read Maddy's mind back about that, her eyes caught on a green sign outside in the night, flying over the windshield.

"That sign says Rockingham, aren't we getting off this road soon?" Red said, not loud enough for anyone at the very front of the RV to hear, where it would have been more use. She was probably wrong, anyway, best to say nothing. They'd been driving on this same road for the past hour, I-73 becoming I-74 and then US 220 without much fanfare.

"Red Kenny, focus." Maddy snapped her fingers, a hint of a smile on her face. It never creased, though, Maddy's face, not even with the widest of smiles. Skin like cream, soft and clearer than it had any business being. It made the freckles on Red's face stand out even more, side by side in photos. Literally side by side; they were almost the exact same height, down to the highest-standing hair, though Red's was dark blond where Maddy's was more light brown, a shade or two separating them. Red always had hers tied back, loose bangs at the front that she'd cut herself with the kitchen scissors. Maddy's was untied and neat, the ends soft in a way Red's never were. "I'm the one asking questions, you're the one with the person, place or thing," Maddy prompted.

Red nodded slowly. Well, even if Maddy also liked to sleep on the left, at least they weren't on the bunks.

"I've asked seven questions already," Maddy said.

"Great." Red couldn't remember her person, place or thing. But really, they'd been driving all day, setting off from home around twelve hours ago, hadn't they played enough road trip games? Red couldn't wait for this to be over so she could finally sleep, whether left side or right. Just get through it. They were supposed to arrive at Gulf Shores around this time tomorrow, meet up with the rest of their friends, that was the plan.

Maddy cleared her throat.

"And what answers did I give, remind me?" Red said.

Maddy breathed out, an almost sigh or an almost laugh, hard to tell. "It was a person, a woman, not a fictional character," she said, counting them off on her fingers. "Someone I would know, but not Kim Kardashian or you."

Red looked up, searching the empty corners of her mind for the memory. "No, sorry," she said, "it's gone."

"Okay, we'll start again," Maddy said, but just then, Simon stumbled out of the small bathroom, saving Red from more Organized Fun™. The door bounced back into him as the RV sped up.

"Simon Yoo, have you been in there this whole time?" Maddy asked, disgusted. "We've played two whole rounds."

Simon pushed his black, loosely waved hair away from his face and held an unsteady finger to his lips, saying, "Shh, a lady never tells."

"Shut the door, then, jeez."

He did, but with his foot, to make some point or other, almost overbalancing as they hurtled along the highway, changing lanes to pass. Wasn't their exit soon? Maybe Red should say something, but now she was watching as Simon waded forward, leaning on the tiny kitchen counter behind her. In one awkward motion, he slid onto the booth beside her, knocking his knees on the table.

Red studied him: his pupils were sitting too large in his dark, round eyes, and there was an incriminating wet patch on the front of his teal-colored Eagles shirt.

"You're drunk already," she said, almost impressed. "I thought you'd only had like three beers."

Simon moved close to whisper in her ear, and Red could smell the sharp metallic tang on his breath. She couldn't miss it; that was how she knew when her dad was lying to her, *No I didn't drink today, Red, I promise.* "Shh," Simon said, "Oliver brought tequila."

"And you just helped yourself?" Maddy asked, overhearing.

In answer, Simon balled both his fists and held them in the air, yelling: "Spring break, baby!"

Red laughed. And anyway, if she just asked, maybe Maddy wouldn't mind sleeping on the right tonight, or for the rest of the week. She could just ask.

"Oliver doesn't like people touching his things," Maddy said quietly, glancing over her shoulder at her brother, sitting just a few feet behind her in the front passenger seat, fiddling with the radio as he chatted to Reyna in the driver's seat. Arthur was standing just behind

Oliver and Reyna, now shooting a closed-mouth smile as he caught Red's eye. Or maybe it was actually Simon he was smiling at.

"Hey, it's my RV, I have a claim to anything in it," Simon hiccupped.

"Your uncle's RV." Maddy felt the need to correct him.

"Weren't you supposed to have a driving shift today too?" Red asked him. The plan was to share the drive equally among the six of them. She had taken the first two-hour shift, to get it out of the way, driving them out of Philly and down I-95 until they stopped for lunch. Arthur had sat with her the whole time, calmly directing her, as though he could tell when she was zoning in and out, or when she was panicking about the size of the RV and how small everything looked from up here. Mind readers everywhere, clearly. But she'd only known Arthur six or seven months; that wasn't fair.

"Reyna and I swapped," Simon said, "on account of the beers I'd already drunk." A wicked smile. Simon had always been able to get away with anything, he was too funny, too quick with it. You couldn't stay mad at him. Well, Maddy could, if she was really trying.

"Hey, Reyna's really cool, by the way," Simon whispered to Maddy, as though she had some claim over the coolness of her brother's girlfriend. But she smiled and took it anyway, a glance over at the couple, picture-perfect, even with their backs turned.

A break in the conversation; now was the time to ask before Red forgot.

"Hey, Maddy, about the sofa bed—"

"—Shit!" Oliver hissed up front, an ugly sound. "This is our exit right here. Move over, Reyna. Now! NOW."

"I can't," Reyna said, suddenly flustered, checking her mirrors and flipping the turn signal.

"They'll move for you, we're bigger, just go," Oliver said, reaching forward like he might grab the wheel himself.

A screeching sound, not from the RV but from Reyna, as she pulled the hulking vehicle across one lane. An angry Chevrolet screamed on its horn, and the guy at the wheel threw up a middle finger, holding it out the window. Red pretended to catch it, slipping it into the chest pocket of her blue-and-yellow-check shirt, treasuring it forever.

"Move, move, move," Oliver barked, and Reyna swerved right again, making the exit just in time. Another horn, this time from a furious Tesla they left behind on the highway.

"We could have just come off at the next one and worked it out. That's what Google Maps is for," Reyna said, slowing down, her voice strange and squished like it was working its way through gritted teeth. Red had never seen Reyna flustered before, or angry, only ever smiling, wider each time she checked in with Oliver's eyes. What was that like, to be in love? She couldn't imagine it; that was why she watched them sometimes, learning by example. But Red should have said something about the exit earlier, shouldn't she? They'd made it almost all day without any raised voices. That was her fault.

"I'm sorry," Oliver said now, tucking Reyna's thick black hair behind her ear so he could squeeze her shoulder, imprinting his fingers. "I just want to get to the campsite ASAP. We're all tired."

Red looked away, leaving them alone in their moment, well, as alone as they could get in an RV with six people, thirty-one feet long. Apparently that extra foot was so important they couldn't round it down.

The world on her side of the RV was dark again. Trees lined the road, but Red could hardly see them, not past her own reflection and the other face hiding beneath it. She had to look away from that too, before she thought about it too much. Not here, not now.

The truck in front slowed as it passed a SPEED LIMIT 35 sign, its brake lights staining the road red ahead of them. The color that followed her wherever she went, and it never meant anything good. But the road moved on, and so did they.

Oh wait, what was it she needed to ask Maddy about again?

A strange yawning in Red's gut, the sound hidden by the wheels on the road. She couldn't be hungry, could she? They'd only stopped for dinner at a rest stop a few hours ago. But the feeling doubled down, twisting again, so she reached out for the bag of chips in front of Maddy. She removed a handful, placing them carefully in her mouth one by one, cheese dust coating her fingertips.

"Oh yeah," Simon said, standing up and sidling out of the booth, heading toward his bunk beyond the mini-kitchen. "And youse all owe me seven bucks for the snacks I got at the gas station."

Red stared down at the chips left in her hand.

"Hey." Maddy leaned over the table. "I'll cover you for the snacks, don't worry about it."

Red swallowed. Looked down even farther to hide her eyes from Maddy. Not worrying wasn't a choice, not one Red had anyway. In her darkest moments, those winter nights when she had to wear her coat to bed, over two pairs of pajamas and five pairs of socks, and still shivered anyway, Red sometimes wished she were Maddy Lavoy. To live in that warm house as though it belonged to her, to have everything they had and everything she didn't anymore.

Stop that. She felt a flush in her cheeks. Shame was a red feeling, a hot one, just like guilt and anger. Why couldn't the Kennys heat their home on guilt and shame alone? But things would get better soon, right? Real soon, that was the plan, what it was all for. And then everything would be different. How freeing it would be to just do or think, and not have to double-think or triple-think, or say *No thank you, maybe next time.* To not beg for extra shifts at work and lose sleep either way. To take another handful of chips just because she wanted to.

Red realized she hadn't said anything yet. "Thanks," she mumbled, keeping her eyes to herself, but she didn't take any more chips, it didn't feel right. She'd just have to live with that feeling in her gut. And maybe it wasn't hunger after all that.

"No worries," Maddy said. There, see, she didn't have any. Maddy had no need for worries. She was one of those people who was good at everything, first try. Well, apart from that time she insisted on taking up the harp. Unless Red was one of Maddy's worries. It did seem that way sometimes.

"Are we in South Carolina yet?" Red said, changing the subject, one thing *she* was good at.

"Not yet," Oliver called behind, though he wasn't the Lavoy she'd asked. "Soon. I think we should be at the campsite in around forty minutes."

"Woohoo, spring break!" Simon yelled again in a high-pitched voice, and somehow he had another bottle of beer in his hand, the refrigerator door swinging open behind him.

"I got it," Arthur said, passing an unsteady Simon in the narrow space between the sofa bed and the dining table, clapping him on the back. Arthur darted forward to catch the refrigerator door and pushed it shut, the dim overhead lights flashing against his gold-framed glasses as he turned. Red liked his glasses, standing out against his tan skin and curly dark brown hair. She wondered whether she needed glasses; faraway things seem to have gotten farther and fuzzier lately. Another thing to add to the to-worry list, because she couldn't do anything about it. Yet. Arthur caught her looking, smiling as he ran a finger over the light stubble on his chin.

"Given up on Twenty Questions, have you?" he asked them both.

"Red forgot her person, place or thing," Maddy said, and that made Red think: Wasn't there something else she'd forgotten, something she wanted to ask Maddy?

"Chip?" Maddy offered the bag to Arthur.

"Ah, I'm good, thanks." He backed away from the bag, almost tripping over the corner of the sofa bed. A look clouded his eyes, and now that she was looking, was there a slight sheen of sweat on his forehead? Red didn't normally catch these things, but this one she did. Did that mean she looked at him too often?

"What's up?" she said. "Deathly allergic to cheese puffs?"

"No, thankfully," Arthur said, feeling his way as he sat down on the sofa bed.

Oh yes, Red needed to ask Maddy about which side she slept on. Shit, Arthur had just said something and she hadn't listened. Best to go with a well-placed "Huh?"

"I said at least I don't feel as dizzy as Simon probably does."

"Carsick?" Red said. "Well, RV-sick?"

"No, it's not that." Arthur shook his head. "Probably far too late to be telling you all this, but I'm not that great with tight spaces." He looked around at the crammed-in furniture and the compact kitchen. "I thought it would be wider—"

"That's what she said!" Simon interrupted.

"For god's sake, Simon, enough with *The Office* references," Maddy said. “He’s been doing that since middle school, before he even knew what it meant.”

“I’m standing right here, Mads, don’t third-person me.”

“Can you all shut up for a second?” Oliver spoke over Maddy’s retort. “We’re trying to navigate over here.”

Red turned back to Arthur. “Well, good thing you’re not spending a whole week in this cramped RV. Oh . . . wait.” Red smiled at him.

“I know, right.”

Arthur was Simon’s friend, really, but he was all of theirs by now. He didn’t go to their high school, he went to one in South Philly, but he and Simon were on the same basketball team, both joined last year sometime. Red guessed Arthur didn’t much like his friends at his own school, because he’d been coming to all their parties and hangouts since senior year began. And that was okay, because she liked having him around. He always asked how she was and how was her day, even though Red usually answered with lies or exaggerated stories with only faint traces of the truth. He showed interest when Red wasn’t interesting at all. And there was that time he dropped her home after that New Year’s Eve party and let her sit in his car, warming up in the dry air of the heater before she had to go inside the cold house and find whatever mess her dad had left for her. Arthur didn’t know that was happening, he thought they were just talking, talking the night away at two in the morning outside her house. A small kindness he never knew he’d given her. She should give him one back.

“We’ll be at the campsite soon, I think,” she said. “You can get out and stretch your legs in the great big outdoors. I’ll come with you.”

“Yeah.” Arthur smiled. “I’ll be fine.” His gaze dropped from her face to the table, where she was resting one hand. “I was meaning to ask earlier, but I didn't want to distract you from driving. What does your hand say?"

"Oh." Red blushed, raising the hand and rubbing at it self-consciously, realizing as she did that there was something written on the back of that one too. To-do lists everywhere, even on her own body. To-do lists and never-get-done lists. "I've got a two-for-one special for you," she said. "On our left hand, we have: *Call AT&T.*"

"Ah, I see. Fascinating. What about?" he asked.

"You know," Red said. "Just to check in with them, see how they're doing, whether they had a good day."

Arthur nodded, a wry smile to match hers. "And did you do it?"

Red pursed her lips, looking at the empty box she'd drawn near her knuckle. "No," she said. "I ran out of time."

"And hand number two?"

"On hand number two," Red said, drawing out the suspense, "we have the very elaborate and detailed instruction: *Pack.*"

"You must have done that one," Arthur said.

"Just about," she replied like it was a joke, but she was telling the truth this time. Packed literally right before she left the house this morning, no time to even double-check her bag against her list. She'd been too busy making sure there was enough food in the house for her dad while she was away.

"Well, if you did it, why haven't you checked it off?" Arthur said, pointing to the small empty box on the see-through flesh of her hand. "Here." He stood up, grabbing one of Maddy's pens from the table that she'd used in an earlier game of Hangman. He uncapped it and leaned toward Red, pressing the felt-tip end against her skin. Gently, he drew two lines: a check mark in the little box. "There you go," he said, standing back to admire his handiwork.

Red looked at her hand. And it felt stupid to admit it to herself, but the sight of that little check mark did change something in her. Small, minuscule, a tiny firework bursting in her head, but it felt good. It always felt good, checking off those boxes. She held out her hand proudly for Maddy to examine and got the nod of approval she was looking for.

Arthur was still watching her, a look in his eyes, a different one that Red couldn't decipher.

"Brazil nuts," Red said.

Arthur's face screwed up. "What?"

"I used to be allergic to them as a kid, but I'm not anymore. Isn't that weird, that a person can just change like that?" she said, fidgeting with the front pocket of her light blue jeans. She'd been sitting here in this spot a long time now. Too long. "My mo—p-parents had to write it on my hand, so I wouldn't forget. Also, does the pattern in the curtains remind anyone of something?" She touched the white-and-blue curtain hanging down next to her, running her hand between the pleats. "It's been bugging me all day, can't work out what it is. A cartoon or something."

"It's just a random pattern," Maddy answered.

"No, it's something. It's something." Red traced her finger over it. Like the silhouette of a character she couldn't quite place. From a book she was read at night, or a TV show? Either way, best not to think back to that time, to when she was little, because of who else might be there.

"Tomatoes," Arthur said, saving her from the memory. "Give me a rash around my mouth. Only when raw, though." He straightened up, as did the wrinkles in his white baseball jersey, navy on the arms. "Anyway, I think I better help with the directions. I'm sensing that Simon is being a hindrance."

"I'm doing a stellar job, thank you very much," Simon said, looking over Oliver's shoulder at an iPhone with a marble orange case; must be Reyna's. There was a map on the screen, a blue dot moving along a highlighted road. The blue dot was them, the six of them and all thirty-one feet of RV. Thank god it wasn't a red dot. Blue was safer.

Arthur sidled to the front, blocking Red's view of the screen, her eyes falling instead to Maddy, who gave her a not-so-subtle wink.

"Huh?"

Maddy shushed her silently, nodding her head ever so slightly in Arthur's direction. "Checks all the boxes," she whispered.

"Stop it," Red warned her.

"You stop it."

They both stopped, because just then Maddy's phone rang, an angry-wasp buzz against the table. The screen lit up with the view from the front camera: the off-white ceiling and a sliver of the underside of Maddy's chin. Across the top was the word *Mom* and *FaceTime video,* with a *slide to answer* button waiting patiently at the bottom.

Maddy's reaction was instant. Too quick. She tensed, bones sharpening beneath her skin. Her hand darted out to grab the phone, holding it up and away to hide it from Red.

Red knew that was what she was doing, she always knew, though Maddy didn't know she knew.

"I'll call her when we get to the campsite," Maddy said, almost too quiet to hear over the wheels, pressing the side button to reject the call. Looking anywhere but at Red.

Mom.

Like Maddy thought Red would split open and bleed just to see the word.

Published by Delacorte Press, an imprint of Random House Children's Books,
a division of Penguin Random House LLC, New York.

"What do you think happened to your mother?"

The word sounded wrong to Bel when he said it. *Mother.* Unnatural. Not quite as bad as *Mom.* That one pushed between her lips, misshapen and mad, like a bloated slug finally breaking free, splatting there on the floor for everyone to stare at. Because everyone *would,* everyone always did. The word didn't belong in her mouth, so Bel didn't say it, not if she could help it. At least there was a coldness to *mother,* a sense of distance.

"It's OK, please take your time," Ramsey said, the vowels clipped and exposed.

Bel looked across at him, avoiding the camera. Lines of concern crisscrossed his black skin, pulling around his eyes as they fixed on Bel's, because she was already taking her time, too much, more than she had in the pre-interviews the past few days. He reached up to scratch his temple, right where his dark coiled hair faded out above his ears. Ramsey Lee: filmmaker, director, from South London—a whole world away, and yet here he was in Gorham, New Hampshire, sitting across from her.

Ramsey cleared his throat.

"Um . . . ," Bel began, choking on that slug. "I don't know."

Ramsey sat back, his chair creaking, and Bel knew from the flicker of disappointment in his face that she was doing a bad job. Worse. It must have been the camera. The camera changed things, the permanence of it. One day thousands of people would watch this, separated from her only by the glass of their television screens. They would analyze every word she said, every pause she took, and have something to say about it. They'd study her face: her warm white skin and the flush of her cheeks, her sharp chin that sharpened more when she spoke and especially when she smiled, her short honey-blond hair, her round gray-blue eyes. *Doesn't she look just like Rachel did,* they'd say, those people beyond the television screen. Bel thought she looked more like her dad, actually. Thanks, though.

"Sorry," Bel added, pressing her eyelids together, bright orange patches where the three softbox lights glared at her. She just had to get through this documentary, pretend to not be hating every second, talk about Rachel, then life could go back to normal, back to not talking about Rachel.

Ramsey shook his head, a smile breaking through.

"Don't worry," he said. "It's a difficult question."

It wasn't, though, not really. And the answer wasn't difficult either. Bel really didn't know what had happened to her. No one did. That was the point of all this.

"I think she was—"

Someone stumbled behind the camera, tripping on a cable that ripped out of the wall. One of the lights flickered and died, swaying on its rickety leg. A hand reached out to grab it before it fell, righting it.

"Oh shit. Sorry, Rams," the tripper said, chasing the loose wire back to the outlet. Now that the light was out, Bel could see him properly for the first time. She couldn't say she'd noticed him before, when Ramsey had introduced the crew, too dazzled by the lights and the camera. He must have been the youngest of the four documentary crew members, couldn't be much older than her. And he was, just maybe, the most ridiculous person Bel had ever seen. He had shoulder-length brown hair that fell in thick curls, pushed off to one side of his pale face, full of angles and shadows. He wore flared tartan pants and a bright purple sweater with little green-and-yellow dinosaurs marching across his chest.

"Sorry," he said again, the *o* giving him away; must be from London too. He grunted as he pushed the plug in and the light sparked back to life, hiding him from Bel. Thank God, that ugly sweater was distracting.

"I told you to gaffer all the wires down, Ash," Ramsey said, shifting to glance behind the box light.

"I did . . . ," came Ash's voice from behind the light, somehow angular, just like his face. "Until the tape ran out."

"Mate, we have like fifty thousand rolls upstairs," Ramsey replied.

"Fifty thousand and one," said the woman standing behind the microphone: a long pole balanced on a tripod, with a fluffy gray head hovering over Bel and Ramsey, just above the shot. Saba, that was what Ramsey had called her, introducing her as *the Sound Person.* She was wearing a huge pair of headphones that dwarfed her face, pushing the brown skin of her cheeks into unnatural folds.

"Sorry," came Ash's voice. "I'll fix it later."

"It's OK," Ramsey said, his face softening for a second. Then, to the man behind the huge camera: "James, why are you panning to Ash?"

"Thought we were aiming for a cinéma vérité style for the doc, that you might want this in," the camera operator replied.

"No, I don't want this in. Let's reset the shot and go for another take. And everyone watch where you're stepping this time."

Ramsey flashed an apologetic smile at Bel, sitting here on a plush couch across from them all, the cushions artfully arranged and rearranged behind her.

"Ash is my brother-in-law," he said, as though in explanation. "Known him since he was eleven. It's his first job, isn't it, Ash? Camera assistant."

Ash: camera assistant. Saba: sound person. James: camera operator. And Ramsey: filmmaker, producer, director. Must have been nice, to have words like that follow your name, words you'd chosen. Bel's were different: *This is Annabel. The daughter of Rachel Price.* That last part said in a knowing whisper. Because even though Rachel was gone, everything existed only in relation to her. Gorham wasn't its own place anymore; it was the town where Rachel Price had lived.

Number 33 Milton Street wasn't Bel's home, it was the house Rachel Price had lived in. Bel's dad, Charlie Price, well, he was *Rachel Price's husband,* even though the Price part had come from him.

"Ash, the clapper," Ramsey reminded him.

"Oh." Ash emerged from behind the light, a black-and-white clapper board clasped between his hands. Printed on it were the words: *The Disappearance of Rachel Price.* The name of the documentary. Below that, a handwritten: *Interview with Bel.* And she was surprised, really, that it didn't just say *Rachel Price's daughter.*

Ash walked in front of the camera, the hems of his pants swishing loudly together.

"Take six," he said, bringing the clapper stick down to the slate with a sharp bang, hurrying out of the shot.

"Let's start again." Ramsey let out a long breath. They'd been here for hours already, and it was starting to show on his face. "Your mum has now been missing for more than sixteen years. In all that time, there has been no sign of her. No activity on her bank accounts, no communication with family, no body found despite extensive searches. Of course there have been *sightings,*" he said, leaning on the word too hard so it came out sideways. "People on the internet who claim to have seen Rachel in Paris. Brazil. Even one a few months ago nearby in North Conway. But of course, these are unsubstantiated claims. Your mum vanished without a trace on February thirteenth, 2008. What do you think happened to her?"

Bel couldn't say *I don't know* again, otherwise she'd never be allowed to leave.

"It's as much a mystery for me as the rest of the world," she said, and from the flash in Ramsey's eyes, she knew that was a better answer. OK, keep going. "I know all the theories people have about what happened. And if I had to pick the one . . ."

Ramsey nodded, urging her on.

"I think she was trying to leave. She left. Then maybe she was killed by an opportunistic killer—that's the term the media uses. Or maybe she got lost in the White Mountains and died in the snow, and an animal got to her remains. That's why we never found her."

Ramsey leaned forward, finger cupping his chin thoughtfully.

"So, Bel, you're saying you think the most likely scenario is that your mother is dead?"

Bel half nodded, staring down at the coffee table in front of her. The full glass bottle of water that was a prop only, she wasn't allowed to drink it. The marble chessboard laid out with all the pieces prepared for battle, her knees pointed down the center in no-man's-land. This repurposed conference room in the Royalty Inn hotel on Main Street was the stage. The water bottle, the chessboard and the cushions were the props. None of this was real to anyone else, it was all for show.

"Yes. I think she's dead. I think she died that day or not long after."

Did she think that? Did it really matter? Gone was gone.

Ramsey was looking at the chessboard too now.

"You say you think your mum was trying to leave," he said, bringing his eyes back. "Do you mean that she was running away?"

Bel shrugged. "I guess."

"But there is compelling evidence that opposes the *ran away* theory. Rachel didn't withdraw any money from her bank account in the days and weeks leading up to her disappearance. If she was planning to run away and start a new life, she would have needed money to do that. Not only that, but she didn't take her wallet containing her ID with her, and she'd left her bank cards at home. Nor did she take her phone. She didn't pack any clothes or belongings. None at all. She didn't even take her coat with her on that freezing day, it was left in the car too, with her phone and wallet."

And me, Bel thought.

"What do you say to that?" Ramsey asked her.

What did he want her to say?

"I don't know." Bel went back to those three words, hid behind them.

Ramsey seemed to sense the barricade, backing off and straightening up.

"You're eighteen now, Bel. You weren't even two years old when Rachel went missing. Twenty-two months old, in fact. And of course, one of the most notable things about this case that sets it apart from all others, was that you were with her. You were with your mum when she disappeared."

"Yes," Bel said, knowing what question was coming next. It didn't matter how many times it was asked; the answer was the same. And it was worse for Bel, trust her.

"And you don't remember anything at all that day? Being in the mall? Being in the car?"

"I don't remember anything," she said flatly. "I was too young to remember. Or to tell anyone what I saw that day."

"And here's the craziest thing." Ramsey leaned forward, words spiking in the middle as he attempted to keep his voice even. "You were a toddler, too young to communicate properly with anyone, with the police. *But* if someone did take Rachel, abduct her from the car where it was found abandoned with you inside, that means you must have seen exactly who it was. You saw them. At one point in time, you must have known, however briefly, the answer to the mystery."

"I know."

Crazy, wasn't it? The craziest thing, in fact.

Bel closed her eyes, three blazing sunspots invading the dark world inside her head. Those lights were just too bright. Were they giving off heat too, or was that just her imagination? Explain why her face was so hot, then.

"Are you OK to continue?" Ramsey asked her.

"Yeah." She didn't have a choice, really. Contracts had been agreed to, waivers and releases signed. And, most importantly, she had promised her dad. She could pretend to be nice, for his sake. Say *yes* and *no* and *sorry* in the right places.

"You really have no memories from that day at all?"

"No." And she wouldn't the next time he asked too. Or the one after that. She had no memory of what happened, no idea. Just what she knew later, when she was old enough to know things: that she had been left behind. Abandoned there in the backseat of the car, however it happened.